THE WITCHES OF MOONSHYNE MANOR

Also by Bianca Marais

Hum If You Don't Know the Words
If You Want to Make God Laugh

For additional books by Bianca Marais,
visit her website, BiancaMarais.com.

THE WITCHES OF MOONSHYNE MANOR

BIANCA MARAIS

mira

Recycling programs for this product may not exist in your area.

ISBN-13: 978-0-7783-3392-0

The Witches of Moonshyne Manor

For questions and comments about the quality of this book, please contact us at CustomerService@Harlequin.com.

Mira
22 Adelaide St. West, 41st Floor
Toronto, Ontario M5H 4E3, Canada
BookClubbish.com

Printed in U.S.A.

For the smart, fierce, kick-ass, resilient,
funny, kind and talented women
I'm lucky enough to have in my life.
Thank you for reminding me every single day
that the most powerful form of magic
is that of sisterhood.
I can't wait to retire with you all
in our very own Moonshyne Manor.
I call dibs on the tree house bedroom!

Witches in the Sisterhood

Ursula:

Clairvoyant witch
Heavyset, bright blue eyes, gray-white pixie cut hairstyle
Timid, second-guesses herself, keeps secrets

Jezebel:

Seductress witch
Long black hair, heavy-lidded brown eyes, beautiful
Caretaker, horny, vicious temper, keeps a roster of lovers

Ivy:

Botanist witch
Tall, gray hair plaited and coiled into a bun, green eyes, wire-rim spectacles, covered in tattoos
Inquisitive, official owner of the manor, keeps tracks of everyone

Tabitha:

Agoraphobe witch
Resting witch face, full afro, wears shoulder pads
Dour, resentful, has a familiar called Widget, keeps a list of slights

Queenie:

Inventor/witch in charge
Bob Marley-esque locs, penchant for Doc Martens
Gruff, impatient, keeps a lot in her pockets

Ruby:

Missing witch
Larger than life, colorful, outlandish
Has kept away

1

Saturday, October 23
Morning

Half an hour before the alarm will be sounded for the first time in decades—drawing four frantic old women and a geriatric crow from all corners of the sprawling manor—Ursula is awoken by insistent knocking, like giant knuckles rapping against glass. It's an ominous sign, to be sure. The first of many.

Trying to rid herself of the sticky cobwebs of sleep, Ursula throws back the covers, groaning as her joints loudly voice their displeasure. She's slept in the buff, as is her usual habit, and as she pads across the room, she's more naked than the day she was born (being, as she is, one of those rare babies who came into the world fully encased in a caul).

Upon reaching the window, the cause of the ruckus is immediately obvious to Ursula: one of the Angel Oak's sturdy branches is thumping against her third-floor window. Strong winds whip through the tree, making it shimmy and shake, giving the impression that it's espousing the old adage to dance like no one's watching, a quality that rather has to be admired in a tree. Either that or it's trembling uncontrollably with fear.

The forest, encroaching at the garden's boundary, looks disquieted. It hangs its head low, bowing to a master who's ordered it to bend the knee. As the charcoal sky churns, not a bird to be seen, the trees in the wood whisper incessantly. Whether they're secrets or warnings, Ursula can't tell, which only unsettles her further.

That infernal billboard that the city recently erected across from the manor property—with its aggressive, gigantic lettering shouting *Critchley Hackle Megacomplex Coming Soon!*—snaps in the wind, issuing small cracks of thunder. A storm is on its way, that much is clear. You don't need to have Ivy's particular powers to know as much.

Turning her back on the ominous view, Ursula heads for the calendar to mark off another mostly sleepless night. It seems impossible that after so many of them—night upon night, strung up after each other seemingly endlessly—only two remain until Ruby's return, upon which Ursula will discover her fate.

Either Ruby knows or she doesn't.

And if she *does* know, there's the chance that she'll want nothing more to do with Ursula. The thought makes her breath hitch, the accompanying stab of pain almost too much to bear. The best she can hope for under the circumstances is that Ruby will forgive her, releasing Ursula from the invisible prison her guilt has sentenced her to.

Too preoccupied with thoughts of Ruby to remember to don her robe, Ursula takes a seat at her mahogany escritoire. She lights a cone of mugwort and sweet laurel incense, watching as the tendril of smoke unfurls, inscribing itself upon the air. Inhaling the sweet scent, she picks up a purple silk pouch and unties it, spilling the contents onto her palm.

The tarot cards are all frayed around the edges, worn down

from countless hours spent jostling through Ursula's hands. Despite their shabbiness, they crackle with electricity, sparks flying as she shuffles them. After cutting the deck in three, Ursula begins laying the cards down, one after the other, on top of the heptagram she carved into the writing desk's surface almost eighty years ago.

The first card, placed in the center, is The Tower. Unfortunate souls tumble from the top of a fortress that's been struck by lightning, flames engulfing it. Ursula experiences a jolt of alarm at the sight of it, for The Tower has to signify the manor, and anything threatening their home, threatens them all.

The second card, placed above the first at the one o'clock position, can only represent Tabitha. It's the Ten of Swords, depicting a person lying facedown with ten swords buried in their back. The last time Ursula saw the card, she'd made a mental note to make an appointment with her acupuncturist, but now, following so soon after The Tower, it makes her shift nervously.

The third, fourth and fifth cards, placed at the three o'clock, four thirty and six o'clock positions, depict a person (who must be Queenie) struggling under too heavy a load; a heart pierced by swords (signifying Ursula); and a horned beast towering above a man and woman who are shackled together (obviously Jezebel). Ursula whimpers to see so many dreaded cards clustered together.

Moving faster now, she lays out the sixth, seventh and eighth cards at the seven thirty, nine and eleven o' clock positions. Ursula gasps as she studies the man crying in his bed, nine swords hovering above him (which can only denote Ursula's guilt as it pertains to Ruby); the armored skeleton on horseback (representing the town of Critchley Hackle); and the two bedraggled souls trudging barefoot through the snow (definitely Ivy). Taking in all eight sinister cards makes Ursula tremble much like the Angel Oak.

Based on the spread, Ursula absolutely *should* sound the alarm immediately, but she's made mistakes in the past—lapses in judgment that resulted in terrible consequences—and so she wants to be a hundred percent certain first.

She shuffles the cards again, laying them down more deliberately this time, only to see the exact same shocking formation, the impending threat even more vivid than before. It couldn't be any clearer if the Goddess herself had sent a homing pigeon with a memo bearing the message *Calamity is on its way! It's knocking at the window, just waiting to be let in!*

And yet, Ursula *still* doesn't sound the alarm, because that's what doubt does: it slips through the chinks in our defenses, eroding all sense of self until the only voice that should matter becomes the one that we don't recognize anymore, the one we trust the least.

As a result of this estrangement from herself, Ursula has developed something of a compulsion, needing to triple-check the signs before she calls attention to them, and so she stands and grabs her wand. She makes her way down the hallway past Ruby's and Jezebel's bedrooms at a bit of a clip before descending the west-wing stairs.

It's just before she reaches Ivy's glass conservatory that Ursula breaks out into a panicked run.

2

Saturday, October 23
Morning

Ten minutes before Jezebel experiences the alarm, she's lying in bed, her black hair fanned over the silk pillow, and her heavy-lidded brown eyes just opening. Her mouth feels cottony, and a hangover headache blankets her temples.

It's Jezebel's turn to make brunch, and she's looking forward to surprising the women with a pancake picnic. It will have to be in Ivy's conservatory, of course, since the October chill will make an outside gathering unpleasant *and* automatically preclude Tabitha from attending due to her debilitating agoraphobia.

This will be one of their last meals without Ruby, and Jezebel, for one, can't wait for her old coconspirator to return to their inner sanctum. It's bewildering how, in Ruby's absence, the sisterhood have gone from being badass witches, who pulled off one of the greatest magical heists of all time, to becoming respectable outcasts whose days are now all carbon copies of each other.

Mornings begin with the downing of a dozen elixirs, tonics and smoothies (which Ivy still refuses to serve in shot glasses despite Jezebel's constant entreaties to do so), followed by a series of stretches to prevent sex injuries (Jezebel) or breaking a hip while putting on their compression socks (everyone except Tabby who won't be seen dead in anything so hideous regardless of the health benefits).

There are regimented mealtimes with everyone taking turns to cook (everyone except Queenie, of course, who burns everything she touches), followed by whatever work needs to be done in the distillery. After which there are planned group activities like bridge or bingo.

How did this happen? Jezebel wonders. *When did I become so old? There was a time that the only group activity I would ever consent to was orgies. The wilder, the better.*

Ruby will set them straight, resuscitating and reviving the dead-on-arrival mess they've become. Assuming Ruby is prepared to come home. Assuming she'll start speaking to them all again.

A loud snork interrupts Jezebel's thoughts, and she rolls over groaning to find a naked man sleeping next to her.

"Ken?" she says in an exaggerated whisper, poking his bare shoulder. "Ken, you need to go before my sisters wake up." He harrumphs in reply, mumbling something Jezebel can't make out because he's lying facedown. "What was that?"

He lifts his head. "I said my name's not Ken."

That's unfortunate but not the first time she's made that mistake. His name definitely rhymes with Ken; of that Jezebel is certain. "Ben?" she chances.

"No." He slumps back down again.

She hazards another guess, quickly running out of options. "Glen?"

"For god's sake, it's Nigel," he snaps, rolling over to lie on his back.

So much for that, Jezebel thinks. "Well, be that as it may, Nigel, you need to go."

He props himself up on his elbows. "You live with your family?" The question is a delayed reaction to her earlier statement.

Jezebel could answer yes, she lives with her family—well, at least, what remains of it—but she knows Nigel doesn't mean it in *that* way. She could explain it to him, but what's the point? He won't remember, and every extra minute that he stays in her bed is another minute that she risks Queenie running into him on his way out.

Not in the mood for another one of Queenie's lectures about the sisterhood's safety after the last two break-ins, Jezebel just says, "Yes, and they won't approve of your being here, I'm afraid, so you'll need to leave."

"I thought we might have another tumble in the old haystack." Nigel's gaze drops to Jezebel's black satin negligee, its bodice pulled tight to display the breasts that have been the downfall of innumerable men and almost as many women. He wiggles his bushy eyebrows suggestively, looking down at his flaccid penis, clearly hoping it will show the same kind of fortitude as it did last night.

Poor fool isn't to know that his raging erection was entirely Jezebel's work, and that she regretted the help almost instantly. Certain men, when gifted a reliably rock-hard member, became like little boys with sticks. Nigel, unfortunately, turned out to be one of them. He was all poke and no stroke, his own pleasure being the entire point of his pointy end. Which had left Jezebel most unfulfilled.

If Nigel were a better lover, like the younger one from last week, Jezebel might be tempted to let him stay. "There won't be any more tumbling," she says, wistfully imagining Nigel taking a tumble down the stairs. "You really need to go." Her thoughts are already on how the inclement-weather ritual room might be the perfect picnic spot, less chance of Ursula's allergies acting up in there than in the conservatory.

But, instead of skedaddling, Nigel lies back down again. "Rustle me up some coffee first like a good girl."

"What did you just say?" Jezebel's voice is pitched low, deceptively calm, like the air holding its breath before a hurricane.

"Some breakfast would be nice too," Nigel says by way of response. "I like my eggs sunny-side up."

Jezebel leaps up, sending the suspended bed swaying back and forth. She lands next to it, hands on her hips, nostrils flaring.

Nigel has clearly never seen a woman move that fast and with such fluidity. It's to his detriment that he notes as much. "Wow, you can really motor for an old girl."

Jezebel's eyes flash with rage, steely-blue sparks flying from them so that they resemble one of Queenie's welding rods. Nigel jolts like he's been shocked with a Taser.

Fury builds inside Jezebel, escaping through her mouth. "Get. Out," she shrieks.

Nigel doesn't move, though whether it's out of obstinacy or shock, it's difficult to tell. Jezebel raises her hand, pointing her index finger just beyond where Nigel sits gaping. His clothes, discarded on the floor last night, begin rising, seemingly of their own volition.

First the shirt, then his trousers. And then his tie, belt, underpants, shoes and socks. As Nigel watches, openmouthed, the loose items of clothing suddenly fuse together as though in the grip of an invisible giant's hand. While keeping her finger trained on the bundle, Jezebel raises her other hand and makes a flicking motion at the bay window.

It flings open with a whooshing sound, and the wind, now unleashed inside, sends the draperies billowing and animates Jezebel's hair. If Nigel were better read, Medusa might spring to mind. With another flick, Jezebel sends the cannon ball of clothing rocketing across the room and out the window.

"Hey!" Nigel objects, bolting upright. "What the hell—"

"Be a good boy and run along, now," Jezebel commands.

Nigel jumps up and starts backing away from her. "You're a crazy bitch, do you know that? What are you getting all hysterical for?"

Well. That. Is. It.

The sparks flying from Jezebel's eyes ratchet up to a pyrotechnic display. Bringing her hands together in a circle, she conjures what looks like a ball of turquoise fire. It crackles ecstatically between her fingers before she draws her hand back and throws it at Nigel with her pitching arm.

He squeals as it strikes him in the chest. A poof of smoke goes up, and then Nigel is gone. In his place, stands a black potbellied pig with a white-streaked face.

"You'll find your clothes around the back on the lawn. Just don't go wandering off into the forest. I'm not coming to save you." Jezebel touches her middle and index fingers to her lips, blowing the pig a kiss. When it finds its target, the pig's eyes glaze over, and it smiles stupidly.

Having issued her instructions, Jezebel shuts the door firmly behind Nigel, returning to bed with a sigh. She splays herself across the silken sheets, closing her eyes as she tries to calm the fire in her blood. Losing her temper is never a good thing. It's best to distract herself so that the mood can't ripen into something truly dangerous.

Without meaning to, Jezebel's thoughts flit to Artemis, the fifty-nine-year-old sustainable-agriculture consultant she met a few months ago to discuss juniper-berry foraging. Artemis, with his dimples like twin canyons, and those amber eyes that positively simmer with mirth. Her imagination lingers on his beautiful hands and his wicked laugh, wondering what both might unleash in her if she'll just allow him to get close enough.

But it's this exact gravitational pull—his power to make her wonder and, more than wonder, yearn—that makes Jezebel wary of him, makes her dismiss his flirtations and keep him firmly at arm's length. He's merely responding to her powers, that and nothing more. A relationship based on magical coercion is one doomed to failure, for a man without agency is not a man who can freely give his heart.

Pushing Artemis from her mind, Jezebel conjures up the memory of a particularly languorous threesome she enjoyed on a sultry Saturday afternoon in Tuscany when she visited Italy in her fifties. She slips her hand beneath her satin panties, thinking that sometimes the best way to get something done is to do it yourself.

Jezebel doesn't yet know that, despite her best efforts, she won't reach climax because the alarm will sound in less than five minutes. It's one that's only ever used when the coven is in peril and the lifelong companions are threatened with being separated. The last time they heard it, thirty-three years ago, they lost two of their sisters.

Moonshyne Manor Grimoire

Ursula's Mugwort & Sweet Laurel Incense Cones Recipe

Ingredients:

3 tsp. ground mugwort
3 tsp. ground sweet laurel
1 tsp. marshmallow root
1 tsp. honey
1 tbsp. water

Equipment:

A brass spell bowl
A mortar and pestle
A piping cone
A toothpick

Directions:

Add the dried mugwort and sweet laurel to a bowl and stir. Grind with a mortar and pestle. Add the marshmallow root. Slowly add the water, stirring all the while. Add the honey and combine well. Put the incense mix inside a small piping cone, pushing it in so it clumps together. Make a hole in the center of the cone with a toothpick. Tap the piping cone hard onto the table six times to loosen it from the sides. Use the toothpick to help push the incense out of the piping cone. Repeat until you've used all the incense mix.

Place the cones on a sunny windowsill to dry. After a day or two, move the cones to an airtight container. Light a cone in a well-ventilated room to summon your clairvoyance.

3

Saturday, October 23
Morning

Ivy squints in the gloom, the storm clouds having doused her usually bright conservatory in darkness. She shakes her head, and the dusk-pink camellias threaded through her gray bun mirror her annoyance. The flowers are ones that she's hybridized herself to hold the melancholy scent of summer rain, Ivy's favorite smell.

As she raises a hand to swipe at her fogged-up glasses, the sleeve of her robe falls back to reveal a forearm covered in vibrant etchings. The curator of the sisterhood's memories, Ivy's tattoos are a kind of photo album. There isn't a pivotal moment of their shared experience that isn't inked onto her skin. Their collective loss and abandonment manifest as thorns and brambles, and their triumphs and happiness are captured as honeycombs and hummingbirds.

Reaching into one of her robe's deep pockets, she withdraws

her elm-wood wand which she twirls as though spinning a baton. *"Claresce,"* Ivy chirps, and a halo of light immediately illuminates her work area.

Pocketing her wand, Ivy turns back to the corpse plant that she personally acquired from Sumatra many, many moon cycles ago. She peers out curiously from behind round wire-rim spectacles, her arresting green eyes sunken into a face that's weathered and lined from a lifetime of exposure to the elements. "Stop being coy, you little bugger, and show me what you've got," Ivy coaxes, running her soil-encrusted fingers along the plant's base.

The *little* part is ironic since the plant towers several feet above Ivy who, in her youth, stood six feet three inches in her stocking feet. She's now, in her greatly advanced age, a mere six foot, puny compared to the plant's twelve. But to be fair, almost everything in the conservatory looms above Ivy, coddled as the plants are.

Ivy recalls how, as a teenager, she started every day with an eight-mile hike across fields and pastures, collecting many of these plant samples alongside riverbeds and in groves. Now, with that new strip mall just two miles to the east, and those McMansion estates that sprung up a year ago like poisonous mushrooms a mile to the west, she chooses to walk the property's perimeter instead. But despite not leaving the Moonshyne Manor grounds, Ivy can't escape the Critchley Hackle townspeople who seem hell-bent on desecrating their land.

Every morning, there are new affronts littered across the property: condoms and empty liquor bottles; McDonald's and Taco Bell boxes charred in the remains of crude fires; words like *bitches* and *whores*—and even worse—carved into trees or spray-painted across rocks. The venom behind them appears, alarmingly, to be escalating.

Just this morning, Ivy had to heal two tree barks, as well as clear up another pit of ash and garbage, before rushing back to the conservatory, gratified to find that the corpse plant's spathe (which looks like a cluster of petals but is actually one giant, modified leaf) was purplish and frilly, a sure sign that it was ready to flower.

The spathe is attached to a huge yellow stalk called the spadix, giving the plant its scientific name, *Amorphophallus titanum* which ridiculously translates to *giant deformed phallus.* (A male botanist clearly named it. A witch would have beheld the stalk and seen that most powerful of all tools, a wand. *Virgula titanum* would be a far better classification for it).

Ivy's eager not just for the rare sighting of the plant's bloom—which only happens once a decade, smells like a rotting animal carcass and has the color of raw steak—but for a chance to get at the highly coveted pollen. She'll freeze some of it and ship it off to prestigious conservatories around the world. The rest she'll keep for the trickier of her elixirs (like the special one that keeps the sisterhood safe) and for powerful spells (like the one Ruby planned to conjure all those years ago).

Ivy's just summoning a stepladder, which comes clattering on its two legs down the pathway, when the morning's first set of footsteps pass outside the conservatory. Ursula's, if Ivy's not mistaken, though she's much more hurried than usual.

What's the big emergency?

As Ivy hitches up the hem of her robe so she can climb unencumbered, a second set of footsteps passes. Actually, a double set: four feet trotting along the hallway. In all likeliness, a pig.

Another of Jezebel's conquests, Ivy thinks, shaking her head, half in amusement and half in envy. *Her life is one big phallus smorgasbord, while I don't have so much as an hors d'oeuvre.* Ivy considers the massive plant in front of her. *Present company notwithstanding.*

Pondering Ursula's haste, Ivy thinks about how on edge Ursula's been lately, but then again, haven't they all, what with Ruby's imminent return? Ivy's nerves fray a bit more every time she thinks about all the potential for conflict in the following days. Who knows how Tabitha will react to the homecoming, considering her deep-seated grudge that none of them have been able to talk her out of? And Ruby will come bearing grievances of her own, make no mistake about that. Her silence has spoken louder than any angry words possibly could.

Worry is like a rocking chair, Ivy tells herself for the umpteenth time that week. *It gives you something to do, but it doesn't get you anywhere.*

It's such a pity that intellectualizing anxiety doesn't actually do anything to diminish it.

4

Saturday, October 23
Morning

Tabitha's seated in the Chesterfield Queen Anne armchair in the ground-floor library, inhaling the intoxicating scent of musty books and old parchments. She turns a flimsy page of a thick volume, the green leather of the book's cover almost perfectly matching her seat's upholstery. The tome is an early edition of Charles Dickens's *Bleak House*, and Tabitha's reading of it is the literary equivalent of marking the time.

Instead of watching sand falling steadily through an hourglass, she devours page after page, each word bringing her closer to what she's waited so long for: Ruby's homecoming and apology. It won't give Tabitha back what she's lost, certainly—some things can never be restored once taken. But Tabitha's sure it would be the jump-start she needs to reclaim her life and move on from this interminable limbo.

It was once noted by one of the other women of the manor—

probably Queenie, since it sounds very much like something she would say—that Tabitha has Resting Witch Face. It wasn't the kindest of observations, but it's certainly an accurate one, for Tabitha's brown cheeks are permanently puckered, giving her the air of someone who's just sucked on a lemon without downing the customary shot of tequila first.

Her dark eyes—anchoring disapproving brows that give the impression they're about to float away—are in constant motion, and she wears her hair in an Afro so resplendent that it resembles a full black moon. Tabitha has a haughty quality to her, as though she looks down on a world that she's decided will disappoint her, a world that has, ironically, lived up to her expectations in that regard.

She hasn't always been this way. There was a time when she was the hurricane's eye of any gathering—hell, she was the person who *threw* the parties, acting as a gateway through which the outside world could enter the insular realm of the cliquey women.

People were drawn to Tabitha as much by her clown-car heart—which was always making room for just one more—as by her fabulous sense of style and her famous menagerie. At any given soiree, guests were likely to see snakes draped around Tabby's neck, or vervet monkeys swinging from her arms, or birds roosting on her head like she was the crow's nest of a pirate ship.

But that was back when she was still able to leave the house to make friends, visit her animals and go shopping. Before Ruby put an end to all that.

Widget, startled by the wind's wailing, swoops down from her favorite spot on the top shelf. The crow glides around a rolling library ladder—an outstretched wing brushing against one of Tabitha's large polka-dot shoulder pads—before alighting on the perch next to her.

"Good girl, Widget," Tabby croons before turning another page, a noise on the stairs stealing her attention.

She looks up as a naked and distracted Ursula comes scurrying down the grand staircase. Tabby raises an eyebrow but says nothing. Everyone is entitled to their eccentricities, after all.

Reaching up, Tabby strokes the crow's wing. The bird doesn't respond to her touch, engrossed as it is with staring out the bay window at the dense forest that encroaches upon the manor from the property's perimeter, dragging its skirt of darkness a step closer every year.

Still, no matter how near the forest gets to the manor, it would never be close enough for Tabby, who wants so desperately to live in the woods with her creatures, her poor, abandoned creatures who call to her day and night but whose howls are especially piercing in the darkest hours.

Suffering as she does from the most terrible insomnia—never getting a moment's rest—Tabby was in the library when Jezebel arrived home with her latest fancy man at around two in the morning.

"Slut," Tabby muttered as Jezebel disappeared up the stairs.

In reply, Widget rasped what Tabby was really thinking. "I wish I were you."

For isn't envy usually the cause of the most vicious judgments that we pass on others, jealousy that they dare to live in ways that we, for whatever reason, cannot or will not? To Tabitha's credit, she takes the crow's gentle chastisements stoically, never denying the astuteness of its observations. After all, thanks to Ruby, Tabby hasn't had the thrill of a one-night stand in decades, hasn't felt the exquisite pleasure of a man's hand upon her bare hip in all that time.

When Tabitha spots the potbellied pig trotting down the stairs, she mutters, "Fool got what he deserved."

Widget caws, "Oh, how I miss passion. How I miss the delicious drama of it all."

Tabitha has seen countless naked men of all ilk doing the walk of shame over the past however many years. She's even occasionally seen the same man twice, though many years apart. She doubts Jezebel recognizes them as repeats; they certainly never recognize Jezebel. Her farewell *obliviscere* spell, blown as a kiss, ensures none of them remember anything that transpired.

It isn't every day that Jezebel sends Tabby a pig. Her visitor must have been a particularly loathsome specimen. "What does she think?" Tabby mutters, regarding the animal who's found its way into the library. "That I've got nothing better to do with my time?"

Widget responds, "Finally! Something interesting." If the crow could rub her wings together with relish, she would.

Tabby makes a clicking noise, and the pig trots over, sniffing the air around her, its eyes not quite finding purchase. She reaches out her hand to its white face and pink snout. The pig tries rooting in her palm, hoping for a treat, but comes away disappointed.

"Off with you," Tabby says. "Go on, out."

The pig turns and walks from the library, coming to a standstill in the foyer, its head cocked at the kitchen.

Sighing again, Tabby looks to the crow, who squawks, *"In hominem muta."*

There's a loud crack and, all at once, the pig is a naked man. He holds no interest at all for Tabby since he clearly isn't their unsettling intruder who's snuck past her not once, but twice, leaving Tabby flummoxed as to how he's managed it. Turning from him, Tabby regards the crow. Widget's feathers are so black that Tabby sometimes expects them to leave a trail of soot. She thinks how grateful she is for her familiar's presence and the security of the manor walls cocooning her.

But isn't that always the way? No sooner do you appreciate something than it gets snatched away.

<u>Moonshyne Manor Grimoire</u>

Jezebel's Candle Magic for Attracting a Lover

What you will need:

1 eight-inch pink pillar candle

1 handful fresh rose petals

1 tbsp. rose essential oil

1 tsp. orris root essential oil

1 tsp. jasmine essential oil

1 tsp. honeysuckle essential oil

1 tsp. gardenia essential oil

1 tsp. ginger essential oil

Equipment:

A sharp knife to carve with

A small bowl as used for spices or soya sauce

A pair of compostable protective gloves

Directions:

Carve your initials and astrological symbol on one side of the candle. Carve your love interest's initials and astrological symbol on the other. (If you cut yourself in the process, Ivy will tell you to put salve on the wound. Don't listen to her. A drop of blood will make the spell stronger.)

Pour all the essential oils into the small bowl. Put on the pair of gloves before tipping the bowl over your palm to empty the oils onto it. Rub your palms together, coating the gloves with the oil. Slather the oils up and down the shaft of the pink candle repeatedly. Sprinkle the fresh rose petals over the candle, getting them to stick to the sides. This is a messy business, but then, so is love.

Remove the gloves and put them in the compost bin. Wash your hands thoroughly, and light the candle.

Let it burn all the way down as you pleasure yourself thinking of your lover.

5

Saturday, October 23
Morning

Ursula pours boiling water into her divination cup, stirring the peppermint leaves. As she returns the copper kettle to its hook, she bends over. Her breasts—unprotected by a robe to secure them—flop down, embracing the cauldron like a long-lost friend. That's where Ursula's standing, next to the walk-in fireplace in the kitchen, cradling a scorched mammary, when she spots a potbellied pig wander into the foyer from the library.

The creature stops and looks her way, turning its head this way and that in appraisal, its pink snout all aquiver. Then, with a loud crack, the pig suddenly morphs into a naked man. The stranger, with a gray mustache and wispy white hair, blinks in surprise to find a kindred spirit as similarly unattired as he is, though he's seemingly unperturbed that he was a farm animal mere seconds before.

As the man assesses Ursula, she sees herself all too clearly through his eyes: her stocky frame and the extra padding that she's accumulated around her midsection over the past twenty years; the large blue veins that snake through her rather pendulous breasts, and the purple varicose ones that climb like vines up her legs; the cellulite that dents her thighs and buttocks, her skin so white that it's almost translucent; the square jaw that's only partially been softened by age; the brilliant blue of her eyes; and the spiked pixie cut of her gray-white hair.

Following his frank examination, the man nods at her wound. "Wearing brassieres more often would've helped you put up a better fight against gravity."

Ursula glances down at the man's testicles, which hang much lower than a young man's would. She wants to suggest that underwire underpants might have prevented gravity from making his goolies look so much like a Newton's cradle that she's absurdly tempted to reach out and flick them, setting them clacking back and forth against one another. But she bites her tongue, a lifetime habit.

The man doffs an imaginary cap and says, "You might want to put some petroleum jelly on that. I've had some experience myself with the...burning of sensitive bits." He winces here, his hand automatically covering his crotch. "They're utterly useless until they heal." With that, he turns, calling over his shoulder, "Have a good day." He strides to the front door, his bare bottom wagging jauntily.

Shaking her head, Ursula gets back to work. She's wasted enough precious time as it is.

6

Saturday, October 23
Morning

In the tunnel that connects the manor to the distillery, Queenie's on her way back after having to tend to yet another piece of broken equipment, one they can't replace due to their financial situation, a dire predicament whose increasing severity is becoming ever harder to hide from the sisterhood.

She kneels on the tracks, pinning back her silvery freeform locs with one hand, and trapping her robe between her knees so it won't get in her way as she peers under the cart.

Flames flicker from torches affixed to the walls, antagonized by the drafts snaking through the tunnel. Their leaping and swaying light is enchanting to the more romantic likes of Ursula and Ivy, but they annoy the living shit out of Queenie.

If they'd gotten the damn manor and distillery rigged up with electricity decades ago like she wanted, she'd have a steady light source, one that would allow her to properly see what the hell the problem is. Plus, it would make dealing with the increasing distillery breakdowns so much easier.

But no. Ivy, Tabby and Ursula view technology as something only required by the magic-deficient. And when Queenie appealed to Jezebel to side with her, Jezebel just shrugged in that annoying way of hers, saying that all the devices she needed were battery-powered anyway, though she was prepared to take Queenie's side if there was likely to be a vote.

There will be no vote now since they can't possibly afford the upgrade.

Queenie gets up and dusts herself off, trying to remember where she put her wand. She checks her lace-up Doc Martens to see if she didn't stick it in one of them like she sometimes does with wrenches or screw drivers. Alas not.

She buries her hands in her pockets. From the one, she withdraws two pencils, a protractor, a magnifying glass, three pipettes, some juniper berries, and a Swiss Army knife. From the others, she pulls out a half-smoked joint, a squeaky dog toy, a Snickers bar, a roll of antacids and three crumpled-up pieces of paper.

One's an old map that she carries everywhere; it's falling apart from being folded and refolded too many times. The other two are bills stamped *ABSOLUTE FINAL DEMAND* in an offensive shade of red. The sight of them sets Queenie's pulse racing, thinking how the sisterhood would have completely overreacted to their arrival if she hadn't had the presence of mind to keep intercepting Ivy's mail.

Luckily, with Ruby coming home in two days' time, there's a good chance none of them ever have to know. Since Ruby got them all into this bloody mess in the first place, she'll just have to help Queenie get them out of it. *And* keep her damn mouth shut about it in the process. It's the very least Ruby can do, all things considered.

Queenie frowns at the papers before returning them to her

pocket. From the rumors she's heard in town, they aren't the only ones struggling to make their payments. Magnus's old place was recently sold too. Swallowing back the lump in her throat that arises at the thought of Magnus, Queenie tears the Snickers wrapper with her teeth and shoves half the chocolate bar into her mouth before returning her attention to the cart.

It, like so many of Queenie's inventions, is something she's salvaged and refurbished for their purposes. Originally belonging to a children's ride at an amusement park, the cart consists of a fiberglass horse pulling Cinderella's pumpkin carriage behind it.

You can either sit on the horse's saddle or in the pumpkin. Queenie, of course, always chooses the horse, and she doesn't ride a ladylike sidesaddle, either. Jezebel rides the horse too, but only because she professes to like something hard between her legs. The others always choose the carriage, taking a literal back seat to Queenie, whose real name is Sybil but who they nicknamed Queenie when she appointed herself as their ruler when they were all still little girls.

The shell of the carriage ride is mounted onto wheels that fit onto the old underground tracks; that's how she usually ferries herself and the supplies back and forth between the manor and the distillery. Unless the cart suddenly breaks down, like now, and she's left fuming and stranded, trying to fix it. Just as she's *always* left to fix *everything.*

Thank the Goddess for her inventions laboratory in the manor's basement. It's where Queenie tinkers with all kinds of appliances and machinery, coaxing them back to fighting fitness. It's also where she draws up her blueprints and brings her fantastical creations to life. The lab is an external manifestation of Queenie's mind, an extension of her soul.

The thought of ever having to leave it makes Queenie's guts churn.

7

Saturday, October 23
Morning

In the remaining three minutes and thirty-seven seconds before Ursula sounds the alarm, she returns to her teacup and saucer on the harvest table and sets about alternately blowing at the liquid and sipping it. She tries ignoring both her headache and the throbbing pain of her burn and, now, her tongue that's being scalded by the hot tea.

When there's just a tablespoon of liquid remaining, Ursula begins the swirling-and-turning ritual, holding the delicate gold-rimmed cup in her left hand while whirling it three times from left to right. With her left hand, she carefully inverts the cup over the saucer, leaving it upside down for a minute, after which she turns it three times and puts it back upright, positioning the handle due south.

The tea leaves are littered all around the cup, but the parts that Ursula focuses on are the ones representing the present moment and the near future. Clustered around the cup's sides is a menacing darkness that makes her yelp. Her eyes dart from it to the rim for an indication of the more imminent danger. There she can discern a frightening mass behind what looks like a unicorn with a disco ball hanging from its horn.

The sight is so alarming that Ursula's fingers seize, the cup slipping from her hand and shattering around her bare feet. With the leaf formation now obliterated, it's impossible for Ursula to check the cup a second time to be *absolutely* certain of what she saw.

She's just considering going through the whole process again when her dull headache suddenly crystallizes to a point before detonating, pain ricocheting around her mind like it's in a room of mirrors. That's when she sees it, the vision.

There can be no mistake. Ivy's plants have let them all down. The protection they've offered the sisterhood has failed, and the castle walls are being breached. Catastrophe is on its way.

Ursula reaches for her wand. She points it heavenward, closes her eyes, and mutters, *"Grave periculum."*

As sparks of silvery-red light erupt from its tip, she feels the alarm as a desolate wind keening through the jagged cracks of her soul.

Jezebel is just building to a crescendo, the wave of her orgasm about to crest, when the alarm sounds. She experiences it as a numbness flooding every cell of her being, obliterating all sensation.

She's plunged into a silent darkness containing no smell, sight, taste or touch. It's the worst possible experience for a self-proclaimed hedonist. Jezebel screams but can't hear her own voice.

It's just as Ivy's making an incision in the side of the blooming corpse plant that the alarm sounds. The scalpel slips, slicing her finger, before it clatters to the ground.

Ivy experiences the alarm as a pollution of the senses: it's like being enveloped by billowing clouds of sulfurous smog. Swaying on the ladder, she gags at the chemical stench. As Ivy reaches out to steady herself against the plant of death, she hears the clinking and clanking of machinery, so loud that it feels like the industrial revolution is playing out in accelerated motion in her head.

Terror wraps itself around her throat with the strength of Japanese wisteria. "Not again," Ivy whispers, certain her old ticker can't possibly withstand a repeat of the heartbreaking loss that came before.

A drop of blood drips from her finger, splattering on the path below. Ivy thinks how strange it is that the bright crimson of it reminds her of the exact shade of lipstick Jezebel wore the night their world was torn apart.

Tabitha hears the alarm differently to the first time.

This time, it manifests as the opening notes of a dirge played on a pipe organ. Her vision darkens, as though shovel after shovel full of sand were being thrown down upon her resting in a lonely grave faceup. Widget feels it as the breaking of both wings.

It's horrifyingly final, and Tabitha gasps for air, snatching at it with both hands as though to cram fistfuls into her mouth.

Queenie is just reaching into the storage space under the horse's saddle to search for the wayward wand when Ursula sounds the alarm. It comes at Queenie from down the length of the tunnel, an invisible blast that knocks her legs out from under her, sending her reeling. In those interminable moments, as Queenie lies on the ground weak and helpless, she feels like she might never be of any use to anyone ever again.

It's a devastating thought. For all her complaining, Queenie often wonders how, if she can't solve her sisters' problems and take care of everything for them, what purpose she possibly serves.

But then slowly, strength begins to return. She flexes her fingers, and when they move, she uses her arms to prop herself up. Wiping the braids back from her eyes, her fingers brush against her wand that's been stuck in her hair this whole time.

Cursing, Queenie stands on trembling legs. Once she's sure they'll hold her weight, she begins running to the manor and her sisters, the two constituting everything that she lives for.

8

Saturday, October 23
Morning

Panicked by the alarm, the women and Widget descend upon the kitchen where they're bewildered to discover a trembling Ursula, who's inexplicably naked and standing there clutching one of her enormous breasts.

Queenie takes in the fallen wand and teacup shards littered around Ursula's bare feet. "What the hell happened?" she demands as the women galvanize into action around Ursula.

Ursula's nerves are shot, and so her thoughts don't take the most direct route in their attempt to answer. As Ursula begins telling a fragmented, highly edited version of events, Ivy dips her finger into the tiny jar of miracle potion she always carries, gently daubing it against the scorch mark on Ursula's breast, careful not to apply more pressure than is required.

Ursula winces but within seconds, the stinging pain begins to subside. She pauses her recounting to murmur her thanks, squeezing Ivy's hand, its birdlike bones squishing together in her grip.

Jezebel whips off her silk kimono revealing her black negligee. She wraps the gown around a naked Ursula, pulling her close to cuddle. "I heard that full bushes are making a comeback after all those years of Brazilian waxes," Jezebel whispers, nodding down. "And your bush is a most resplendent one, indeed."

"Thank you, Jez," Ursula says, smiling at how Jezebel never fails to make her feel better about herself.

Queenie tuts her impatience, and Ursula resumes the story. When she gets to the part about the naked man, all heads, Widget's included, turn as one to Jezebel who shrugs as though to say *But of course the naked man was mine.*

"Did you sound the alarm because of that?" Queenie asks. "Did he attack you? Was he the intruder who's broken in before?" Each rapid-fire question is like a shove to the chest, though Queenie intends them to be an embrace, her way of saying she's sorry she didn't protect Ursula.

"No." Ursula explains about the vision that came to her after the man left, wanting them to think that was the only sign of imminent danger, that she didn't second-guess both the cards *and* a tea reading.

"What was the vision?" Queenie prods. "What did you see?" And then something terrible seems to occur to her. Her voice pitches low, fear threaded through it, stitching the words with dread. "It wasn't about Ruby, was it?"

Just the mention of Ruby is enough to release a thousand butterflies flitting through Ursula's belly. If the sisterhood knew Ursula's part in everything that happened with Ruby, they'd never forgive her.

Ursula shakes her head, thinking of the two ominous signs she saw in the tea leaves: the one on the rim, indicating the present, and the one on the sides, alluding to the near future. She nudges away the sight of the darkness, knowing that Charon the Ferryman will only arrive in a few days' time, which still gives them time to deal with the terrifying prospect of being paid a visit by one of the most powerful dark wizards alive.

For now, Ursula focuses on the more pressing concern. "I saw an advancing mob of townsmen. They're all headed this way as we speak."

"For the love of the Goddess, why the hell didn't you lead with that?" Queenie demands, back to looking fantastically annoyed. "Is this about Ruby? Some kind of protest about her coming home?"

"No," Ursula says. "I don't think so. They're all walking behind a crane with a wrecking ball."

Ivy scoffs. "A crane and wrecking ball? Headed here? Impossible!" The manor was left to Ivy sixty-six years ago when her great-aunt Mirabelle died; it's unthinkable that anyone would try to take it from them. "They don't have the authority to tear the house down," Ivy declares crisply, turning to their ruler, confident that she'll clear this all up as she usually does. "Tell them, Queenie."

But Queenie doesn't tell them. Instead, her gaze drops, her combative questions dying on lips that are now drawn into a grim line. The *ABSOLUTE FINAL DEMAND* bills and useless map burn in her pocket.

Moonshyne Manor Grimoire

Jezebel's Full Bush Care

Waxed and bare nether regions are so last decade.
Grow out your lady bush and embrace those gray hairs,
nature's way of bedazzling your glorious vajayjay with
silver filaments, tinsel for your cooch.

Ingredients:

½ cup grape seed oil
¼ cup jojoba oil
2 drops peppermint essential oil
2 drops rosemary essential oil
2 drops lemon grass essential oil
1 drop camphor essential oil
5 drops lavender essential oil

Equipment:

A small tincture bottle

Instructions:

Pour all of the oils into a tincture bottle and mix together by shaking it. Apply 5 drops of the tincture to your full bush, using your fingers to massage it into your pubic hair. Let your fingers linger there as you luxuriate in being the full-bushed goddess that you are.

Moonshyne Manor Grimoire

Ursula's Tea-Leaf Reading Instructions

Ingredients:

1 pinch loose peppermint tea leaves
1 cup hot water

Equipment:

A white teacup and saucer

Instructions:

Place a pinch of the peppermint tea leaves directly into the cup and pour hot water over them. While the water cools, reflect on your intentions. When the temperature allows, begin sipping the tea. When there is approximately a tablespoon of liquid remaining in the cup, begin the swirling-and-turning ritual. Hold the cup in your left hand, swirl it three times from left to right. Then, still with your left hand, carefully turn the cup over a saucer. Leave it upside down for a minute, then rotate it three times. Turn the cup back upright, positioning the handle due south. The tea leaves should be stuck to the cup in a variety of clusters for you to interpret.

The five types of symbols you're most likely to encounter are animals, mythical beings, objects, letters and numbers. The cup is divided into three sections for prophesying. The rim symbolizes the present, the sides represent the near future, and the bottom of the cup signifies the far future. Trust your instincts to interpret the clusters correctly.

9

Saturday, October 23
Midday

It's a surprise when the doorbell rings seven minutes later since one never expects an advancing mob to be quite so polite.

The women are now fully dressed and clustered together. Well, all of them except Tabitha, who's nowhere to be seen. They reach out, interlinking their pinky fingers like they used to when they were little girls, and silently count to three, all of them squeezing at the same time, before releasing each other's hands and reaching into their pockets for their wands.

Queenie steps up to the threshold, the women squaring up behind her as Tabitha joins them from the library. Queenie tugs at the intricately carved double doors, and they swing inward, dragging the wind inside. It carries burnished fall leaves in its wake, raining down over the women like confetti.

Ivy, Jezebel and Ursula smile to be anointed by the Goddess. Queenie frowns, swatting the leaves out of her face. The women peer over Queenie's shoulder, expecting to be faced with men brandishing the requisite pitchforks and burning torches. What they encounter instead is a girl who looks very much like a sprite.

She has skin as pale as milk and white hair that corkscrews in all directions, giving her a dandelion-esque quality. Her eyes are an arresting blue that brings to mind the lapis lazuli crystals they all wear strung from leather cords around their necks to ward off psychic attacks. She looks familiar to Ivy, who can't think why that may be.

The wind buffets the girl, who appears to be about twelve, but it's difficult to say. She seems unperturbed, bracing against its onslaught by standing with her feet wide apart. A blue scarf trails behind her, fluttering like bunting at a festival. She has her hands buried in a red coat that's quite a few sizes too big for her. The coat triggers something for Ivy too, a memory that's just out of reach.

Misunderstanding the girl's presence, Queenie says, "We won't take any cookies today, dear, but do come back another time."

"Oh, I'm not a Girl Scout," the girl chirps, sounding *exactly* like a Girl Scout. "I'm Persephone. President of the Critchley Hackle chapter of the Young Feminists of the World Association."

Wondering if she's having an acid flashback from her youth, Queenie says, "I beg your pardon?"

Persephone, seeming to realize the advanced age of the women, speaks louder and slower, drawing out her syllables. "I'm Per-seph-o-nee. The pres-ah-dent of the Critch-ley Hack-kill Chap-ter of the Young Fem-ah-nists of the Wor-ld Ah-so-see-ay-shun."

"I heard you the first time, dear," Queenie says. "I'm just wondering what you're doing at our door."

"Oh, I'm here to fight the patriarchy," the girl replies, smiling widely.

Queenie turns back to the women to check that they're all hearing what she's hearing. Their incredulous faces assure her that they are. "'Fight the patriarchy'?" she parrots.

"Yes." Persephone nods. "They're, like, on their way here right now to knock down your distillery and house." She inflects the sentence like it's a question. "And we're here to prevent that from happening."

Peering past the girl, Queenie searches for reinforcements. "*We?* The rest of your…er…association are here?"

Persephone flushes. "Well, no. So far, I'm the only member of the Critchley Hackle chapter. But Ruth Bader Ginsburg is here with me, so that makes two of us." With that, she slaps her thigh, calling, "Ruth!" An Italian greyhound wearing a crocheted collar bounds to her side.

Queenie is still taking in this new development, and so it falls to Ivy to ask the obvious question. "How did you know they were coming?"

Before Persephone can reply, there's a rumble as a huge crane trundles into view at the property's edge. It turns off from the road, ignoring their long tree-lined driveway, heading straight at them over the lawn. A menacing wrecking ball hangs from an enormous arm, swaying as the imposing machine lurches its way closer. At least a hundred men of all ages march behind it, holding aloft placards and cell phones, filming their advance upon the manor.

Some wear Viking hats, which they cling to so as to stop the wind from snatching them away. Some are decked out in fur and face paint, while others wear camo gear, looking like they're either going hunting or to war, maybe both. They're all chanting something, but the words are indistinct because of the noise of the crane.

Jezebel spots a familiar face in the throng. *Fucking Nigel.*

He clearly found his clothes because he's properly attired for a witch hunt.

As the men and the machinery make their way down the lawn, Queenie steps around Persephone. The sisters crowd behind Queenie on the porch while Tabitha remains hovering in the doorway, its threshold a border she cannot cross.

"They look angry." Queenie turns back to Ivy. "Are you sure that last batch of calming elixir we put in the booze was strong enough?"

Ivy sniffs, incensed that her quality control and ingredients are being questioned. "Of course it was. Every single batch is always the exact same strength."

"Maybe that's the problem," Jezebel muses. "Their tolerance has probably gotten higher."

Widget glides past, settling on the porch railing. "They might need a stronger dose for the same effect," she caws.

Ruth Bader Ginsburg, apparently not a fan of talking birds, growls softly until Persephone shushes her. The girl looks at the crow, clearly wanting to ask questions but restraining herself.

When the crane comes to a standstill, as close to the manor as it can get with the enormous Angel Oak standing guard, its engine switches off, and the sisterhood can finally make out what the crowd is chanting.

"Heave-ho, heave-ho. Moonshyne's witches have got to go! Heave-ho, heave-ho. Moonshyne's witches have got to go!"

The women's spines stiffen as they tut and groan. They all have the exact same thought, which Widget verbalizes. "Not this shit again."

10

Saturday, October 23
Afternoon

Some of the men take occasional breaks from shouting to lubricate their throats, swigging from cans and bottles, none of which are from the Moonshyne Distillery. Their drinks all appear to bear the same unfamiliar purple branding.

Ivy studies the crowd, surprised to spot a few of the women who in the past have visited the manor under the protection of darkness to ask for the sisterhood's help. Some have come for assistance with fertility, others for remedies to stop their men from straying or being violent. As long as Ivy lives, she will never reconcile herself with the immense betrayal she feels when women turn against other women.

Queenie's eyelid twitches as she waits the mob out, irritated that the men need this additional time to preen and posture. She searches the crowd but doesn't see Critchley Hackle's mayor, Will Stoughton, or the bank manager, John Hathorne.

It's going to be another member of the town council who will step up, then. That, in itself, is interesting.

Queenie is proved right when Cotton Mather, the reverend of Critchley Hackle's megachurch, breaks away from the pack a few minutes later. He's in his sixties with a clean-shaven head and a neatly trimmed goatee. Two lines have carved themselves between his eyebrows, like twin exclamation marks. They're the sign of a man who takes great pleasure in frowning.

Not a fool by any means, the reverend isn't in his usual suit and tie. He's attired similarly to the rest of the group in hunting camo, though of a much higher quality and price point. His outfit says *I'm one of you. But I'm also so much better than you*, a message so subtle that his followers don't get it. They just see the camouflage they want to see and not the truth that it's disguising.

As the chanting ratchets up a notch, Queenie says, "Ursula—"

"I'm on it." Ursula puts her hand on Persephone's shoulder, pulling the girl back so that she's enveloped by the women, their cloaks obscuring her. As the dog follows her mistress into the thicket, Widget takes flight, soaring to the crane's tip where she comes to rest, tucking her wings neatly to her sides.

"Videos off," the reverend calls, and his men obey, lowering their arms and tucking away their phones. Once he's sure that all recording has ceased, he strides forward. "Sybil," Cotton growls, jutting his chin toward her in acknowledgment.

"Cotton," she replies, hands on hips.

"That's *Reverend Mather* to you."

"And that's *Queenie* to you," she counters.

"You're no queen," he spits.

"And I don't revere you, so just plain old *Cotton* it will have to be." It's the wrong thing to say, and Queenie knows it, but she's sick of always having to filter her thoughts in these dealings with the outside world, of having to pound away to soften them so they're sufficiently palatable for the tender egos of men like Cotton Mather and his ilk.

"You gonna take that kind of disrespect from her, Cotton?" someone yells from the crowd as other voices chime in, heckling their leader. "You gonna put that bitch in her place, or what?"

Cotton bristles. "See what you've done?" he asks Queenie. "See how you've upset my men?"

What Queenie wants to say is something she saw graffitied onto a wall in town: *Behold my field of fucks. Lay thine eyes upon it, and thou shalt see that it is barren.* Fifty years ago, these men would have tossed the N-word at her like grenades. Now, they just think it. Instead, she shrugs and says, "It's a pity your men are so sensitive."

A projectile is suddenly flung from the crowd and narrowly misses an unflinching Queenie, the bottle smashing behind her. There's laughter and jeering from the mob. Queenie's hands clench, and her nostrils flare. She's about to head down the porch steps to confront the idiot who threw the bottle when two things happen at once.

Ivy begins to recite under her breath, and Jezebel steps away from the women to lean against the porch railing, cocking her hip. The wind whips Jezebel's hair into a frenzy, framing her face. It's as she bites her plump lower lip that the first bolt of lightning tears through the sky, dragging its accompanying thunder just a few beats behind it.

The flare of it is like a heavenly flashbulb, lighting Jezebel up as hundreds of leaves twirl down dizzyingly upon her. Despite the threat of the storm, bottles fall away from lips, fists ease open, and jaws hang a bit slack as the men gaze upon her. It doesn't matter that she's almost eighty and that her powers have weakened considerably over the years. Jezebel still casts a mighty spell. Even the reverend feels her effect, though he recovers faster than the others.

"Good day to you, Reverend Mather," Jezebel says in that

seductive drawl of hers. Her voice is raised to be heard above the onslaught of the coming storm. "To what do we owe the pleasure of this visit? Are you here for a sneak preview of the small-batch lavender gin we're releasing next month? If so, we'd happily set up a tasting area for you and your friends in the distillery."

At this, a few of the men break ranks, so mesmerized that they forget why they've come, thinking artisanal lavender gin poured by the infamous Jezebel Jones is exactly what the doctor ordered.

"Back in line." The reverend's voice is raised in rebuke. The men look dazed as they return to their positions. Those who are there with women receive withering looks. "That's not why we came." The reverend flashes a shit-eating grin.

Jezebel inclines her head. "Then, why *did* you?"

"To demolish this den of iniquity."

"On whose authority?" Queenie calls.

"The town's authority. You're well behind on your mortgage payments and property taxes. We're here to foreclose and recoup the costs."

"We still have a week and a half to make those payments."

The reverend laughs. "We both know that's not going to happen. No one will give you another loan."

Queenie glances back at Tabitha, who's still standing at the threshold to the manor. Understanding what Queenie needs, Tabby nods, her gaze flicking up to Widget who's still perched at the top of the crane. The old crow takes flight in the direction of the town, cawing loudly as her wings carve through the air, struggling against the onslaught of the wind.

"Knocking our home down now, when we still have nine days to legally stay here, would be breaking the law, Cotton," Queenie says. "We'd be forced to call the police on you."

"Good luck with that," Cotton replies, smiling widely. "And

good luck finding an attorney to represent you. Or a judge who'd hear your case."

Upon scanning the crowd, Queenie finds Clyde and Randy, the town's two lawyers, as well as Elmer, its only judge, huddled together on the periphery. They shoot her sympathetic looks, all of them indebted to the witches for having helped their wives or children in some way. They aren't bad men, they're just ones whose hands are tied. Turning her gaze from them, Queenie recognizes three of the fools wearing Viking hats as members of the police department. One of them tips his hat's horns at her when their eyes meet. Another's hand goes to his firearm.

"It's people like you who are holding Critchley Hackle back," Cotton calls again, an evangelical quality to his voice. The men, sheep that they are, respond with a chorus of *Amens*. "We're trying to launch this fine city into a God-fearing future." More *Amens* follow.

"You think what God wants is more Walmarts and fast-food joints?" Queenie scoffs.

"God wants an end to abominations like you," Cotton calls, and his men answer. "He wants this town run by men who are prepared to fight against the evil in our midst."

"And all this time I thought God said that the meek would inherit the earth?"

Something flashes in the reverend's eyes then, a burst of light like a purple flare.

Ivy keeps up her steady incantation behind Queenie, and another fissure of lightning cleaves the sky, the thunder so loud this time that it makes Queenie's teeth rattle. The first splat of rain falls, followed quickly by dozens of its paratrooping comrades. And then the rain is pelting down hard enough to make all those manly men grimace, looking around for cover.

"Hold steady," Cotton calls to them as though this were a war, and he were their commanding officer. "It's just a bit of rain. No one ever died from some water."

On the contrary, Queenie thinks, *millions of people the world over have died from some water. Isn't the Old Testament proof of that?* Not to mention the thousands of witches over the centuries who were subjected to the so-called swimming test, dragged to nearby lakes or rivers, stripped and bound, and then tossed in. Ironically, the supposedly innocent would drown while the guilty would bob to the surface just in time for them to be burned at the stake.

As Queenie looks at Cotton Mather, she still can't understand why, for so long, people feared the witches instead of the men who burned them alive.

Lightning strikes nearby, and Queenie thinks how mixing it with water is a surefire recipe for disaster. But she isn't going to point that out to any of the damn fools trespassing on their property. Especially not the one sitting in the crane, which is nothing if not the perfect conduit for electricity being flung from the sky.

"I'd suggest you all get off that porch if you don't want to become a part of the rubble," the reverend calls to the women, his voice whipped away by the wind.

The crane rumbles to life.

"Ivy," Queenie pleads, her locs flapping wildly in the wind, slapping against her face, "now would be a *really* good time to get that crane fried."

Ivy, eyes closed and fingers pressed against her temples, continues muttering, sweat beading her forehead. She positively thrums with exertion as the pink camellias in her hair begin to droop. Queenie's gaze darts from Ivy to the heavens and then back again. But despite Ivy's best efforts, no more lightning strikes.

The crane lurches forward, its arm beginning to move back and forth in small increments to build up momentum for the wrecking ball. The men scatter from its path as though wanting to avoid getting pummeled by the massive swinging ball.

They regroup under the Angel Oak, which Queenie can't help but notice is the only protection from the deluge.

"Wimps," she mutters darkly, watching as face paint drips down from beards, making a few of the men more recognizable. And then turning her attention to the sisterhood, Queenie calls, "Quick, we need a circle." The women gather around. "Ivy," Queenie pleads again, panicked, the whoosh of the wrecking ball warming up behind them, "we really need that lightning bolt. We really, *really* need it right now."

The women, except Tabitha—who's still restrained by the manor's threshold—all come together, joining hands as they surround Ivy. They close their eyes, ostensibly turning inward, but this is when they're most connected, each of their individual energy being harnessed at its maximum capacity for the sake of the group. Their hands tingle with the force of the power and love coursing between them.

The sisters focus on Ivy, pouring all of their collective energy into her. She, in turn, focuses on the heavens, which spit and crackle, darken and roil. But, inexplicably, still no further heavenly intervention comes. And then, seemingly out of nowhere, a dog barks.

Suddenly remembering Persephone, the women all break apart, spinning around to check on her. There's some consternation to discover the white-haired girl handcuffed to one of the manor doors' giant wrought iron handles, Ruth Bader Ginsburg tucked under her other arm.

"What the hell—"

But Queenie's cry is interrupted by the reverend calling out, "Stop the ball. Stop the ball! That's the mayor's daughter."

Queenie groans inwardly. *Now we're really in shit.*

"Down with the patriarchy!" Persephone yells, her cheeks flushed.

11

Saturday, October 23
Afternoon

Cotton Mather storms up to the manor, joining the witches who are clustered on the porch. Queenie's not the only one shooting nervous glances at the mayor's daughter, who has complicated things so thoroughly with her presence. They're all thinking how the girl is going to bring hell raining down upon their heads.

As the reverend nears Queenie, the sisters close ranks around her, forming a protective wall. They may be pissed off with her, but they aren't about to let anything happen to her.

"You've taken this innocent child hostage!" Cotton splutters.

Queenie's about to reply that they didn't even know who the girl was, when Persephone yells to be heard above Cotton. "I have *not* been taken hostage."

The reverend's face takes on a puce hue that makes his face

look bruised. "You don't know what you're saying. You've been bewitched by these—"

"I am not bewitched." Persephone juts her chin out. "I came here voluntarily to prevent a miscarriage of justice."

Cotton Mather gawks at her like he's never heard anything so ridiculous as a girl knowing her own mind. Ignoring Persephone, he jabs a finger against Queenie's chest. "Wait until the mayor gets here. He'll have your ass put in jail so fast—"

"Could you please stop shouting?" Persephone cries out, flinching.

"Why? Am I *triggering* you?" the reverend sneers.

"No, you're *spitting* all over me. It feels like biological warfare getting so much of your slobber on my face."

Cotton is briefly speechless, gawping at Persephone, before turning and calling for help with her handcuffs.

The three bedraggled police officers, huddled under the Angel Oak, look relieved to be summoned. The tree's been dropping enormous acorns upon them at an alarming rate, a surprising turn of events because it's already late October and, from what they can tell, there are no actual acorns on any of the branches.

"Where are the keys?" one of them asks Persephone.

"In my pocket."

He reaches in, yanking at something. But whatever it is, it won't release. It just keeps on coming, dozens of multicolored scarves all tied together unfurling in a seemingly endless chain. "What the f—"

Queenie has to resist the urge to laugh.

"Other pocket," Persephone says, deadpan.

The officer reaches in there, and this time extracts an enormous bouquet of fake flowers.

"I'll use my own key," the officer mutters.

But upon attempting to open the cuffs, he discovers his universal ones don't work. Another of the cops steps forward to struggle with the lock.

When he jostles Ruth Bader Ginsburg, Persephone's grin disappears. "You hurt my dog and I'll report you for animal abuse. Can't you see how old and fragile she is?"

Ruth Bader Ginsburg may appear so, but she's also clearly fierce and has strong side-eye game. The dog growls every time one of the cops gets too close, repeatedly forcing them to back off.

When the policemen give up, Persephone motions Queenie over by cocking her head. "These are maximum-security handcuffs," Persephone whispers. "It was difficult getting my hands on them, but I suspected we may need them for this eventuality."

"Bit of a gamble, don't you think?" Queenie says, admiring the girl's courage. "Resisting cops could end badly." Queenie knows this only too well from personal experience.

"Oh, I'm white," Persephone replies, shrugging. "We all know nothing bad will happen to me, so I'm leaning into that."

Queenie snorts and shakes her head. "Out of the mouths of babes."

Despite the complications that Persephone's presence brings, Queenie has to respect the girl's chutzpah. It's the kind of energy Queenie remembers them all having back when they were around her age, when their blazing indignation still burned bright, not yet extinguished by decades of having to face the same shit over and over again, nothing ever changing.

An underling is promptly dispatched to head to the hardware store to purchase a ceramic tungsten-carbide saw blade, but that just makes Persephone grin even wider. "They only work on standard cuffs," she informs Queenie from the corner of her mouth.

Despite all the attention, and the towering authority figures surrounding the girl, Queenie thinks she looks very much like someone thoroughly enjoying herself. Her eyes are shiny as magpie treasure, and her pale cheeks are flushed. The kerfuffle has suited her, making her look less anemic.

As the girl's father is called to the scene by the reverend, the storm continues to rage, though it's a Faulkner kind of storm: full of sound and fury, signifying little without the lightning strikes Ivy conjured it to produce. Unable to demolish the house with the girl so firmly attached to it, the crane operator announces that he'll be off as he has another job booked two towns over. And unlike *this* job, they're paying him time and half because it's a Saturday.

"Good riddance," Queenie calls, waving him off just as a local reporter pulls up the drive.

His arrival is the equivalent of a rotten log being lifted from the dank forest floor: it sends most of the men scattering like the kind of slimy insects who prefer decay to sunlight. The judge and lawyers skedaddle, not wanting to be put in the sticky predicament of having to account for their presence at a modern-day witch hunt.

Queenie waves them goodbye too, smiling as she mutters obscenities under her breath.

The journalist, sopping wet after dashing from his car to the porch, bypasses Queenie and walks straight up to Persephone. "Hello, young lady. Could you tell me why you're staging this protest?"

In reply, Persephone hands Ruth Bader Ginsburg across to him. "My arm's going numb. Could you hold my dog for a minute? If she likes you, I might give you an interview."

Queenie snorts as the journalist takes the dog, cradling it awkwardly. He smiles as he straightens Ruth Bader Ginsburg's crocheted collar, patting her on the head, which has the effect of lulling her to sleep. Queenie can relate; it's been a damn busy morning, and she's equally tuckered out.

A car door slams, and Queenie looks up to see Persephone's

father, Will Stoughton, arriving on scene. The mayor of Critchley Hackle is a large man, both in personality and in girth. He looks to be in his midfifties and has an air of general neglect about him, like a lawn that hasn't been mowed in months. While he wears a nice-enough jacket, it's plain to see that the shirt under it is creased as all hell.

He has pouches under his eyes and a florid complexion. His five-o'clock shadow appears to have shown up six hours too early, like an overeager prom date. As he thumps up the manor's stairs, dripping wet, he curses under his breath that his loafers are now completely covered in mud.

Queenie looks to the sisterhood. As one, they all orbit around Persephone, creating a barrier between the girl and her ill-tempered father.

Ivy draws herself up to her full height, formidable despite her exhaustion. Ursula takes a deep breath, her considerable bosom expanding, making her appear wider than she is, as she links arms with Jezebel, who no longer looks quite so coquettish: there's rage simmering below the surface, waiting to erupt at the slightest provocation. Tabby glowers from the open door.

"Phony, what in tarnation is the meaning of this?" Will Stoughton demands, peering past all of them.

"I told you not to call me that," Persephone replies, scowling.

Her father rolls his eyes. "It's just a nickname, pumpkin."

"So is Stout, but you don't like it when people call *you* that."

Queenie barks a laugh, and William Stoughton flushes. He takes a deep breath and pulls his jacket closed around his paunch, trying to do up one of the buttons. Shaking his head, he motions to Persephone. "Come, we're going home. You don't belong here."

"Women belong in all places where decisions are being made." Persephone raises her chin, making Queenie proud.

The mayor huffs, eyes raised heavenward. He's wondering the same thing that all fathers of teenage girls eventually do.

Whatever happened to his obedient little girl? One day, not too long ago, she was sugar and spice and all things nice, and now she's hot peppers and sass, blowing smoke up his ass.

"How in the blazes does handcuffing yourself to the witches' door—"

It's at this point that Queenie intercedes. "What I'd be interested to know is how your daughter knew about the demolition crew, Mayor Stoughton." The journalist steps forward, mouth open, but Queenie shushes him. "I'd dare say it's a case of little pitchers having big ears. And if Persephone overheard a conversation about it, that points to collusion on your part. Collusion *and* sanction. Which I'm sure Mr., er…" Queenie trails off, motioning at the journalist.

He jumps in, readjusting Ruth Bader Ginsburg in his arms. "Reggie Collins."

Queenie thanks him before turning back to Stoughton. "Which I'm sure Mr. Collins would be interested in exploring further."

"I would, yes," the reporter confirms, his voice dipping low when Ruth Bader Ginsburg suddenly opens a beady eye and growls at him.

"I'd be prepared to give a statement telling you everything," Persephone says to the bespectacled reporter before turning back to her father, "unless you promise not to knock down their house until their time is officially up. It's only fair, Daddy."

As the mayor runs his fingers through his buzz cut, thinking through all the implications, Queenie leans in close and murmurs, "Mr. Collins can be made to forget this whole exchange, if that's what's bothering you."

William Stoughton squirms as he struggles with this offer, wondering what means would be employed by witches to make someone forget a whole episode.

Persephone pulls her cell phone from her pocket. "A Tik-

Tok or two of me crying would get a lot of attention, especially when I show the world that you're picking on little old ladies."

Queenie has no idea what a TikTok is, but it sounds exactly like the kind of powerful weapon they need, and so she's all for it.

They have Mayor Stoughton by the short and curlies, and he knows it. He doesn't even try to claim innocence or bluff his way out of it. He just heaves his large shoulders and sighs. "You have until the close of business in nine days," he mutters gruffly to Queenie.

"Until midnight, actually," she shoots back. All contracts entered into by witches have that clause built into them.

"Fine."

Something begins ticking nearby. It takes Queenie a moment to realize it's a Deathwatch beetle counting down the time. They don't have a minute to waste.

12

Saturday, October 23
Afternoon

As Queenie makes her way to Ivy's laboratory on the second floor, she'd never admit to feeling overwhelmed, since that would suggest she isn't capable of dealing with everything, which she is, of course. Still, it's a lot she's having to juggle.

There are her suspicions about what's happening with the townsmen that need to be confirmed, after which she'll have to come up with a plan for how to deal with that fallout. They also have to get the manor ready for Ruby's homecoming in two days, and after that, they'll have another two days in which to retrieve the treasure so that Queenie can hand it over to Charon the Ferryman in what will hopefully be a seamless transaction.

Following that, Queenie has only five days in which to make the payment to the bank, squaring everything up, and she's not stupid enough to believe the men of the town council will make that easy for her. She wouldn't be at all surprised if they have a few dirty tricks up their sleeves to prevent her from settling the debt. The Goddess knows the men enjoy tormenting the sisterhood.

And only after all of that is taken care of will the real work begin, because Ruby's homecoming will save them from the immediate threat of homelessness but it won't solve the larger, ongoing issues. Queenie has to make the business more profitable going forward so that they don't end up back here again in another year or two. She needs to figure out what's causing all the breakdowns in the distillery and then ensure that their sales improve.

When Queenie reaches the lab, her knock goes unanswered. She's just about to backtrack her route down the hallway to see if Ivy's in the conservatory, when Ivy comes bustling around the corner, robe dripping, and hair plastered to her face.

"Sorry I'm late." Ivy swipes mud from her forehead. "The lawn needed tending after that bloody crane churned everything up. And I had to bolster the Angel Oak. It was thoroughly depleted after having to produce all of those acorns."

Queenie nods, intrigued. While most people are only interested in the effects of magic, what fascinates her is the science of it. For that's what magic is, harnessing and bending natural laws in ways that most people can't. "How did you go about strengthening it?"

Ivy extracts a key from her pocket, opening the lab's door. She never used to lock the room: this is a new security measure Queenie suggested following the break-ins. "All parts of a tree need the sugars that its leaves produce through photosynthesis," Ivy explains, waving her wand at the wall sconces that obediently burst into flame. "Before a tree sheds its leaves, it extracts as much of their sugars as possible, sending them down the tree, to feed the branches, trunk and roots."

"Pressler's law." Queenie nods.

Ivy dips her head. "Exactly. I had to get some of those sugars back up the trunk again so the tree could sprout new leaves."

"And photosynthesize more sugars to replace the ones it lost today," Queenie finishes for her. "Genius!" Queenie's amazed that Ivy had the power left to work such intricate magic after depleting herself so thoroughly by conjuring the storm. She produces her own wand, pointing it at Ivy, muttering, *"Sicca."*

Ivy, who's come to a halt at one of her workstations, begins to dry off in a puff of steam. "Thank you." She dusts off her hands, and her lip quivers as she says, "But what if it was all for nothing? What if that wrecking ball comes back in nine days, joined by a fleet of bulldozers, to raze everything to the ground?"

"I'm not going to let that happen." Queenie returns her wand to her pocket, maintaining eye contact with Ivy all the while. "Trust me, I'm going to fix everything before then, okay?"

Ivy nods, turning brusque. "I assume you didn't ask me to meet you here for a lesson in dendrology magic?"

"No." Queenie hands Ivy a Snickers bar. "I came to bring you lunch since we all skipped breakfast."

Ivy eyes it suspiciously. "That's hardly a meal."

"It's all we have time for." Queenie shrugs and adds, "It has peanuts. They're vegetables, right?" Queenie winks and Ivy laughs, taking the Snickers with a thanks and tearing into it.

Once the chocolate bar has been devoured, Queenie plonks a bag down on the table, withdrawing a few cans and bottles discarded by the mob. The beer cans are a bright metallic purple, and the tequila bottles have clear glass with purple labels. The brand's logo depicts the letters *SWT* engulfed by flames. "I need you to run some tests on these."

"And what exactly am I testing for?" Ivy asks, eyebrows raised.

Queenie tells her, causing Ivy's brows to shoot up even

higher. "Did you see that strange gleam in Cotton's eyes earlier?" she asks.

Ivy sighs. "He always has a maniacal gleam in his eyes, Queenie. He's a fanatic."

"It was more than that. Like a purple spark that was otherworldly. And definitely more than just good old-fashioned misogyny."

Ivy sighs. "What you're asking is difficult to test for. I don't suppose you have any of the men's blood?"

"No, but that could always be arranged." Queenie wiggles her eyebrows.

"Never mind the blood." Ivy sighs again, adjusting her glasses as she thinks. "This is going to be incredibly difficult."

"Just see what you can do," Queenie says. She turns to go, already thinking ahead to everything that still needs to be done.

"Where are you going?" Ivy asks, annoyed. "I thought you might stay and help."

"I've got to have a chat with Widget as soon as she returns, and then I have another errand to send her on. We'll convene later." When Queenie reaches the door, she stalls and turns around, needing to get something off her chest. "I'm… I'm sorry about everything." It's a struggle for Queenie to get the words out, like pushing boulders up a hill. "Today was all my fault."

"How so?" Ivy asks, head cocked. "I mean, I agree. You absolutely should have told me about the financial troubles right from the start. I'm furious with you that you didn't. But how's the mob your fault?"

Queenie shrugs. It's her job to protect the women. It's something she promised on Mirabelle's deathbed that she would do. When Queenie swore an oath to the matriarch who had taken all of them in, she was serious about it. The thought that she's let Mirabelle down fills her with a bubbling shame.

As though reading her mind, Ivy says, "Just as I can't do everything, Queenie, neither can you. Nor should you be expected to. We're all just doing the best we can."

Queenie nods her thanks. Ivy could have made this so much harder for her, and she appreciates that she didn't. Heading down to the library, Queenie thinks that once her suspicions are confirmed, she'll have to figure out a way of dealing with the problem of the townsmen. But first, she needs to know who's behind the scheme, orchestrating all of it.

It's exhausting to be under constant attack, threats coming from all sides. Queenie takes a deep breath to steel herself for what's still to come.

<u>Moonshyne Manor Grimoire</u>

Ivy's Dendrology Magic

Plant Tonic:

Ingredients:
¼ cup Epsom salts
2 cups urine (witch's urine is best, but that of the magic-deficient will work just fine in a pinch)
2 cups wood ash (no charcoal or anything containing lighter fluid)
+/-20 lbs grass clippings/green weeds/pruned green leaves
3 gallons water
1 dandelion

Equipment:
A 5-gallon bucket
Empty milk jugs

Instructions:
In the 5-gallon bucket, mix the Epsom salts, urine and wood ash. Fill the rest of the bucket about halfway with grass clippings, pruned green leaves or green weeds pulled right from the ground. Thank the trees from which you've pruned the leaves.

Fill the bucket to the top with water and drop the dandelion into the mixture while giving thanks to the Goddess. Point your wand at the mixture and say Convenite. *Allow the mixture to steep for three days. After steeping, strain the tea or decant into empty milk jugs. Before use, dilute by 50% by mixing half water and half tonic into a watering can. Apply the tonic by pouring it directly onto the soil around your plants.*

Note: Steep for three days only as you want to avoid fermentation. Use the concentrate within a day or two.

13

Saturday, October 23
Evening

Ivy points a shaky hand at the parlor's fireplace and mutters, *"Incende."* When the flames leap to her command, she's ridiculously gratified to have achieved such a mundane task considering how utterly depleted she is.

The old house creaks and sighs, relieved to have survived the storm's onslaught. Something taps in the walls, the manor's steady heartbeat. The trees just beyond the window murmur assurances, as the fire crackles and pops an upbeat melody.

A creature howls from the forest; it's so plaintive—like the sound of unrequited love—that it sends goose bumps up Ivy's arms. Night has fallen, and the witching hour is upon them. Or at least, the witching hour for elderly witches who can't be arsed to stay up until three in the morning like they used to in their prime.

Despite her exhaustion, Ivy didn't try for a nap. How could

she with everything that needed doing, like erasing the journalist's memory, running those tests Queenie asked for and checking on the corpse plant after her incision was interrupted by the alarm.

Despite all her care and attention, the plant flowered without Ivy being there to witness its dramatic show. Its entire blooming will be over by morning, the spathe already dead. At any other time, her heart would be broken by missing out on the process, but now with the threat of losing the manor hanging over them, Ivy doesn't have the emotional bandwidth to be disappointed. Especially since the entire conservatory could be demolished in just over a week. If anything, what she feels when thinking about it is a simmering anger, a resentment that she isn't sure where to direct.

Remembering her sliced finger, Ivy checks it only to find that the tip is inflamed. Sighing, she reaches into her pocket for some salve, thinking that what she really needs is her entire aching body to be soaked in a bathtub full of it. Her stomach growls, reminding her that it's there and is very empty, one Snickers bar not enough to sustain her.

As the warmth of the fire begins working its magic on her stiff joints, Ivy looks around the parlor, taking in its coffered, twenty-five-foot ceiling, ornamented with carved columns and fanned wooden arches that resemble a peacock's gilded plumage.

The fireplace is limestone-topped with the DuBois coat of arms inset with lapis lazuli. The elaborate hand-carved couches scattered about the room are upholstered in mint-green and burgundy velvet, rumpled with age, and passementerie-trimmed. Heavy brocade curtains, with gold-tasseled tiebacks, cast the already-dark room into a curated gloominess.

The shabbiness of the once-opulent room feels too much like a chastisement, and so Ivy snaps her fingers and closes her eyes. When she opens them again, the parlor as it was before is gone. It's now completely adorned with ivy-covered walls, Nepal ivy to be exact, with its leathery leaves, the glossy dark green of them juxtaposed against the almost yellow midrib and veins.

The carpet has also disappeared and been replaced by silky forklet moss. Ivy kicks off her boots and wrestles off her socks, threading her bare toes through the moss's sponginess, reveling in the exquisite sensation.

Ivy's asked the others if the house does this for them, offering up its little tricks. They all claim to not know what she's talking about, and so Ivy has come to understand that the manor becomes a chameleon only for her, who it apparently defers to. It must have once done the same for Great-Aunt Mirabelle before transferring its allegiance to Ivy after her aunt's death.

After snapping her fingers again, the old parlor is back. Hovering above the room, looking down from her lofty perch, is the life-size oil portrait of Great-Aunt Mirabelle DuBois, auburn hair piled upon her head in a lavish swirl, pinned up with a peacock feather hairpiece. She's young in the painting, probably in her thirties, and yet there's no sign of the fashion of the times, no corset or bustles to be seen.

Instead, she's wearing a man's suit, tailored to fit her curvaceous form, and she brandishes a smoldering cigarette tapering from a sleek jade holder. There's something rakish about her, a mischievous quality to her green eyes that the artist captured perfectly.

Ivy never knew her aunt at that age, of course. They only met when Mirabelle was the same age, more or less, as Ivy is now. How ancient she seemed to Ivy then with her crevassed face, powdered cheeks, bright red lipstick bleeding into the cracks of her lips, and eyes surrounded by cobwebby wrinkles.

It's uncomfortable comparing herself to the older woman who, at the same age, was not only successfully raising and tutoring six little girls but also thoroughly maintaining the manor, while beginning to make plans to one day hand it over to Ivy. And look at what Ivy has managed to do with Mirabelle's legacy: the house is falling to ruin around them and about to be wrecked by the town council unless Ruby—who hasn't lived here in decades—can help them save it.

It's infuriating to be in this predicament, and Ivy, who's usually so even-keeled, is thrown off-kilter by her rage. She takes a few deep breaths, trying not to dwell on it, thinking instead how apt it is that Mirabelle is on display in this room, since this is where they've always gathered for important meetings.

It's where Ivy was first introduced to both Mirabelle *and* the manor when she arrived late one night eighty years ago, orphaned at the age of seven after both of her parents died within a month of each other. Her father first, from tuberculosis, and then her mother, Mezula, from poisoning.

Mezula was an apothecary by trade, and so there was talk of tinctures having gone off, or perhaps some kind of mishap with the mixing of dangerous ingredients, but Great-Aunt Mirabelle scoffed at that, saying Mezula was too skilled a practitioner for that.

"Death by her own hand" is what she told Ivy. "Death by broken heart. Your mother didn't want to live after she failed to save your father." Mirabelle had cupped Ivy's chin, leaning in close to impart her wisdom. "Remember that, darling girl. No matter how great our powers," she'd said, "death's power is greater still. The closest thing we will ever have to it is love."

But what was the point of love, Ivy had wondered, when it propelled you to act in such impetuous ways? When it made you abandon your daughter who needed you desperately, when it caused you to throw yourself headlong into the chasm of death because you could not live without it? If that's what romantic love was, then Ivy wanted no part of it. She considers her avoidance of it a wise decision in light of what went on to happen with Ruby, Magnus and Ursula.

What Ivy remembers of that very first year living with her eccentric aunt in her enormous house is how the manor worked so hard to amuse and distract her, alcoves calling to her and furniture skittering about as it played an elaborate game of cat and mouse.

She recalls too the strange comings and goings at all hours of the night, hooded women arriving on the doorstep, only to disappear into the woods hours later. When Ivy asked about the women as her great-aunt tucked her into bed one night, Mirabelle explained that they were members of her sisterhood.

"Mark this, my child," Mirabelle said. "The strongest alliances you will ever have in your life will be with the women you choose as your family."

"But you don't get to choose your family." Ivy was confused. "You're born into one."

"You get two families," Mirabelle clarified, tucking a wayward strand of hair behind Ivy's ear. "The one you're bonded to by blood ties, and the one you're bonded to by a force far greater than blood. Choice is a mighty powerful thing, Ivy. When the time comes, choose your sisters wisely."

But Ivy didn't get to choose the members of her sisterhood like Mirabelle had, because the manor chose each of them for her, drawing them to Ivy, one by one, by the power of its enormous gravity.

Just over a year after Ivy arrived and was beginning to feel lonely, she was startled awake in the early hours of the morning by an approaching buggy and horses. Flinging off her covers, Ivy rushed down the long hallway to the reading window overlooking the driveway. Pressing her nose and palms against the icy glass, she looked down, recognizing Anastasia, one of Mirabelle's mysterious nighttime visitors.

With her was a blonde girl, a year or two younger than Ivy, who looked up at the manor with an expression akin to recognition. From eavesdropping, Ivy learned that the six-year-old was called Ursula and that her mother had been murdered in her bed by an unknown assailant. The child, having been born covered with a caul, apparently had second sight and could describe the man perfectly despite not having seen him.

In the following weeks, Ivy overheard other conversations, darker ones. Based on Ursula's description of the murderer, Mirabelle's sisterhood had identified and tracked him down. They left the manor late one moonless night, flying east in a loose formation. They returned just before daybreak looking exhausted but satisfied. To the best of Ivy's knowledge, whatever they'd done was never referred to again.

Ursula was the manor's first gift, bequeathed like a cat might present its master with a mouse.

Though a year had passed between Ivy's and Ursula's arrivals, it was a mere day after Ursula showed up that a six-year-old Ruby arrived. The redheaded, violet-eyed child had apparently been abandoned on the steps of an orphanage with a note pinned to her pajamas. It read *Take it. There's something wrong with it.* The orphanage clearly agreed with its author, playing a game of pass the parcel as they sent Ruby on.

Ivy recalls how, on the night Ruby arrived, Ursula joined her out on the porch, arms outstretched, the two girls falling into each other like those finding the key to the lock of themselves.

Anyone else might have considered that a strange second gift, more a present for Ursula than for Ivy. But the manor knew how Ivy felt about attachments despite her loneliness, how much easier it was for her to tend to her plants than to the little girls whose damaged souls throbbed with such need. And so the manor gave Ivy two sisters who didn't need her all that much as long as they had each other.

Four months later, Ursula's head snapped up. Eyes wide, looking past Ivy and Ruby at something neither of them could see, she whispered, "Another one's coming."

An hour later, the three girls watched from the reading window as six-year-old Queenie—covered in scorch marks, her dress dusty with soot—was ushered inside. She'd been orphaned when both of her inventor parents were killed in an explosion at their factory. After a month in an orphanage, Queenie was shipped off to Mirabelle when Queenie almost set the orphanage's kitchen alight during an experiment of her own.

Queenie was the manor's best gift, the closest Ivy would come to having a true soul mate.

Two years later, Ursula made another prediction of an imminent arrival. The girls, all aware by then that formal introductions were always done in the parlor, dashed there to find hiding places so they'd have front-row seats to the action. It was from behind one of the dusty drapes that Ivy caught her first glimpse of the raven-haired Jezebel, who was asleep and cradled in the hairy arms of a mountain of a man. His name was Marvin, and he was a trucker who'd almost knocked Jezebel over as she wandered, thumb in mouth, into oncoming traffic.

That gift was the one that kept Ursula and Ruby occupied, leaving Ivy and Queenie to their own cerebral devices.

A year and a half after that, Ivy was out in the garden when an eight-year-old Tabitha arrived on foot, walking out of the forest, clutching a suitcase in one hand and a strange-looking egg in the other. She was mute for the first two years, not saying a word about how she got there or who her parents were.

This last gift would be given twice, though it would take Ivy years to understand that.

The manor wasn't the only one to give its gifts. Mirabelle's final gift to her grand-niece was suffering illness long enough for Ivy to legally take ownership of the manor without anyone being able to contest her claim to it. Well, *successfully* contest her claim, because despite Mirabelle's best efforts, of course there was a challenge from that bloody awful Bartholomew Gedney.

And now, Ivy thinks, here they are, all these years after overcoming the Gedneys, about to fail regardless of their efforts, about to have Mirabelle's legacy razed. Without the manor, can there even be a sisterhood? If the house is what brought them all together, what will keep them together if the manor is no more?

Ivy brushes angry tears away as the sisters all come filing into the room, Jezebel bringing up the rear, heading for the drinks cart.

14

Saturday, October 23
Evening

The black bottle Jezebel's searching for on the antique drinks trolley is short and squat with a white skull and crossbones painted on it, Ivy's idea of a joke.

Pick your poison is something Ivy likes to say, and it's advice Jezebel can wholeheartedly get on board with. *We're all going to die*, is her philosophy, *but not all of us are smart enough to choose our executioners.*

Spotting the menacing-looking bottle on the trolley's second tier, Jezebel reaches for it, its contents a rather lovely pink pepper and rosemary infused gin. Ivy makes it in small batches exclusively for the women of the manor. That's why it isn't in the usual Moonshyne Distillery branded bottle that looks like a gilded cage refracting prisms of light.

Jezebel mixes three perfect dirty martinis, adding just enough olive juice to give them a briny tang. With a gentle flick of her wrist, she floats them across the room to where Queenie and Ivy sit in mismatched wingback chairs positioned next to each other. The two of them pluck the glasses from midair, murmuring their appreciation.

"Are you sure you won't have one, Ursula?" Jezebel asks, head cocked and voice coaxing. "It's been a really rough day. Why don't you give yourself a night off? You deserve it."

Ursula pauses her knitting, the clacking of the needles abruptly stopping. Though she looks tempted by the offer, she replies with a reluctant "No, thank you."

"Oh, stop being such a martyr," Ivy gripes, shaking her head.

Jezebel startles, surprised by Ivy's tone. Ursula looks stung.

"Come on. Just have one," Jezebel says gently, already turning to mix Ursula something sweeter that will appeal to taste buds that aren't used to hard liquor. "The worst has already happened, so it's not like you need to have your wits about you."

Tabitha isn't drinking, either, but Jezebel doesn't bother trying to cajole her. Instead, after mixing a vodka sour that tastes like county-fair lemonade, she tosses a hazelnut Tabby's way. Widget snatches it from the air, cawing appreciatively.

"Don't spoil her," Tabitha says, reaching up reflexively to stroke the crow on its perch next to her.

"Thank you for being so thoughtful" is how Widget translates it.

Jezebel smiles, enjoying the role of the doting hostess. There was a time, as the baby of the group, when everyone did her bidding, taking care of Jezebel's every need and most of her demands. But after what happened that night, everything falling apart so spectacularly, Jezebel found that the only thing that made her feel better was reversing those roles and taking care of the shattered sisterhood instead. It sometimes takes tragedy to reveal parts of ourselves that we never knew were there.

Once Jezebel sends bowls of snacks across to everyone, she takes a seat on the couch next to Ursula, in what used to be Ruby's old spot. She hands over the cocktail and gives Ursula's knee a squeeze. Taking a deep sip of her own martini, Jezebel says, "This is good shit, as always." She raises her glass in Ivy's direction.

Smiling grimly from her place next to the fire, Ivy raises her drink in return. The women let go of the two *Y*-shaped glasses, and they float across the marble table toward each other, coming to rest directly under the chandelier. They clink together, like it's a celebration rather than a commiseration, before boomeranging back to their respective owners, all without spilling a drop.

Everyone's famished, and they're quick to tuck into the bowls of toasted kale chips, pita and hummus, falafel, celery sticks and baba ghanoush. Queenie usually runs their meetings, but there's an unspoken understanding that she's lost that privilege for now, and so all eyes turn to Ivy.

"I let you down today," Ivy says crisply, wiping her mouth. "I don't know what happened." She shakes her head, the withered pink camellias drooping sorrowfully. "Actually, scrap that. I do. I'm getting old. I just don't have it in me anymore." Her voice cracks as she says it, the admission costing more than she'd care to admit.

If these were any other women, they might chime in with protests, denying the veracity of Ivy's words, insisting that she *does* still have it in her, of *course* she does. But these are the women of the sisterhood. And while they argue and bicker, complain and taunt—while they sometimes either greatly omit or wildly embellish—what they never do is flat out lie, not about the important things.

"We're all getting old, Ivy," Jezebel says. "None of us has the power that we used to."

If they did, Jezebel would've had the men lined up in the distillery for that gin tasting she'd offered as a diversion, all of them having forgotten what they'd come for. She sighs at the thought, at how powerful she used to be and what a traitorous mistress time is. If she favors you, she'll gift you with additional years, but in return she will demand payment of that which you're most loath to part with: your beauty and vitality, your power and health.

How true it is that youth is wasted on the young. *Give me my eighteen-year-old body and energy,* Jezebel thinks, *but with these seventy-nine years of experience, and I would be unstoppable.*

"It's not your fault, Ivy," Ursula adds, frowning. "We're vulnerable, and they know it. That's exactly why they've launched this attack now."

"But who is *they*?" Jezebel asks. "The town council? Is that how Stout's daughter knew about what was happening? Because he's in on it?"

"It doesn't make sense," Ursula replies, absentmindedly cradling her breast, which is still tender. "They need us for the distillery because we're the only ones in the county with a license to produce liquor."

Ivy rubs at her forehead, evidence that she's still battling a postconjuring headache. "In case you haven't noticed," she says, sounding annoyed, "much has changed. Look at all those fast-food chains moving in. And the big developments and strip malls that have been going up. Critchley Hackle is not the same town it used to be."

Taking a tiny sip of her vodka sour, Ursula asks, "But why would there be an uprising like this *now* after so many years of peace?"

"Because of this." Queenie reaches down next to her for the cans and bottles Ivy returned to her.

Jezebel reaches for them. "An artisanal brewery *and* a distillery in one?" She whistles, impressed despite herself. "I've never seen this company's products before. I wonder what *SWT* stands for?"

"Salem Witch Trials," Queenie replies, relaying the infor-

mation Widget was able to gather after flying to downtown Critchley Hackle and finding the mayor, Will Stoughton, and the bank manager, John Hathorne, sitting in the mayor's office with an out-of-towner. "They were consulting drawn-up plans showing the development of something called..." Queenie uses air quotes, her tone thick with sarcasm "...Men's World."

"What?" Jezebel almost chokes on her martini. "You can't be serious?"

"Oh, but I am," Queenie says. "It's apparently a high-concept recreation venue, kinda like Disney World, but for grown-ass men. It has a megadistillery and brewery attached to a golf course, and it includes a shooting range, a paintball course and a strip club."

"Booze, naked women and guns," Ursula muses. "What could possibly go wrong?"

"Where will the development be?" Jezebel asks. "Here in Critchley Hackle?" Jezebel can tell just by looking at Queenie that she's not going to like the answer.

"It's going to be here," Queenie replies. "*Right* here, on this property."

Moonshyne Manor Distillery Recipes

Ivy's Pink Pepper and Rosemary Infused Gin

Ingredients:
1 bottle of Moonshyne Manor vodka
3 tbsp. juniper berries
1 tbsp. Indian coriander seeds
5 large sprigs of fresh rosemary
1 tsp. dried lemon zest
1 tsp. whole allspice berries
2 tsp. Red Kampot peppercorns
2 tsp. pink peppercorns

Equipment:
A quart jar
Fine mesh sieve

Instructions:
Put the juniper in a quart jar and add the Moonshyne Manor vodka. Cap the jar tightly and let it infuse for twelve hours or overnight. After a twelve-hour presoak, add the rest of the herbs and spices to the vodka. Let it sit and infuse for a further seventy-two hours.

Strain the infused gin into another jar using a fine mesh sieve. Store in a bottle or jar in a cool, dark place for up to a year. Enjoy in a dirty martini.

Jezebel's addition:
The dirtier the martini, the better. Just like a lover's mind.

15

Saturday, October 23
Evening

"What?" Ivy yelps, spilling her martini down the front of her robe. "You can't be bloody serious?"

Ursula gasps as the puzzle pieces fall into place. "That billboard across the road. The one that says *Critchley Hackle Megacomplex Coming Soon!* We thought they put it there because we're near the off-ramp from the highway, but it's because they're planning to build right here."

"Exactly." Queenie's furious with herself for not having recognized the billboard for the literal bad sign that it was. They shouldn't have been blindsided like this; she should have seen it coming. "We have a hundred acres of prime real estate with a whole distillery already set up." Queenie rubs at her tired eyes as she turns back to Ivy, saying, "And we're just outside Critchley Hackle city center, while also not being too far from Oxbridge,

Flanders Falls and Titssup. None of those towns have their own golf courses, shooting ranges, paintball courses or strip clubs."

"But they'd need more land than just ours," Ivy splutters.

"They have it." Queenie's shoulders drop in defeat, as she pops yet another antacid. "All the properties around ours have been bought up, including…" she swallows deeply, trying again "…including Magnus's old land."

The women all wince as though a communal bruise is being prodded. It's why they never allow themselves to speak of him.

"The new owners ran into financial difficulties so they had to sell up. That gives the developers seventy acres in total," Queenie continues. "And since we weren't prepared to sell all those years ago, he's now coming after our land with force."

"He?" Ivy's widened eyes are magnified by her spectacles. "You can't possibly mean Bartholomew Gedney. He died almost sixty years ago."

"You know better than anyone how impossible some weeds are to kill," Queenie replies, feeling that old loathing anew. "You can burn them to the ground or poison them, but they just keep on coming right back, generation after generation."

"His son, you mean?" Ivy asks, realization dawning. "The one who came sniffing around to buy the land just before everything happened with Ruby?"

"His grandson, actually," Queenie clarifies, so mad she could spit. "Brad Gedney owns the Salem Witch Trials craft brewery and distillery, and if the name isn't a clear enough announcement of his intentions, then I don't know what is."

"But why?" Ursula asks, blue eyes flashing. "Why would he be coming for us?"

"Because misogyny is an Ivy League family sport, didn't you know?" Queenie replies, her tone grim.

She thinks back to the day after Mirabelle died and a twenty-one-year-old Ivy inherited the manor, how Ursula foretold the arrival of Mirabelle's long-lost cousin, Bartholomew Gedney, who arrived as predicted on their doorstep, contract in hand, to make Ivy an offer on the property.

Bartholomew wasn't a big man by any means—there was actually a squirrelly quality to him, with his slight, hunched frame and rodent's face—but his immense arrogance made him loom large in the doorway despite his being eighty years old.

It was a pitiful sum he was offering, and Queenie—already stepping into the breach that Mirabelle's passing had created—said as much, suggesting he take his offer on a long walk off a short pier. Having a young woman, and a Black one at that, speak to him in such a manner enraged Bartholomew, who came back a week later, insisting that going forward he'd only deal with Ivy.

He presented Ivy with a marginally higher offer and then a slightly higher offer still, returning another three times until Ivy made it clear that the manor wasn't for sale to *him* at any price. It didn't matter that he was her relative. Had his own cousin, Mirabelle, wished to sell the manor to him, she would have.

Retaliating, Bartholomew called Ivy and her wards freaks of nature, claiming everyone knew they were witches, and what witches deserved was to be burned at the stake. He sneered at Queenie and Tabitha, saying that if Blacks weren't allowed to ride on buses with white people, they sure as shit shouldn't be allowed to live with them. When he left, he swore that Ivy would rue the day she'd turned him down.

Things went quiet for a while after that, until one day, when Mirabelle's ancient lawyer, the lovely Mr. Faulks, informed Ivy that Gedney was trying to contest the veracity of Mirabelle's will. Luckily, Mirabelle, along with Mr. Faulks, had ensured that the will was ironclad. Still, they were a shaky few weeks.

"Did Mirabelle ever tell you Bartholomew's particular beef with her?" Ursula asks, gazing at the fire.

"No," Ivy replies, "just that he blamed her for all his problems, but she said he wasn't worth the wasted breath it would take to elaborate." There's a vein bulging in Ivy's temple, and her face is flushed.

Jezebel delivers a fresh round of cocktails. "So, this Brad Gedney has the town council in his pocket? That's why they tried to knock the manor down?"

"Exactly." Queenie gratefully accepts her martini. "We wouldn't sell the land to his grandfather sixty-five years ago, nor to his father thirty-three years ago, and now he's resorted to skulduggery to get it. He's waiting in the wings to buy the land cheap and start development on Men's World as soon as John Hathorne and the bank foreclose." Just saying the words is like pouring Queenie's blood into a cauldron and cranking up the heat.

For a moment, there's nothing but the sound of hissing issuing from the fireplace, and the occasional rattling of pipes in the walls, the manor expressing its rage on the women's behalf. Widget hops down from her perch to stand on the chair's armrest, her feathers rustling as she preens. Another howl pierces the night, and Tabitha stirs.

It's Jezebel who breaks the silence. "So, the town's been buying their drinks from Brad Gedney?" When Queenie nods, Jezebel murmurs, "I guess that explains why our orders have been falling way down. And why the men came for us today."

The sisterhood have been medicating, as they refer to it, the distillery's liquor with one of Ivy's concoctions for the past almost three and half decades. After one too many witch hunts, the women agreed that the safest option for all concerned was to administer a soothing draft to the men of Critchley Hackle whose tempers needed adjusting.

Ivy began experimenting with various concoctions, finding that a combination of Bupleurum, St. Benedict's thistle, skullcap, passionflower and corpse-plant pollen to be the most effective. Various ways of administering the elixir were suggested and eliminated, with the women ultimately deciding to infuse the distillery's various spirits with the potion. Just one drink, taken as was customary with Sunday lunch, was enough to calm those who needed it, while having no effect at all, from what they could tell, on those who didn't.

Whatever ethical concerns have arisen over the years with regards to the morality of controlling people in this way, the sisterhood tell themselves they aren't the only ones benefiting from it. The whole town has flourished. Marriages have thrived. Wives have been treated more lovingly. Children have better role models to look up to. Much has been achieved with the men's energy being channeled in positive outlets.

"But," Jezebel says, brow puckered, "the men were way more aggressive than we've ever seen them before. How do you explain that?"

Moonshyne Manor Distillery Recipes

Jezebel's Pepper and Rosemary Infused Dirty Martini

Ingredients:

2½ oz. of Ivy's special batch pepper and rosemary infused gin
½ oz. black olive brine
½ oz. dry vermouth
½ tablespoon ground black pepper
Lemon slice
Garnish: olives of choice

Equipment:

Cocktail shaker or mixing glass
Martini glass

Instructions:

Start by rimming a martini glass (not that kind of rimming, you dirty minx!). Place the ground pepper in a dish, run a lemon wedge along the edge of the glass, then dip the glass into the pepper and twist to rim. Set aside. In a mixing glass with ice, add the gin, olive brine and vermouth. Stir until chilled.

Strain into the prepped glass and garnish with an olive. Best consumed while naked and aroused.

16

Saturday, October 23
Evening

"Well, I had a theory about that," Queenie says, shooting Ivy a look of what Ivy construes to be disappointment, making her bristle, "but Ivy wasn't able to figure out how to extract the—"

"Why don't we all just pile on top of Ivy!" Ivy yells, standing. "I'm not a bloody miracle worker, you know! There's no laboratory in the world that can accurately test the amount of serotonin in a person's brain, and there are no specific diagnostic criteria." Her pulse is racing, anger chafing against the inside of her chest and stomach like sandpaper. Ivy pitches her martini glass at the fire where it shatters into smithereens.

The sisterhood stare back at her with wide eyes and open mouths, shocked by her outburst, as though they aren't the very ones pushing her over the edge. *Do this, Ivy! Do that, Ivy! Come up with an elixir to save us, Ivy! Take care of the manor so we'll al-*

ways have somewhere to live, Ivy! It's horseshit, is what it is. Utter horseshit, and Ivy isn't having it.

"Why didn't you run the tests yourself, Queenie, if you're so smart?" Ivy demands. "You sit here criticizing me and my plants—"

"I wasn't criticizing," Queenie says, throwing up her hands. "I was just saying—"

"Well, don't! Who the hell do you think you are, finding fault with me? After what you did? This is all your fault, so stop pointing fingers—"

Queenie turns to Jezebel. "Did you see that?" she asks, before turning to Ursula. "With her eyes? Did you see what happened?"

"The flash of purple?" Jezebel asks.

"Yes!" Queenie looks triumphant as she turns back to Ivy. "Did you drink from any of the bottles or cans I brought to the lab earlier?"

Ivy stiffens at what she perceives to be another criticism. "I was thirsty. It was exhausting tending to the tree, and the lawn and the reporter. There wasn't time to take a lunch break, so excuse me if I had a beer to quench my thirst. It was the only thing on hand."

"You did it," Queenie says, smiling. "You ran the test, and you got our answer."

"What's that supposed to mean?" Ivy asks, fingers itching to pick up something else and throw it.

Queenie walks over to Ivy slowly, as though approaching a dangerous creature. "I suspected something was being put in that alcohol to cause anger and aggression. And you've just proven it."

Jezebel's eyes widen. "You mean Brad Gedney is not just canceling out what we've been doing, he's making all the men hyperagitated?"

"Yes, exactly."

"That definitely can't be good for us," Jezebel says, giving Ivy a long stare, still too nervous to come near her.

"No shit," Queenie adds. "I'd say that's quite an understatement." She withdraws her wand and points it at Ivy, muttering, *"Cessa."*

All at once, the wildfire that's raging out of control through Ivy's veins is doused. The anger steams for a few moments before disappearing completely. She's left shaken, hollowed out. More than that, she's mortified by her loss of control. "I'm... I'm so sorry. That was hideous of me. I'm so sorry." She turns to Queenie, taking her friend's hand. "Forgive me. I don't know what came over me."

"There's nothing to forgive," Queenie replies. "That wasn't you speaking. It's whatever was put in those drinks."

Queenie helps settle Ivy back down in her chair as Jezebel rushes to pour Ivy another cocktail. Her hand trembles as she hands it to Ivy, just as Ivy's hand trembles as she accepts it. They all give Ivy a few moments to collect herself, shooting her concerned glances.

Finally, when Ivy feels composed, she looks around at the sisterhood whose eyes glitter with the light of the reflected flames. "We have to ask ourselves, why now? Why did they come today instead of just waiting until the bank forecloses?"

Ursula gasps, looking a little flushed from all the drama and her half-finished cocktail. "You don't think this Brad knows about Ruby?"

"It doesn't seem possible, but the timing is most suspicious," Queenie replies, returning to her seat. "Since Ruby's the only one who knows where the goods are hidden."

Ivy feels something icy settle in her belly. "It's almost as if Brad and the council know she's the only one who can save us."

Jezebel's voice is strained when she says, "Ruby hasn't spoken to any of us in thirty-three years. How...how do we even know she's prepared to come home on Monday?"

It's what Ivy's been wondering too. It's what they've all probably been thinking, though this is the first time one of them has verbalized it. How will Ruby react when she sees them all? Will she rebuff them, as she's done in the past, or will she have moved beyond that?

Ivy looks at Ursula, knowing she'll have the answer.

Ursula takes her hands away from her knitting. Instead of the needles dropping, they just continue their clacking as she reaches for her vodka sour. What's unspooling from the needles is a purple cashmere scarf, one that Ivy knows, without asking, is intended for Ruby.

"All the signs point to Ruby coming home." Ursula finishes off her drink. "Both the cards and the tea leaves. My crystal ball too." She's clearly aiming for a note of confidence, but there's something hesitant in her tone.

"There's something you're not telling us," Ivy ventures. "What is it?"

Ursula flushes as though caught out. "It's nothing, really. Just a bit of a fog that I'm seeing."

"Fog?" Queenie asks. "Like bad weather?"

"I can't be sure. It could be literal fog, certainly."

Ivy remembers something Great-Aunt Mirabelle used to say. "For every fog in October, a snow in the winter."

"Are you sure you were looking at your crystal ball and not a snow globe?" Queenie asks in all earnestness. When everyone except Ursula titters, Queenie adds, "It's just you won't admit that you need glasses."

"This fog?" Ivy prompts to smooth things over. "It has something to do with Ruby's homecoming?"

"Yes," Ursula says, nodding. "I see it every time, but I have no idea what it means. I just know that it's going to be a problem for us."

Queenie waves it off. "A little fog never hurt anyone. So long as she's coming home, that's all that matters."

Ivy knows Ursula well enough to suspect that there's something else she's not saying, something worse. But she also knows there's no point in pushing her further on it. Ursula can dig in her heels, becoming mulish when she feels cornered.

Ivy looks to Tabitha, all too aware that she's been the elephant in the room, the topic they've all been skirting around. Considering Tabby hasn't left the manor in thirty-three years, what will become of her if the wrecking ball returns in nine days? Will they be able to get Tabby beyond the door if they need to?

It's late now, and the women are all tired. Exhaustion has crept into Ivy's bones, as heavy as lead. It's also tugging insistently at her eyelids. "Okay," she says, standing with a groan, everything stiff and aching. "That's enough for one day. We have a busy day ahead of us tomorrow with getting everything ready for Ruby. I'm off to bed."

All the women, except Tabitha, rise.

"Did Widget check on Persephone?" Ursula gathers up her knitting.

They invited Persephone to stay once she was freed of the handcuffs, but the girl declined the offer, saying she had a lot of homework to do and social-media platforms to update. Whatever those are.

Tabitha, clearly affronted that Ursula even needs to ask, doesn't reply. She just puckers her cheeks and glowers, keeping her eyes on the fire. Widget opens her beak to say something but then seems to change her mind, casting Ursula a sympathetic look but remaining silent.

"Persephone's fine," Queenie replies. "Widget reported that it all looked peaceful on the home front an hour ago."

The women follow Ursula out through the door to the mudroom, walking in single file.

"That child worries me," Jezebel says. "She seems so lost."

Certainly, no more lost than any of us were at the same age, Ivy thinks. The child reminds Ivy of someone, but she hasn't figured out who just yet. Perhaps it's themselves, all of them floundering their way into womanhood.

When Ursula suddenly comes to a stop, Ivy sidesteps her in time, but Jezebel doesn't. She walks straight into the back of Ursula. But she doesn't react to the impact. Her vision is clouded over as she stares at that which none of the rest of them can see. It's a common-enough occurrence, and so they're patient as they wait her out.

After a minute, Ursula snaps out of it. She smiles and nods. "Persephone will be coming back soon enough." And then she turns to Queenie who's bringing up the rear. "And when she does, let her in."

Queenie rolls her eyes. "Who made me the resident doorman? Is it because I'm Black?" And then she tuts. "You know we don't allow guests, Ursula."

"This one we must. And when I say, 'Let her in,' Queenie," Ursula clarifies, first tapping Queenie's temple and then her heart, "I don't just mean through the door."

Ivy smiles, thinking how much she's looking forward to seeing this play out. Out of all of them, Queenie's the most bristly, the least inclined to welcome outsiders. Plus, she was never any good at girlhood, even when experiencing it herself.

17

Sunday, October 24
Afternoon

A harried-looking Queenie answers Persephone's knock the next afternoon, opening the door a crack and peering out. The old woman glowers at Ruth Bader Ginsburg who glowers back.

Persephone's spirits sink as she realizes that Queenie doesn't look happy to see them. She wonders why it is that she seems to spend a lot of time being exactly where she's not wanted, home and school being just two of those many places.

Still, Persephone forces a bright smile. "Hi. I thought I'd come by and help out," she chirps.

"Help out?" Queenie echoes, clearly distracted.

"Yes, with the fundraising efforts," Persephone clarifies, launching into the sales pitch she practiced while cycling over. "I have some ideas for a GoFundMe campaign, but we're going to need a social-media presence obviously, and of course we need to figure out, like, what your brand is because, if you don't mind my saying, big yikes, you all don't currently have the best optics—"

"Whoa." Queenie holds up a hand, her expression dazed. "You're saying a whole lot of words that mean nothing to me."

"Oh, sorry," Persephone says, shaking her head, making her white curls bounce. "I keep forgetting how ancient you are."

Queenie draws breath to speak, but before she can get any words out, a pink van pulls up. A man hops out and rummages in the back of it before trotting up the porch steps, holding aloft a huge bouquet of red roses that partially obscures his face.

"I have another delivery for Jezebel," he says, peering around it. "They're getting bigger every week," he gripes. "This one barely fit in the back."

"She's keeping you in business, Roy, so what are you complaining about?" Queenie counters.

The man grumbles, holding a device out for Queenie to sign. She scrunches up her eyes and scrawls something illegible, after which he thrusts the flowers at her. The tires of his van kick up gravel as he drives off.

"Just a sec," Queenie says, disappearing inside. "Jezebel, there's another bunch of flowers from Artemis," she calls. "Can't you make the poor fool forget you? We have enough damn flowers in the conservatory." And then Queenie reappears, sans bouquet, looking at Persephone as though she's trying to place her. "Uh..."

Before Persephone can launch into her spiel again, a series of bangs issue from behind Queenie.

Ruth Bader Ginsburg growls from next to Persephone, the dog's thin frame trembling. Persephone reaches down to pick her up.

"Could you excuse me for a minute?" Queenie asks. Without waiting for an answer, she withdraws her head and closes the door, hollering something until the noise quietens down.

And then she's back, head stuck through the crack once more. "Look, kid, now really isn't a good time." Queenie's barely managed to get the words out when they're punctuated by a shrieking that makes her wince.

Persephone's eyes widen. "Are you having a ritual?" Horror makes her voice hitch as she tries to peer around Queenie. "Or some kind of sacrifice? You're not slaughtering animals, are you? I'm totally cool with magic just so long as its cruelty-free."

"Magic?" Queenie scoffs. "Whatever gave you that idea?"

"The whole town says you're witches." Persephone blinks and cocks her head. "So I just assumed—"

There's another explosion behind Queenie, who mutters from behind gritted teeth, "For the love of the Goddess." Turning back to Persephone, she smiles grimly and says, "Just one moment, please."

And then the door's closed again, and Queenie is shouting. It's muffled, but Persephone has had a lot of practice eavesdropping, and so she can still make out every word.

"For fuck's sake. That child is here asking about magic and sacrifices and shit, and I'm trying to throw her off the scent, which is pretty much impossible to do with all the magic you bitches are so loudly doing."

The bangs fizzle out, and then there's murmuring that Persephone can't make out, and when Queenie opens the door again, a cloud of pink smoke wafts out. "Sorry about that. As I was saying, there's no sacrifices or witches—"

"But I just heard you say you're trying to throw me off the scent which is pretty fuc—"

"Okay!" Queenie yells, dropping her head in defeat and rubbing at her eyes. "I...er... I obviously didn't think you could hear that." And then she mutters, "You children with your perfect hearing and excellent health. Pure showing off is what it is."

"Also," Persephone continues, "I'm not a child. I'm fifteen." When Queenie looks skeptical, Persephone throws her hands up. "I'm small for my age, okay? And I have a baby face, I know. No one ever takes me seriously because of it. It's a major pain in the ass."

Queenie regards the girl more seriously now, taking her in. "If you want to look your age, it doesn't help wearing clothes that are at least three sizes too big for you. It makes it look like you're playing dress-up."

Persephone looks down at the red coat that's her favorite. "I got it from my mother, and I like it. And I don't appreciate my clothing being policed. Women should be allowed to wear whatever they want." She nods at Queenie's robe. "You clearly do."

"Touché." Queenie nods, a glint of respect in her eyes.

"And also, you shouldn't call other women *bitches*. It's antifeminist."

"Ah, who's the one doing the policing now? And you're wrong, by the way," Queenie says, relaxing now that she's no longer on the back foot. "Words have power, which is exactly why you need to reclaim them. When you take something that was meant to demean you and you turn it into a term of endearment or a badge of honor, you take all the sting out of it. And that means you win."

Persephone looks skeptical. "It didn't *sound* like a term of endearment when you called them that."

Queenie scowls. "Yeah, well, that's because I'm not particularly good with affection."

"Okay." Persephone nods, putting Ruth Bader Ginsburg down again and digging her hands deeper into the coat's pockets as though steeling herself. "Look, I don't care that you're witches, okay?"

"We're not—"

"I saw the way your friend conjured that storm yesterday," Persephone says, voice raised, "and I actually think it's, like, really cool. I've always wanted to do magic. That's why I've been learning to become a magician, which isn't as lit as doing *real* magic, obviously, but it was fun yesterday, with the cops, wasn't it?" She mimes the policeman pulling all those scarves out of her pocket.

Queenie smiles. "I might have taken a mental picture or two for prosperity."

"And I absolutely *love Charmed* and Hilltowne. I'd be thrilled to find out I'm like one of the sisters."

Queenie raises an eyebrow. "You're saying words that have no meaning again."

Persephone's jaw drops. "You don't know Macy, Mel and Maggie?"

"No, why? Does he live in the neighborhood?" Taking in Persephone's incredulous expression, Queenie adds defensively, "Look, you can't expect me to keep up with everyone's comings and goings. It's not like we get a lot of visitors—"

"Yeah, I can see that," Persephone huffs. "Because I've been here for more than five minutes," she says, ready to go back home, "and I haven't been invited in to join you bitches."

Queenie flinches.

"What?" Persephone asks, eyes wide. "I thought you, like, said that was okay?"

From inside, a voice calls out, "Remember what I told you about letting her in, Queenie!"

Shaking her head, Queenie mutters, "For the love of the Goddess, just come inside." She opens the door wide and ushers Persephone and Ruth Bader Ginsburg in.

Having grown up hearing all the kids in Critchley Hackle speaking of how the house is haunted by ghosts and patrolled by monsters, Persephone's disappointed by how lovely it is. There's a grand double staircase, like the kind you only see in train stations where streams of people have to move in opposite directions. Persephone eyes the gleaming banisters, thinking how fun it would be to slide down them.

A huge chandelier is suspended directly above her in the foyer, shining brilliantly but swaying ominously. There are doors that open to what looks like a library on the left, as well as a room and passage on the right. A corridor leads off through the middle of the dual staircase. The same three old women from yesterday are all frozen in place in various spots around the room, covered in streaks of dirt, looking shifty as all hell. They tuck things away in their robe pockets, smiling innocently while issuing a chorus of *hello*s.

All around them in the foyer are mops and brooms, pails filled with sudsy water, feather dusters and various kinds of polish. A few cleaning rags lie in heaps upon the floor as though they dropped there just a moment ago. The bouquet from earlier sits in a vase on a side table. All the roses have disappeared in what looks like a fire; only their scorched stems remain.

Ruth Bader Ginsburg growls at the vase, and Persephone shushes her as she wonders which witch is which. There was so much happening yesterday that she only really caught Queenie's name. She doesn't want to be rude and confess as much, but thinks it might become awkward down the line if she doesn't.

The plump woman with the short pixie cut and bright blue eyes seems to sense her indecision, saying, "We didn't have time to get properly acquainted yesterday. I'm Ursula. And this," she says, pointing at the beautiful woman with jet-black hair, "is Jezebel." She turns and gestures at the tall woman with the crown of flowers. "That's Ivy." And indicating the vase that RBG was growling at, she says, "And that's Tabitha."

"Umm," Persephone says, perplexed, looking between Ursula and the table, "there's no one there."

Ursula claps a hand over her mouth just as Queenie curses under her breath.

"For fuck's sake, Ursula," cries the crow, sweeping into the room.

18

Sunday, October 24
Afternoon

Ursula groans. Of course, Persephone can't see Tabby standing there in her '80s polka-dot robe with its ginormous shoulder pads and wine-colored stain on the left breast. The girl isn't a witch so she can't make out the ghost in their midst. She obviously didn't see her the day before, either, just Ursula and the other three sisters, along with the talking crow which, while unusual, isn't unheard of.

Persephone isn't to know that Tabby has been dead for thirty-three years, the ghost somehow confined to the manor, unable to even cross the threshold onto the porch. And that while the sisterhood are all able to see her—and can feel the waves of hostility emanating from her—Tabby's only able to communicate and conjure through her familiar, Widget, who's almost thirty-four, and won't be around much longer to act as Tabitha's conduit to the living world.

No one knows what will become of Tabby if the manor is destroyed, if she'll be obliterated along with it or if she's tied to the grounds, cursed to wander whatever part of Men's World will go up where the manor once stood. All they know is that the gravity of the manor pulled Tabby back to it in the moment of her death, refusing to relinquish her to whatever waited beyond. And that the manor has kept her here all this time despite Ursula's treachery, the role she played in Tabby's death.

All eyes are on Ursula, including Persephone's piercing blue ones. They feel like a laser dissecting Ursula as the girl stands there, hands in her coat pockets, shoulders hunched against the oppressive silence.

Ursula's about to blame her mistake on senility—laugh it off as a senior moment—when something clearly dawns on Persephone, some kind of understanding.

The girl tilts her head and then raises her chin as though summoning courage. The gesture feels strangely familiar. Persephone takes a few tentative steps over to where Widget is hovering above Tabby's shoulder. Ruth Bader Ginsburg begins to growl softly, insistently, one paw held up as her emaciated-looking frame trembles violently.

Persephone reaches down and picks the dog up, shifting her weight as she tucks it into her side. She touches her forehead to the dog's, though her eyes don't leave the spot where Tabitha stands. It must look strange, the way the crow just floats there in midair without using its wings to stay airborne. On the verge of stepping through Tabitha—a terrible faux pas which would incense Tabby beyond measure—Persephone suddenly stops.

Ursula looks from the white-haired girl wearing the oversized red coat to Tabby who's regarding Persephone with a mixture of disdain and curiosity. Persephone is the first person outside of the sisterhood that's been in Tabby's vicinity since the last party they ever had at the manor, held the weekend before Ursula sounded that first alarm. She's as much a curiosity to Tabitha as the ghost is to the girl.

Every group needs a disruptor, someone who yanks its members out of their comfort zones. For the coven, that person was once Tabby. Insisting that being recluses made them even bigger targets—and only further perpetuated the belief that they had something to hide, something therefore to be ashamed of—Tabitha opened their doors to anyone remotely interesting or entertaining.

Since almost no one in Critchley Hackle met that criteria, she had to find them farther afield, which luckily hadn't been that difficult. Tabby had built up a reputation by then for being an expert in the field of exotic animals. She was regularly invited to speak at symposiums and conferences all over the world, her travels bringing her in contact with all kinds of fascinating people.

Most of Tabitha's gatherings were just-for-the-hell-of-it soirees, but that last one was a particularly special occasion, her fiftieth birthday *and* a blowing off of steam ahead of what was to come. The guest list was an eclectic mix of circus folk, zookeepers, breeders, vets, biologists, conservationists, game rangers, wildlife experts, entertainment-industry people and those who didn't work in the field but who loved animals, that being Tabby's only other criterion when making new friends.

Ursula recalls how hilarious Tabby thought it was to make witches the theme of the party. "Just think, we already have all the props. We hardly have to go to any effort at all," she'd said, adding that it was also a good way to disguise the magic she wanted to use.

Everyone was roped into the preparations, and as much as the sisterhood complained about the events—pretending to only attend them to humor Tabby—they all secretly loved them for different reasons.

Ivy enjoyed the company because she loved trading ideas and sharing knowledge; the guests were all living, breathing textbooks she could study and learn from. Plus, those who loved fauna were often predisposed to liking flora too, and Ivy got to talk plants with those who had an interest in them.

Queenie treasured having appreciative test subjects for her inventions, the sisterhood having long tired of humoring the accidents and explosions that often accompanied each new creation, many of which they didn't see the point to, since why were they even necessary when magic could be used instead?

What Ruby had loved most was having an audience to dress up for and perform in front of. Her shows consisted of cabaret, singing, comedic interludes and dancing. She often changed costumes in between sets and had perfected the art of making a grand entrance down the sweeping staircase, sometimes using it as her stage for an entire set.

Jezebel thrilled at the flirting and delighted in the seduction. The more men and women who could leave their parties utterly besotted with her, the better. Some nights, she'd have so many aspiring lovers trailing her that some guests mistook it for a conga line.

What Ursula liked most was being exposed to new auras and palms to read, the intimacy of being invited into a life and being allowed to rummage around in the dark corners of it. She was sympathetic to the brokenhearted who wore brittle smiles to mask their pain. It was reassuring to tell them that they would recover and move on, that new love awaited them just around the corner. It made her wonder if the same might ever be possible for herself.

As the women all prepared for Tabby's fiftieth, they scattered cauldrons throughout the manor, filling them with strong punch, and bewitching mist to swirl and bubble over their rims. Black helium balloons covered with tiny rhinestones bobbed up at the ceiling, creating the impression of the starry night sky in every room. Suspended disco balls reflected the light of a thousand floating candles, while broomsticks whizzed back and forth overhead.

Once the party started, a baby Widget (who hadn't yet learned to speak) flitted from shoulder to shoulder, cawing like some harbinger of death, as a dozen yellow-eyed black cats threaded through the guests' legs, hopping into any laps they could find.

Ursula was set up in the library, dressed as a fortune-teller, doing tarot readings, crystal-ball gazing and palmistry while also people-watching. Jezebel, looking like the Cher character from *The Witches of Eastwick*, was enticing people into hidden alcoves.

Queenie, in a Wicked Witch of the West costume, was in her element showing off her various inventions, including the silent fireworks (so as not to upset any of Tabby's creatures) and the broomstick zip line that ran from Jezebel's third-floor bay window.

Ivy, dressed as Witch Hazel, sat with the circus folk playing a game of one-upmanship as they showed off all of their tattoos. Ruby was supposed to put on a show like she did at all of the parties, which Ursula was very much looking forward to, but this time, much to Ursula's chagrin, she'd demurred and chosen instead to spend the night cuddled up with that awful beau of hers, Magnus.

The two of them sat together on a couch in the corner of the living room, a difficult feat considering how Ruby's pink monstrosity of a ball gown took up most of the seat on its own.

A DJ, whose equipment ran off a gasoline-powered portable generator, played George Harrison's "Got My Mind Set on You," as Ruby gazed at Magnus, so smitten that nothing else in the room could divert her attention. It pained Ursula to look at their cozy little tableau and his smug face, and yet she couldn't stop herself from darting covert looks at them all night.

And threading all of these people together like beads on

a necklace was Tabby, the belle of the ball in a formfitting Morticia Addams sheath, circulating from group to group, head thrown back in laughter, various animals either wrapped around, flying above or trailing behind her.

Considering how incredibly vital she looked that night, it's still difficult to believe that within three days, Tabby would be dead.

It's only now, seeing how hungrily Tabby eyes Persephone, that Ursula realizes just how much Tabitha's missed all that company. How awful it must have been to go from being the center of attention to being invisible.

Persephone closes her eyes and holds her free hand up like a mime's. She moves it around and then freezes, nodding. "It's warmer here in this spot," she says which surprises everyone. "I thought ghosts were supposed to make a room colder, but this feels lovely, like being next to the fire. I like it."

And then the impossible happens. Tabby's lips, forever tugged down in that perpetual rictus of disapproval, twitch.

"I heard there were ghosts in the manor," Persephone continues, tracing the air in front of her as she traces Tabby's outline, "but I thought they would be scary. This one feels friendly."

Queenie splutters at this, but Tabby's mouth turns upward into something resembling a smile. And then Tabitha reaches out and pets Ruth Bader Ginsburg, who immediately stops trembling.

"Good dog," Widget crows. "What a good dog."

And just like that, Tabitha's made her first new friend in a long time.

19

Sunday, October 24
Afternoon

"Witches and ghosts," Persephone says, thrilled beyond measure, as she watches Widget retreat into the library with who she assumes is Tabby, the ghost. "It's so cool."

And not just cool but encouraging too. If the manor can have a ghost, then maybe her house has one too. It's something she's never dared allow herself to consider.

Persephone wishes that she'd built up the courage to defy her father sooner. He's always forbidden her from going near the manor, telling her that the women are dangerous and unhinged, and that witches are nothing more than Satan worshippers who shouldn't be romanticized. He even confiscated her copy of *A Discovery of Witches*, refusing to take her trick-or-treating the one year that she dressed up as Diana Bishop.

But after she heard him plotting in his study with those awful council men, John Hathorne and Cotton Mather—along with that sinister out-of-towner, Brad Gedney—she knew she couldn't just stand by without trying to help the witches.

"How did Tabby die?" Persephone asks. "Was she sick?" She swallows thickly, her voice lowered. "Was it cancer?"

Queenie sighs deeply, the topic clearly a painful one. "She wasn't sick, no. In fact, she'd just hit her stride. I'd never seen her more luminous."

"So, what happened?"

"A whole lot went wrong," Queenie says, voice strained. "Terribly, terribly wrong. Sometimes, it doesn't matter how well you plan, or how much you try to see every eventuality, life will still blindside you, letting you know who's boss and how very little is actually within your control." When Persephone waits Queenie out, hoping for more, Queenie adds, "You'll have to ask Tabby for the details yourself."

"Why can't you tell me?" Persephone asks, trotting behind Queenie as she turns and starts ascending again.

"Knowing a person's story doesn't mean you have the right to tell it. And sometimes the right to hear it has to be earned."

At the top of the stairs, they get to a huge glass-walled room filled with what looks like a jungle. Persephone is brought up short at its threshold, gawping as she turns to Queenie for an explanation.

"That's Ivy's conservatory," Queenie says, coming to a stop just outside it. "She can give you a tour another time. You like plants?"

"I guess?" Persephone shrugs, thinking about the sad ones in her home, the ones that have all wilted and died, probably from trying to feed off the toxic atmosphere.

"Yeah, I never used to be big on them, either." Queenie's voice softens. "But you'll be surprised at how useful they can be."

"This place is massive. How many rooms does it have?" Persephone asks, turning on her heel as she takes it all in, thinking how she's likely to get lost if she ever has to navigate it by herself.

"Well, let's see," Queenie says, scrunching up her face in concentration as she leads Persephone down a corridor to a bench at the reading window overlooking the front of the property. They both sit, and Queenie runs through a mental list. "Downstairs, there's the library, office, kitchen, dining room, parlor, bathroom, rage room and inclement-weather ritual room." She counts them off on her fingers. Before Persephone can ask what a rage room is, Queenie continues, "And up here, there's Ivy's lab. Tabby's, Ivy's and my bedrooms are also on this floor, along with the two bathrooms, two storage rooms and the bilious room."

"Do you mean *billiards room*?" Persephone asks, confused.

"Definitely not." Queenie smiles mysteriously. "And then upstairs, there's another three bedrooms for Ursula, Jezebel and Ruby, along with the two bathrooms and the secret room."

"What's in the secret room?"

"Can't tell you," Queenie says, winking. "It's a secret. And then, of course, there's the various storage rooms, and in the basement, there's my lab."

"You have two labs?" Persephone asks, impressed.

"They're quite different. Ivy's is more a traditional chemistry one for plant extraction and mixing her elixirs. Mine is for making my inventions. I call it a lab, but it's more like an auto-repair shop." Queenie looks around the space like someone seeing it for the first time. "Our whole lives are here. Our livelihood and everything that makes us who we are…it's all tied up in this house. If we lose it, we lose everything."

"It sounds like the house is one of your best friends," Persephone ventures.

"Oh, she's more than that," Queenie says, misty-eyed, reaching out and rubbing the wall as though it were a nervous mare.

"She's been a mother and father, a best friend and a fairy godmother all rolled into one."

"Can't you magic the money you need?" Persephone asks, looking at her hands, knowing from her father that talk of money makes adults uncomfortable. She picks at her bluish-gray nail varnish on her thumb before gnawing on the nail. "What's the point of all those powers if you can't use them to save your home?"

Queenie sighs, standing. "That's unfortunately not how any of our magic works. We each manipulate the laws of physics in different ways, but none of us can conjure money or gold out of thin air without working a forbidden spell. Believe me, we've tried."

"What about other witches who can help you?" Persephone asks, inspiration striking. "The first rule of TYFOWA is—"

Queenie holds up her hand. "Tiff what now?"

"TYFOWA. The Young Feminists of the World Association," Persephone explains. "Their first rule is that you have a responsibility to the other women of the world. It's your duty to help uplift and empower them. Isn't there a witches' council or something that does the same for other witches?"

"I don't think so," Queenie says, frowning. "At least, I've never heard of one. I know there are other witches out there, obviously, but it's not like we've unionized or anything."

"This is why you all need the internet and social media to connect with each other," Persephone mutters, tucking her hands in her pockets. She shakes her head and then tries again. "What about the women of Critchley Hackle? I know they come here sometimes for tarot readings or potions." When Queenie shoots her a curious look, Persephone replies, "I read about it in my mother's journals. She called it *medicine* and *guidance*, but it's easy enough to read between the lines. Don't you think the women of the town will help you?"

Queenie sighs again, a heavier one this time. She yanks at

a tendril of loose wallpaper, peeling it away like it's the manor's sunburned skin. "The women of the town have come to us for decades when they had nowhere else to turn. But they had to come under the cloak of darkness because consorting with witches was almost as bad as *being* a witch. If those same women united now in our defense, it would be tantamount to admitting their involvement with magic. And you heard what the reverend said yesterday about the town coming for us. The women's hands are tied."

"That's not fair!" Persephone tugs at one of her corkscrew curls, something she does when she's worked up. "They ask for your help for decades but then refuse to help you when you need theirs?"

"You can't ask people to give what they don't have." Queenie smiles and reaches for Persephone's hand, steering it away from her hair. She squeezes it, saying, "I can see that you're a fellow doer like me. Someone who can't listen to other people's problems without wanting to step in and help. But we have a plan to save the manor, okay?" When Persephone nods, Queenie says, "Come on. Let me show you the bilious room, Ruby's favorite."

"Who's Ruby?" Persephone asks.

The question startles Queenie who drops Persephone's hand as though she's been scalded.

20

Sunday, October 24
Afternoon

"She was…she *is* one of our sisterhood," Queenie says, correcting herself.

"I don't think I met her. Is she also a ghost?"

"No, Ruby had to go away," Queenie replies slowly, trying to find the words to articulate their collective pain over something that was set in motion all those years ago by the life-changing decision Ruby made. Ruby herself and Tabby paid the highest prices for it, of course, but they've all had to live with the terrible consequences. "She's been gone for a long time, but she's coming home tomorrow."

"Is that why you're all cleaning the place up? For her?"

"Yes." Queenie tries to smile her sadness away. "Ruby's always liked pretty things and reflective surfaces. All the better to see herself in." She laughs and then looks around, feeling like she needs to explain herself as much to the manor as to Persephone. "We've let the place fall to ruin a bit over the years, more from sadness, I think, than laziness. And now we're trying to buff the old girl to a shine to welcome Ruby home."

Queenie stops at a door on the left, turning the creaky handle and stepping inside. Persephone follows and gasps to see the whole room is painted red, including the ceiling, walls and floor. It's like stepping into the very heart of the manor. Queenie draws her wand from her pocket, pointing it at the wall sconces. *"Incende,"* she mutters, and the torches suddenly light up, flames dancing where there were no flames before.

"That's so lit," Persephone squeals, clapping her hands.

Queenie laughs at her reaction and the pun before turning serious. "Listen," she starts. She's reluctant to have this conversation, but it must be broached. "I really hate to ask this of you because you should always be wary of adults asking you to keep secrets, but you can't tell anyone about what you've seen here today or anything that I've told—"

"I know." Persephone nods. "Muggles don't understand the magical world."

"Huh?"

"Never mind." Persephone laughs. "Don't worry. My lips are sealed."

Queenie nods. "I appreciate it. It's just that it could be extremely dangerous for us. People fear what they don't understand, and fear makes them do reckless things."

Queenie watches the girl taking in the room and is surprised by how much she's enjoying her company. She doesn't understand Ursula's insistence that she form a relationship with the child, but Ursula's visions work in mysterious ways. If she says it's important that Queenie let her in, then it is. Queenie's learned from firsthand experience to never ignore one of Ursula's visions, or tragedy was sure to befall them.

Still, it's a lot easier to do than Queenie would've thought. There's something about the girl that reminds her not just of herself at that age but of all of them. Persephone has the same lost quality to her, that same floundering, abandoned air that makes Queenie feel protective of her even as she's asking Persephone to help protect the sisterhood.

Queenie turns to an enormous table that's covered by what looks like a huge white sheet. She points her wand at it and says, *"Veni."*

Persephone watches, awestruck, as the white sheet is ripped away from the table, flying at Queenie, who catches it with the hand that isn't holding the wand.

"OMG," Persephone gasps. "That is so sick." And then she turns to the table, frowning. "So, it *is* a billiards table."

Queenie folds up the white sheet and then points her wand at it, making it disappear. "Not exactly." Persephone squeals at the trick which is exactly what Queenie was aiming for. "Take a closer look."

Persephone walks up to the table, circling it. She counts the six pockets, one in each of the four corners, and one midway along each of the longest sides. The girl sinks her hands into them, taking note of how big they are, more like giant salad bowls than pockets.

As she runs her hand along the table's scarlet cloth, she comments on how it feels hardier and more durable that regular felt. She also studies the table's eight legs, each one ornately carved in what appears to be a dark, almost black, wood.

Queenie answers Persephone's question before she asks it. "It's slate."

There are what appear to be scorch marks all over the table. Persephone studies the burns along the room's walls *and* above the table where, mounted on the ceiling, are what look like six giant metal pinball paddles aligned directly above the six pockets. Two basketball hoops, with chain netting, hang from the walls at the foot and head of the table.

"The walls, ceiling and floor have been treated with a fireproof coating," Queenie says.

"Where are the balls and cues?" Persephone asks.

"There aren't any. You play with a wand and a fireball."

There's a black iron stove shaped like a pyramid in the corner of the room. A dozen steel mesh masks and chain-mail gloves hang from hooks on the wall.

Queenie waves her wand, zapping cobwebs and dust. She flicks the black scorchproof curtains aside to open the windows for some air. "This is Ruby's favorite game, and one of the only things she couldn't get Ursula to do with her. It became our thing, mine and hers, the way we'd let off steam on particularly tough days. She always whipped my ass. It's how I got this," she says, hitching up her sleeve and showing Persephone an oddly shaped scar.

"Sick," Persephone says, turning her head at an angle. "It looks a bit like Marge Simpson."

"Who?"

"Never mind." Persephone laughs. "So that's why the game is called *bilious*? Because the injuries can make you feel super nauseated?"

"Exactly," Queenie says, laughing. "It's also known as the lionheart game. You can't play this game half-heartedly; it doesn't let you. You play with all your might to win." She caresses the table like greeting an old friend. "I haven't played bilious since Ruby left so I'm more than a bit rusty. And, of course, we're both a lot older than we used to be. But maybe..." Queenie says, feeling wistful "...maybe we can play again when she gets home."

Straight after Ruby saves us from near ruin.

Persephone aches hearing the emotion in Queenie's words. Queenie's revealing a lot despite everything she isn't saying. Persephone knows because she's become a master at listening to the silence between words, to all that goes unsaid, because that's where the most important truths hide in plain sight. There's so much her own father won't speak about, that he'll pretend to speak about but actually talk *around* when Persephone asks him the questions that burn in her rib cage, keeping her up at night.

She's learned that adults communicate in strange ways that often don't resemble communication at all. Like how a sweating tumbler full of whiskey can mean the observance of an important anniversary, because of how it appears on the same July day every year, staining the table's wood until its surface eventually looks like interlaced Melero Rings—a staple of every magician's bag of tricks—rising up through the polish.

And how another kind of ring finally taken off can leave a thin band of white skin that looks more vulnerable than newly born mice. And also how muffled sounds in the middle of the night, too high-pitched to be words, can sound like steam escaping a valve on a pressure cooker, and how crying without tears can sound like that, and how the absence of tears doesn't signify the absence of pain but, in fact, just the opposite.

At least their friend Ruby is coming back; at least there's that. Not everyone comes back.

Wanting to understand, Persephone asks, "Where has Ruby been all this time?"

Queenie sighs, shoulders slumped. "Prison," she says. "She's been in prison."

Moonshyne Manor Grimoire

Ivy's Miracle Compress for Burns

Ingredients:

1 tbsp. chamomile tea
1 tbsp. marigold tea
1 tbsp. aloe vera tea
2 cups water

Equipment:

A copper kettle or small, heavy-bottomed cauldron
A dish towel
Gauze
A bowl
A wooden spoon

Instructions:

Boil the water in the small, heavy-bottomed cauldron or copper kettle. Mix the tea leaves in a bowl and pour the boiling water over the dry herbs. Cover with a dish towel and let steep for 10 minutes. As the tea infuses, thank the Goddess for her bounty in between muttering curse words at whatever had the temerity to burn you.

Remind yourself:
Rather a localized burn than being torched at the stake.

Add the gauze to the mix, stirring with a wooden spoon to ensure the gauze is completely submerged. Squeeze out excess liquid while keeping the gauze moist and apply the gauze to the burned area. Keep it there for 10 minutes.

21

Monday, October 25
Afternoon

Ursula and Queenie are parked outside the prison gates in Queenie's black 1947 Cadillac convertible, a car so big it looks more like a luxury cruise liner than a motor vehicle. Checking the time again, Ursula wonders if the minute hand on her wristwatch has stopped working. It's barely moved, and there are *still* ten excruciating minutes to go.

Her stomach feels like a pit of writhing snakes, anxiety squirming against terror, entwining with guilt and hope. She thinks she's going to be sick and wonders if the color of her face matches that of her clothes. It's late October, colder than usual, and the outfit Ursula's wearing was chosen for aesthetics rather than practicality. She's out of her usual drab robe, wearing a newly purchased shimmery emerald-green pantsuit, because Ruby always insisted green was Ursula's color.

Ursula's even wearing makeup that she had to ask Jezebel to

apply since she doesn't have any herself, not anymore; she hasn't bought cosmetics since before Ruby was led away in handcuffs. And as Ursula learned this morning, when her old eyeshadow crumbled to dust in her hand, they apparently have a shelf life of less than three decades.

Queenie could clearly not care less about her own appearance. She's in her functional black robe, the one that's double-lined to guard against the midfall chill. The only nod to the occasion is that her Docs aren't the standard black lace-ups but a customized pair painted with witch's knot symbols interwoven with machine cogs. Her silver locs are tied back from her bare face, and she's wearing her square-framed driving glasses.

Only the way Queenie taps her fingers against the steering wheel after popping one of her antacids betrays her nervousness. "Are you sure Ruby's being released at noon?" Queenie asks, looking at the prison gate.

"That's what they said when I called," Ursula says, checking her hair and makeup again in the rearview mirror.

Not used to layering a more filtered face over her usual craggy one, Ursula swiped at her eyes a few minutes ago and managed to smudge her mascara. She doesn't remember this from the last time she bothered with all this titivation, how faces seem to have silent earthquakes all their own, in which tectonic plates shift and crevices open. How areas that were previously smooth are now shot through with cracks into which powders can collect, highlighting the very flaws one is trying to camouflage.

After a minute, Queenie says, "You don't think anyone else might be coming to get Ruby?" She nods over at the only other car in the parking lot, a black Lincoln Navigator that pulled up ten minutes after Queenie and Ruby arrived. The windows are blacked out so it's impossible to see who's inside.

Ursula's brows lurch upward, alarmed at the thought. "Like who?"

They're both thinking about Magnus, how he would've been there to pick Ruby up if he could have. But then, Ruby wouldn't have gone to prison in the first place if it weren't for Magnus, so it's the kind of argument that, if examined too closely, chases and eats its own tail.

"We can't rule out that Ruby didn't make friends while inside," Queenie says. "She's been gone a really long time. And hasn't spoken to us during any of it."

Ursula sighs, trying to swallow back the dread that's been building for weeks. How much easier this all would've been if Ruby hadn't cast a spell to make herself invisible to Widget, ensuring that the crow couldn't check on her during flybys. Or even before that, if Ruby had just allowed the sisterhood to visit so they could see for themselves how she was doing.

But that's such a reductive thought.

If Ursula's going to play that game, it's easier to think how, if Ruby had just allowed the sisterhood to rescue her as they'd attempted, they wouldn't even be in this position. Remembering that night, Ursula can still see Queenie hovering over the prison on her Harley broomstick, a rope ladder hanging from the side, as the rest of the sisters flew in formation, Ivy blasting a hole into the roof of Ruby's cell.

But if the Goddess helps those who help themselves, then the same has to be said for those who are being sprung from jail. A lifeline, when thrown your way, must be grasped. A ladder must be climbed. Calling for the guards to patch up the hole in your ceiling isn't the most effective method of seizing the day or taking advantage of the cavalry who've charged in to rescue you.

"I'm sure she's expecting us," Ursula says, when what she really means is *I hope she's expecting me.*

For who else would wait for so patiently for Ruby other than her best friend and soul mate? Who else would count down the 12,076 sleeps, crossing them off her calendar every single morning, other than the person who knows Ruby best and loves her most? Who else, but Ursula, would do all of this despite being so utterly wounded by Ruby's rejection of her? Most people, when treated this way, would move on. Not Ursula.

"Besides, all the signs pointed to us definitely fetching her today," she says.

"Yeah, but you also saw fog in the signs, and the day couldn't be clearer," Queenie adds, nodding at the cloudless sky.

Ursula shrugs, opening the door and getting out. When Queenie makes as if to follow her, Ursula holds up a hand, shaking her head. Queenie seems to understand. Or, if not, she at least respects Ursula's wishes. Queenie sighs and leans back in her seat, fingers energetically tapping out "The Shoop Shoop Song" beat on the steering wheel as though arthritis hasn't registered on Queenie's radar.

Ursula takes a few steps toward the gate, the satiny fabric of her outfit swooshing around her. It feels strange to be in trousers when most of her life has been spent in robes. There's such freedom of movement in a loose dress that it can't be a coincidence that retirement meccas are filled with older women who've rejected underwire bras and restrictive clothing in favor of gauzy caftans and flowing muumuus.

Of course, Ruby wouldn't have aged the way Ursula has, capitulating in this way.

Ruby always made an effort. Comfort was never a consideration; only style counted. Ursula doesn't want Ruby to see that she's given up, become complacent. Ruby's motto would have aligned with Dylan Thomas's, to not go gentle into that good night.

That's what Ruby would've done if she hadn't been arrested and forced to spend so much of her life behind bars. Who knows what that's done to her? Ursula tried, in the beginning, to send Ruby care packages with face masks and skin-care potions Ivy had concocted especially for her. But when the twentieth box was sent back unopened, Ursula gave up.

Has Ruby managed to age not just gracefully but fabulously, like she always swore she'd do? Is that even possible in a correctional facility? And not just any facility but *this* particular one, truly the last place Ruby should ever have been sent to?

And suddenly the gate is whirring open, and Ursula snaps from her reverie. There's a figure walking from the office down the drive, clutching a small bag.

Something builds in Ursula then, like how water pulls back from the shore to feed an approaching wave, giving it the momentum to crest. It's a gathering, an inhalation before the scream which manifests as a razor-sharp question, the kind that slices to the heart of things: What if the reason Ruby has rejected her all these years is because Ruby knows what Ursula did?

If she does, who would have told her? One of the members of the sisterhood? Ursula turns her head, regarding Queenie. *Surely not?*

22

Monday, October 25
Afternoon

Queenie watches as Ursula takes a few tentative steps toward the opening gate as unsteady as a toddler testing its legs. She wonders if Ursula knows the truth, if she has enough self-awareness to admit that she's in love with Ruby, and always has been, probably since she first laid eyes on her all those many years ago.

Love is such a tricky beast, Queenie thinks, more capricious than the damaged mortals it dwells in. It can hit like a lightning bolt on a summer's day when there isn't a damn cloud in the sky. It can strike like a baseball bat to the kneecaps during your own birthday party. Of course, it can be beautiful too, redeeming rather than debilitating, but not everyone has that kind of karma.

For Ursula, love has been a blade to the Achilles heel. And it's been excruciating for the sisterhood to witness.

Watching Ursula stiffen now, as though steeling herself against a possible attack, Queenie wants to look away but can't. It's too compelling. Perhaps some stories are just so big, so utterly large in scope, that they draw others into their gravity. Like now. Even as this moment's playing out—one that Queenie is merely a spectator to—she knows it will imprint itself on her psyche like a meteor scooping out a space for itself at its collision site.

Queenie wonders if it would have made any difference had they said something to Ursula when she and Ruby were thirteen, and Ursula watched, crestfallen, as Ruby plastered her walls with pictures of Clark Gable, Cary Grant and Humphrey Bogart. Or when Ursula was eighteen and listened, clearly heartbroken, as Ruby chattered nonstop about her first real crush, Brendan Fisher, a beautiful boy she'd started a conversation with at the drive-in two towns over.

Should they have pulled Ursula aside when she was twenty-five and she and Ruby still slept entwined, like twin vines wrapping around one another, only with one clinging that much more fiercely than the other? Or when they were thirty and Ursula turned down a proposal, telling her suitor that her heart already belonged to another?

While the sisterhood believe in honesty, they don't condone the brutal kind. Had Ursula asked for their advice, they would have given it, gently and with love. But she never did, perhaps because she knew what they would say and didn't want to hear it. Sometimes what we want is for the world to maintain the charade we've constructed for ourselves, a hall of mirrors reflecting back our own warped perception of reality.

As the figure leaving the prison gets closer now, Queenie has the uneasy sense that she's being watched. Tearing her gaze away from Ruby, she looks around the parking lot, noticing that the Lincoln Navigator's back window has been lowered.

She peers over her driving glasses, breath catching when she spots the man who's watching her.

Without ever having seen him, Queenie knows exactly who he is. Brad Gedney bears a striking resemblance to both his father and his grandfather. His gaunt face appears to lack muscle or fat, giving the impression of a skull that's been draped with skin, almost like a tablecloth disguising a scuffed table.

He has protruding eyes that burn with what might be mistaken for fever, but since Queenie has seen it before in the older Gedneys, she can identify it for what it is: zealotry. A jagged scar bisects one of his eyebrows, giving him a permanently startled expression.

He nods at Queenie, once, the motion barely perceptible, as though he isn't prepared to waste even the tiniest bit of energy on her. A startling thought occurs to her then, as she thinks back to finding her office in disarray, as though someone had been rifling through her desk and drawers. And then discovering the sooty footprints throughout the ground floor a few weeks later.

Could Brad Gedney have been inside the manor? The thought sends a shiver through her.

Satisfied that some kind of message has been delivered, Gedney closes his window, and the Navigator pulls away.

23

Monday, October 25
Afternoon

What Ursula spots, through the diamonds of the chain-link fence, is someone carrying a small bag, someone who can't possibly be Ruby. Not with that short white hair and those drooping cheeks and the soft jaw covered with days-old stubble.

But then Ursula does a double take, recognizing the tilt of the head and the set of the shoulders. There's no denying that the lone figure is, in fact, Ruby. She's wearing trousers that hang from boyish hips, and a man's shirt that sits flat against her chest.

As Ruby takes her last few steps from the Dayton Correctional Facility for Men, Ursula thinks, *Oh, Ruby.* And something cracks inside her like fissures shot through a block of ice.

Ruby looks like an old man, which is exactly what some might consider her to be. Certainly, the same people who sentenced Ruby to all those years of incarceration with men would think as much.

And it's heartbreaking now to see Ruby this way, as though stripped naked in her most vulnerable moment. It's not only that she's presenting as a man, when she'd so vehemently chosen to present as a woman just before her incarceration, but also that she looks so disheveled. It's such an invasion of privacy, because Ruby would never have allowed herself to be seen this way, not ever in all the time Ursula's known her.

What comes to Ursula then is the memory of a six-year-old Ruby, a few days after her arrival at the manor, sitting across from Ursula on the floor of Ruby's room, playing with a trunk of Victorian dolls Mirabelle had dragged down for them from the attic.

"Look at her hair," Ruby said, reaching for one of the dolls in the play chest. "It's just like mine."

As Ruby brushed the doll's fiery tresses with a miniature comb, Ursula watched her, transfixed, thinking how the beautiful little girl looked *exactly* like the porcelain-skinned doll. Ursula, with her sturdy body and stubby nose, didn't possess such feminine beauty. She came from plainer stock, more plow horse than show pony.

Ursula gazed at Ruby's long eyelashes and Cupid's-bow lips and the smattering of delightful freckles. She wasn't envious, as one might expect. Somehow Ruby's delicacy and grace felt like her own, something Ruby had gifted Ursula with when she'd befriended her. She was proud to know her and grateful to be in her proximity, soaking up the reflected rays of her light.

And then, just as Ruby reached into the trunk for a bonnet to fit on the doll, the impossible happened. Ruby flickered, as though she were a mirage, and when Ursula blinked again, the little girl was gone.

In her place was a pale-skinned, freckled, redheaded boy. He was still wearing Ruby's dress, but the long tresses had somehow shrunken back into his skull, and the delicacy of his features had hardened into something ruddier, more elementally masculine.

Ursula's mouth fell open just as the little boy appeared to realize what had happened. He watched her carefully, assessing her response as though he were testing her. When it seemed that Ursula wasn't going to scream or attack him, the boy swapped out the bonnet for a white ribbon, tying the doll's hair with it.

"This happens sometimes," he said matter-of-factly.

Ursula wasn't sure what to make of it. Was this still her friend, or had another person entirely taken her place? "Is that you, Ruby?"

"Yes," the boy replied. "I'm still me. I'll just be boy until I can change back."

"Change back?" Ursula asked, confused but wanting to understand.

And then it all came out. How Ruby was born in a boy's body but was able to shift to presenting as a girl when she wanted to, which was quite often, though not all the time, since there were occasions when she quite liked being a boy. Her growing powers meant she was able to maintain the girlish state for longer with each passing year, but she still struggled to make the transformation stick for more than a few days at a time.

After Ruby's mother, Garnet, had been killed in a car accident, Ruby was sent to live with her grandfather, her only living relative. She'd never met him prior to that because her mother had been estranged from him. Grandpa Hank wouldn't let Ruby call him Grandpa since he maintained Garnet wasn't his real daughter, that his wife must have had a fling with a traveling salesman to birth such a peculiar peacock of a child, what with her flaming-red hair and her pale complexion so very different from his own ruddy one.

It was obvious, from the appalled looks he often cast Ruby's way, that he also considered *her* peculiar, the worst possible quality a person could have in his brown-and-beige world. Because he fled any room Ruby entered, she'd managed to hide her transitioning powers from him for over a month. But upon discovering them, he'd left Ruby at a boys' orphanage fifty miles away with a note stuck to her pajamas saying *Take it. There's something wrong with it.*

"I'm glad," Ruby said, shrugging off his abandonment like it was nothing. "He was horrible."

Ruby had been kicked out of the orphanage two days prior when she'd changed back into a girl upon waking, scaring the morning matron who thought the little girl had sneaked in during the night to test out the beds like Goldilocks.

"There weren't others like me," Ruby said, looking disappointed. "Most kids are boring. They're just boys or girls."

Ursula, not wanting to be considered boring, said, "I'm just a girl, but I can see things other people can't."

Ruby brightened. "Yeah? Like what?"

"I can see when bad men are coming," Ursula said, swapping out a dark-haired doll for a blond one. "And sometimes when nice people will come. Like I saw with you."

"Can you see something now?" Ruby asked, rummaging in the trunk for a purse.

"No," Ursula sighed. "I can't do it when I'm trying. I have to wait for it to happen."

"That's like with me. I can't stay a girl for long when I'm sad," Ruby confided. "It won't work then." And then Ruby shot Ursula a worried look. "Will Mirabelle send me to a boys' orphanage when she finds out?"

Ursula didn't know what Mirabelle might do, having only been at the manor a day longer than Ruby. All she knew was that they couldn't take that chance. "How long before you're able to turn back again?" she asked.

"Probably a day, maybe less if I'm able to think only happy thoughts."

"I'll help you," Ursula said, putting her doll down and fixing all of her attention on Ruby. "What makes you happy?"

There was a pause as Ruby thought it over. "I like music. And I like singing and dancing."

"Okay," Ursula said, thinking hard. "Stay here. I'll be back."

Within half an hour, Ursula had managed to convince Mirabelle to move the clunky gramophone up from the parlor to Ursula's room. Despite Mirabelle's obvious reservations about Ursula being old enough to play with the expensive device, she gave in when Ursula told her that she needed the music to make Ruby happy.

Once the gramophone was placed on the escritoire in Ursula's room, Mirabelle taught Ursula how to crank the handle, after which she handed over a few records—Bing Crosby, Fred Astaire, Billie Holiday and Fats Waller—showing Ursula how to remove the records from their sleeves and hold them by the edges, placing them gently on the turntable, so as not to get scratched by the spindle.

After Mirabelle left, Ursula ferried Ruby—who was wrapped in a blanket as a kind of disguise—to her room where she put on Fats Waller's "It's a Sin to Tell a Lie." Within a few minutes, Ruby was shaking her booty so hard that the blanket jiggled wildly with little bursts of seismic joy. The children shrieked with laughter, their dancing becoming wilder each time they played the song.

Ruby changed back into a girl within twelve hours, the fastest she'd ever managed it. And when Mirabelle discovered their secret soon afterward, they didn't need to worry about it anymore.

As long as Ursula had known her, Ruby had always embraced the two bookends of her genders, as well as the spectrum of ones in between. She was a chameleon who was able to alter her appearance at will, suffering no trauma over her identity, and feeling fully supported and understood within their tiny community.

Regardless of whether she presented as a burly dark-haired man or a slight blond one; or as a redheaded, curvaceous woman or a green-haired elfin one; or an androgynous person or an agender one, what was always consistent was how well-groomed and stylish Ruby was.

And now here she is, looking so utterly scruffy and unkempt.

Oh, Ruby. What have they done to you? Ursula thinks, blinking back tears. And then Ruby has passed through the gate. The moment Ursula has been waiting thirty-three years for is finally upon them. Terror snatches Ursula's breath away so that she fears she might begin hyperventilating.

How will Ruby react to her considering everything that's happened? Will she curse Ursula, sending her away? Will she give her the silent treatment, refusing to acknowledge her?

What Ursula isn't expecting is for Ruby to look around the parking lot as though searching for someone who isn't there. Seeming to give up on them, she spots Ursula, heading for her. Ruby comes to a stop in front of her, smiling as she reaches out to touch Ursula's face. Ursula wants to weep with relief at the sensation of Ruby's fingers upon her cheek. Is it possible that Ruby has forgiven her, that Ursula is being granted an absolution she doesn't deserve?

"Ruby," she whispers, the word weighted with a lifetime of love. "Oh, Ruby. How I've missed you."

Ruby runs her finger along Ursula's jaw as though tracing the scalloped edge of an old photograph. She smiles, but then her hand drops away, and her eyes fog over. She tightens her grip on her bag, pulling it close as though using it as a shield. "Oh, I'm so sorry," she says, suddenly unsure, eyebrows furrowed. "Do I know you?"

24

Monday, October 25
Afternoon

Jezebel paces the length of the foyer, from the library—past the grand staircase across to Queenie's office—and then back again, shooting dirty looks at the bits of the manor that now gleam too richly for her taste.

Thanks to the hours of buffing and shining Queenie forced them all to do yesterday, spiders have been encouraged to pack up their webs and go pitch them elsewhere, peeling wallpaper has been coaxed into reuniting with surfaces it formally separated from years ago, and mold and damp have been persuaded to do some drying out like aging rock stars sent to rehab.

Jezebel hates it, much preferring the manor's previous air of genteel grubbiness. And despite all these efforts being made for Ruby's homecoming, Jezebel is certain Ruby will hate it too. Ursula might have always been Ruby's soul mate, but Jezebel was her partner in crime. Being the two misfits of the group, they were always simpatico when it came to these kinds of things, similarly embracing a healthy level of debauchery, while having a sincere appreciation for delinquents (both in building and human form).

It's only now that Ruby's really coming home—and saving them all from losing their home in the process—that Jezebel allows herself to admit just how much she's missed that connection, how much it always meant to her having a true kindred spirit. Truth be told, Jezebel's been lost without Ruby who was always a mirror for Jezebel, never allowing her to lose sight of who she was.

It's not like Jezebel hasn't tried to keep things at the manor lively and fun. There's still cocktail hour and the occasional skinny-dipping, not to mention naked romps into the forest for solstices, equinoxes and hunter's moons. Jezebel even managed to cajole everyone into playing strip poker one night a few months ago, but it didn't end well when Ivy caught a cold and Queenie almost set herself alight from sitting too close to the fire.

Aging gracefully is a bore. Aging disgracefully is something to be proud of.

And now that Ruby's coming home, Jezebel's looking forward to shaking things up again, to rediscovering that part of herself that isn't secretly comforted by the regimented routine of it all, how their lives are like a well-choreographed play with the entrances and exits carefully timed, everyone knowing their lines and no one going off script.

Plus, if anyone can talk Jezebel out of her recurring thoughts of Artemis—those pesky fantasies that keep intruding, making her wonder what it might be like to truly love a man for the first time in her life—it will be Ruby. After all, just look at how Ruby's great love affair ended up. Look at what she got from letting down her guard and daring to believe in a happy-ever-after.

It's Ivy trotting down the stairs that interrupts Jezebel's musings. Ivy is in her usual state of disarray from her work in the conservatory, mulch down the front of her robe, and dirt streaked across the bridge of her nose because of constantly pushing her spectacles up with grubby fingers. Instead of the usual dusk-pink camellias, Ivy's gray hair is threaded with purple orchids, Ruby's favorites.

"Did I hear a car?" Ivy asks, craning her head to listen.

"I don't think so." Jezebel adjusts her leather lace-up bustier just in case, opening the door to double-check, before closing it again with a disappointed sigh.

Tabitha joins them from the library, lips moving, though, of course, they can't hear a word. Ivy and Jezebel automatically turn to Widget who has flown in ahead of Tabby, coming to rest on a banister. "What if something happened?" Widget rasps. "What if she isn't coming?"

"Ursula saw her homecoming in the cards again this morning," Ivy replies crisply, considering the matter settled.

"Is it just me," Jezebel ventures, "or has anyone else noticed something a bit *off* about Ursula lately?"

"Off?" Ivy asks, brow furrowed. "Off how?"

Jezebel licks her thumb, reaching forward to wipe the dirt from Ivy's nose. "Like she's off her game. She missed predicting both of the break-ins that we've had. And didn't you get the sense that Ursula was hiding something from us on Saturday when she sounded the alarm? That she's been hiding things for a while?"

Jezebel can see she's touched a nerve because Ivy isn't flat out dismissing it. But just as Ivy opens her mouth to answer, there's the unmistakable crunch of tires in the driveway and the sound of the Caddy's engine.

"It's them!" Jezebel squeals.

Something crackles between the triangle of women, the air physically charged with the strength of their collective emotions. It's been a while since that happened, and they all smile at its occurrence, even Tabby who always looks so dour, radiating waves of negativity regardless of the lovely sentiments that come out of Widget's beak.

Despite their anticipation, they each remain motionless. Even Widget is frozen to the spot, black eyes gleaming like beads stitched to a feathered ball gown.

What they're all acutely aware of is how, when someone leaves, what we retain of them is a kind of time-stamped Polaroid in which they're perfectly preserved, just as they were in their moment of departure.

But life marches relentlessly on, and nothing stays the same. Not mountains, not coastlines. Certainly not people. So the person who leaves is almost always not the same person who returns. And those who are left behind are just as eroded as those who go; no one is left unscathed, not even if they've stayed in the same place. *Especially* not then, for there are none who are quite so transformed as those who feel so utterly abandoned.

What the women all woke up to thirty-three years ago, before everything went wrong, was a complete faith in the sisterhood's bond. But then Tabby was killed, and Ruby was led away in cuffs, screaming as she tried to drag herself toward the two sheet-covered bodies being loaded into the ambulance. Connections that had always felt as sturdy as chains were revealed to be gossamer-thin, as easy to sever as the threads of a spider's web.

"How much do you think prison has changed her?" Jezebel asks.

"I have no idea, but we're about to find out," Ivy replies, her voice as shaky as Jezebel's legs feel.

Ruby might be back now, but Jezebel knows there's sometimes no *going* back. And that's what they're all terrified of. Perhaps even more terrifying than losing the manor to Brad

Gedney and his cohorts is losing what they once had, losing the sisterhood and themselves in the process.

The Goddess knows Ruby and Tabitha have lost the most, but there's always more to lose.

Moonshyne Manor Grimoire

Jezebel's Sex Goddess Natural Lube

Ingredients*:*

¼ cup fractionated organic coconut oil
¼ cup aloe gel
6 drops ylang-ylang essential oil
2 drops black pepper essential oil
2 drops peppermint essential oil
2 drops of sea buckthorn oil

Equipment:

A glass jar

Instructions:

Combine all ingredients in the glass jar. Shake well. Keep it by your bedside, and use as much as desired during intimacy or sensual massage.

Hot tip: blow on the lube to make it tingle before using.
(I promise you'll thank me later.)

25

Monday, October 25
Afternoon

Tabitha's waited thirty-three years for an apology. That's what all the literature says, that ghosts linger because of the injustice they feel. She's convinced the anticipation of it—the waiting for the password that will set her free—is what's kept her chained to the manor, unable to even venture into the forest to take comfort from her animals. Perhaps today's the day when she'll finally be vindicated, released by those two magical words.

Nothing else has worked up until now. While Tabitha has no idea why she was yanked back here to the manor when she took her last breath—all those lights flashing around her, punctuating her passing—she's tried everything to move on. But trying to cross the manor's threshold feels like walking into a giant marshmallow, the outside world gently pushing her back inside. And it's impossible to die once you're already dead. No amount of throwing yourself down the stairs or being careless around fires actually works.

Maybe today's the day.

But maybe not.

Tabby can already tell something's wrong from where she's standing waiting in the foyer alone after Jezebel and Ivy rushed out to greet Ruby. Their initial excited chattering out on the porch turned to yelps of surprise, which have since swiftly devolved into a bewildered silence.

Has Ruby changed that much? Is seeing her that much of a shock? Tabitha doesn't have to wait long for the answer.

Ruby is the first person through the door, though it takes Tabby a second to recognize her, considering her vastly changed form. This white-haired old man—essentially a stranger—is a complete surprise. Despite that, Tabby can't think of him as a *he*. Even with that stubble and those bushy eyebrows, even with the nose and ear hair, Ruby is...well, Ruby.

She's trailed by an openmouthed Jezebel and a frowning Ivy. Queenie and Ursula, bringing up the rear, have no expressions at all, just the shellacked look of the shell-shocked.

"There she is," Ruby exclaims, spotting Tabitha and rushing at her. "The birthday girl." Ruby tries to gather Tabby into a hug. When Ruby's arms close upon themselves, rather than being met with the resistance of a body, she doesn't appear to notice. Instead, she looks around the foyer, confused. "Where are all the decorations we planned? The guests will be here soon."

"What the fuck are you talking about?" Tabitha snaps.

"What decorations do you mean, Ruby?" Widget croaks, head twitching from side to side.

"Oh, you've taught her to speak," Ruby says, smiling and clapping. "Good for you! You were hoping she would learn before the party." And then Ruby turns, smiling at each of them in turn, hands clasped coquettishly to her chest. "I have the perfect costume for tonight. Magnus is going to love it."

And suddenly, with a feeling like an anchor thrown overboard, Tabby realizes what's happened. Ruby has somehow reverted back to the day of Tabby's fiftieth birthday party, before Tabby was killed and Ruby was arrested. It's bewildering, of course, having someone think they're living a day that happened thirty-three years ago.

But more than that, it's enraging because, thanks to Ruby, that birthday was the very last one in which Tabby ever got to draw breath.

Had she known then that she'd be dead within three days, Tabby wouldn't have dieted ahead of the party, hell-bent as she was on fitting into her skintight dress. Instead, she would've reached for every dish in sight, savoring each exquisitely nuanced flavor, the sweet and sour, the tangy and salty. She would've drunk more on the night too, downing glass after glass of champagne, relishing the delicious fizzing of the bubbles as they effervesced lustily against her tongue.

Had Tabby known that was the last weekend she'd ever feel any kind of sensation, she would have appreciated it every time another person bumped against her in the throng, warm bodies all pushed together. She would have reached out to touch people all night long and gone on Queenie's zip line over and over and over again, reveling in the wind caressing her face and threading its fingers through her hair. She would've let go of the handles to plummet into the water—November cold be damned—and she would have shivered ecstatically, teeth clattering together in a percussion of joy.

But she didn't know.

That's the thing about a death that silently creeps up on you, hunting you through the long grass, not making its presence known until it pounces, claws unsheathed. You don't know it's coming. And so you think you have all the time in the world to shriek and dance, to laugh and eat, to drink and swim and make love.

And here Ruby is, the cause of Tabitha's untimely death, acting like it never happened, making Tabby second-guess herself, allowing her to snatch at the flimsy hope that it's all just been one long, awful dream that she's finally awakening from.

But the expression on the other women's faces confirms it's Ruby, and not Tabitha, who's lost her grasp on reality. Queenie's mouth is set in a grim line while Ivy wrings her hands. Ursula's eyes are misted over with tears, and Jezebel's mouth is twisted in a dubious smile, as though she's waiting for a punch line she suspects will never come.

Sensing their unease, Ruby turns from Tabitha, regarding the women behind her. "What? Why are you all looking at me like that?" And then she swipes at her nose. "Is there a bat hanging from the cave?"

It's Ivy who takes charge, swallowing deeply before forcing a smile. "No, darling. You look perfect, as always." Her voice is gruff with emotion.

And Ruby smiles in response. It's a dazzling smile they all know and love, one they've missed too much to extinguish now. They all look to Ursula, who steps forward and takes one of Ruby's hands, after which Jezebel walks around and takes the other.

"It's time to open your room," Queenie says, holding aloft an ornate key and following Ivy up the stairs, the rest of the women trailing in their wake.

Tabitha's miffed enough that she considers holding back and returning to the library, but there's something irresistible about the six of them being together again. Five of them are now covered in liver spots and move stiffly, age having hibernated in joints that will never see the spring again. One of them is dead, and another is so vastly changed that she wouldn't be recognizable to anyone but the sisterhood. They're not who they were more than three decades before, but they don't have to be.

They're reunited, and for now, that is enough. And so Tabitha joins them as they welcome Ruby home, wanting to partake in the celebration before they have to deal with the inevitable devastating fallout.

26

Monday, October 25
Afternoon

Charon the Ferryman will be coming for me in two days, and I don't have the treasure. I've promised something that I don't have to one of the most powerful dark wizards in the world. It's a thought that's on repeat in Queenie's mind, like the chorus to a particularly gut-wrenching song. It's giving her a stress headache which isn't helped by all the noise.

There's a grunt of exertion punctuated by the sound of porcelain smashing into hundreds of tiny shards. It's followed by another noise just like it. And then another. The explosions have a demented rhythm all of their own. Grunt, crash. Grunt, crash. Grunt, crash.

The door leading off from the parlor to the rage room is closed, but Queenie can still hear Jezebel's exertions each time she pitches a cup or saucer against the wall. Sometimes, judging by the spectacular shattering, Queenie can tell it's a gravy boat or a salad bowl that have met their end. Then a vase, its death throes as dramatic as a galaxy being born.

There was a time when Queenie used magic to reconstruct them, but that kind of sorcery is like eyesight: it gets worse with age, so you end up needing younger witches to thread that particular kind of supernatural needle. Which they unfortunately have a dearth of.

After that, she began buying china and porcelain dinnerware sets by the dozen in estate sales around the county. She hasn't bought any in a while, Jezebel becoming more even-keeled with age. Queenie would make a mental note to lock the kitchen cupboards until she's able to replenish the stock, but what's the damn point?

If Ruby doesn't even consistently remember who they are and has reverted to the time *before* the heist, then she won't remember where she hid the treasure. And without the treasure, not only will Queenie have to deal with the fallout of the arrangements she made for selling them to Charon (the thought of which makes her guts churn), they'll also lose the manor, including the rage room *and* all the crockery.

And the Goddess alone knows what will happen to Tabby.

Ruby was Queenie's backup plan. Hell, truth be told, Ruby was her *only* plan. For the first time, Queenie allows herself to seriously consider the threat of homelessness. Where would they even go? How could they possibly leave Tabby?

There's no point in trying to talk about it with the others until Jezebel has worked off all of her rage. There's another sound of something being smashed, and Ursula flinches in a jolt of seismic activity. Unable to take it anymore, Ursula uses both arms to wrestle herself up from the couch.

She heads for the corner of the parlor where she sorts through their considerable record collection. Upon finding what she's looking for, she places the record on the gramophone's turntable and then cranks the handle. When she lowers the needle, it makes that little staticky noise as it tickles a tune from the record.

"Beat the intro," Ursula calls to Queenie, a game they've always played.

An upbeat trumpet intro blasts from the horn. It takes a second for Queenie to place it and then, "It's 'Hellzapoppin'' by Louis Armstrong," she calls out to be heard above the music and smashing.

Ursula gives her a half-hearted thumbs-up.

When Louis rasps the opening line about the roof being about to tumble in—his timbre so deep that it's like his voice is drilling for oil—Queenie finds herself, despite everything, smiling and nodding along, tapping her foot as she remembers her twenty-first birthday. That was the night they all flew out to Queens, Tabby clinging to Queenie's waist, because she was deathly afraid of heights and refused to ride her own broom.

Jezebel was only fifteen then, but there were times when the rage room just didn't cut it, when her fury was so immense that inanimate objects weren't enough to vent with. She'd sneak out occasionally, flying to the city, where she'd linger on deserted streets, waiting for some predator or another to pounce. And then she'd beat the living shit out of them.

It was on one such night, as Jezebel was coming out of an alleyway—her knuckles bloody after having taken on an attacker who was twice her age and triple her size—that she met Rosco, a handsome eighteen-year-old musician. Smitten with Jezebel (whose rescue he'd tried to come to before quickly determining that she didn't need it), Rosco told her that Louis Armstrong would be playing a secret gig at a jazz club the following week and that he could get Jezebel and her friends in the door.

What a night that was, sneaking in an underage Jezebel and Tabby, the women and girls arriving windswept and red-cheeked from their travels. They'd boogied all night, "Hellzapoppin'" bringing down the house.

Despite the general air of panic, the music has a similar effect on the rest of them. Ivy's tensed shoulders begin to ease, and her posture relaxes; she traces the outline of a red mandevilla vine that's on her left wrist, a self-soothing mechanism. Tabitha's expression dims to a few degrees less dour.

Ursula comes back to sit down, absentmindedly stroking her knuckles. Her arthritis must be acting up again. Ivy, noticing it as Queenie does, digs into one of her pockets, fishing a few things out from its depths before finding what she's looking for. She hands a tin of salve across to Ursula, who accepts it, murmuring her thanks. As Ursula massages it into her joints, the scent of tree sap fills the room.

The cacophony from the next room suddenly falls silent.

The door leading off to the rage room is flung open, and Jezebel enters the parlor, flushed from all that exercise. She changed out of her leather bustier celebratory outfit after it became clear that there would be no celebrating. Jezebel straightens her robe now as she removes a teacup handle from her hair.

Flinging it into the fireplace, she asks in a chipper voice, "Who wants cocktails?" She wipes her brow with her forearm as she heads for the drinks trolley.

"Can I have a cup of tea instead? Jasmine, if possible," Ivy asks.

"I'll have a virgin cocktail, please," Ursula murmurs, not looking up from rubbing the salve over her joints.

Queenie hesitates, the cocktail sounding good. But she feels like she's choosing a well-balanced approach, the best of both worlds, when she requests a coffee liqueur. She hopes it won't aggravate her stress-induced reflux which will only make Ivy try to force that hideous slippery elm brew on her.

Once they're seated—all of them except Ruby, who's napping—Jezebel takes a sip of her cocktail and exhales, a protracted sigh. “So,” she says, her gaze still on her drink as though she doesn’t trust herself to look at the others, “what the actual fuck was that?”

27

Monday, October 25
Afternoon

The question is like the tugging of a knot. Ursula shakes her head, tears loosened by the motion. They spill over, dripping from her cheeks onto her breasts. "She didn't remember me," she murmurs, her voice cracking. "She came out the prison gates, walked right over and asked if she knew me."

It's the first time Queenie's heard what transpired. Not being there as the two women were reunited, she didn't know what Ruby said to Ursula; all she saw was the fallout, Ursula's dazed and brittle expression as she led Ruby to the car.

"She didn't know me at first, either," Queenie says, half trying to make Ursula feel better, and half stating this fact to herself, testing how she feels about it. "At least we now know what the fog was that Ursula was seeing."

"During the drive home, she asked us arbitrary questions,"

Ursula adds. "Like what we did for a living and where we lived. It was like making polite conversation with a stranger on a bus."

"And then, when we pulled up outside, something seemed to shift," Queenie says, taking a sip of her liqueur and pulling a face, wishing she'd just asked for the damn cocktail. "She called us by our names, like she actually remembered us, telling us to hurry up for the party."

Ivy produces a giant seed from her pocket that looks like an avocado pit, only bigger. She cups it, closing her eyes, and a stem and root system begin to unfurl from it. But the coloring is all wrong, black instead of green, betraying her inner turmoil. "I'm thinking it's some kind of dementia like Alzheimer's, only different, because our brains aren't like those of the magic-deficient."

"That's what I was thinking too," Queenie says. "Her symptoms don't match any known malady, but that's to be expected, I guess. Magic affects the brain in its own way, so who knows how our types of dementia manifest?"

"But if Ruby has some affliction and can't remember anything..." Ursula ventures.

"Then, we're screwed," Queenie replies, closing her eyes and rubbing hard at them with the side of a balled-up fist. "Without Ruby guiding us to where she hid the treasure, we're completely and utterly fucked."

As much as Queenie is personally concerned for Ruby, the more pressing issue right now is finding a way to keep their home. With just eight days left until the bank forecloses, they're running out of time. Plus, there's the other, even more urgent matter so it's crucial that they find where Ruby hid the treasure.

Queenie clears her throat, wishing she didn't have to share this news. "We have a problem."

"No shit," Jezebel quips.

"No, another problem. Perhaps a bigger one." She frees two antacids from their roll and shoves them in her mouth.

"What could possibly be bigger than losing the manor?" Ivy asks, head dipped low as she regards Queenie over her spectacles, irritation threaded through her voice.

Queenie chews and swallows, wishing the words would circle and disappear down the drain of her throat.

Before she can answer, Ursula blurts, "Charon the Ferryman's coming in two days."

Widget squawks, flapping her wings in agitation, as Ivy drops her cup, the tea splashing over the rug.

"What?" Jezebel yelps. "Why?"

Queenie withdraws her wand, muttering an incantation to right Ivy's cup and dry the tea in a puff of steam. "I thought Ruby would reveal where the goods were hidden just as soon as she was home. And I needed the reassurance that we actually had a buyer for the artifact, one who could pay up really quickly."

"But Charon, of all people?" Ivy asks, eyes wide. "After what he did to Great-Aunt Mirabelle when she turned to him for help with that whole Anastasia debacle?"

Queenie winces. She's deliberately avoided thinking about those four long days when Mirabelle just disappeared, the girls all thinking they'd lost her forever. While Mirabelle never got into the details of what had happened with Charon and Anastasia, she returned looking wretched, emphatically cautioning them against ever making deals with dark wizards.

"Charon is evil, yes," Queenie says, "but he's also wealthy and is known for being honorable when it comes to keeping his word. Plus, it's not like we could just sell the artifact on a street corner or on that—" she flaps her hand "—internet thingy. We *need* him." She turns to Ursula. "How did you know about the Ferryman?"

"I saw it in the tea leaves," Ursula replies, "as a blackness descending upon us in the near future. But I didn't know you'd be stupid enough to cut a deal with him."

Their collective fear does nothing to calm Queenie. "I thought it was a simple case of supply and demand. That we'd have the artifact, which he'd want, making him a no-brainer for the highest bidder. How was I supposed to know Ruby wouldn't be able to produce what I'd already promised him?"

Ursula groans, and Jezebel tuts.

Widget hops from foot to foot, cawing, "He's going to kill us all."

If that's the crow's translation of what Tabby just said, then Queenie's glad she couldn't hear the actual words. "We need to find Ruby's hiding place," Queenie says. "It's nonnegotiable. We *have* to."

"What about your map?" Ivy asks, referring to the map of hiding places Queenie drew up soon after Ruby was arrested.

Unlike classic treasure maps, it's littered with many *X*s, all the places Queenie thought Ruby might possibly have buried or hidden the jewels and the artifact. Like under her favorite tree in the forest, the Japanese maple they do their rituals under, or in the flower bed she dug as a joke in the shape of a penis. And in the hollow of the Angel Oak, where Ruby once hid Jezebel's vibrator, confusing the shit out of a squirrel, who nevertheless embraced the windfall of a new back massager.

Between them arriving home and what followed after, none of them remember Ruby leaving the manor that night. But since Ruby's bedroom and the usual spots in the manor were thoroughly searched and didn't yield anything, Queenie couldn't completely eliminate outside hiding places. And so they'd searched everywhere.

"The map's useless." Queenie pulls it from her pocket and unfolds it for what feels like the millionth time. The paper's coming apart at the seams, only held together by fraying magic. "It's nothing but places where *X* doesn't mark the damn spot."

The drawing mocks Queenie. She crumples it into a ball

and pitches it at the fire whose flames ravenously swallow it in a puff of cerulean smoke.

Tabby's lips move, and Widget suddenly straightens, pacing back and forth along the armrest. "Maybe Ruby's just tired," Widget rasps, head cocked. "Maybe prison took a terrible toll. Maybe she wakes up tomorrow and is thinking more clearly."

"I've got some thoughts about a memory-stimulation device," Queenie says, "but in the meantime, we each need to do our part to try and jog Ruby's memories loose."

"What if that's upsetting for her?" Ursula asks. "Or frightening? It can't be easy for her living this way."

"You know what will be harder for her than this?" Queenie snaps. "Dementia *and* homelessness."

Before Ursula can reply, three ominous bangs burst through the silence. The women all startle. There's someone at their door, rapping on the brass door knocker.

Ursula trembles visibly. "Oh, my Goddess, it's him! The Ferryman's come early."

Queenie stands. As the others rise with her, she gestures for them to sit. "It's not Charon," she says, feigning certainty. "You know that's not how he arrives. He doesn't knock at the damn door like some garden-variety visitor." She shivers despite herself. "It's probably just Persephone. I get the sense that poor girl doesn't much like spending time at home."

Once Queenie reaches the double doors in the foyer, she takes a deep breath and pulls one of them open. Having half convinced herself it will be the girl, she's startled to see a man waiting at the threshold. Queenie goes cold at the sight of Brad Gedney. "What do you want?"

"Is that any way to greet a guest?" Brad replies smugly.

"Guests need to be invited. Otherwise, they're just flotsam who've washed up on your doorstep."

"Then, a guest I must be since I was, in fact, invited."

Queenie snorts, about to tell him off, when she hears a breathless, girlish laugh behind her.

"Magnus! Oh, Magnus, darling. You're here."

Queenie turns to see Ruby standing at the top of the stairs. Her jaw drops at the sight. Ruby's not only a woman once more, but she's dressed in the pink meringue she wore as her Glinda the Good Witch costume for Tabby's fiftieth. The sleeves are puffed up enormously, and she's wearing that ridiculous crown that looks like something better suited to the Pope. Ruby sweeps down the staircase, making an entrance, eyes shining as she beholds Brad Gedney.

He pushes his way past Queenie into the foyer, holding out his arms, smiling like the snake he is, looking like he might start laughing at any second. "Ruby, honey. There you are."

"I was so scared you wouldn't come." Ruby runs to Brad, taking his hands in hers.

"Oh," he replies, arrogance dripping from every word, "I wouldn't have missed this for the world."

This isn't something Queenie can deal with on her own, and while she's never been one to ask for help, she hears herself calling for Ivy.

Moonshyne Manor Distillery Recipes

Jezebel's County Fair Vodka Sour for Ursula

Ingredients:

2 oz Moonshyne Manor vodka
1 oz fresh lemon juice
1 oz simple syrup
2 dashes angostura bitters
1 egg white
Cocktail cherry and lemon wedge
Ice

Equipment:

Cocktail shaker

Instructions:

Add the vodka, lemon juice, lime juice, syrup, bitters and egg white to a cocktail shaker without any ice. Shake as hard as you can while doing a sexy shimmy. Add ice to the cocktail shaker. Shake, shake, shake that booty and the shaker. Strain into a glass and gently add ice. Garnish with a lemon wedge and a cocktail cherry.

28

Monday, October 25
Afternoon

It's definitely not the girl who's visiting, that much is clear. After hearing Queenie calling for her, Ivy rushes, wand drawn, to the foyer, the rest of the women bobbing in her wake.

"What on earth is going on?" she asks, appearing from the mudroom just behind the grand staircase, stopping short at the ludicrous sight that greets her.

There Ruby is, inexplicably resplendent as Glinda the Good Witch, arms thrown around the waist of a man, as Queenie tries to pull them apart. Judging by the man's pointy features and sloping shoulders, he can only be Brad Gedney. Terror squeezes Ivy's gut, making her legs go weak. She reaches out to steady herself against the banister.

"Let go of her!" Queenie yells, tugging at Ruby's arm, trying to pull her from him.

He tightens his grip of Ruby's shoulders. "She invited me," Brad replies, unperturbed. "Tell her, darling," he instructs Ruby.

"There's no way she invited you," Queenie hisses. "She doesn't even know you!"

"Of course she does," he replies. "Unlike *some* people," he says, leering at Ivy and the cavalry who are standing off to the side in shocked silence, "*I* actually visited her while she was in prison."

Queenie looks like she's been slapped. "We tried to visit her. Dozens and dozens of times but—" She is not willing to admit the truth to Brad Gedney, of all people.

"But what?" he asks. "She didn't want to see you? Who can blame her for not wanting to see the very people who let her take the fall for their own crimes?"

"I beg your pardon." Ivy has drawn herself up to her full height as she marches over to Brad. "If I were you, I'd be very careful with what I was implying."

"Oh, I'm not implying it. I'm flat out accusing you of it." He turns to Ruby and cups her chin, the gesture more aggressive than affectionate. Ruby's cheeks pucker where he's gripping her. "They staged the heist and then blamed you for it, didn't they?"

The word sears itself to Ivy's brain. *Heist.* How does Brad know about that?

Ruby looks confused for a moment, her gaze flicking between Ivy and Queenie and back to Brad who she is pressed up against. "Come, now, my love. Let's not fight," she says in a conciliatory tone, trying for a tentative smile. "We have a party to get to, Magnus." Ruby flicks her wavy red hair over her shoulder.

It's Ursula who steps forward then. "Magnus?" Her eyes widen. "She thinks *you're* Magnus?"

Brad shrugs, neither confirming nor denying the assertion, just maintaining that shit-eating grin. While the hair color and age are similar, it seems impossible that Ruby could make that kind of mistake. Magnus was a handsome man, full of life, whereas Brad has a sinister quality to him. Plus, there's that jagged scar snaking down from his forehead into his eyebrow which Magnus never had. It must be another manifestation of Ruby's dementia.

"Ruby," Ursula says, touching her friend on one of the elbow-length gloves, "this isn't Magnus."

"It is!" Ruby insists.

"No, Ruby," Ursula replies, shaking her head. "Darling, Magnus died—"

"No!" It's guttural, this denial, Ruby swatting Ursula away along with the terrible thing that she's claiming. "No. Magnus did *not* die." She glowers, looking on the verge of tears. "This is Magnus." She reaches out and pats Brad's cheek, clearly reassured.

Brad smiles, placing his hand over hers. "That's right. I'm right here."

Ivy's had enough of this farce. She's about to demand that Brad leave when she begins to feel the air crackle. It becomes static, all their hair starting to rise. *Bloody hell*, she realizes. *Jezebel is about to lose her shit.* They absolutely can't allow Brad to witness the eruption, as certain as it is to be accompanied by magic. Not everyone can have their memories erased or be hypnotized: some people are too stubborn to be suggestible, and Ivy would bet the manor that Brad is one of them.

"Ursula," Ivy barks, "why don't you take Jezebel and Ruby to the kitchen to check on the punch and hors d'oeuvres ahead of all of our guests arriving?" When Ruby appears reluctant to go, Ivy adds, "Magnus will be along shortly, darling."

Ruby looks to Brad who, now that he's made his point, is clearly tiring of the charade. He nods at her in a run-along-now way.

Ursula snaps out of her daze, grasping Ruby's hand and tugging at her. As the two women head for the kitchen, Ruby blowing Brad a kiss, Ursula links her arm through Jezebel's, pulling her along with them. There's a zapping sound as they make contact, like hundreds of tiny blue lightning strikes.

Jezebel growls but allows herself to be swept away as Ursula murmurs calming words in her ear.

"Quite the temper your friend has," Brad comments, smirking.

"What is it that you want?" Queenie asks. "Why are you here?"

"Can't I visit my good friend Ruby without having ulterior motives?" he asks.

Ivy has to resist the urge to turn him into compost. "I want you to leave," she says. "You aren't welcome here, no matter what Ruby says."

"You know she isn't of sound mind," Queenie adds, infuriated. "You know she thinks you're Magnus. What kind of person takes advantage of someone vulnerable that way?"

"I don't know," he retorts wryly. "Why don't you ask your friend Ivy the same thing?"

"What?" Ivy gasps. "What are you talking about?"

"You and your great-aunt, Mirabelle. Quite the con artists and fraudsters, the both of you. Talk about taking advantage of people. The two of you wrote the book on the subject."

Ivy's at a loss for words. It looks as though Queenie's about to launch a barrage of questions when Widget suddenly swoops across the room, instructed by Tabby to fly at Brad Gedney's face.

Brad screams and swats at the sharp beak heading straight for his eye. The crow dodges his hand and rises again before circling back for another go. Widget dives, her whole body now an arrow, and Brad ducks, hands protecting his head as Widget swoops past.

Brad glares at Tabby, who's been standing quietly off to the side this whole time. "Control your familiar," he says.

"That's exactly what I'm doing, fuckhead," Widget squawks.

As the crow loops around for another attack, Brad turns and stalks from the house, clearly shaken. He screams that he'll be back, that the women can't keep him away.

"Huh, a man afraid of birds." Ivy is surprised by his fear and gloats in their triumph. That's why it takes a few seconds for the realization to dawn. When it does, she gasps.

"What?" a distracted Queenie asks, locking the door.

Ivy looks from Queenie to Tabby. "He could see Tabby."

"Oh, shit," Queenie says, eyes widening. "*And* he knows about the heist." Her expression turns grim. "We're going to need Ursula to get some answers from Ruby."

29

Monday, October 25
Evening

It's the first time Ursula's been in Ruby's room in a third of a century. She marvels at how it looks almost exactly as she remembers, only tidier without all the clothes and feather boas flung over armoires and chairs or lying in heaps on the bed and floor. It smells the same too, like talc and perfume and cotton candy.

It's bizarre to have something from the past so perfectly preserved when everything else has changed so spectacularly. The last time Ursula was in here was the night of Tabby's party when she and Ruby got ready together, a tradition they'd upheld ever since their excited titivations ahead of all the childhood parties Mirabelle threw for them.

Ursula remembers how Ruby had leaned in close that night, her breath fluttering against Ursula's eyelashes as she carefully applied the makeup for Ursula's fortune-teller costume.

Never one for wearing cosmetics, Ursula nevertheless always jumped at any opportunity to have Ruby apply them for her. Not because of Ruby's skill with the brush, or the alchemy she worked in transforming a face from something awfully plain into something almost pretty. But because of how, for that half an hour, Ursula would be the object of Ruby's undivided attention; how Ruby gazed at her like she was the only person in the world—touching her face as she turned her chin this way and that—hovering so close that Ursula could almost hear Ruby's heartbeat and could pretend that it galloped for her and her alone.

After Ruby had finished Ursula's makeup and then added gold earrings and a turquoise headscarf, it was Ursula's turn to help Ruby into her enormous, hooped skirt. As she did so, Ruby thrummed with excitement, speaking of everything she was looking forward to: seeing Magnus that night, the upcoming heist that would play out in three days' time, and how everything would change after that. She was eager to take control of her destiny, tired of being helpless in the face of her powers' whims.

Despite Ruby's candor, Ursula had sensed that there was something Ruby wasn't telling her, something else that was making her smile that much wider and laugh that much more raucously. When she'd asked Ruby about it, as she placed that ridiculous crown on Ruby's head to finish off her Glinda costume, Ruby denied that she was keeping anything from her best friend.

It was frustrating, having Ursula's gift for clairvoyance but being unable to use it when it came to Ruby. There was something about their connection that prevented Ursula from delving into Ruby's mind and heart the way Ursula could with strangers. Ursula always likened it to how, when you stood too close to someone, you couldn't see all their features clearly, just a freckle or two, or a scar, on the topography of their faces. It was only in stepping back that any perspective was gained.

She'd always assumed it was a quirk of her gift—a limitation of her powers—that prevented her from ever skulking in the dark corners of Ruby's psyche. Ursula never suspected the truth until later, that another of Ruby's powers was that she could cast protective shields, like the one she'd always used to stop Ursula from prying.

Like the one she used to stop Widget from spying for the sisterhood. That's how Ursula would find out that Ruby had known all along how to keep a wall between herself and Ursula, one Ursula could never scale no matter how desperately she climbed.

It was only later at the party that Ursula discovered the truth, which was that Ruby *did* have a secret, exactly as she'd suspected.

Ursula now turns to Ruby who she's sitting next to on the dressing-table bench. Ruby's enormous dress spills over, almost pushing Ursula from the seat. Their eyes meet in the Hollywood vanity mirror which is framed by dozens of Polaroids of all of them taken over the years.

"It's awful that we had to cancel the party," Ruby says, sighing. "Poor Tabby. She was so looking forward to it. I don't understand what wildlife emergency she was called away for."

"Rhino extinction," Ursula blurts, the first thing that comes to her.

"Oh. I thought you were going to say wildfires or something," Ruby replies. After a beat, she adds, "If the rhinos are extinct, what's the emergency?"

Thinking how Ruby's explanation would have been a much better one had she just thought of it, Ursula tries to brush it off. "Who knows? It's all top secret, hush-hush, for Tabby's work at the Ministry of…uh… Extinction."

The Ruby of old would have called bullshit on it, but this

one smiles vaguely and nods, as though that makes perfect sense.

"I can't believe Magnus left without saying goodbye," Ruby says, crestfallen.

"He also had an emergency," Ursula says. "The horses all came down with something." It's jarring, hearing herself echo what really happened all those years ago. She's scared Ruby will latch onto that memory, recognizing this excuse for the lie it is, but she doesn't.

Instead, she stands, looking stricken. "Are they okay? Should I go there?" Ruby asks, standing.

"No," Ursula yelps and then seeing Ruby's alarmed expression says, "It's not necessary. He called a few minutes ago to say they're all fine. And that he sends his love and will see you tomorrow."

Ursula hasn't left Ruby's side all night, and so Ruby should know no such call came through. And yet she nods, seemingly placated. "Will you help me get undressed?" she asks. "Take off all of my layers?"

Ursula blinks, confused. "Your layers. I thought… I mean…"

"I couldn't do it myself," Ruby says, eyes dropping. "It wouldn't work, so I had to do it the old-fashioned way."

Ever since Ruby's childhood, if she chose to present as a woman but couldn't summon enough magic to do so, she'd dress in drag because she said it made her feel more like herself. The drag was only ever a temporary solution, something to fall back on until she could call on her powers once again.

Ursula senses Ruby's shame that the magic wouldn't allow itself to be summoned this time and feels something sink in the quicksand of her chest. "Of course I'll help with your layers. I'd be honored to."

Muscle memory kicks in, and Ursula reaches out and tugs at one of Ruby's eyelash strips, pulling it off gently before doing the second. Picking up a bottle of rubbing alcohol, Ursula uses it to soak a cotton ball before dabbing it around Ruby's hairline.

She gently lifts the lace front of the red-haired wig, swiping under it to get at the spirit gum that's keeping the wig affixed to Ruby's skin. Once most of the glue is loosened, the wig pulls free of Ruby's head, exposing the stocking cap underneath.

Ursula hands Ruby the hairpiece, expecting her to place it on one of the many mannequin heads because she's always so fastidious about taking proper care of them. Instead, Ruby just lets the wig fall to the dresser, and Ursula picks it up, putting it away herself. She then reaches for the clip-on earrings and the choker necklace, storing them in one of the drawers filled with all of Ruby's jewelry.

After that, Ursula undoes the stocking cap. What's left of Ruby's real hair springs up from under it, making Ruby look like a newly hatched bird. Ursula then brings in the big guns: cold cream and more cotton balls to excavate layer after layer of foundation and powder, mascara and lipstick.

It always used to surprise Ursula how, when Ruby's dramatic fake eyebrows disappeared, the real ones would be revealed below, looking sheepish about how ordinary they are. Then again, that was true of most of Ruby's features, the process uncannily like watching a photograph developing in reverse, so that it went from a being a resplendent color image to just a white sheet of paper.

As Ursula works, one of the cotton balls snags against the stubble of Ruby's jawline, needing to be replaced with a fresh one. After almost ten minutes of these meditative, repetitive actions, Ursula's able to declare, "Okay, makeup's all off! Now, let's get this dress off."

Ruby stands and allows Ursula to lead her to the middle of the room. She turns so Ursula can tug at the dress's zipper. Once it falls to a heap around Ruby's ankles, Ruby steps out of it. She's wearing underpants but the moment is still shockingly intimate.

"Okay, arms up and boobs off," Ursula says to mask her discomfort.

Ruby raises her arms, and Ursula pulls the silicone breast plate off.

"Gentle on the tits," Ruby's muffled voice calls as it always used to. "They're expensive." And there Ruby stands, chest fuzz and five-o'clock shadow exposed, vulnerable without the face paint and body armor. "Thank you," she says shyly.

"You're welcome."

And then their eyes meet and hold steady. Ursula feels that old familiar flutter followed by the quickening, as though her entire core has contracted to a pinpoint. After all this time, it's still there.

And then Ruby blinks, her expression darkening. "I'm sorry. I've forgotten your name."

Something shatters inside Ursula, like a crystal vase in Jezebel's rage room. She swallows back the lump that's swelled up in her throat. "It's Ursula," she whispers. "My name is Ursula."

"And I'm Ruby." It's more of a question than a statement.

"Yes, you're my Ruby Tuesday."

Ruby wraps her arms around Ursula as though clinging to a life preserver. The feeling is entirely mutual when Ursula responds in kind.

They stand like that for seconds, minutes, hours, an eternity. And then, thinking of Charon, and their dire predicament, and of Tabby and what might become of her, Ursula forces herself to ask what Queenie needs her to. "Where is the treasure hidden, Ruby?" she whispers into Ruby's ear.

"Treasure?"

"Yes, darling, the treasure from the museum. Where did you hide it?"

Ruby is quiet for a few seconds and then giggles. "I hid it in the safest place."

Ursula's heart rattles her rib cage. "Which is where?" She holds her breath.

"The fire," Ruby says simply. "No one can touch it there."

Moonshyne Manor Grimoire

Ruby's Shaving Cream Potion

Ingredients*:*
2 ½ oz shea butter
2 ½ oz coconut oil
3 tbsp. castile soap
2 tbsp. sweet almond oil
6 drops witch hazel oil

Equipment:
A small, heavy-bottomed cauldron or saucepan
A wooden spoon
A bowl
A hand mixer
A 4-or 6-oz. glass container with lid

Instructions:
Add the coconut oil and shea butter to the cauldron or saucepan. Warm over low heat until melted and then allow to cool. Add the oil, soap and essential oil, and stir clockwise. Once the mixture is close to room temperature, transfer it to the bowl. Allow to cool and harden, which could take up to an hour or two.

Once the mixture is hard, remove the bowl from fridge. If the mixture is too firm to beat with a mixer, allow it to soften a little. Use a hand mixer to whip the mixture for at least 2 to 3 minutes until it's fluffy.

Once sufficiently whipped, transfer the shaving cream to the container and close with a lid. Use on your face, legs, underarms and around your nether bits.

30

Tuesday, October 26
Morning

Ursula heads to the basement the old-fashioned way, using the stairs rather than going into Queenie's office to take the fireman's pole down. *Firefighter's pole*, she can mentally hear Persephone correct her.

She's exhausted after yet another sleepless night, the ongoing run of which she was hoping would end with Ruby's homecoming and the granting of her forgiveness. There's nothing quite like a guilty conscience to keep you from getting any rest: it wants you awake for every excruciating second that it twists the knife in your gut.

Now, on top of her guilt, what Ursula feels is heartbreak over what Ruby's going through. And the catastrophic implications of her memory loss for the rest of them. They've pinned so much hope on Ruby saving them when Ruby doesn't even have the power to save herself. Despite Ursula's prodding for more information, Ruby wouldn't say anything more than the treasure being in the fire, an assertion that makes absolutely no sense.

Queenie will be able to figure it out. With Charon arriving tomorrow, and only five days left in which to pay the bank, Queenie *has* to make sense of it.

When Ursula reaches the door, she can hear the usual drone of the generator—Queenie insisting that she needs electricity down here in the lab—and intermittent *dzzt dzzt* sounds, which are tame compared to the noises that usually escape.

Ursula doesn't bother knocking. Queenie is usually so consumed by whatever she's creating that she wouldn't hear it anyway. Instead, she opens the door and, stepping inside, is immediately accosted by the smell of burning metal. She scrunches up her nose, wondering how Queenie can stand the stench of it.

The overhead industrial lights strung up along crisscrossing wires are also an assault on the senses. Ursula squints in the glare of them as she makes her way to one of the workstations where Queenie is bent over some contraption. She has bicycle pant-leg cuffs attached to her robe sleeves to stop them from getting in the way of whatever she's doing.

Knowing better than to address Queenie when she's busy, especially with something that's giving off sparks like a Fourth of July fireworks display, Ursula hovers off to the side, waiting for Queenie to acknowledge her.

"Pass me that wrench," Queenie says, lifting the protective hood from her face after she's finished welding what has to be the latest invention, the one she's working on for Ruby.

Ursula complies, heading for the toolbox. She rummages around in it until she finds it, passing it across.

"I tried to find you last night after I spoke to Ruby," Ursula says.

"I flew to the city to chat with a neurologist I met at one of Tabby's parties. We've kept in touch over the years." She tightens a bolt with more vigor than is probably required. "What did Ruby say?"

"She laughed and said she hid it in the fire, the safest place for it."

Queenie stops torquing the wrench. "The fire?"

"I know. It doesn't make any sense." Ursula has to take a deep, steadying breath to get out the rest of it. "She forgot who I was again. I don't know how much stock we can put into what she says."

Queenie sighs like that's exactly the answer she was expecting. She lowers the hood again. "Stand back."

There's more welding, blue sparks flying. When Queenie finishes, she turns back to Ursula, mask still on. "And you're not able to see anything in the cards or leaves?"

It's something Queenie has been asking year after year for decades. Usually, Ursula bristles at the question because what she does, her power, is not the same as Queenie's. What Queenie excels at is science. There are known variables and laws that govern the principles she adheres to. Queenie can predict outcomes; every time she does the same experiment under the same conditions, she'll get the same result.

That's not how Ursula's gift works. It's unreliable, every vision obscure. If she isn't able to interpret the signs properly, the vision means less than nothing. At least nothing would have no consequences. Something interpreted the wrong way can have all kinds of unforeseen ripple effects. Each time Ursula reads the signs, she alters the future. It's a terrible burden to live with.

"You haven't seen any visions that can help us?" Queenie prompts.

"No," Ursula replies. "But then I never get anything about Ruby at all." If she did, she would have foreseen everything that happened the day of the heist, and she would have been able to prevent it.

"This kinda affects all of us, not just Ruby," Queenie grumbles, but there's no venom in it.

Ursula might not have seen it in the leaves or cards, but she does have something that could help them. She just doesn't know how she can explain it without inviting questions about the night Tabby died. Besides, Ursula's not even sure how much help it might be, so why draw attention to it just yet?

Queenie sighs and then removes her welding hood stepping back from her invention that looks like a weird motorcycle helmet, the kind Queenie should probably wear when on her customized broomstick, a Harley-Davidsonstick.

But on closer inspection, Ursula sees that there are wires like tentacles hanging from it. "You really think this might help?"

"I have no idea, but we've got to try something."

"How does it work?" Ursula knows she won't understand a word of it, but Queenie loves explaining the mechanics of her inventions.

"It's based on something called neurofeedback, which is a kind of biofeedback. It teaches self-control of brain functions by measuring brain waves and providing a feedback signal."

Ursula can feel her eyes glazing over as Queenie continues explaining. All she can understand is that Queenie will make Ruby wear the helmet just as soon as it's finished being built. And that she'll be trying to stimulate Ruby's brain in some way to see if they can rattle memories loose.

"Also," Queenie adds at the end, "you'll need to put Ruby on a ketogenic diet. It's shown good results with symptomatic improvement of Alzheimer's, so it might work with her too. Certainly can't hurt."

Ursula nods, making a mental note to ask Ivy what a ketogenic diet is, since it will be a much shorter explanation than if Queenie gives it.

Queenie returns her attention to what looks like a blueprint, jotting a few notes on it after muttering a calculation.

"The meeting with Charon isn't going to go well tomorrow, Queenie," Ursula blurts. She watches her friend keenly, trying to get a reading on what Queenie is feeling, not easy since she's the consummate poker player. The shadows cast by the overhead lights make it even harder, with Queenie's eyes lost in deep pockets of darkness.

Queenie snorts. "No shit. I promised a dark wizard something I don't have. How could it go any other way but tits up?"

"He's going to demand a price you can't pay."

There's a beat before Queenie asks, "What price?"

Ursula shakes her head. "I don't know. I can't see it clearly, but it's something terrible, so please just be careful."

"His favorite currency is the power of youth," Queenie says. "And he'll find none here. We can't pay what we don't have."

Queenie has a point, and so Ursula moves on from Charon, asking the question that's been troubling her. "What do you think it means that Brad's been visiting Ruby in prison?"

"That he knows about the heist, which is way more than we gave him credit for." Queenie picks up a circuit board, inspecting it. "At least we know she hasn't told him anything useful about the treasure."

"How can we be sure?"

"Because he would have taken it already. He wouldn't still be sniffing around for information." Queenie reaches for her soldering iron. "I've been thinking about the break-ins. It never made sense that nothing was stolen, just rifled through. And I never thought too much about the sooty footprints at the time, but I think that Ruby told Brad the same thing about fire and that he's been in the manor, checking the fireplaces."

Ursula gasps. "You think she might have hidden the goods in one of them and told him about it?"

"It won't hurt to check. The manor essentially only has two fire chimneys that extend up three floors." Queenie puts the soldering iron down again and begins counting on her fingers.

"There's the two fireplaces in the kitchen, the two in Ivy's bedroom, the one in Tabitha's room, and the one in your room that also backs onto the secret room."

"There's also the ritual fire in the forest," Ursula adds. "And what about the wall sconces in her room, in case she magicked the treasure into the flames somehow?"

"Or any of the wall sconces for that matter," Queenie adds. "Check the ritual candles too, as well as the AGA oven in the kitchen. Get everyone together and check everywhere."

Ursula nods.

"Also," Queenie says, "I'm thinking that all those unexplained breakages in the distillery now make sense. He's been tampering with the tanks and equipment causing all of our problems."

"And his being able to see Tabby?" Ursula asks. "But her not seeing him during any of the break-ins? What do you think that means?"

Queenie is silent for a moment. When she speaks, she sounds scared. "It means he's far more dangerous than we first thought."

31

Wednesday, October 27
Afternoon

Persephone feels smaller than usual standing next to Ivy and Jezebel in the Moonshyne Manor Distillery. Even Ivy, who towers over Persephone, is dwarfed by the huge metal tanks that are scattered throughout the place, silver and bronze pipes rising from them in columns that bring to mind the pipe organ at the megachurch Persephone's father forces them to go to every Sunday, the one run by that awful Reverend Cotton Mather.

They're standing at a metal table surrounded by glass beakers. Jezebel yawns, covering her mouth, setting off Ivy who yawns like a lion, proudly and languidly. The women are both bleary-eyed, and dark smudges hang like hammocks under their eyes.

When Jezebel yawns yet again, Persephone raises an eyebrow. "Did you, like, have big parties the last two nights?"

"Hmm?" Jezebel asks.

"For Ruby's homecoming. You look like you've both been up a few nights in a row."

"No parties," Jezebel murmurs. "More like a scavenger hunt where every item on the list was hidden up a fireplace or in a flame."

Ivy snorts.

It's clearly an inside joke. When the women don't elaborate, Persephone lets it drop. She watches Ruth Bader Ginsburg walk from tank to tank, sniffing each one delicately before moving on. Persephone has to keep an eye on her: Ruth Bader Ginsburg has big-dick energy, lifting her leg against things instead of squatting. Persephone's father says it's unseemly, but Persephone thinks the dog's nonconformation to gender stereotypes is something to be admired.

Ivy reaches for one of the glass beakers, pouring clear liquid from a bottle into it before swishing it around. Jezebel hands her another beaker, which Ivy holds up to the light and examines before adding it to the first one. Once Ivy's done with that, Jezebel passes across a pipette, and Ivy then drips a few drops into the concoction before stirring it with a tiny spoon Jezebel gives her.

Their movements are economical but graceful, each of them anticipating the other's next move and synchronizing their own accordingly. Persephone wonders if they can see the beauty in how they're choreographing their own dance.

The last time Persephone experienced anything similar was the final time she and her mother did their weekly Sunday-afternoon baking together, Persephone passing the ingredients across a split second before her mother had to ask for them.

She thinks of how sometimes the most sacred conversations we'll ever have are the ones that require no words, and how there are very few people in our lives who we'll ever speak that silent language with.

Still, despite how lovely it is, Persephone wonders why the

women do everything manually. "Can't you magic all of that?" Persephone asks, nodding at the pipette and beaker.

"You mean like the *Look, Ma, no hands* kind of magic?" Jezebel asks.

"Totally," Persephone says, imagining everything floating across the room.

Jezebel smiles. "Using magic can sometimes be more mentally and physically taxing than just doing something without it. You need to decide when and how to use it. It gets harder the older you get."

"Oh." Persephone never thought about it that way, but it makes total sense. Even her own form of magic requires a lot of concentration. *Speaking of which*... "Wanna see one of *my* magic tricks?"

Jezebel claps her hands, delighted. "Yes!"

Persephone pulls a pack of cards from her pocket, putting the box on the table, before shuffling and fanning the cards out. "Okay, pick a card by tapping it," she says, holding the deck out to Jezebel.

Jezebel studies it thoughtfully, tapping a card off to the right.

"Okay, let's see it," Persephone says, flipping it over to show Jezebel. "It's the queen of hearts. Now I'm gonna put your card back into the deck."

Persephone shuffles it. With a flourish, one of the cards comes flying out of the deck like it's about to be juggled. Jezebel yelps and claps as Persephone snatches it from the air.

"This is the ace of spades, not your card," Persephone says. "Because your card is now under the card box."

"What?" Jezebel says, looking at the box on the table. "No way!"

Persephone reaches over, moving the box aside, and picking up the card under it. "Ta-da! The queen of hearts."

"That's amazing," Jezebel squeals as Ivy smiles.

"Thanks," Persephone says, thinking that she'd much rather

be able to do real magic. She returns the cards to the box and puts them back in her pocket. As she does so, her fingers connect with the folded piece of paper, the reason she's here today. "Is Queenie around?" Her knocking at the manor door didn't summon anyone which is when she wandered off to the distillery, finding Ivy and Jezebel there. "I didn't see her at the house."

"She has a…meeting," Jezebel replies.

Persephone notices the pause and then the covert look Jezebel and Ivy share, like there's something they're worried about but don't want to discuss.

"Oh." Persephone has a ton of questions about Ruby, most of them fueled by her discovery earlier at the town library. But she'll wait until she can talk with Queenie, since she was the one to reveal where Ruby has been all this time.

As Ivy moves between tables and shelves, reaching for this and that, her robe sleeves fall away, revealing the bright tattoos that cover her arms and taper off at her wrists. They fascinate Persephone, not just as another form of silent communication but because of how mesmerizing they are.

Ivy catches her looking and smiles. "You like tattoos?"

"Yeah, but my father says I can't get any."

"Well, you're still young," Ivy says, shrugging. "Better to wait until you're older."

"My dad says they look okay when women are young and firm but look ridiculous when they get old and saggy." Persephone uses air quotes on the *old and saggy* part, rolling her eyes at her father's misogyny.

Jezebel snorts, shaking her head.

Ivy puts the beaker down, giving Persephone her full attention.

She pulls up a sleeve, turning her forearm so that Persephone can see what she's pointing at. "See that?" she asks, indicating an intricate purple flower that looks like it's thrown its petal arms up in celebration.

Persephone nods.

"That's Arethusa bulbosa or Dragon's Mouth. It's a leafless orchid that grows in bogs and swamps. It's been Ruby's favorite flower ever since she saw it in one of my botany textbooks when she was twelve," Ivy says, stroking the tattoo. "The orchid is rare, joyful and beautiful, just like Ruby. I managed to grow her one for her thirtieth birthday, and she said it was the best gift anyone had ever given her."

"That's so cool," Persephone murmurs, trying to reconcile this Ruby that Ivy's talking about with the menacing one written about in the tabloid article.

Ivy turns her arm again so Persephone can see the inside of it at her wrinkly bicep. "And you see this?" she asks, pointing at an exuberant flower with purple, blue and yellow petals. "This is a Black Joker Siberian iris. And this," she says, indicating a lush orange flower, "is a flame azalea. They were my mother's favorite flowers. She died when I was really young, and time has erased so many of my memories of her. But these flowers? They're all I *know* to be true about her."

Ivy points out other plants and leaves, insects and birds, explaining their significance. "They're all memories. And memories only become more precious with age when it's so difficult to hang on to them." Her eyes mist up then like she's going to cry.

"Also," Jezebel adds, resting her hand of Ivy's arm, "we don't lose the right to tell our stories just because our flesh is sagging. If anything, age and experiences give us even more right to speak and be heard."

Ivy composes herself, and the two women go back to what they were doing. After a few moments, Ivy asks, "What does your mother say about your father's sexism and ageism?"

"Not much," Persephone says, "since she's dead." It comes out more harshly than she intended, more of an accusation than the mere stating of a fact.

The women both stop what they're doing, their hands stilling as they regard Persephone, heads cocked, already sympathetic. And it's only now that she's in the company of it—that innate intuition that women have, that immediate impulse to comfort—that Persephone realizes how much she's missed it, how lonely she's been this past year.

She doesn't mean to cry, doesn't even know she's doing it, until Jezebel murmurs, "Oh, honey," and opens her arms to gather Persephone in, cradling the girl's head to her chest, rubbing her back in gentle circles. Ivy hovers next to them, clearly not as comfortable with affection, but still interested, still present and engaged.

That's been the hardest part of the past year for Persephone, having her father disengage so completely at a time when she's needed him most.

"How did she die?" Jezebel asks.

Persephone pulls away, sniffing. "It was cancer, just over a year ago," she says, noticing how her tears have left a wet splotch on Jezebel's robe. "She had all the treatments, but when none of it worked, she came home so she could die in peace surrounded by her family."

"That's understandable," Ivy murmurs.

Persephone shakes her head and scoffs, feeling the betrayal anew. "Only, Dad was never home. As soon as she arrived back, he started spending all of his time drinking at the bar." Persephone shoots a dark look at the nearby bottles of liquor. "The more he drank, the less he cared. And he's been like that ever since. I think he blames me," Persephone says. It's the first time she has dared verbalize the thought.

"Why do you think that?" Jezebel asks, and Persephone's grateful that she didn't just flat out dismiss the notion, that she is taking her seriously.

"She had uterine cancer when she was younger. They treated her for it, but the doctors wanted her to have a hysterectomy. But she wouldn't because she wanted to have a child." Persephone struggles to speak past the lump that has risen in her throat. "She promised my dad she'd go for one after I was born, but then I started nagging for a baby sister, and so she didn't."

Jezebel takes her hand and says, "Her death was not your fault. Your mother made her own decisions for her own reasons. I know that's hard to believe, but that's because we're so programmed to always blame ourselves."

"What do you mean?" Persephone asks.

"Most of those school shootings are done by boys because they blame everyone else for their problems. But most people who cut or starve themselves are girls because we blame ourselves. And that's dangerous because it's a self-administered poison. Don't be the one feeding yourself poison, okay?"

"Okay."

Jezebel tugs at Persephone's hand, saying, "Come, let's go."

"Are we going to see Ruby?" Persephone asks, excited and nervous to meet the outlaw she's read so much about.

"Later. Ruby and Ursula are planning a walk to the forest. I have a rage room I want to introduce you to."

Moonshyne Manor Grimoire

Ivy's Tattoo Aftercare Salve

Ingredients:

2 tbsp. beeswax
1½ tbsp. coconut oil
1 tbsp. mango butter
1 tsp. sesame oil
4 drops frankincense essential oil
4 drops myrrh essential oil

Equipment:

A small, heavy-bottomed cauldron or saucepan
A wooden spoon
A round tin salve container

Instructions:

In the small, heavy-bottomed cauldron or saucepan, heat the beeswax over the lowest heat possible. When the beeswax is nearly melted, add in the coconut oil, mango butter, sesame oil and essential oils. Once it's all combined, pour the mixture into the salve container. It will solidify in approximately 6–12 hours.

Apply the salve twice a day to your new tattoo.

Moonshyne Manor Grimoire

Ivy's Instructions for Getting That Perfect Beach Body

Instructions:

Blend yourself a healthy smoothie that's chockablock full of vitamins and minerals because you want to support that amazing body of yours, the one that ferries you through the world, allowing you to experience so many of its joys.

Then have some chocolate cake or a cocktail because life is short and broccoli tastes like feet.

Find a beach. Strip down to your bathing suit or your birthday suit, whichever you prefer. And there you have it.

You're on a beach and you and your body are perfect. Now, go enjoy it.

32

Wednesday, October 27
Afternoon

The forest makes Ursula uneasy. The rest of the sisterhood assume it's because she's developed a fear of the creatures after Tabitha died and stopped being able to offer the women her protection. The beasts have become that much wilder, and therefore more menacing, since Tabby stopped visiting them.

But that's not why Ursula hates coming here.

It's guilt, pure and simple, that plagues her. Being here, seeing the creatures that Tabby tended to with such care all her life—knowing that Ursula is the reason why Tabby is kept away from that which she loves most—is what makes the visits so unbearable.

You'd think seeing Tabby every day, forever immortalized as a ghost in what she was wearing when she died, would be the real torment. Instead, Ursula finds the spirit's presence comforting. At least some part of Tabby remains, some essence of her that's able to communicate with them and partake of their lives, albeit in a greatly diminished way.

As Ursula and Ruby approach the forest's fringe, Ursula withdraws her wand, pointing it down and away like a loaded gun she's scared might go off in her hands. She doesn't want to do accidental harm when spooked.

To hell with Queenie for making me do this. Ursula begged Queenie to send Ivy instead, since she enters the forest fairly regularly anyway to tend to the trees, but Queenie said Ivy was otherwise occupied in the distillery and that everyone had to play their part. Since this was the place where so much of their lives unfolded, they had to visit it with Ruby.

Despite being told that they were hiking into forest, Ruby insisted on wearing high-heeled boots, an impractical choice that Ursula could not talk her out of. The more Ursula pleaded with Ruby to change them, the more Ruby jutted her jaw, her face a picture of dogged stubbornness. Something about the expression took Ursula back to the six-year-old Ruby, determined to do something simply because Mirabelle had expressly forbidden it.

There's a childlike quality to this Ruby that breaks Ursula's heart, mostly because she herself cannot return to that state with her friend. Ursula has been left behind once again.

"Are we having a picnic?" It's the fourth time Ruby has asked despite there being no basket or blanket or any evidence at all that they might be taking a meal outside.

Ursula's answered in the negative each time. She's so tired after all the searching of the fireplaces, wall sconces, candles and stoves last night, and then herding Ruby to bed twice after finding her wandering around in the foyer, that she has to check her impatience. "No, darling," she repeats. "We're just coming to check on something."

"Oh, that's a pity. A picnic would have been nice."

Ruby's cheeks are pink from the cold, and she doesn't appear to feel that her nose is dripping steadily like a leaky faucet. Ursula reaches into her pocket for a tissue, pulling it out and dabbing at Ruby's nostrils. Ruby turns her head and pulls away like a fractious toddler, but she doesn't say anything beyond making a disapproving grunt.

Ursula pulls her coat tighter around herself before checking to see that Ruby's own coat is fastened up to her neck and that her purple cashmere scarf is tied properly. She takes a deep breath as they enter the first row of trees that serve as the border between the lawn and the forest: apt, since the two spaces feel like they're worlds apart.

The cultivated manor gardens still retain the lingering scent of mud and rain, along with the mulchy fragrance of fall leaves raked into decomposing piles. But the forest smells like melancholy and rejuvenation, like an old friend who's changed perfumes, so that reuniting with them is at once familiar *and* disorientating.

It immediately gets louder as soon as they're within the confines of the woods. Creatures chatter and caw, bark and twitter. The trees rustle and sway as critters hop from branch to branch, making Ursula tighten her grip on her wand.

"Are we going to have a picnic?" Ruby asks again, looking around at the dappled sunlight, perhaps thinking as Ursula does how the smudges of light appear to have been daubed onto a wet canvas, the yellow and gold tones overlaying rich emeralds and sepias.

Ruby sounds so hopeful that Ursula can't bear to disappoint her yet again. She reaches into one of her pockets, pulling out the pack of Big Berry Adventure Tic Tacs she bought knowing that Ruby would love their plum and lavender tones; Ruby's always insisted that anything purple tastes like happiness, hence all the purple icing on every one of her birthday cakes.

Ursula rattles the pack now like maracas. "Yes, we're having a picnic."

Ruby claps her hands. "Splendid!"

The path threaded between the ferns and ground cover is overgrown, but Ursula is still able to make out the spine of it. "This way," she says, stepping in front of Ruby, so that they're now walking in single file rather than side by side.

It's easier this way, having Ruby behind her so that Ursula doesn't have to look at her unmade face as she presents once again as a man, except for her women's clothes which go back several decades and are now way too big and hang from Ruby's diminished form. The bust of the dress gapes obscenely.

But breasts are not what make a woman. Ursula knows this to be true from all the women who've come to consult Ivy for tinctures to help fight nausea after weeks of chemotherapy, after sacrificing their breasts in order to live. It seems a high price to pay, but then Ursula has always suspected the gods of terrible misogyny.

Ursula's chest is the most impressive of any of the sisterhood—even larger than Jezebel's—and it's one that Ruby always used to be vocally envious of. Ursula wonders what it would be like to lose that part of herself that she has always been both proud of *and* taken for granted, something Ruby's never had the luxury of doing. How can it be that mounds of fat and tissue make women feel like women, and how that which so often defines them can betray them so spectacularly?

It's all so ridiculous, what makes men feel masculine and women feminine. Truth be told, Ursula has never felt feminine, not one day in her life, not even with her substantial bosom. She's always felt like such a tomboy and had to be schooled by Ruby in their teens on how to look and act more womanly.

But why was that so important?

Ursula's so lost in her musings that she doesn't notice Ruby's no longer behind her until she hears a shriek, followed by an anguished moan.

33

Wednesday, October 27
Afternoon

Ursula spins around, heart racing and wand brandished, expecting calamity. What she sees is Ruby standing, eyes cast down and face contorted in a mask of fear. Ursula looks to see if a snake or some other frightening creature has threatened her but sees nothing on the path.

"What's wrong?" Ursula asks.

"It's a hole," Ruby says, her voice shaking. "A hole that's going to swallow me."

Ursula casts her gaze about, looking for the menacing pit. "Where?" she asks, confused. "I don't see anything."

"Here it is. Right here." Ruby's voice is shrill as she points at a patch of shade where the forest's canopy cover is so dense that no sunlight can pierce it.

"That's just a shadow," Ursula says, laughing. "It's not a hole."

But Ruby has burst into tears now, and she stands there frozen, seemingly unable to take a step forward.

"Oh, Ruby." Ursula rushes back to take Ruby's hand. She pulls her close, wrapping her arms around her, trying to still the quaking of her body. "We'll go around, see? We'll just go around it." Once she's calmed Ruby, Ursula steers Ruby off the path and around deep shadows, taking her via a patch of bright sunlight, murmuring for Ruby to be careful in her heels.

How can we possibly give any credence to what Ruby's saying about the treasure, Ursula thinks, *when a mere shadow can make her unravel to this degree? Is the memory even in there to be accessed, or are we all chasing a figment of Ruby's imagination?*

The rest of the walk passes without incident as Ursula searches for splotches of light to serve as their stepping-stones. When they pass the stream, Ruby bends over it, gazing at her reflection.

"Who's that strange man?" she asks, pointing to her face mirrored back at her.

"That's a very dear friend," Ursula replies sadly, leading Ruby on.

A few paces on, a capuchin monkey swings through the trees, dropping to the forest floor. It cocks its head, regarding them. Ursula knows it's not Klepto, the monkey they released into the forest the morning after Tabby's death, but it's still likely to be Klepto's offspring. She wishes so much that Tabby could be here to see it. As she thinks it, the capuchin scampers off.

They're just approaching the Japanese maple that overlooks the ritual circle when something swoops overhead. Ursula ducks, covering her head with her arms, expecting talons sinking into flesh, exacting their revenge. Ursula knows she deserves to be sliced open by Tabby's creatures for what she did, but the instinct for survival is strong regardless.

But no claws pierce her skin so she looks up to see a falcizard gliding past her head. It has the scaly body and tail of a lizard but the wings and head of a falcon. This is the kind of creature that hatched from the egg Tabby walked out of the forest clutching all those decades ago.

Somehow, despite Tabitha arriving with only one such egg, the falcizard multiplied, not only shedding its tail in moments of danger as lizards are wont to do but shedding parts of itself in order to replicate. And now there are dozens of them in the forest. The creature lands in the sprawling Japanese maple, issuing high-pitched clicks that Ursula recalls are a sign that it's calm. Ruby seems equally unperturbed by its presence.

Ursula steers Ruby to the ritual circle, the place they've always gathered for their Wheel of the Year celebrations Mirabelle invited each of the girls upon their thirteenth birthday to join her sisterhood here to initiate them into the ancient ways. Only Jezebel never got to join the older women, being just three months short of thirteen when Mirabelle died.

This is where the sisterhood buried Mirabelle. It's also where Tabby was laid to a state of perpetual unrest. This is where they've celebrated birthdays and milestones like the successful conjuring of tricky spells and learning to ride a broomstick. It's where they marked important rites of passage like the giving of their virginity (none of them allowing their virginity to be carelessly lost or, worse, taken).

Jezebel, despite being the youngest, was the first to have her virginity-giving ritual at sixteen. Ruby was the next in line at the age of twenty-two, with Tabitha being the third at twenty. Tabby was followed by Ivy, aged twenty-five, and then Queenie, who was twenty-four at the time.

Ursula was the last to have the ritual, when she was thirty. Though her maidenhead was freely given to a man, she'd held on to it all that time, hoping to bequeath it to the true love of her life, Ruby.

Ursula knows it was considered odd, even degenerate, back in the day to be attracted to both men and women, as well as those who lived in the in-between, for Ruby's various fluid states attracted Ursula as much as her womanly one did. Ursula didn't think of herself as being attracted to men or women per se, but to the souls inhabiting those forms. Just as Ruby found it boring to *be* just one gender, Ursula found it tiresome to be constrained to loving just one.

Ruby's soul has always been Ursula's brightest beacon; Ursula is a moth to Ruby's flame, throwing herself into the fire again and again, regardless of how much it scorches.

Ursula looks at Ruby now, wondering if she might finally be able to confess that love.

How strange that, despite everything they've shared and how close they once were—*Like twins!* everyone used to say, which didn't help matters at all since that would have made Ursula's feelings for Ruby a form of incest—Ursula has never confessed her feelings for Ruby aloud. Not to anyone, and certainly not to Ruby.

Ursula and Ruby each sit on one of the six large boulders that form the circle of the ritual area. She forces herself to look at the two gravestones just off to the side, wishing she'd remembered to bring some irises to lay on Mirabelle's grave. None of them have ever brought flowers for Tabby's.

Ruby wraps her new scarf tighter around her neck, sinking her hands into her coat pockets. She looks like an old man, it's true—one with white stubble and cheeks drooping into jowls—but she still *seems* like a woman to Ursula.

If ever there was a time for Ursula to confess her love, now would surely be it. After all, what does she have to lose? If Ruby laughs at her, it won't quite devastate her as it would have all those years ago, since Ursula isn't even sure that Ruby could process what she'd be saying in order to truly understand it.

She tells herself this, that Ruby's reply won't matter, but Ursula isn't a witch for nothing: she recognizes the power of words. How the correct one uttered at the appropriate time can make magic happen. How the wrong ones whispered into a phone can cause the collapse of everything that one holds dear.

Words that remain unspoken too long have a way of festering. Words are meant to be set free, not kept caged; they're a lot like birds that way.

Ursula's just busy gathering the three words from the corners of her psyche—no, six words, because just the three might be misconstrued; six words, followed by another nine, are what are needed to ensure the meaning is understood. She's just readying herself to utter them when Ruby interrupts her thoughts.

"Fire!" Ruby exclaims.

It takes a moment for Ursula to focus. "What's that, darling?"

Ruby points at the center of the ritual circle where the fire is usually conjured. "Fire. The safest place." She giggles, covering her mouth.

Something prickles along the back of Ursula's neck. *Is this it? Is this where Ruby hid the treasure?*

Moonshyne Manor Grimoire

Mirabelle's Instructions for a Full Moon Sisterhood Ritual

Instructions:

Gather with your sisterhood an hour before midnight on the night of a full moon. Wear whatever is most comfortable and will allow for freedom of movement: a robe, a muumuu, or your birthday suit (not recommended in winter). Fill your goblets with wine, mulled wine or green tea. Drink of the goblet as thirstily as you drink from the fountain of life. Enter the Moonshyne Manor Forest (or another wooded area of your choice) in single file, taking care not to unduly disturb its plants or creatures. Step within the sanctity of the ritual stone circle and then form your own circle within its womb. Light ritual candles, or sparklers, or use your wands to write your blazing names upon the night, or entreat fireflies to shine their light upon you.

Thank the Goddess for nature's bounty and for the powers she has gifted you with. Work whatever magic you need to, whether it's summoning charms or protective shields. Sing your songs, whether they're ancient tunes passed down from cradle to grave or modern anthems. Belt them out even if your voice is warbly. Dance as though possessed by joy.

You are with your sisterhood, and nothing can harm you. You are more blessed than you could possibly know.

34

Wednesday, October 27
Afternoon

Ursula stands, wand outstretched. Pulse racing, she conjures their ritual fire as Ruby claps with delight. Ursula's hand trembles as she tries a summoning spell first. When that elicits no reaction, she tries a revealing charm. Still nothing. There's nothing hidden in the fire.

Ursula's shoulders slump along with her spirits. Crestfallen, she casts her gaze about. And then she has a thought. Perhaps Ruby buried the goods under where the fire usually would be. They've had dozens of rituals right here since Ruby went to prison. Who's to say they haven't been conjuring flames directly above that which they sought?

Ursula lowers herself to one knee with a groan. Her joints are too old for this kind of nonsense. But still, she drops to the other and bends over at the waist. She begins scraping at the muddy ground, wishing she'd brought a shovel with her. It's only when she breaks a fingernail, tearing it cleanly away, that she remembers to use her wand.

That's been happening more and more lately, Ursula doing things the hardest way possible, almost as though she were punishing herself with tedious labor instead of calling upon the magical power that's her birthright, the same power that couldn't save Ruby.

Ursula points her wand at the earth, drawing air through her teeth before muttering, *"Fode."*

The soil begins flying as though an invisible dog were digging up a bone. It piles up across from Ursula, the hole getting ever deeper. Remembering Ruby's reaction to the shadow earlier, Ursula looks to Ruby to see if she's scared. But Ruby sits transfixed, a vague smile settled on her lips.

The hole gets more cavernous as the mound of soil grows. *Please, please, please,* Ursula pleads. *Please let this be it! Let this be the answer to all of our problems.* And suddenly, the digging stops as a box is unearthed. It rises up to settle in Ursula's outstretched hands. Her heart thumps against her breastbone, excitement making her pulse race. *Is this it? Is this the treasure?*

Ursula brushes dirt off what looks like an old cigar box. Her fingers tremble as she opens the lid. She expects to see flashes of sparking light from the jewels and the curve of the ancient Egyptian wand. When she spots ivory, she thinks they've found it. Ursula lets out a whoop.

But then it registers that something's wrong.

The box contains bones, a full skeleton, in fact. It's neither the jewels nor the priceless wand. It's the remains of some creature who was given a burial here many moon cycles ago, the box serving as a casket.

Disappointment floods through Ursula, leaving her weak. This was their last chance, the last hope of finding the treasure. Without it, they're well and truly fucked.

"Are we going back now for the party?" Ruby asks, forgetting the picnic and getting up. "The guests should be here soon."

Ursula sighs, struggling to her feet. "Yes, darling."

"I have a secret," Ruby whispers gleefully. "Do you want to hear it?"

Ursula's spirits lift again. Has Ruby remembered something that could help them? "Yes, Ruby Tuesday. Always. What's your secret?"

Ruby walks over to Ursula, cupping her hand around Ursula's ear as she whispers. "Magnus asked me to marry him."

I know, Ursula wants to say.

She thinks back to the night of Tabby's fiftieth birthday party when she'd looked up to see Magnus standing there, gray-blond hair swept back, white beard neatly trimmed. His eyes, a piercing blue, were similar to Ursula's own. He was dressed as a wizard, in the kind of get-up that Ursula had always imagined Gandalf might wear.

"I brought you a cocktail," Magnus said, putting a martini glass filled with a cherry-colored liquid down on the table. "It's a Ruby Tuesday," he explained, smiling, "your nickname for Ruby. I know you don't really drink alcohol, so it started off as a virgin, I promise, but Ruby thoroughly seduced and corrupted it before I could get it here," he said, laughing, "and now I must warn you that there's rye whiskey and Amaro in it."

Ursula found his clumsy attempts at ingratiating himself to be tedious and futile. She was never going to warm to him. Why couldn't he just accept that, so they could get on with disliking one another? At least there was honesty in that.

"Thanks," Ursula said, pushing the glass to the side.

When it became clear he wasn't delivering the drink and then departing, Ursula was about to brush Magnus off, saying she had to go to the washroom, when she spotted Ruby standing off in the shadows watching them. Ruby had obviously forced Magnus to come speak with Ursula, wanting her beau and her best friend to love one another as much as she loved each of them and stupidly believing such a thing were possible.

"I don't suppose I could trouble you for a reading?" Magnus asked, smiling too widely for Ursula's liking.

Not a fool by any means, knowing that Ruby was gauging her reaction, she'd smiled back and said, "Of course. Take a seat."

As Magnus sat across from her, Ursula asked, "Cards, crystal ball or palm?" Nine times out of ten, men chose the crystal ball, finding the pictures on the cards to be either too unsettling or silly, and the contact of palmistry too intimate.

He considered the question for a moment, surprising her when he answered, "Palm, please."

Ursula nodded. "Which is your dominant hand?"

"I'm left-handed," he replied.

"Then, give me that one."

He did so, and Ursula reached out reluctantly, taking it in hers before turning it over. She grudgingly admitted that he had nice hands. A man who worked with horses, as opposed to one who sat behind a desk, Magnus had strong palms that were slightly calloused. His fingers were long but not too spindly, and his nails were clean and well looked after but not overly fussed over.

Ursula was about to consider his palm's mounts and plains when her sight blurred and a vision came to her: Magnus on bended knee, looking up at Ruby, who was radiant, smiling like Ursula has never seen her smile before. *Yes, yes, a million times, yes*, Ruby said in the vision, swatting at her mascara as she began to cry tears of happiness.

Ursula leaped up, dropping Magnus's hand. "I'm sorry," she mumbled. "I think I ate something that hasn't agreed with me." And then she fled.

That vision was the catalyst for every terrible thing that followed.

Moonshyne Manor Distillery Recipes

Ruby Tuesday Cocktail

Ingredients:

1.5 oz. Moonshyne Manor vodka
1 oz. Moonshyne Manor peach schnapps
1 oz. Moonshyne Manor coconut rum
3 oz. fresh cranberry juice
3 oz. pineapple juice
½ oz. cherry syrup
1 fresh cherry for garnish
Ice

Equipment:

A cocktail shaker
A glass tumbler

Instructions:

Add all the ingredients except the cherry and ice to the cocktail shaker. Shake as though you're in a conga line holding the maracas. Pour into the tumbler after filling it with ice. Garnish with the fresh cherry.

35

Wednesday, October 27
Evening

Queenie checks her watch as she sits waiting in her laboratory. It's 5:49 p.m. Charon the Ferryman will arrive at 6:00 p.m., at the moment of day's death, summoned by the magic Queenie conjured a week ago, using the kind of spell that constitutes a contract, the binding kind with no loopholes that allow for it to be undone if the witch has a change of heart.

As a distraction from her mounting anxiety, Queenie focuses all of her attention on the number six. Pythagoreans believed it to be the first perfect number, one of only four that the ancient Greeks recognized in existence. Six is the atomic number of carbon, the basis of all life on earth.

Hexagons have six sides and are the shape that best fill a plane with equal size units, leaving no wasted space. With the pull of surface tension in each of the six directions, it's the structure that's most mechanically stable, which is why even though bees make their honeycombs circular, when the wax hardens into place, the end result is hexagonal.

It's also the number of women in the sisterhood, the reason why no further orphans were ever added to their number, the manor viewing them as strong and, therefore, complete.

She's had six antacids in the past hour. And Mirabelle passed away sixty-six years ago.

Queenie thinks back to when Mirabelle was dying, how the old woman created the Moonshyne Manor Grimoire for her girls. Knowing that she wouldn't be around much longer to answer their questions or to offer guidance in their magical education, Mirabelle composed the grimoire to serve as her voice, allowing her to speak from beyond the grave.

The textbook of magic included instructions on how to perform spells and charms, create magical objects like talismans and amulets, mix potions and elixirs, and summon or invoke deities or demons.

Queenie can still vividly recall sitting next to Mirabelle's bed in what is now Queenie's own bedroom, the old woman propped up against pillows, looking too frail to bear the weight of the enormous book on her lap. It appeared to take all of Mirabelle's strength to undo the two metal buckles of the belts stretched across the leather cover and to open the grimoire by its handmade brass corners.

While there were dozens of pages that she'd left blank for the girls to complete when they grew into their own powers—discovering magic they wanted to pass on to future generations, as they learned their own truths—she flipped to the very back of it.

Mirabelle crooked a gnarled finger, beckoning Queenie closer. Her voice was scratchy like a record that had been played too many times. "You see this?" she asked, pointing to two pages in which incantations were written in such a cramped scrawl that it was obvious that the very act of committing them to paper had been painful for the old woman. "There are only two spells in this book that you should never use. These are them."

"Then, why bother to include them?" Queenie grumbled, so deeply affected by Mirabelle's decline that she'd become even more confrontational and gruff than usual in those last weeks.

Mirabelle sighed. "It is unfortunately your nature, Queenie, to never ask for, nor accept, any help. Your self-sufficiency is both your second-greatest weakness and your second-greatest strength."

Queenie matched Mirabelle's sigh with one of her own but couldn't stop her mouth from twitching into a smile. "Only my second-greatest? So, what's my first?"

"That you will do anything, absolutely anything, for those you love."

The old woman's watery green eyes searched Queenie's face, perhaps waiting for the younger woman's customary quarrelsomeness, but she didn't have it in her to be combative. There was no point in denying it. Not now when Queenie would have laid down her own life for Mirabelle's, knowing how much the girls needed her, so much more than they would ever need Queenie.

Satisfied that there was no objection—that Queenie might be argumentative but wasn't blind to who she was—Mirabelle continued. "There might come a time when you're desperate, unsure of where to turn, when the only way out is doing something previously unthinkable. Or when your love for another is so great that you'd do the unimaginable for them."

It immediately occurred to Queenie that she didn't need to wait for such a time, that she was already experiencing it right then as she watched Mirabelle dying.

"Don't even think about it," Mirabelle said, always seeming to know exactly what was on Queenie's mind.

How prophetic her words had turned out to be, considering

that it was their love of Ruby that led the sisterhood to contemplate doing the inconceivable and use one of the forbidden spells. And it was that decision which had set off the ripple effect of unintended consequences.

Queenie can feel six o'clock approaching. It terrifies her that she has no real plan and no alternative that she can offer Charon. He's coming for the powerful Heka Wand of Isis, which she doesn't have. Nor does she have anything of equal value to offer him instead. All she can do is throw herself upon his mercy and ask for additional time to retrieve it. The dark wizard is terrifying, but he's rumored to be fair. Still, a man known for keeping his own word will expect the same from those he does business with.

What's the worst that could happen? Queenie wonders.

Before she can answer her own question, the overhead lights flicker and are extinguished. The darkness gathers upon itself like a magnet attracting millions of black iron filings. There's a density to it so that the inky air becomes like syrup, clogging Queenie's nose and mouth. She chokes on it, panicking as it fills her ears and pours into her soul. And then it becomes even more claustrophobic, the darkness morphing from a liquid to a solid that presses down on her like cave walls closing in.

The darkness speaks. "Queenie." In its mouth, her name sounds like a hiss.

For all Queenie knows, Charon could be a snake speaking with forked tongue. No one can be certain what he looks like, only that he manifests in the darkness, that perhaps he *is* the darkness itself.

Fear rings through her like a bell, just one protracted note stretching to infinity. Queenie has never felt quite so exposed or helpless.

She swallows, her tongue sticking to the roof of her mouth. "Charon."

Queenie waits for the Ferryman to speak, but no further

words come. The lab is silent as a tomb. She's never heard it this quiet, because the basement is a part of the manor, and the manor is an extension of the sisterhood. Like the women, it makes its opinions known, either muttering darkly or sighing theatrically. It murmurs in its sleep, grumbling about the injustice of old bones and plumbing that doesn't work as well as it once used to. It wheezes and tsks, harrumphs and bellows. What it doesn't do is keep its own counsel.

And as the silence expands, the black hole of it swallowing everything with the force of its gravity, Queenie has the strangest sensation that the basement has detached from the manor, that she and the lab are now cast adrift on the River Styx, the Ferryman of Hades carrying them between the worlds of the living and the dead.

Even as she thinks it, she feels something icy pressing down on her tongue. Queenie gags, spitting it out in panic. It's a disk, something metal. Her fingers lose all sensation when she realizes that it's a coin, the payment for a corpse to be ferried into the afterlife.

"You do not have what you promised me." The voice materializes from everywhere and nowhere so that it's impossible to pinpoint its source.

Queenie begins turning around slowly, unsure of where to face, not wanting to have her back to Charon. "There was a complication," she says, her voice quivering. "I thought I'd have it today, but there was a problem with recovering it. But I'll have it soon," she adds desperately.

"Soon?" the Ferryman mocks.

"Yes. I promise, soon. Just give me a few more days." Queenie's legs are trembling now. Her pulse cracks like a whip, racing, racing, racing. She's so light-headed, it's like she's floating outside her body.

"You will be punished for this."

Queenie winces and swallows again. "Yes." *Is this it?* The moment he kills her.

And then from far away, as though the words were being shouted across galaxies, Queenie hears her name being called. It's so disorienting that it takes her a moment to realize what's happening. The voice is Persephone's. The girl is making her way down the basement steps calling Queenie's name again.

Queenie goes cold. *No. No. No. No.*

The darkness smiles. Queenie can feel its lips curling around her.

"The girl," it says.

"No." It comes out more forcefully than Queenie intended.

She pictures Persephone, with her childlike face and those corkscrew curls, with her lost-girl air and her eagerness to please. Queenie's not sure how it happened, but ever since the girl arrived unannounced on their doorstep to fight for them, she has burrowed deeply under Queenie's skin.

Queenie makes her voice soft, pleading, "Not the girl. Name your price. I'll give you anything. Just not the girl."

But the darkness will not be reasoned with. "That is my punishment. You have until midnight on All Hallows' Eve to get me the wand. If you do not have what you've promised me, I will take the girl."

With that, he flicks something, and then her right wrist is clamped by what looks like a pulsating purple bracelet made up entirely of hot light.

"You have one hundred and one hours left," Charon says. "Let this serve as a constant reminder that time is running out."

36

Wednesday, October 27
Evening: one hundred and one hours left

"Queenie?" Persephone calls. "Are you down here?"

The staircase is narrow, and the steps appear to be shifting under Persephone's feet, making her feel unmoored, like a balloon that a toddler has lost its grasp of. She's used to electricity and the constancy of light bulbs, ones that aren't mercurial, sputtering with indecision about whether or not they're prepared to provide light.

"Queenie?" Persephone calls again. Ruth Bader Ginsburg whines next to her, looking like she wants to bolt. She's probably still skittish after listening to all that plate throwing.

Persephone's regretting venturing down here on her own. After bidding Jezebel farewell in the rage room, saying she could see herself out, Persephone saw the door leading down to the basement and spontaneously decided to check if Queenie was down here after taking her meeting.

She's not as steady on her feet as she'd like to be. Flinging those missiles in the rage room sapped all of Persephone's strength. It's as if she's been propped up this past year purely by righteous anger alone; now that it's all been drained, she feels like one of those inflatable tube figures you see flapping about at car dealerships.

Persephone reaches the bottom of the stairs. When Ruth Bader Ginsburg whines again, she bends down to pick her up, raising her hand to knock at the door. Her knuckles freeze in midair when she hears voices. Pressing her ear against the door, she recognizes one of them as Queenie's, but the other sounds *off* somehow, like a cross between a snake and a cat, or a punctured tire that's slowly deflating. Its hissing sends ripples of goose bumps up Persephone's arms. She's just about to turn around and retrace her steps when the door flings open.

Queenie stands there, framed by darkness, dripping with perspiration like she's run a marathon. "What the hell are you doing here?" she yells, eyes wide and crazed looking.

"I-I'm sorry," Persephone stammers, starting to back away. Ruth Bader Ginsburg growls.

"Who gave you permission to be down here?" Queenie demands.

The old woman is furious for some reason, and Persephone can't understand why. It's more anger than an unannounced visit warrants. "I just… I just wanted to—" Persephone can't quite grasp at the words she needs to explain herself. Instead, she reaches into the pocket of her mother's red coat, pulling out the printout that she made in the library. She tries unfolding it to show Queenie, but her hands shake so much that she drops it.

"What?" Queenie asks, hands on hips. "What is it?"

Persephone bends to retrieve the newspaper article, handing it across to Queenie by way of answer.

Queenie glares at her, like she's pinning the fact of Persephone's existence to the face of the earth—almost like she's scared the girl will disappear before her very eyes—before she unfolds the paper. When she sees the copy of the tabloid article, Queenie's shoulders drop. "Where did you get this?" she says sighing, her voice dipped low.

Persephone swallows and says, "At the library in their microfiche section. The librarian helped me narrow down the search based on the information I gave her."

Queenie closes her eyes as though willing Persephone and the printout to disappear. But then she sighs, opening them again and says, "You'd better come inside."

There's a tiny part of Persephone that wants to be mutinous and leave, telling Queenie that she knows when she isn't wanted. But it appears there's a part of her that's more lonely and curious than she is stubborn, and so that part wins. She trails Queenie into the tar-black room, noticing the strange purple bracelet on Queenie's wrist and how its light looks like it's throbbing.

It seems to take Queenie a few seconds to realize that they're standing in the dark. When she does, she disappears, and a moment later there's the sound of an engine chugging.

Overhead lights flicker on, and Persephone looks around the room for the person Queenie was speaking with a few moments ago. There's no one else there; they're completely alone. Unable to admit that she was eavesdropping—and therefore prevented from straight out asking who Queenie was speaking with—Persephone asks a different question instead. "Is that a generator you just switched on?"

"Yeah, it's solar-powered," Queenie says. "Green energy at Ivy's insistence. I rigged all the solar panels up on the roof myself one night on my Harley-Davidsonstick."

"Cool. Is that, like, a broom?"

"Yeah." Queenie looks at Persephone weirdly. It's intense, like she's trying to figure something out.

The old woman is acting super strange, and it's creeping Persephone out. She sets Ruth Bader Ginsburg down and notices that the dog is acting weirdly too, shivering and turning in tight circles, sniffing the air. Persephone strokes RBG's flank, murmuring reassurances. Once the dog calms, Persephone walks around the perimeter of the room, studying all the blueprints that have been tacked up against the walls.

Some of them are on yellowed parchment, their ink having faded with time so that the drawings look like anemic versions of themselves, while others are bolder—the lines crisper and more assertive—undoubtedly more recent.

"What's this?" Persephone asks, squinting at an older drawing that looks like a mechanical spider.

"An Arachnid Martin," Queenie replies. "A hybridized form of the 1915 Aston Martin Coal Scuttle, designed to climb walls."

"You made that?" Persephone asks, incredulous.

"No, I tried testing a prototype, but I couldn't get the tarsal claws of the vehicle to work effectively. Sticky magic is tricky," she grumbles. "It's easy enough to get something to cling to a surface, but to get it to unstick just as quickly so it can advance up a building is more complicated than you might think. The vehicle kept leaving legs behind." Queenie shakes her head, clearly frustrated with the failure. "Ivy said it was damaging the manor, so I wasn't able to work out the kinks."

Once Persephone has thoroughly perused the walls—including checking out a blueprint of what looks like a flying saucer with suction cups affixed to it—she comes back to where Queenie's standing. "Is that an invention too?" she asks, nodding at Queenie's wrist.

Queenie shakes her head, frowning. "No." She looks up from the article she's been reading and clears her throat. "You can't believe anything you read in the tabloids, you know."

Persephone looks at the title of the article for what feels like the hundredth time: *Witchcraft Killer Murders Three in Bonnie and Clyde Shoot-Out.*

"There's a ton they left out and made up," Queenie says. "To understand what happened that night, you need to understand what came before." She moves a wrench and a screwdriver out of the way before taking a seat on the bench. "I'd say you should speak to Ruby herself to get all the details, but I'm afraid that won't be possible."

"Why not?"

Queenie swallows hard and clears her throat again, composing herself before she speaks. Her voice is huskier than usual when she does. "She has Alzheimer's, or a magical form of it, and there's a lot she's forgotten. She remembers the day of Tabitha's party, but memories of what happened after that don't seem to be within her grasp to retrieve."

Suddenly, Ivy's sadness from earlier makes more sense to Persephone. As do Ivy's words: *Memories only become more precious with age when it's so difficult to hang on to them.*

"So will you tell me what happened that night?" Persephone asks.

Queenie thinks for a minute and then nods. "Yeah. I mean, why not? It can't hurt to get a fresh set of eyes on old memories. Maybe something will stand out to you that we've missed."

37

Thirty-three years ago: a month before the heist

Queenie unclipped one of the buckles of her harness, her stomach still doing somersaults. She was buzzed from successfully testing out the Yanker, a mechanism that pulled her up from her lab in the basement into her ground-floor office. Between that and the newly installed firefighter's pole, her commute time was now reduced, allowing for more time spent inventing.

Checking her watch, Queenie saw she was running late for the big meeting. "Shit."

After she'd fully extricated herself from the Yanker, Queenie bolted through the doorway and then sprinted the shortest route to the parlor.

Jezebel and Ursula were already seated in their usual spots, two large pizzas laid out before them on the table. Ivy and Tabitha were huddled together at an open window.

"Ursula," Jezebel said, "be a darling and pour me a drink,

will you? I'm thinking a Between the Sheets would go down a treat."

Ursula stood, trained by a lifetime of caretaking to do Jezebel's bidding without complaint.

"Since you're up," Queenie said, "could I have one too, please?"

Ruby wasn't there yet, which irked Queenie, since Ruby was the one who'd called the mysterious emergency meeting, insisting everyone be there on time.

Queenie grabbed a slice of pizza, cramming it into her mouth as she walked over to where Ivy and Tabby were standing, engrossed with something happening outside the window. "What are you two up to?" she asked, mouth still full.

In answer, Tabby's baby crow, Widget, flew through the window, landing on Tabby's hand. She cradled the bird before pinching its beak open as Ivy used a dropper to get an iridescent liquid into its gullet.

"Widget hasn't been feeling well," Tabby said. "Ivy's mixed up a tonic for her."

"That should stimulate her appetite," Ivy said as the little crow shook her head, trying to expel the medicine from her mouth.

Widget looked very much like she wanted to utter an expletive, but none was forthcoming. "She's still not speaking?" Queenie asked.

"Not a word," Tabby replied, stroking the crow's head with her finger.

"Wonder who she takes after, then?" Queenie asked, alluding to Tabitha's own silence for those first two years at the manor. "Don't worry," Queenie added. "She'll speak when she has something to say."

Tabby smiled and nodded, looking down at her familiar with an expression of such love that it almost took Queenie's breath away. It never ceased to amaze Queenie how the women of the sisterhood—motherless from too early an age, and never becoming biological mothers themselves—had found myriad ways to mother other things.

Ivy lavished all of her maternal affection on her plants, which thrived under the care of her green thumb. For Tabby, it was her creatures who benefited from her endless ministrations. For Ursula, it was all the women who came to her, supposedly so that they could be told their future through the laying down of cards but who actually just needed to know that everything would be okay in the end. It seemed that for those whose souls overflowed with an abundance of maternal instincts, there would always be something or someone in need of nurturing.

Ivy withdrew two envelopes from her robe pocket, holding one of them out to Queenie, interrupting her train of thought.

"What's this?" Queenie took the envelope and turned it over. *Ms. Ivy DuBois* was typed on the front of it.

"Another offer on the property from one of the Gedneys. This time, from Bartholomew's son, Bart Jr."

"What is it with those people?" Tabby huffed.

Queenie scowled. "I hope you told him to—"

"Take a long walk off a short pier?" Ivy said and laughed. "It just so happens that I did."

"What about the other letter?" Tabby nodded at the second envelope. "That looks like it's from the University of Edinburgh," she said, studying the red, blue and yellow emblem. "Don't tell me you're turning down another invitation to collaborate?"

Ivy waved it off. "You know I don't like leaving the manor. Besides, I don't have any formal qualifications—"

"Oh, good, you're all here," Ruby called, sweeping into the room and coming to a stop in front of the fireplace. She was carrying a parcel wrapped in purple silk which she set down on the coffee table next to the pizzas.

Ruby's hair was a vivid pink that day, cascading around her shoulders and tumbling over a matching pink dress. Her abundant eyeshadow, rouge and bright lipstick were all the exact same pink shade. She clapped her hands like a kindergarten teacher trying to get the attention of wayward children. "Please, could you all take a seat."

As they made their way to join the others, Queenie muttered to Tabby, "I'm getting heartburn just looking at that get-up. Is it just me, or does it bring to mind Pepto Bismol?"

Ruby, overhearing the remark, shook her head and tutted. "You should have said *Pepto Abysmal*, Queenie. That would have been much funnier. Don't ever give up your day job to become a drag queen, darling."

"Touché." Queenie laughed. She accepted an orange cocktail in a coupe glass from Ursula before sitting.

The women quickly settled down, private conversations ceasing as they turned to Ruby, curious as to what her news could be. Everyone's expressions were open, receptive to whatever was to come, except for Ursula who looked pensive and sat fidgeting with the lapis lazuli pendant hanging from her neck.

Queenie had assumed Ursula would know what this was about since Ruby always confided in Ursula first. Now she realized that not only was Ursula as much in the dark as the rest of them, she also wasn't very happy about it.

Ruby took a deep breath before saying, "I've decided that I want to present as a woman all the time."

The declaration was met with silence as the women all looked around, confused. It was a bewildered Ivy who spoke first. "But, darling," she said, "you already *are* a woman."

"True," Ruby said. "I mean, we all know that I *am* a woman, but I don't consistently present as such. I'm only able to keep my outward appearance consistent with who I really am when I'm feeling strong enough to sustain the shift. And that's no longer good enough. I want to permanently look exactly how I feel."

"How..." Tabby considered before trying again. "How would you go about doing that?"

"With magic, of course!" Ruby leaned forward and opened the purple silk-wrapped parcel to reveal the Moonshyne Manor Grimoire.

Queenie went cold, knowing even before Ruby opened the book that she would be paging to one of the last two spells, the ones Mirabelle had so vehemently cautioned Queenie against using.

Which is exactly what Ruby did just as soon as she got the buckles unclasped and the grimoire opened. "There's a spell that grants the object of the incantation anything they want, no matter how great."

"Is that true?" Ursula asked, her voice like a creaky door. She leaned forward, craning her neck to see the page which was too far away to make anything out. Ursula had never spent much time with the grimoire, not requiring it for potions or elixirs like the rest of them did, since her own powers came from deep within herself.

Ivy paled. "But...that's one of the forbidden spells."

"That spell requires a powerful talisman," Queenie interjected, all heads turning to her, "a rare magical artifact like the Book of Thoth or Galdrabók. That's its secret ingredient. Without it, we can't perform the spell no matter how much we might like to."

Queenie expected Ruby to look crestfallen at the news, but she brightened instead. "It just so happens that I know exactly where we can get our hands on such an artifact." Ruby pulled a newspaper clipping from where she'd tucked it into the grimoire, passing it along to Ivy who glanced at it before handing it to Queenie.

It was about a collection of rare artifacts from ancient Egypt that would be on loan to the city's Rothschild Museum in a month's time. The picture in the article showed a curved wand that was made from hippopotamus ivory and resembled a boomerang with hieroglyphs carved on it. "The Heka Wand of Isis," Queenie murmured, awestruck. She whistled appreciatively. "That definitely qualifies."

"The collection will only be there for a week. We just need to come up with a plan to liberate it," Ruby said, excitement bubbling through her words, like champagne effervescing over a bottle's mouth.

"You mean *steal* it," Ursula corrected, her tone as prim as her rigid spine.

Ruby shrugged. "Call it what you want, but I personally think it's a victimless crime. Ancient magical relics belong to the descendants of the magical, not the stupid museums of the magic-deficient who don't understand our powers." When Ursula just pursed her lips tighter, Ruby doubled down. "The point of magical artifacts is that they've been imbued with power. We owe it to them to work powerful magic with them, instead of just letting them gather dust in stuffy old collections."

"What about the sacrifice?" Ivy asked, her voice pitched so low that Queenie had to strain to hear it.

"That's what I was wondering," Tabitha said, looking pained. "You know we want you to be happy, Ruby, but it *is* a huge sacrifice."

"What sacrifice?" Ursula asked, looking from Ivy to Tabby, but neither of the women would meet her eye.

"I think you should be the one to tell her," Queenie said, gazing steadily at Ruby.

"Tell me what?" Ursula asked. Ruby flushed, keeping her eyes downcast. When it became clear Ruby wouldn't be the one filling Ursula in on whatever the rest of them knew, Ursula turned to Queenie. "Tell me what?" she repeated, more insistently this time.

Queenie sighed and said, "Any witch who performs that particular spell has to give up her own magical powers as payment for that which she asks."

Moonshyne Manor Grimoire

A Spell to Grant the Deepest Longing of Your Yearning Heart

Ingredients:

1 gallon rainwater from Puerto Rico
½ gallon black rhino urine
3 drops Cuchumatan golden toad saliva
1 drop scorpion venom
10 tears shed by a virtuous man
3 oz. corpse-plant pollen
1 flower from the lady's slipper orchid
1000-karat rough tanzanite stone, mined from the foothills of Mount Kilimanjaro during a total lunar eclipse
1 eyelash from a ruling British monarch
2 oz. placenta powder from a sextuplet birth
1 powerful magical artifact
**Secret ingredient*

Equipment:

A large heavy-bottomed cauldron
A ritual fire
A large wooden paddle
A potion chalice
A ladle

Instructions:

By the light of a full moon, gather in the forest at midnight and light a ritual fire over which you must place the cauldron. Add the liquid ingredients in order, including the tears, saliva and venom.

Once they begin to bubble, add the rest of the ingredients in order, one by one, stirring the potion clockwise after each addition. When the potion begins to glow a mercury-silver, reminiscent of the light of the moon, drop the magical artifact into the center of the cauldron, taking care not to create a splash. Use your wand to extract the secret ingredient, and add it last.

Using a ladle to extract 12 fluid oz. of the potion, and pouring it into a chalice, hold the chalice up to the moonlight and utter the incantation, Muta in donum volutissimum.

Drink the potion. Once you have swallowed the last drop, the deepest longing of your yearning heart will be granted. There is no undoing this spell so be careful what you wish for.

38

Thirty-three years ago: a month before the heist

Ursula gasped. "You all knew there was a spell like that in the grimoire?"

The rest of the sisterhood shifted uncomfortably in their seats. Jezebel gazed into her cocktail like it was a crystal ball containing the answers to all of life's mysteries. Ivy tapped her fingers together and then kicked off her shoes, threading her toes through the carpet. Tabitha became wholly absorbed with one of Widget's tail feathers, and Queenie closed her eyes, trying to block all of them out.

When she opened them again, Ursula wore a stricken expression as though betrayal had settled like a stone upon her chest. Whatever feelings Queenie had about the matter, it was clear that they would have to take a back seat to Ursula's.

"Why would you leave a dangerous spell like that in there in the first place?" Ursula asked, looking from Queenie to Ivy.

It was Ivy who answered. "Great-Aunt Mirabelle wrote

down every one of those spells for a reason. The grimoire is her legacy—it's all that remains of the generations of knowledge that were passed down to her—and it's not for us to—"

"Oh, shut it, Ivy," Ursula snapped. "I'm not in the mood for one of your lectures right now." Ursula turned back to Ruby, incredulous. "You'd be prepared to give up your powers? To stop being a witch so that you could, what?" she scoffed. "Become a woman full-time?"

Ruby squared her shoulders, finally meeting Ursula's gaze. "I *am* a woman full-time. But yes, I'd do it to *present* as such full-time."

"But..." Ursula floundered, grappling for words "...that's just preposterous."

"Why?" Ruby challenged, jaw jutted. "Why is that so inconceivable to you?"

Ursula threw up her hands, clearly exasperated that she even needed to explain it. "Your magical powers allow you to present as a woman seventy percent of the time—"

"Exactly!" Ruby said, eyes flashing. "Which means that the other thirty percent of the time, I'm stuck in limbo, not looking how I feel—"

"But you've never had a problem with being either a man or any of the in-between ones," Ursula said, getting to her feet. She walked around the couch as though she needed to put an additional barrier between herself and Ruby besides the coffee table. Leaning her hands on its backrest for support, she said, "You quite liked the gender fluidity."

"That's true. I did. But now things have changed."

"And by *things*, you mean Magnus," Ursula tutted.

Oh, shit, Queenie thought. *Now the gloves come off.* None of them had seen very much of Magnus beyond the most basic of introductions. Whenever he came over, Ruby quickly ferried him off to her room, though whether that was because she was ashamed of him, or of them, Queenie couldn't tell.

Ruby had a history of dating the wrong guys, even those she knew for certain were dirty cheats, and so there was always the chance that this was another of those cases, Ruby keeping her man away from them so that she wouldn't have to listen to them tell her she could do better.

"This has nothing to do with Magnus," Ruby snapped. "This is about me. *I've* changed, Ursula," Ruby said, placing her hands over her heart. "Can't you understand that I'm older now and know myself better? That something I once enjoyed is no longer enjoyable, and so I choose to change it because it's in my power to do so?"

"But, you almost always present as a woman anyway," Ursula insisted again, running out of arguments.

"You're missing the point," Ruby said, frustrated. "I want to live with the certainty that when I'm a woman, I'm not likely to suddenly swap over, either because I'm coming down with something, or because I'm stressed, or because my mojo is running out."

"But to give up your powers for it?"

Ruby shrugged. "It's hardly that much of a concession."

Ursula's jaw dropped. "How can you possibly say that? We're witches, Ruby. Our powers make us who we are."

"No, *your* powers make *you* who you are. You identify as a witch first and foremost, but I don't. The only thing I use my abilities for is metamorphosis magic to keep me from morphing back. All of my energy is conserved for that. I have no reserves left for the kinds of magic the rest of you work."

"That's not true!" Ursula turned from Ruby to the rest of them. "Tell her that's not true."

"When did you last see me conjure anything?" Ruby asked. "When did you last see me work any kind of spell that wasn't related to staying in my truest form?"

Ursula opened her mouth, clearly intending to let forth a

stream of examples, but the stream appeared to be in drought. Try as she might, not even a few drops trickled from her tongue.

Seeing Ursula's struggle, Queenie considered the multitude of tiny acts of magic they all performed every single day, from lighting fires and opening windows to sending each other bowls of vegetables or fresh bread across the dining room table or summoning books from high shelves in the library or cleaning up spills and fixing things that had succumbed to gravity's effects.

Queenie thought of Jezebel's many charms and Ivy's myriad potions and Tabitha's conjurings and Ursula's incantations. Despite being the member of the sisterhood who relied least on magic, in the last hour alone Queenie had used it to summon various tools and blueprints, as well as tidy up the lab and reinforce the elastic strands beneath the nylon sheath of the Yanker.

For the life of her, she couldn't recall when last she'd seen Ruby use magic for any mundane tasks or for their rituals.

"I..." Ursula shook her head, unable to answer. "I'm sure..." But it was no use. She'd clearly reached the same conclusion that Queenie had.

Ruby, sensing Ursula's dismay, made her way behind the back of Tabby and Jezebel's couch to where her friend stood. She reached for Ursula's hands, holding them in her own. "Don't beat yourself up for not noticing." She turned to the rest of them, taking in their similarly dazed expressions. "Don't any of you feel bad about that. I've become somewhat of an expert at hiding it from you." She turned back to Ursula. "We only have so much magical power, and my metamorphosis magic uses up an inordinate amount. And that's what I've prioritized mine for."

It had never occurred to Queenie that their magic could run out. It had always been right there at her fingertips whenever she needed it. There had always been frustrating limitations, to be sure, and ways in which she hadn't been able to command her powers as she might've liked. But that buzzing in her veins?

That crackling of energy? It had never stilled, and she couldn't imagine what it would be like if it suddenly did.

"What about your shape-shifting?" Ursula asked. "Won't you miss doing that?"

"It *is* a lovely parlor trick," Ruby admitted. "Something I loved using to mess with you all when we were younger." She smiled at the memory, and they all smiled along with her, wistful for a simpler time. "But now that I know who I am, I don't want to be anyone else ever again."

"Can't we siphon off some of our own magic for you?" Ursula asked, turning to Queenie. "We all have excess powers that we don't use on a daily basis that we should be able to grant Ruby. Isn't there a spell in the grimoire for that? Or a device you can invent that will enable that?"

The wheels began turning, but before Queenie could think it through, Ruby spoke. "I refuse to take powers from any of you, Ursula," she said sadly, releasing Ursula's hands. "I'm not a charity case asking for handouts."

"They're not—"

"Are you saying you won't love me anymore if I'm not a witch?" Ruby asked, her eyes filling with tears. "Is that what this is about?"

"Of course not!"

"Then, why do you insist on pinning that identity on me when I keep telling you it's not one that fits?"

Ursula's mouth gaped as though desperately wanting to form words but finding itself wholly incapable of the task.

"This is all I want," Ruby said, an aura of calm settling upon her. "And I'm going to do this with or without your help." She sighed. "You don't need to be involved in how I go about making it happen, Ursula, but I know my mind, and I really need you to respect and support my decision."

Queenie stood, walking to where Ruby and Ursula were.

Tabby, Jezebel and Ivy rose as one, trailing her. They circled the two friends whose arms were now wrapped around each other.

When Ruby and Ursula broke apart, the women huddled together, arms around one another's waists.

"You promise you won't stop loving me just because I'm a not a witch anymore?" Ruby asked, eyes watery.

"Witch, please," Queenie said. "Never gonna happen."

39

Thirty-three years ago: the morning of the heist

Three days after Tabitha's fiftieth birthday party, the witches of Moonshyne Manor gathered in the kitchen at sunrise.

Though the house had been cleaned the day before (a full day *after* the party, since they'd needed the whole of Saturday to recover from the celebrations), evidence of the festivities still remained. Glitter twinkled from the cracks between the floorboards, hardened candle wax remained puddled in wayward corners, and leftover food and alcohol lined the kitchen's surfaces.

The women had all insisted that Ursula do her customary daily checks and balances in front of them—hoping that their collective energy would bring good luck—and so she brought her tarot cards and crystal ball down to the kitchen where everyone was already gathered around the harvest table, waiting for the copper kettle to boil.

Ursula began with the tea leaves, using a special blend that

Ivy had grown in the conservatory. She let Ruby pick the cup and saucer in which the tea was made and then proceeded with the swirling-and-turning ritual. After the cup was turned upside down over the saucer and then righted and properly positioned, Ursula studied its sides. "Huh," she murmured.

"What?" Queenie asked just as Ruby cried, "What is it?"

Ursula squinted at the clusters of leaves. "I'm not able to see a clear answer."

Queenie plucked Ivy's glasses from her face, handing them across to Ursula. "Maybe these will help. Put them on."

Ursula clucked, handing the spectacles back to a scowling Ivy. "I don't need glasses, Queenie," she said. "The leaves are giving contradictory signs."

"What do you mean?"

"I'm seeing both success *and* peril in the near future."

"Well, there's success in there, at least," Ruby said. "That has to be a good sign, right?" She looked around, hoping for agreement. Jezebel reached out and squeezed her shoulder.

Ursula wasn't convinced, but Ruby was eager for her to move on so she set the cup aside and reached for her amethyst crystal ball. The sisterhood knew to hush when Ursula was scrying, and they all went still, trying to breathe as quietly as possible so Ursula could clear her mind. Flames crackled in the fireplaces, and the sweet perfume of the jasmine tea permeated the room, but Ursula wasn't aware of either. Her focus was on the shining purple orb, her conduit to a higher level of consciousness.

For five excruciating minutes, the women gazed at Ursula, who gazed into the sphere. Finally, she blinked and shook her head.

"What?" Queenie and Ruby asked in desperate unison.

"Conflicting messages again."

There was a collective exhalation, Ruby's betraying her frustration. "The cards are always best, anyway," she said. "Forget the rest."

Since it was Ruby's big day, Ursula handed her the tarot cards. They were still wrapped in their purple silk pouch. "You know what to do," Ursula said.

Indeed Ruby did, for they'd done this hundreds of times over the years, Ruby usually consulting the cards to see if an errant lover was likely to repent and return, or if someone more rakish and mysterious might be lurking in the future. Ruby cupped the pouch in her palms and closed her eyes as she considered her question.

She projected not only all of her intention into the cards but all of her desperate hope too, when she asked, "Will the heist go well today?" Ruby then released the oversize cards from the pouch, shuffling them awkwardly, before picking out the eight cards that Ursula would base her reading on. Ruby handed them across reluctantly, looking clammy and green-faced.

As Ursula began flipping the cards over, laying them out, one by one in her usual heptagram formation, Ruby turned away and began pacing between the two enormous fireplaces that bookended the kitchen.

Queenie stood behind Ursula, leaning in so close as she peered over her shoulder that Ursula snapped, "Could you please give me some room to work?"

Queenie made a show of throwing her hands up and stepping back, but her breath remained hot on Ursula's neck. They all peered at the familiar pictures as though studying a family photo album. While they'd seen the cards hundreds of times, none of them had Ursula's gift of clairvoyance, and they looked anxiously from the cards to Ursula's face, waiting for her verdict.

It must be said that there was a moment then in which Ursula considered lying about what the formation foretold. She could lie and say it wasn't a good day for the heist, but she knew Ruby well enough to know that she wouldn't change her mind. The week-long exhibit at the Rothschild Museum was at its end, and that night was the last one before it moved on.

If the heist didn't happen today, Ruby would want to follow the exhibit so they could try again and again until they succeeded. And so there was nothing for Ursula to do but to study the cards and say, "It appears there will be a slight hiccup or two, but nothing we can't overcome."

Ruby whooped from across the room, rushing at the sisterhood who threw their arms around each other.

Little did they all know that when Ruby had focused her intent on the cards, she'd asked the wrong question.

40

Thirty-three years ago: the evening of the heist

Ivy's storm arrived right on time, just after sunset and half an hour after the Rothschild Museum had closed for the night. Jagged bolts of lightning tore at the sky's seams, rending the fabric of the heavens. Thunder rattled the windows like a banshee pounding against the glass, desperate to get inside. Fat raindrops began to pelt Jezebel, who stood just outside the museum's entrance, wearing a fur coat and not much else.

The fur was fake, obviously, since Tabitha wouldn't have allowed otherwise, but Jezebel's near nakedness was very real. As was what was about to transpire with Jimmy, the young security guard from the Bronx, who reminded Jezebel of the hot young actor Rob Lowe, who she'd been seeing in all her celebrity gossip magazines.

Their imminent rendezvous would be a repeat performance of what had already happened twice before in what Jezebel had labeled *test runs*. She might not have been a scientist like

Queenie or Ivy, but she was nothing if not thorough in her research methodology.

The storm, though, was a new detail. As was the young man who lingered outside the museum, hat pulled low and head bent over a newspaper. Jezebel didn't want to take the chance of being spotted and remembered, and so she held back. When the man finally tucked his paper away, dashing across the street, Jezebel made her move.

She had to rap against the glass doors harder than usual to be heard above nature's ruckus. When Jimmy came into view, already smiling wolfishly as he unclipped the ring of keys from his belt, Jezebel let her coat fall slightly open.

Seduction, in her experience, was all about building anticipation. The sooner you could whet someone's appetite and the longer you could hold out satiating it, the better.

Jimmy unlocked the door, trying to pry the rest of Jezebel's coat open with the force of his gaze.

She stepped inside and smiled coquettishly. "Excuse me, sir," she purred. "I believe I left my purse inside while I was perusing your fine collection of boners—oops, I mean *bones*—an hour ago. Could you please help me find it?" She tugged her lip down with her finger, gazing up at the guard from beneath lowered lashes. Her red-painted nails, perfectly matching the crimson shade of her lipstick, gleamed under the overhead lights.

"Why, certainly, ma'am," Jimmy replied, tipping his hat in a reenactment of the first time Jezebel had carried out this charade a few weeks ago when she'd actually gone through the motions of visiting the museum and supposedly losing a purse.

"You're too kind," Jezebel murmured.

Before Jimmy could lock the door, Jezebel flicked her wrist, aiming a blocking charm at it. While the key turned in the lock, Jimmy failed to notice the customary click of a lock engaging because of the noise of the raging storm.

"Please follow me." Jimmy smirked as he motioned Jezebel to the security desk.

As per the last two visits, he would make a big show of searching for the purse in the Lost and Found bin, before leading her back to the security office to supposedly search a bigger bin there, while actually searching her nether regions. The office was the only place in the museum, besides the washrooms, where there were no cameras, and where it was, therefore, safe to get up to shenanigans.

Jimmy wasn't a man of many words during sex, which was disappointing as Jezebel enjoyed scintillating dirty talk as much as the next gal, but there was something about climaxing that seemed to unleash his words. As he'd lain panting and spent after their first coupling, he'd told her how there was supposed to be a second guard, Tony, on duty with him, but luckily for them, he was always late.

Tony apparently had to hotfoot it to the museum from his other security job at the docks. Jimmy said he covered for Tony for that first forty-five minutes to an hour of the shift, explaining how it wasn't a big deal since the day guard helped clear the visitors out before the museum closed, after which it was quiet anyway.

"Is Tony here?" Jezebel asked now, just to be on the safe side.

"Nah. We have the place to ourselves for at least another forty minutes." Jimmy turned back and wiggled his eyebrows, shooting her a devilish grin.

As Jezebel followed Jimmy to the desk, her stiletto boots clacked across the marble floor serving as a kind of foreplay. Young Jimmy had a heel fetish, insisting Jezebel kept her boots on whenever they fucked, and Jezebel had a security-guard fetish, insisting Jimmy kept most of his uniform on, so it all worked out.

Queenie's original plan for the heist hadn't involved any kind of seduction, and certainly no fucking at all, since she was of the mind that women could pull off a perfectly good robbery without needing to have sex with anyone. But Jezebel had called bullshit on that after spotting the young security guard during an early reconnaissance mission.

Knowing what was about to happen in exactly one minute, Jezebel set about capturing Jimmy's attention so thoroughly that he wouldn't allow himself to be distracted. Once they reached the desk and Jimmy began fake-searching through the Lost and Found box for her purse, Jezebel positioned herself with her back to the security cameras. She let the coat slip all the way open, revealing the red lace corset and garters she'd chosen for the occasion.

Jimmy's eyes almost bugged right out of his head like a cartoon character's. It was the last thing she saw before the power went out, right on schedule.

"Shit," Jimmy muttered from the darkness in front of her.

"I'm sure the generator will switch on shortly," Jezebel said.

He cursed again as he stumbled into the desk. "It's only programmed to kick in half an hour after the power fails, so that its juice isn't wasted on brief cuts caused by power surges."

Jezebel smiled. That had been one of the few things they couldn't be a hundred percent certain of, and now it was one less thing to worry about. "You have a flashlight, right?" Jezebel asked.

"Yeah, why? You scared of the dark, Vivian?" he teased, using the name she'd given him when they first met.

"No," she said. "I just want you to shine it on me later so this outfit doesn't go to complete waste." Jezebel could hear Jimmy gulping. "You're not going to let this ruin our plans, are you?" she murmured. "The power will either come back on soon or the generator will kick in. Might as well have some fun in the dark while we wait."

Jimmy hesitated for three whole seconds. Jezebel could be sure that's how long it took because she counted each one of them. His answer came in the form of him navigating his way around the desk. Jezebel turned when he came up behind her, pinning her against the desk. His hand reached out and found its way under her coat, cupping her breast as he leaned in to kiss her neck.

Jezebel gasped as his tongue flicked against her pulse point, the warm heat of it making her squirm. They kissed passionately, Jimmy pressing against her so that she could feel his growing excitement. When he reached down to caress her, Jezebel came to her senses. "Not here," she murmured. "I don't want people from the street seeing us when the lights are restored."

"You don't strike me as the shy type," Jimmy teased, but he withdrew his hand and made his way back to behind the desk where he reached under it for a flashlight.

Flicking it on, he trailed its yellow beam as it guided their way to the back room where the darkened security screens stood lined up against the wall. Jezebel pointed a finger at where she knew the server thing was positioned, muttering a spell to wipe its memory so there would be no trace of her arrival on any of the surveillance footage.

"What did you say?" Jimmy asked, tugging on her other hand and pulling her in close as he leaned back against a table.

"Nothing," Jezebel whispered, kissing him. "Nothing at all."

As the sex hormones—oxytocin, dopamine and serotonin—flooded her senses, Jezebel forgot to conduct the silencing spell Queenie had instructed her to conjure just as soon as she got Jimmy inside the office. By the time she remembered, when she was straddling Jimmy as he sat on one of the chairs, she figured it didn't matter. Jezebel was sure they wouldn't hear a thing over the sound of their own gasps of pleasure.

She would be proven wrong in exactly twenty-four minutes.

41

Thirty-three years ago: the evening of the heist

Queenie and Tabby watched from a porte cochere across the street as the flashlight lit up, its beam bobbing across the lobby until it was out of sight.

"That's our cue." Queenie used her wand to shoot sparks of green light into the air, the miniflare acting as a thumbs-up for Ivy and Ursula, who stood under an awning two buildings across, keeping dry as Ivy continued to wreak stormy havoc. "Let's give it another minute just to make sure Jimmy doesn't come back to the desk for something."

Once the time was up, Queenie dashed across the deserted road, so focused on what was to come that she barely noticed the rain that was pelting down upon them. When they got to the museum's entrance, a furry little head suddenly popped out of the top of Tabby's coat.

Queenie nodded at it, and Tabby glanced down, zipping up the coat around the bump bulging from her torso as she patted at it affectionately. Had any casual observers been standing around (foolishly casually observing rather than taking shelter from the storm that was walloping the city), they might have thought Tabitha was being protective of a pregnant belly, passing judgment on her considering she was fifty years old. But Queenie was relieved to see the street was still deserted, the man with the newspaper having disappeared, and so there wouldn't be any witnesses to the strange sight.

Certain they hadn't attracted any attention, Queenie gently tugged on the door, careful not to make any noise. It obediently opened, and she sighed with relief as they stepped through. With the sun having dissolved, and the formidable storm clouds now buttressing the sky, the space was as black as Lucifer's soul.

Queenie reached for her wand, pointing it at Tabby, muttering, *"Sicca."* Once Tabby's clothes were dry, Queenie did the same for her own. It was as much for safety as for comfort. They didn't want to be dripping across a marble floor, turning it into a watery slipping hazard.

Putting her wand away, Queenie withdrew three pairs of goggles from one of her coat's many hidden pockets. She put one on, the darkness instantly morphing into a stunning emerald green, forms untangling themselves from the sticky blackness to stand out in sharp relief against other discernible shapes.

Queenie handed the other two goggles across to Tabby, who donned hers and then opened her coat, nudging Klepto. The capuchin monkey immediately unwrapped his arms from around her chest and clambered up to stand on her shoulder.

Tabby handed him the smaller pair of goggles, which he delightedly snatched from her grasp, before expertly slipping them on. Klepto hopped from foot to foot on Tabby's shoulders, doing a happy dance over his windfall, but well-trained enough to remain silent despite his obvious, delirious simian delight. Queenie couldn't help but envy him. If only people were so easily pleased.

The tiny night-vision goggles for Klepto had proven challenging for Queenie, but since monkeys couldn't see at night—due to their eyes not having tapetum lucidum, the light-reflecting surface that made certain animals nocturnal—it was an invention he couldn't do without.

She'd finally perfected their design a week ago, relieved when Klepto took to them—wanting to wear them all the time, and staring at himself in every reflective surface when he did—since she didn't fancy the idea of having to magic the device to the little primate's face. Nor was she sure that Tabby would have let her.

Having already done a thorough reconnaissance of the museum's layout, Queenie knew that what they were seeking was at a back corner, and that they had to pass through a maze of display cases, plinths and partitions to get there.

They were both dressed all in black, in trousers instead of robes, since Queenie didn't want to take the chance of flapping fabric snagging on the corners of pedestals, potentially pulling artifacts down in their wake. Their split-toed jika-tabi boots allowed them to move quietly across the marble floors as they zigzagged their way past the permanent Aztec jewelry collection to the special itinerant exhibit.

Finally coming to a stop at the pedestal they were seeking, Queenie didn't need to read its information plaque. She'd memorized it on previous visits.

Title: The Heka Wand of Isis
Period: Middle Kingdom
Dynasty: Dynasty 12–13
Date: ca. 1981–1640 B.C.E.
Geography: From Egypt
Medium: Hippopotamus ivory
Dimensions: L. 13 1/16 × W. 2 1/16 × H. 4 7/8 × Th. 3/8 in

Credit Line: Miriam Cartwright Collection, Bequest of Miriam V. Cartwright, 1917

The Heka Wand of Isis was discovered in the tomb of an ancient Egyptian woman who served as a high priestess to Hathor, the goddess of motherhood, love, joy, fertility, dance and beauty.

The wand is carved out of hippopotamus ivory and still retains the shape of a hippopotamus tusk-line canine.

One side of the wand is decorated with the carved figures of protective female deities that carry knives to ward off evil.

These wands are believed to have provided some form of supernatural safeguarding to women during pregnancy and childbirth.

They were also placed in tombs to offer protection to the deceased at her rebirth.

"You ready?" Queenie whispered, and Tabby nodded. Queenie withdrew her wand again and pointed it at the top of the towering display case that held the curved ivory relic. Its ends were suspended on two thin wires to give the impression that it was floating in midair, making it look even more like a boomerang. The white of it gleamed strangely in the green light of the world created by the night-vision goggles.

A high-pitched cry suddenly tore through the room, ricocheting off all the glass and marble surfaces. Queenie dropped her wand in fright. It clattered against the floor, skittering out of sight.

Moonshyne Manor Grimoire

Ivy's Directions for Making a Wand

Use that Google thingy on the interwebs to learn about the properties of different types of wood.

Choose one that speaks to the kind of witch you want to be or the kind of magic you want to perform.

Go into the Moonshyne Manor Forest during the waxing moon period, before noon, as that's the most auspicious time to harvest your wand with a knife or hacksaw in a clean cut. Never damage a tree or harvest from a protected tree. The best wands are around 12"–15" long and the same diameter as your middle finger, though the base where you hold it can be wider. Ask the tree for permission to take its wood. Place your hand over the wound where you took the wood and direct healing energy into it as you thank the tree for its sacrifice to your magic. Leave an offering of fruit or nuts for Tabby's creatures at the base of the tree. If you're working with green wood, strip the bark off and place the wand in a warm, dry place to season. This will take as long as it takes, usually around a month.

To personalize the wand, oil it to bring out the wood's natural beauty. You can also attach crystals by wrapping them with copper wire. Carve runes or other symbols into the wand's shaft.

42

Thirty-three years ago: the evening of the heist

Tabby's pulse was thundering fiercely as adrenaline surged through her. She ducked, shushing Klepto who'd cried out at the noise. As Tabby tried to balance on her haunches with the capuchin bobbing around on her shoulders, she struggled to hear anything over the sound of blood whooshing past her eardrums.

When another moan pierced the silence, this one very clearly one of pleasure, Queenie hissed, "For fuck's sake."

Jezebel was clearly enjoying the heist more than they were.

Queenie crouched, searching for her wand. When she didn't spot it, she got down on all fours, crawling around as she searched under nearby pedestals until she finally let out a grunt of satisfaction, her hand closing around it.

She stood, dusting herself off as another groan issued from the back office. Queenie stilled, cocking her head.

"What is it?" Tabby whispered, alarmed.

"If we can hear Jezebel," Queenie replied in a hushed tone, "that means she didn't work the silencing spell on the office like she was supposed to."

"Shit. Can't we work it here instead?" Tabby asked, reaching for her wand.

"This space is too big. It won't work. That's why she had to do it in there."

A protracted moan, followed by a few whimpers, issued from the office.

Tabby looking around, considering. "Should I try to get back there and cast the spell from the doorway?"

Queenie shook her head. "We're running out of time. Let's hope she makes enough noise to disguise any we might make." Queenie aimed her wand at the top of the display. "Let's try this again," she muttered. *"Aperi."*

Tabby was expecting the acrylic top of the display case to come off with a soft pop, after which Queenie would use her wand to direct it to the floor where she would gently set it down. That's how it had played out during all the test runs. But nothing happened now.

Queenie tried again. *"Aperi."*

Still nothing. Queenie regarded her wand, checking for some kind of damage but finding none. She shrugged, shooting a dark look at Tabby, who reached for her own wand, trying to perform the same spell.

But nothing. "Shit," Tabby whispered again.

Their magic wasn't working for some reason. It had worked in the lobby when Queenie had dried them both off. One wand might malfunction, but two? Highly unlikely. There had to be something about the concentrated collection of magical artifacts that was interfering with their powers.

Tabby began to panic. Ruby had been so excited and hopeful that morning; the thought of disappointing her was devastating. With this being the last day of the exhibit, it wasn't like they could just come back another night.

She was beginning to spiral when Queenie held up a hand, whispering, "Don't worry. I brought a backup, just in case."

Of course you did, Tabby thought, so relieved that she considered leaning forward and planting a kiss on Queenie, whose complex brain worked a magic all of its own, which was probably why she wasn't quite as enamored with their powers as the rest of them were. She had never relied on magic alone—putting more faith in her inventions than in her magical abilities—which could sometimes be annoying.

But sometimes, like now, it totally saved their asses.

Tabby watched as Queenie reached into various hidden pockets, pulling assorted paraphernalia from them. She set everything on the floor and knelt down, turning the items this way and that like puzzle pieces, as she deftly assembled them into something that, when it was done, resembled a flying saucer with suction cups under it.

Pulling a remote control from another pocket, Queenie stood with her device, handing it across to Tabby, who took it gingerly. Queenie flicked a switch, and the contraption in Tabby's hands began thrumming, so that it felt like she was holding a huge insect. Queenie flicked another switch, and mechanical wings suddenly sprouted from the sides of the saucer's lid.

It tugged away from Tabby's hands, and so she let it go, watching in wonder as it soared into the air, alighting on the display case as though it were a huge flower waiting to be pollinated. There was a soft buzzing as the saucer rotated back and forth, and then, with a muted pop, a circle of acrylic came away from the case's top, pulled away by the suction cups. As Queenie returned the contraption to the floor, she nodded at Tabby.

This was her cue.

"Klepto," Tabby whispered, pointing at the display case. "Go fetch for Mama."

The capuchin leaped from Tabitha's shoulder, both arms outstretched as he grabbed for the top of the display case. When he latched onto it, he tugged himself up and within seconds he'd hopped over the edge of the circular hole, and was dangling down the inside of the case. Just as they'd practiced in the fake booth Queenie had set up in her lab, Klepto reached for one end of the wand. He gently tugged at it to release it from the wire hook, before yanking it free.

Clutching the wand under an armpit, Klepto pulled himself out of the display case with the arm he was hanging from, before launching himself back down at Tabby. Klepto' s part in the operation had taken less than a minute, and Tabby breathed a sigh of relief as she snatched him from the air, proud of how well he'd performed.

It was as the capuchin grabbed at Tabby that he lost his grip on the wand. It fell, and the sound of it striking the marble floor was like a gunshot.

43

Thirty-three years ago: the evening of the heist

"Freeze! Stand and put your hands up where I can see 'em," a voice called from behind the flashlight that was pointed their way, blinding Queenie where she was crouched.

"I feel like that's a contradiction," she croaked, annoyed beyond measure by their damn helplessness. "Should we freeze or should we stand? Because we sure as hell can't do both." Queenie squinted, turning her face away from the light.

She was still clutching her wand, which she'd instinctively drawn just as soon as they'd heard Jimmy advancing. She'd even tried to fire off a disarming spell or two, forgetting that the wand was useless. Perhaps if they could get to the lobby, outside the triangulation of whatever force field was working against them, their wands would work once more.

"Drop the stick, smart-ass, or whatever the fuck that is you're holding, and *then* put your hands up," Jimmy called, his words punctuated by the sound of a firearm being cocked.

With a loaded weapon trained on her, Queenie had no choice but to comply. She placed her wand on the ground before raising her hands. From next to her, Tabby did the same. Klepto followed suit a second later.

There was much Queenie was berating herself for. Like not factoring in exactly what the Heka Wand of Isis weighed when they did their simulations. She must have made the fake artifact lighter than the real one, because Klepto never once lost control of the fake during all their practice runs. She blamed the stupid museum plaque for that; it gave all the artifact's dimensions except the weight.

What kind of so-called information was that? It was half-assed was what it was, and Queenie had a strong mind to write a letter of complaint to the curator of the exhibit.

She was also beating herself up for not testing any spells near the exhibit. Queenie, like an idiot, had just assumed their magic would work in here, but as everyone knew, assumption was the mother of all fuckups. As an experienced scientist, how had she made such a rookie mistake?

All variables should have been considered and tested as they tried to simulate the exact conditions of the museum. They'd gotten close enough, even sourcing the same materials the museum used for their display cabinets, and building the pedestals to those exact specifications to test that Klepto could make the leap comfortably.

But Queenie hadn't thought about how the powerful magical artifact they were trying to steal might affect their own powers. And now they were in deep shit because of it.

Stupid, so stupid of me, she seethed.

It was as she was mentally kicking her own ass that the lights came on. Not all of them but staggered ones dotted around the room that looked like backup lighting. It was still dark outside, Ivy's storm-induced power outage ongoing. These lights had to be fueled by a generator, which meant that their half-hour window had passed. Had Klepto not dropped the artifact, they would have just made their escape.

Queenie could now clearly make out Jimmy the guard. He was standing a few feet away, flashlight in one hand and his gun in the other. His shirt was rumpled and untucked, and his belt was unbuckled. His thick black hair stood up in all directions like a seductress had recently been running her red-nailed fingers through it.

Speaking of which, where the fuck is Jezebel? Queenie cast her gaze behind Jimmy but saw nothing. Maybe she was hidden somewhere, about to pull some kind of stealth attack to redeem herself for the silencing-spell failure. Had Jezebel just done what Queenie had asked her to do, none of this would be happening. Why was it that if you wanted something done properly, you always had to do it your damn self?

No longer needing the flashlight, Jimmy threw it to the side, bringing both of his hands to the grip of the weapon, steadying his aim. "Get up," he instructed, taking two steps back.

Queenie and Tabby stood, their knees creaking in protest. Queenie was just thinking through all of their dwindling options—from using Klepto to create a diversion to finding something that could serve as a weapon to somehow picking up her wand and getting Jimmy to direct them all to the foyer where she might be able to use it to cursing the fact that the only two witches, Jezebel and Ivy, who could work their magic without wands were the two who weren't here right now—when the front door of the museum swung open with a bang and a man in a security guard's uniform came rushing in.

He was at least thirty years older, forty pounds heavier and three inches shorter than Jimmy, and not nearly as good-looking with his bulbous nose and fleshy chin.

"Yo, Jimmy, what the hell is goin' on, man?" he asked in a thick Brooklyn accent as he made his way over, weapon drawn.

He came to a stop next to the younger man, staring at Klepto. "Is that a fuckin' monkey or am I having a fuckin' stroke?"

"Tony," Jimmy said. "Shit, man, I've never been so happy to see your ugly ass. We've got a robbery in progress. And they almost got away with it too. I was in the back with Vivian, my lady friend I told you about," he said. "I wouldn't have heard nothin' if the monkey hadn't dropped whatever the fuck that is." He nodded at the Heka Wand of Isis lying on the floor.

"I have a cousin who's got a dick shaped like that. Can never pee straight into the toilet. You don't want to stand next to old Frankie at a urinal," Tony said as he looked around. "Where's that broad of yours now?" he asked.

"Handcuffed to the chair in the back," Jimmy said, the corner of his lip curling up into a smile.

"Why?" Tony asked, surprised. "She one of the suspects?"

"Nah. She let me tie her up before I spanked her."

Queenie thought she'd have a heart attack right there and then.

"You fuckin' kids, man," Tony said, laughing and shaking his head. "You gonna go call the cops?"

"Yeah," Jimmy said. "Watch 'em for me, okay?" He handed Tony his weapon.

Tony took the gun. "I'm afraid I'm going to have to ask you to put your hands up," he said, pointing the weapon at Jimmy.

"What the fuck?" Jimmy did a double take, waiting for the punch line.

Which came when, right before their eyes, Tony morphed from an overweight, middle-aged cop into a gorgeous, pink-haired Ruby. She turned to a gaping Queenie and said, "Close your mouth. You're going to catch flies."

44

Wednesday, October 27
Evening: one hundred hours left

"Wait. What?" Persephone squeals. "Tony the security guard turned out to actually be Ruby?"

"Yeah," Queenie says, smiling at the memory. "She intercepted him as he was coming in, and then she worked her metamorphosis magic to take his form."

Persephone listens, trying to keep up, as Queenie launches into a long-winded explanation of how Ruby's powers used to work, how she could not only move back and forth between a spectrum of genders but also change her appearance, depending on who she'd last been in proximity to.

"Think of it like a chameleon who changes its colors depending on the kind of surface it's standing on," Queenie says. "She touched Tony at the entrance of the museum before Ivy used magic to disarm him. And that's who she was able to become."

"But what about the power coming back on? Didn't that

start the security cameras going again?" Persephone asks. Ruth Bader Ginsburg taps Persephone's leg with her paw. She reaches down to pick the dog up.

"Yeah, but we were able to go to those server thingies and wipe out their memory." Queenie shakes her head. "The magic-deficients' technology can be really cool, but it has a lot of weaknesses. Memory override is one of them."

"What happened next?"

"We put the fake artifact in the display case and closed it back up. I erased Jimmy's memory, much like we did with the server, and then did the same for the real Tony."

Something dawns on Persephone. "So, no one ever even knew there was a heist because you replaced the artifact with the fake?" She looks at the blueprint from earlier, the one with the blade and suction cups, understanding now what it was designed for. "That's so smart. My kind of magic uses decoys all the time too. I've gotten quite good at making them myself."

Queenie stands and stretches, looking restless. "Well, that's the way it was supposed to play out, but unfortunately that's not how it went. Klepto stole some other stuff."

"The monkey?" Persephone yelps, shocked.

"Yeah. I mean, we should have seen that coming," Queenie says, grinning as she scratches her ear. "Tabby didn't name him Klepto for nothing. While we were busy with the cleanup operation, Klepto got into a few other display cabinets, helping his little simian self to some jewels."

Persephone's heard of cat burglars, but this is next-level. She can't help giggling as she imagines the jewelry-thief monkey running amok in the museum. She wonders if she can train Ruth Bader Ginsburg to do the same.

"We only realized what happened once we got home and emptied out the bag with the artifact and found the jewels in there," Queenie says and begins pacing.

"So the heist went well, just as Ursula's cards said it would when Ruby asked her question," Persephone says.

"Yeah," Queenie replies, reaching for a screwdriver, which she begins twirling like a baton. "With just those few predicted hiccups, which we overcame as the cards said."

Persephone looks down at the article she brought from the library that Queenie's placed on her worktop. *Witchcraft Killer Murders Three in Bonnie and Clyde Shoot-Out.*

"But, I don't understand," she says. "I thought that was the same night Tabby died and Ruby was arrested?"

"It was, but that all happened later. After we got home."

Persephone thinks it through and nods. "That's why you said Ruby asked the cards the wrong question. Because she asked if the heist would go well and not if the whole day would go well."

"Exactly," Queenie says, tapping her forehead with the screwdriver.

Persephone looks from the article to Queenie's tired, crevassed face. She remembers that when Ursula looked at the tea leaves the morning of the heist, she saw what she thought was a contradiction: success and peril in the near future. "So, what happened later that night?"

Before Queenie can reply, Persephone's cell phone rings, the display showing that it's her father. She checks the time, realizing she should have been home half an hour ago. After answering and telling him she'll see him soon, Persephone says, "I'm sorry. I have to head home."

Queenie waves it off. "Don't worry about it. We have a long day tomorrow anyway. I should get some shut-eye."

As Persephone trails Queenie around the workstations on their way out, she asks, "Why? What's happening?"

"I've built a Memory Jogger that we're going to try out on Ruby to see if we can jog some recollections loose."

Persephone thinks about the day her mother died, how she was the one to come home and find her. At least, she's been told that's the case, and that she then called 9-1-1. Persephone can't remember any of it.

The trauma counselor she saw for a few sessions afterward said that the mind does that sometimes to protect itself, that it's best not to force some memories, because they will reveal themselves only when we're strong enough to cope with remembering.

Persephone considers the tabloid article and how traumatic it all sounds. "Maybe the memories shouldn't be jogged loose. Maybe it's better for Ruby if she forgets."

"I'm afraid we don't have a choice," Queenie replies, shoulders slumped. She lifts her arm, staring at the strange glowing bracelet before looking back at Persephone with a pained expression. "She has to remember. She just *has* to."

45

Friday, October 29
Afternoon: fifty-six hours left

Ivy wishes yet again that they could have done this in the parlor. Tempers are running high, fuses are short and a cold cocktail (or four) would definitely help smooth things over. Her elixir, brewed especially for the disgruntled townsmen, would do better to be slipped into their own drinks today.

What's that they say about getting a taste of one's own medicine? Ivy thinks wryly. *Oh, the irony!*

They're a day behind schedule thanks to yesterday's issues with Queenie's Memory Jogger. The invention didn't so much jog as crawl, and even that's an overly generous assessment. In truth, it twitched once or twice before succumbing to dramatic death throes. The session with Ruby yesterday morning had to be abandoned so Queenie could go back to the drawing board, more than an entire day wasted when they have precious few to begin with.

Queenie hasn't slept in over thirty-four hours. The bags under her eyes, along with her snappish demeanor, betray her exhaustion. She refuses to speak about the shackle of light Charon branded on her wrist—or what transpired during their meeting—but the bracelet seems to be getting warmer with every passing hour, and Queenie fidgets with it constantly.

Ivy's pestered Queenie about it, of course. As have the others. Whatever the cuff signifies, it's bound to be terrifying. But Queenie's mulishly stubborn, and she'll only divulge the details when she's good and ready. If Ivy's being completely honest, there's a cowardly part of herself that's relieved not to know, that's quite happy to be kept in the dark.

If the memory device fails again, Ivy doesn't want to witness the fallout. She's not even prepared to entertain the thought. *It's going to work*, she tells herself. *It has to.*

"Ruby Tuesday," Ursula calls in that overly chirpy voice she now uses, the one that grates on Ivy's nerves, "can you take a seat over here like you did yesterday?" Ursula maneuvers Ruby around a workbench to a straight-backed chair.

"Are we playing musical chairs?" Ruby asks, exactly as she did yesterday.

"Yes, darling," Ursula replies, another echo from the day before.

"I don't want to." Ruby crosses her arms over her chest, a mulish expression stamped on her face.

They're all so accustomed to the sense of déjà vu that Ruby's homecoming has established as the new normal that her abrupt deviation from the script stops them short.

"What do you mean?" Ursula asks.

"I don't want to play," Ruby says. "I want to go outside and have a picnic."

Yesterday, Ruby had meekly taken a seat in the chair, letting Queenie fit the strange-looking helmet over her head. Now they all look around at each other, at a complete loss, hoping for some divine inspiration.

"How about we play musical chairs first and the winner gets to carry the picnic basket?" Ivy tries. It's a tactic that she used on the sisterhood when they were little girls, their competitive natures often motivating them when entreaties failed.

"I'm not a child, Ivy," Ruby says now. "Don't talk to me like I'm a child."

Ivy flushes. How easy it is to lose sight of that when Ruby has reverted to such a helpless state, when she's bewildered so much of the time, unable to perform even simple tasks. Chastened, Ivy says, "Of course you're not a child. I'm sorry, Ruby."

They all stand in awkward silence, probably thinking that while they want to afford Ruby the dignity she deserves, they *do* have to manage her like they would a child in order to keep her safe. Both Tabitha and Ursula have discovered Ruby downstairs in the early hours of the morning, skulking around the foyer. They're terrified she's going to wander off outside and get lost. Queenie has promised to make some kind of protective device for the front door just as soon as she perfects the Memory Jogger.

Ruby regards Ivy suspiciously, as though she knows she's being managed. Ursula hovers off to the side, wringing her hands. Jezebel looks pained, as though bearing witness to this moment somehow degrades them all. Tabitha glowers from the corner as Widget hangs her head. And Queenie looks like she's had enough coffee to power a small city. Her one eye twitches, and she grinds her teeth, the masseter muscles of her jaw bulging.

Jezebel forces a smile. "How about I bring the picnic down here and magic it to look like outside? Would you like that, Ruby?"

Ruby nods, only slightly mollified, the recalcitrant frown not easing completely.

Ivy shoots Jezebel a grateful look as Jezebel heads for the door. The room is only slightly less crowded now with four witches, a crow and a ghost standing among the workstations, benches and various pieces of equipment.

"Will you take a seat now, Ruby?" Queenie asks, impatient to get started. "We'll do the picnic afterward."

"I don't want to."

There's silence, no one daring to look at each other, but everyone wondering, *What now?*

"Why don't we each have a turn with the Memory Jogger?" Ursula says brightly, heading for the chair. "I know my memory isn't what it used to be. Just recently, I forgot to put on my robe, and I ran around the whole house naked," she tells Ruby.

"Like Jezebel?" Ruby asks, smiling.

Ursula laughs. "Yes, *exactly* like Jezebel." And then she turns to Queenie, nodding at the helmet on the table. "Can I have the first turn?"

"Be my guest," Queenie says, ushering Ursula into the seat and then picking up the helmet to affix it over her head.

"I'm hoping the Memory Jogger can help me find my lucky rabbit's foot which I seem to have lost," Ursula says.

"Losing it couldn't have been very lucky for the rabbit, either," Widget caws.

Queenie hooks everything up to Ursula and then fiddles with the dials and switches on the control board. Satisfied that everything's working, Queenie turns on the device, and there's that gentle thrumming, same as yesterday. Ivy holds her breath, expecting the whole system to suddenly shut down again, refusing to be resuscitated no matter how much Queenie pounds, yells or cajoles.

But the thrumming continues, and Queenie smiles in triumph, turning a dial as she cranks a lever like she's playing the slots at a casino in Old Vegas. Ivy half expects Ursula's eyes to start spinning, flashing the cherries, dollar symbols and big red 7s, and for Queenie to announce a jackpot.

Unfortunately, it's not nearly that exciting. Queenie just asks Ursula a few standard questions, which she answers, Queenie calibrating the device all the while with the flick of a switch here and the tug of a lever there. The contraption responds each time by whirring or clacking, its own kind of muttering to match its creator's.

After five minutes of this, Ursula's eyes suddenly light up. "The rabbit's foot is in Queenie's Caddy!" she declares, delighted. "I left it in there when we went to fetch Ruby."

Everyone claps, and Ivy can't help the optimism that flares in her chest.

"Who wants to go next?" Ursula asks, struggling to remove the helmet.

"I will." Ivy takes it from Ursula and sits down, submitting to all of Queenie's ministrations as she gets the machine set up.

When the contraption is whirring at optimal pitch, Queenie asks, "What is it you want to remember?"

"There's a fungus name that's been at the tip of my tongue for days." This has been happening more and more lately. It's infuriating, like having an itch on the brain that can't be scratched. Ivy's started using words like *thingumajig* and *whatchamacallit* as placeholders until the proper terms suddenly come to her three weeks later, sometimes only after stubbing a toe on the way to the bathroom at two in the morning.

As Queenie does her thing with the control board, she says, "Picture the fungus you have in mind."

Ivy conjures a mental image of it, picturing the bloodlike fluid secreted on its surface. She's just beginning to feel claustrophobic in the mask when something rattles loose in her mind, the word dropping with a thwack like candy from a gumball dispenser. *"Hydnellum peckii!"* Ivy exclaims.

"Bless you," Ursula says as a joke, before turning to Ruby.

“Look how much fun we’ve had. Are you ready for your turn now?”

As Ivy gets up, taking the helmet off, Ruby asks, “What about Tabby? She hasn’t been yet.”

All eyes turn to Tabitha, almost like in the old days when she used to be so much the center of attention, rather than merely a ghost, an afterthought, a memory.

46

Friday, October 29
Afternoon: fifty-five hours left

"It's your turn, Tabby," Ruby says. "What do you want to remember?"

The question is asked so innocently and with such sincerity that Tabby almost doesn't feel the slice of it into her heart, or actually—to be more accurate—where her heart would be if she still had one if it hadn't stopped beating on that ill-fated night.

Too much of it can be recalled in vivid detail, like the seven stallions rearing up on hind legs, eyes white with churning fear, as well as the mental snapshot of a sequined dress throwing off hundreds of sparks of light. But so much of it is lost as well, just swirling mist where something concrete should be.

Since Tabby's never been able to leave the manor and hasn't encountered any other ghosts within its walls, she doesn't know if it's normal to not remember all the events leading up to your death. She also wonders why she would have stayed behind as a ghost when Mirabelle didn't. And what about the others? When they die, will they move on without her, leaving her alone?

Regardless, Tabby feels she's owed those memories. It seems that the least the universe can do, when snatching your life away, is to allow you to recall those last minutes in which breath made your rib cage rise and fall, animating your body so that it could move through the world.

It seems, though, that the universe has a sense of humor. It may have snatched Tabitha's memories from her, but hasn't it also done the same for Ruby, albeit in a different way? If Tabby was a victim of chance that night—someone who was accidentally taken because they were at the wrong place at the wrong time—then Ruby was the perpetrator of that bait and switch, the reason Tabby was there in the first place.

She may not remember much, but she remembers that, which is how she knows, without a doubt, that the apology owed to her is Ruby's.

And now here Ruby is, asking Tabby what it is she most wants to recall, when there couldn't possibly be anything else. And while Tabby suspects Ruby is the key to unlocking everything—and making sense of that night and why Tabby's still stuck here—she can't even ask Ruby because Ruby's mind is an old field blanketed with fresh snow.

Of course, Queenie's Memory Jogger machine won't work on Tabby. It's not made for the dead.

And so Tabby directs a dour look Ruby's way and says, "You want to know what I want to remember, Ruby? I want to remember how I ended up dead because of you."

Widget splays her wings and bobs her head. "My head is already crammed full of every happy memory we ever made together, Ruby. There isn't room for anything else."

Tabby thinks for the thousandth time how people don't deserve animals, not with their love that's given so unconditionally and their souls that are so completely unblemished.

Widget doesn't lie or cover for Tabitha; she wouldn't know how to since there isn't an ounce of guile in the crow. What Widget does is see through Tabby's pain—one that manifests in the speaking of ruthless truths—to tap into the emotional essence underlying it.

Which is simply that Tabby misses her sisters and her old life desperately because she counted herself so incredibly lucky to have lived as she did. What Tabby does is mask her heartbreak with harshness because that's the only bearable way to go on. And Widget ensures that Tabby isn't even more alone in death than she otherwise would be.

They're all surprised when Ruby claps her hands, suddenly delighted. "I want *my* head to be full of those memories too," she exclaims, taking the helmet from Ivy and sitting down. "I want those memories that the birdie has," she says, beaming at Widget.

Queenie's relief is palpable as she begins calibrating the Memory Jogger.

Jezebel returns just then, but Ruby doesn't even notice the arrival of the picnic basket that she's been asking for so incessantly. Jezebel clears a workstation to overlay it with a red gingham tablecloth, and Ivy goes to assist her.

Once the picnic is unpacked, the two of them walk around the lab, casting spells to create the illusion of being outside on a summer's day. Along with trees and lawn and sunlight, they conjure a gentle breeze that carries flitting butterflies of every rainbow hue.

They've tried doing this once before for Tabby, magicking her forest inside the library, but it felt like being taunted with a cheap knockoff of a reality she would never get to experience again.

As Queenie begins asking Ruby questions, Tabby knows Jezebel and Ivy are listening as attentively as she is.

"What is your full name?" Queenie asks.

There's a beat before Ruby replies. "My name is Ruben."

Tabby hasn't heard Ruby refer to herself as Ruben since she confided, a few days after Tabby's arrival, that that was the name she'd been given at birth, but that she'd later changed it to something that felt more like her.

"And what's your last name?" Queenie asks, voice strained as she cranks another lever.

"It's…it's…" Ruby looks perplexed. "Is it *Between*?" she asks. "Ruben Between?"

It's close to the last name Ruby chose for herself when she was thirteen, but it isn't right.

Queenie continues to ask Ruby questions about her age, her address, what year it is, what four plus four equals, who the president is. Ruby doesn't answer any of them correctly. She thinks she's still fifty-two, which is how old she was when Tabby died. She knows she lives at Moonshyne Manor but can't remember the street name (Gwillimbury) or the number (13). She thinks it 1988, that four plus four equals forty-four, and that the US president is "one of those Bushes who need trimming."

Tabitha holds out no hope at all for the Memory Jogger, but she's surprised to find herself wishing beyond all reason that it might work. After all, it's Tabby's very existence that depends on it.

Queenie begins turning a few knobs, flipping some switches, cranking one lever while turning a dial. After the device vibrates for a few moments, Queenie begins asking Ruby all the questions again, starting at the beginning.

This time, Ruby gets her full name right, declaring it to be Rubilicious Faloolah Minx Betwixt. It's a mouthful of a name chosen by a scrap of a girl on the verge of womanhood, the kind of name you donned as armor against a world that was always going to see you as a target because you dared to be different.

And if Ruby can remember a name like that, isn't it possible that she can remember the rest of it too?

When Ruby answers the next question correctly, the sisterhood begin clapping and cheering Ruby on. Each correct answer buoys their spirits enormously.

And now, Queenie is steering Ruby to the day she seems stuck in, Tabby's fiftieth birthday.

"What costume did you wear for the party?" Queenie asks.

"I went as Glinda the Good Witch in that glorious pink frock."

"Who did Jezebel go as?"

There's a pause, and they hold their collective breath. "I can't remember the character's name, but Cher played her in *The Witches of Eastwick*. It was a *très risqué* costume."

"Yeah, baby," Jezebel says in her huskiest Cher voice, doing a sexy shimmy paired with a smile cracked open like happiness has been chiseled onto her face.

Queenie asks a few more questions about the party and then moves on to the day of the heist. "On that night at the Rothschild Museum, what were we there to steal?"

Ruby scrunches up her brow in concentration. "The Heka thingy of Asses."

Queenie smiles, thrilled with the hilariously mangled answer. "And who did you use metamorphosis magic to transform into that night?"

"That security guard," Ruby says. "The ugly one that Jezebel wasn't shtupping."

Jezebel barks a laugh. Something ticklish brushes against the back of Tabby's throat, or where her throat used to be. The sensation is so rare that it takes Tabby a moment to realize it's a laugh building up, wanting to escape. It's so wonderful to have the old, scandalous Ruby back that Tabby's disappointed when Queenie moves on, her tone serious now, because this is it, this is where everything's been leading the whole time.

Come on, Ruby. You can do it.

"When we came home that night," Queenie says, "where did

you hide the Heka wand and the three necklaces that Klepto stole?"

"Two necklaces," Ruby shoots back.

"What?" Queenie blinks, surprised.

Ruby shakes her head. "Two necklaces, not three."

Queenie looks nervous now, like she's not sure how much emphasis to place on the number of necklaces—whether getting agreement on them is imperative before moving on or whether she should just gloss over that detail. She seems to reach a decision to let the number go and to focus on the hiding place instead. "Okay, where did you hide the Heka wand and the two necklaces?"

Ruby nods, satisfied that Queenie agrees with her. "In the fire," she says with that sly grin.

"Which fire?" Queenie asks.

"The safest one."

Queenie's tone betrays her frustration. "Is it the one in the forest where we do our rituals? Or the one in the parlor where Mirabelle's portrait can watch over it, keeping it safe? Maybe in one of the bedrooms where no one can come at night to steal from us while we're sleeping?"

"The fire that only I can get to," Ruby says.

Queenie recalibrates the device, making it rattle as she cranks it up to its full capacity.

"Which fire is the one that only you can get to?" Queenie asks.

Something registers on Ruby's face. It's like mist suddenly clearing, revealing a breathtaking view. "The one in—" But before Ruby can finish, the helmet gives off sparks as the control board begins to smoke. And then there's a bang, the power going out.

Ruby jumps up, bewildered and panicked, pulling off the helmet. "Why am I here?" She has the expression of someone facing a firing squad. And then she sees her face in the helmet's reflection. "Who's that man? Why does he keep following me?"

Tabitha wants to cry. Because that's it. The Memory Jogger was their last hope to save the manor. If they lose their home and it gets knocked down by a wrecking ball in three days, that means Tabby gets obliterated along with it. Since the moment she woke up in the manor on the night she died, Tabby's never been able to leave its walls.

But when there are no longer any walls holding her in, what will become of her?

Moonshyne Manor Grimoire

Ivy's Balm for Stiff Joints
(Not to be confused with Jezebel's recipe for a stiff joint)

Ingredients:
3 tsp. beeswax
1 drop sweet birch essential oil
2 drops cayenne essential oil
1 drop ginger essential oil
1 drop cinnamon essential oil
1 drop willow bark essential oil
1 drop magnesium oil
1 drop menthol essential oil
1 drop black pepper essential oil
1 drop peppermint essential oil
1 drop nettle essential oil

Equipment:
A small, heavy-bottomed cauldron or saucepan
A wooden spoon
A round tin salve container

Instructions:
In the small, heavy-bottomed cauldron or saucepan, heat the beeswax over the lowest heat possible. When the beeswax is nearly melted, add in the essential oils. Pour the mixture into the round tin salve container. It will firm up in approximately 6–12 hours.

Apply the balm to stiff, aching joints.

47

Saturday, October 30
Afternoon: thirty-three hours left

"Does anyone know where Tabby is?" Queenie asks. Having already waited an additional ten minutes in the parlor before starting the meeting, she doesn't want to have to push it out even further. Every minute counts when you're in a frantic race against time.

Ivy shakes her head as she traces the outline of the red mandevilla-vine tattoo on her left wrist. "I haven't seen her at all since we left your lab yesterday."

The scene of the epic failure, Queenie thinks, feeling the crushing sense of defeat all over again. She hangs her head and swallows deeply. She's never felt so utterly disappointed in herself; the taste of it is acrid in her mouth, commingling with that of her antacids. The Memory Jogger is fried beyond the point where it can be fixed. And there isn't time to build a new one.

Jezebel hands a virgin cocktail to Ruby before sitting down. “I haven’t seen her since then, either.”

Their experience tallies up with Queenie’s. Tabby’s disappearance should make this meeting easier, but somehow it doesn’t. Not having Tabitha here just makes it worse, as though Tabby’s already gone before the manor’s been destroyed. “And Ursula?”

Ivy answers. “She said she had to run an errand. I’m sure she’ll be back any minute.”

Queenie nods, careful not to lift her gaze above the line of faces. She can feel the heat of Mirabelle’s glower radiating from her portrait: it pulses in waves. Queenie’s terrified to meet her eyes and see the judgement in them.

That tactic doesn’t stop Mirabelle’s voice from coming through, strong and clear in its I-damn-well-told-you-so tone. *“You will do anything, absolutely anything, for those you love.”*

It’s true, Queenie *will* do anything for those she loves. But this? Project-managing their leaving of the manor so as to prevent them from being crushed by the wrecking ball on Monday morning? It’s too much, something she shouldn’t be expected to do.

And yet, since this is all her fault—thanks to her complete and utter inability to seek out help, thanks to her belief that she’s only ever good enough when she’s making the world easier for others to traverse—it’s the least she can do.

Plus, there’s the more urgent matter of Charon, something Queenie’s tried putting off thinking about because it’s the worst kind of problem, the kind she can find no solution to, no matter how much she circles it, coming at it from every angle. Ursula warned Queenie that he’d dictate too high a price, and Queenie hasn’t told the sisterhood what payment the Ferryman has demanded, but she suspects they assume it’s her life. None of them know that it’s Persephone’s life that hangs in the balance if Queenie can’t produce the Heka wand.

She has a plan, which is to offer herself instead of Persephone to the Ferryman. She's eighty-five years old; she's lived a long and fruitful life. This isn't the way she wanted to go, but she tells herself she can do it, make that sacrifice. The only problem is that Queenie has no idea if Charon will accept it.

A young soul can empower a dark wizard to do stronger magic, but an experienced witch's soul can have just as much force if used the right way. Queenie is hoping that she can convince him or figure out a way to sweeten the deal.

She *has* to because it's not like they can even conjure the forbidden spell to help them fight Charon: they need the Heka wand to perform that kind of magic.

Queenie glares at the purple bracelet pulsing on her wrist. The heat it radiates is becoming more than an unpleasant annoyance. She tries not to think about how hot it will eventually get.

She reaches for her tumbler of acorn cauldron whiskey that Jezebel poured on the rocks at her request, since the initially proffered frothing pink cocktail felt too festive for what was about to transpire. Queenie takes a deep sip, the alcohol searing the feelings that are all knotted in her throat. She is about to suggest that they begin without Ursula and Tabby, when they hear the front door slam.

Ursula comes fluttering into the room, trailing the cold behind her like a shadow. "Sorry I'm late!" As she bends to kiss Ruby on the cheek, she unwinds her green scarf that's embroidered with gold moons. "Where's Tabby?" she asks, setting her shopping bag down and taking a seat next to Ruby. Ursula accepts a martini glass from Jezebel without any of her usual reluctance.

"Is Tabby the little black birdie?" Ruby asks. "I saw her last night flying around and around the front garden." And then she shakes her head, looking sad. "It sounded like she was crying."

Before Queenie can process that information, Ursula declares, "I have news!" She reaches into her shopping bag and withdraws two bundles, setting them down on the coffee table.

Ursula looks so impressed with herself that Queenie inspects the bundles more closely only to discover that they're wads of cash. Jezebel whoops as Ivy gasps. "What the hell?" Queenie asks, doing a double take.

"I've cashed out my savings," Ursula says, going a bit pink as she says it. "And I want the sisterhood to have it."

"What savings?" Queenie's never heard Ursula mention of any kind of savings. They've all lived mostly hand to mouth, scrounging up money as and when they needed it, careful not to use their powers in ways that would attract even more unwanted attention than what the townsmen already paid them.

Ursula's cheeks turn a mottled fuchsia. "My inheritance, I should say."

"Inheritance?" Ivy squawks, knowing full well she's the only one of the sisterhood to have officially inherited anything from family.

"Yes. There was some money left over from the sale of Mother's house. That friend of Mirabelle's, the one who brought me here, put the proceeds from the sale into a trust which I then had access to when I was twenty-one."

"Why didn't you ever mention anything about it?" Ivy asks, clearly as suspicious as Queenie is.

Ursula waves it off. "To be quite honest, I forgot all about it until recently when our money woes began." She clears her throat. "And I realized how unfair it was that we've all just always expected Queenie to have to deal with everything when we should have taken equal responsibility."

Queenie is overcome with an emotion that's so foreign to her that it takes a moment to identify it as gratitude. It's ridiculous how much she appreciates Ursula's comment, how it helps ease the guilt.

"How much is it?" Ruby asks which is what everyone is wondering.

"Fifty thousand dollars," Ursula replies, her expression hopeful as she looks from Ivy's face to Queenie's. "Will it help pay the bank off?"

Ivy closes her eyes and shakes her head sadly. "It might if they were amenable to working with us as we pay off our delinquent debt. But we owe the bank half a million dollars. And they've made it clear they won't accept a penny less."

"And," Queenie adds, "considering we only have until midnight tomorrow to pay it all off and we're not going to find the Heka wand before that—" she pauses, shooting a quick look at Ruby, who's smiling back at her "—it's time to face the harsh reality that we're going to have to leave our home." Queenie swallows deeply and then turns back to Ursula, who looks crushed. "Thank you for trying to help and for making this money available to us. It won't save the manor, but it will help finding somewhere else to live so much easier."

And then, before she's likely to break down completely, Queenie reaches for her clipboard and starts going over all the tasks that need to be completed before the wrecking ball arrives.

It seems almost inconceivable that the manor house will no longer exist by this time on Monday. How is that even possible for a building with a gravity so large that it not only drew all the scatterlings of the sisterhood to it in the first place but that it also sucked Tabitha back from the abyss, refusing to concede her to the afterlife?

The manor is the seventh member of the sisterhood. Having lost one of them to death and another to the black hole of dementia, Queenie has no idea how they can survive another loss. But if she has to give her own life to save Persephone's, she wants to go knowing that the sisterhood will be as fine as they can possibly be. Which means trying to figure out a way for Tabby to leave the manor with them.

48

Saturday, October 30
Evening: twenty-nine hours left

As Persephone and Ruth Bader Ginsburg wander from room to room in the manor, Persephone has a sense of what it must feel like to be Tabby. The witches are all so focused on lists Queenie handed out prior to Persephone's arrival, that they barely take any notice of their visitors.

There's a pall in the air, like she's arrived in the middle of a funeral. Or, no, not a funeral exactly. More like she's arrived on someone's deathbed as their family gathers around them to say their last goodbyes. It's an awful thing to witness someone's grief and not be a part of it, to see them suffering and not be able to do anything to ease their pain.

If Persephone can't help save the sisterhood's home, then she can at least make their transition from it as smooth as possible by offering what little assistance she can. After walking past the parlor and hearing Ursula cursing, Persephone joins her in there.

That's how she meets Ruby for the first time. The old woman, seated next to Ursula, has unshaved cheeks and is wearing a wig that's slightly askew. Her bright pink lipstick has been haphazardly applied, but her eyes are bright and clear, and she grasps Persephone's hand tightly as Ursula introduces her.

"Ruby, this is—"

"Sarah-Jane Mortimer," Ruby finishes, beaming before reaching down and stroking Ruth Bader Ginsburg.

Something inside Persephone clangs like a bell.

"No, dear," Ursula says, smiling at Persephone apologetically. "It's Persephone Stoughton, the mayor's daughter."

"No, it's Sarah-Jane," Ruby says, smiling and nodding. And then she points at the red coat Persephone's wearing. "In your favorite coat." And then she taps her forehead with a finger. "I remember." Ruby winks slyly.

Ursula looks confused, but Persephone has figured it out. "You knew my mother," she says. "This used to be her coat." Persephone wants to ask Ruby more but knows the old woman is struggling with memory issues. That Ruby thinks Persephone is Sarah-Jane is a testament to the degree of confusion she's experiencing. And so, she resists the urge and turns to Ursula instead, asking, "What are you trying to do?"

"It's my job to find us a rental, but all the offices are closed, and I can't get anyone on the phone. It's the weekend. How am I going to speak with someone who can help me?"

"You don't need to," Persephone says, steering Ursula away from what she assumes is a telephone (even though it has a strange spinning contraption full of holes), and sits her down in one of the wingback chairs. "We can get it all done without you having to speak at all." Persephone pulls her iPhone out. "Okay, tell me what kind of place you're looking for."

Ursula reads from Queenie's list. "We need a five-bedroom house with two laboratories, a conservatory and a distillery attached. A rage room would be an added bonus. As would a large garden so that we can bring some of Tabby's creatures with us. We need it to be ghost-friendly, but I'm not sure if that will be stated on the listing. And it needs to be available to move in on Monday."

Persephone scratches her head and tugs at a curl. "I don't think you're very likely to find another place that's set up like this. Maybe we just look for the biggest property we can find that suits your budget?"

Ursula peers over Persephone's shoulder as she pulls up a few apps, adjusting the filters to conduct her multiple searches. Ruth Bader Ginsburg hops up onto the sofa, settling onto Ruby's lap.

When, after ten minutes, Persephone finds a long-term rental of a dilapidated-looking farmhouse with five bedrooms, a barn on the verge of collapse, a basement, a huge greenhouse that's shattered (but could possibly be restored to its former glory) and a few acres of land that have gone to seed, Ursula looks at her like she's a miracle worker.

Even more so when Persephone somehow magically pulls up pictures of the property and sends the owner an email, which they then reply to within seconds, clearly overjoyed that anyone would consider their property a suitable rental.

"The farmhouse is a quarter of the square footage of the manor, but you might be able to turn the barn into a distillery if you fix it up. And the basement could serve as a communal lab for Queenie and Ivy. And once the greenhouse is fixed..." Persephone is thinking how much work the rental is going to need. But at least it means the sisterhood won't experience homelessness.

Once Ursula crosses finding a new home off her list, she has to move on to the next item, which appears to be taking down and securing the oil portrait of that fabulous woman in the suit, who Ursula tells Persephone is Mirabelle, the woman who took them all in. And as Ursula sets about doing so, chatting with Mirabelle all the while, Persephone bids her and Ruby farewell,

Ruth Bader Ginsburg in reluctant tow, the dog clearly wanting to stay with Ruby.

Persephone finds Queenie and Ivy in Ivy's lab where she helps them book a moving van online. When she comments that the one they're ordering is too tiny to clear out even one of the manor's rooms, they smile and brush off her concerns, saying they have ways to alter space so that the rules of science no longer apply.

"Forget all that *No two objects can occupy the same space* nonsense," Queenie says before thanking Persephone for the help and turning back to her list that looks triple the length of anyone else's.

"About the Heka wand," Persephone ventures. "I was thinking I could spend today and tomorrow helping you find it."

"No," Queenie snaps, her expression suddenly stern. "Thank you, but you've already been a huge help with the move."

"I-I don't mind at all," Persephone stammers. "I really want to help. And tomorrow—"

"No!" Queenie's looking at her weirdly again. Like she can't decide whether to march Persephone off the property or hug her fiercely, holding on for dear life. "Tomorrow's going to be a sad day for us. It's probably best that we spend it alone, just the six of us."

"Okay, sure," Persephone says, trying not to sound as hurt as she feels that Queenie doesn't want her around.

The sound of porcelain shattering draws Persephone to the rage room. She spots Jezebel inside and is about to join her before she sees the tears that run in rivulets down the beautiful woman's face.

As Persephone furtively watches, Jezebel drops a plate with a clunk and walks over to a wall, nuzzling her forehead against it. Jezebel strokes the wall, whispering to it, and Persephone is jolted by the memory of her own leave-taking, of those last hours with her mother when she knew the end was near, when she'd resigned herself to the fact that the force of her love wouldn't be enough to keep her mother tethered to life.

Jezebel's grief is too similar to Persephone's, the kind she still hasn't quite come to grips with even after this past year, that she's unable to bear witness to it without falling apart herself.

And so she leaves, going in search of Tabitha which was her real reason for coming here today. As much as she's liked helping the witches, Persephone's had a niggling feeling that if she can just put all the pieces of the puzzle together, she can help them find the wand. The only thing she doesn't know is what happened the night Tabby died and Ruby got arrested. Perhaps those details are the key to unlocking everything.

It's harder to spot a ghost than you'd think. Persephone can't see Tabby like the witches can, so she's in search of an energy or temperature shift. It means she has to walk through each empty room multiple times, back and forth, as though walking a grid. Ruth Bader Ginsburg isn't much help: she trails Persephone, making it clear she wants to be picked up.

An hour later, Persephone's about to give up when she hears the crow's squawk coming from the library, which she searched quite thoroughly earlier without any luck.

"Over here, child," Widget rasps.

Persephone enters the library and can tell immediately just by the way Widget is focused on it that Tabby is sitting in the green leather armchair. The crow's head is twitching this way and that, her beak darting as though stitching the ghost to the air.

Widget speaks from a perch next to Tabby. "You seem quite determined to find me. You've come with questions, haven't you?"

Ruth Bader Ginsburg growls at the crow, quivering with excitement. Persephone shushes her, and the dog settles down, not taking her eyes off the bird.

Persephone isn't sure how to make eye contact with a ghost. And she doesn't want to guess wrong and be staring at the wrong thing. And so she turns to Widget who the conversation will be conducted through.

"You want to know about how I died." Widget's head is tilted to the side.

"Yes, but only if you're comfortable telling me."

Ruby and Ursula wander in just then, looking sweaty and disgruntled after having to wrestle the portrait from the wall to wrap it up. "So, this is where you've been, Tabby," Ursula says. "We've been looking for you everywhere." They each take a seat, Ursula looking from Tabby to Persephone expectantly. "What are you two talking about?"

Drawn by the voices, Queenie and Ivy, who are clutching clipboards, join them in the library, a sweaty and tear-streaked Jezebel trailing them.

"Another meeting?" Jezebel asks, rolling her eyes.

"The girl wants to know about the night I died," Widget squawks.

Ursula goes pale. "Perhaps that's a discussion for another time."

There's silence as Widget considers this. And then she speaks. "I'm tied to the manor because of what happened that night. And the manor will be no more in thirty-six hours when the wrecking ball arrives. Talking about it might help Ruby remember something about the wand. If nothing else, perhaps she'll remember that she's the reason I'm dead."

<u>Moonshyne Manor Grimoire</u>

Ivy's Elixir of Life
Smoothie for Seniors

Ingredients:

1 cup frozen cranberries
1 cup fresh or frozen mango
½ apple, peeled
½ tsp. freshly grated ginger
¼ tsp. ground cardamom
1 tsp. organic cinnamon powder
1 tbsp. cacao nibs
3 tbsp. hemp seeds
1 cup water

Equipment:

A smoothie blender
~~*A glass*~~
Jezebel's amendment: shot glasses

Instructions:

Combine the ingredients in a blender, and pulse until smooth. Pour into a glass and savor nature's bounty.

Jezebel's amendment: shot glasses and knock 'em back one by one like you're at a nightclub about to go wild on the dance floor.

49

Thirty-three years ago: the evening of the heist

It was close to ten o'clock on the night of the heist when Tabitha headed for the parlor through the mudroom entrance, Widget perched on her shoulder, and Klepto hanging from her back.

She set Klepto down upon the coffee table where he began capering around, thrilled to be allowed inside, and then she held out her hand to Widget who hopped onto it. Ferrying the crow up to her face, Tabby kissed her beak which incensed Klepto, who shrieked, arms outstretched.

"Don't be jealous, Klepto," Tabitha said, scooping him up with her free hand so she could balance him on her hip like a fractious toddler. "There's a lot of love to go around." She nuzzled the black spot at the top of the capuchin's head. "Good job tonight, even if you did go on a thieving spree."

"Widget's looking so much better after the tincture," Ivy

said as she arrived. "She's filled out quite a bit too. Is she talking yet?"

"Not yet," Tabby said, for once not too bothered by it. Queenie was right. Widget would speak when she had something to say. For now, it was enough to see her familiar looking so robust. "Thank you for being a miracle worker."

Ivy brushed off the compliment as Queenie arrived. Queenie had changed out of her heist pants and was back in her drab house robe, making Tabby second-guess donning her new polka-dot party robe with its ginormous shoulder pads. But then Jezebel and Ruby both swept in, similarly festively attired. Ruby was in a silver sequined gown, paired with silver stilettos, while Jezebel had matched her dress to her bright red lipstick.

Ruby was clutching a magnum of Veuve Clicquot in one hand and brandishing a large sword in the other. She looked around the room. "Where's Ursula?"

"I don't know," Tabitha replied. She'd last seen Ursula just over an hour after they'd gotten home. The phone had rung, and Ursula had dashed to answer it as Tabitha headed upstairs. "I'm sure she'll be down shortly."

Jezebel returned from the drinks cart, setting down six champagne flutes. "She'd better hurry before we finish all the bubbly."

"Did you know *Veuve* means *widow*?" Ruby asked, sliding the saber along the seam of the bottle to the lip. "The widow, Madame Clicquot, was the first woman to run a champagne house." She struck the lip with a theatrical flourish. The glass neck dramatically broke away with the cork, which shot off like a meteor, before it struck the roof and plummeted back down to the floor with a thunk. "It's a boy," Ruby cackled, as champagne gushed from the bottle's severed neck, Jezebel trying to get as much of the foam into the glasses as possible.

Tabby put Widget on her perch and released Klepto to explore the room. This kind of freedom wouldn't usually be allowed, but considering the monkey had played such a big role in the night's success, she figured he may as well benefit from everyone's gratitude.

Once they each had a glass of bubbly, Tabitha raised hers in Ruby's direction. "Here's to the Widow Clicquot and to Tony," she said, laughing, "who saved our asses."

The sisterhood followed her lead, raising their glasses and chorusing. "To Tony!"

Ruby blushed and smiled broadly, doing a small curtsy.

The women all sat down and over the next half an hour proceeded to go over the details of the heist at least a dozen times, rehashing the best parts and embellishing them with each retelling. The moment when Ruby tricked Queenie, Tabby and Jimmy into believing she was the other security guard was by far the most exciting bit, with the most ridiculous being Jezebel having to be rescued from her handcuffs.

But instead of being embarrassed by the incident, Jezebel was still glowing from what she claimed was some of the best sex of her life. "Don't knock having-sex-while-tied-up-during-a-heist until you've tried it," she'd said, winking lasciviously.

Queenie shook her head, obviously too amused by Jezebel's antics to be annoyed with her.

Tabitha was just beginning to worry about Ursula, wondering if she should head upstairs to check on her, when Ursula swept into the room, cheeks pink.

"Where have you been?" Ruby called, patting the empty spot next to her on the settee.

"I sat down for a minute and must have fallen asleep. I guess the excitement of the day got to me." Ursula sat, and Ruby leaned over to kiss her cheek, enveloping her in a hug before handing her a glass of champagne.

"It's a pity you have to wait twenty-two days until the full moon before you can work the spell," Tabby said to Ruby. "I'm sure you're eager to get on with it."

Ruby shrugged philosophically. "I've waited all this time. What's another three weeks?" And then she grimaced. "Besides, that spell is really complicated, and I used up a lot of my power tonight shape-shifting. It's probably going to take me a while to recover enough strength to be able to work it."

As though to prove Ruby's point, her face suddenly flickered on and off, like the power had gone out of it. One second she had her usual recognizable features, and then her face was a blank canvas. And then, instead of the pink-haired woman sitting across from Tabby, there was a middle-aged, auburn-haired man.

Ruby sighed and shrugged. "Only three more weeks of this to go!"

"What have you done with the artifact?" Queenie asked. "You don't want to leave something that valuable lying around." She shot a look at Klepto. "Not with old Sticky Fingers lurking about."

Klepto shrieked just then, and the women all turned to find him with his hand inside a vase, withdrawing a sterling silver punch ladle.

"See what I mean?" Queenie said. "Make sure he doesn't head to the nearest pawn shop to hock that."

"Klepto, leave it," Tabby said, shooting him a dark look so he'd know she wasn't messing around.

He dropped it, muttering all the while.

"Don't worry," Ruby said laughing, "I've hidden the Heka wand and the jewels somewhere only I can get to them. I'm not taking any chances—" A high-pitched trill silenced her.

Queenie checked her watch. "It's almost eleven. Who'd be calling now?"

Ursula quickly stood to go answer the phone. "Good evening. Moonshyne Manor." She listened, frowning, and then held out the phone. "It's for you, Ruby. It's Magnus."

Ruby's whole face lit up, a glow illuminating it from the

inside as though a sun was rising inside of her. She rushed to where Ursula stood, taking the receiver from her. "Magnus, darling—" Whatever she was going to say died in her throat. As Ruby listened, her brows shot up, knotting together. She looked to Tabitha and said, "We'll be right there."

"What is it?" Ursula asked, eyes wide, as Ruby slammed the receiver down.

Ruby ignored the question. "Tabby, get your vet's bag. Magnus's horses need our help." She then turned to Queenie. "Will you drive us there? Tabby hates flying."

"Of course," Queenie replied, "but what—"

"I don't think any of you should go," Ursula said as Tabby picked up Klepto and Widget, heading for the foyer.

"What?" Ruby demanded, disbelieving. "What are you talking about?"

"I have a feeling that something really bad is going to happen if you go." Ursula had risen and was blocking Ruby's way.

"Something bad *is* going to happen if we don't get there to help Magnus's poor stallions."

"No, something worse than the stallions." Ursula's voice was frantic now, pleading. "Please don't go."

"We have to!"

"No." Ursula was tugging on Ruby's arm.

Tabby didn't hear the rest of Ursula's entreaties as she turned onto the grand staircase, taking the steps two at a time on her way up to her room. Once she'd secured Klepto in a large cage—not ideal, but it would have to do until they got back and she could release him into the forest—Tabitha grabbed her bag of supplies. She ran through a mental checklist, ensuring she had everything, from anesthetic and sutures to antidotes and bronchodilators, as she headed out again.

The sixty-two breaths that she took as Ruby hustled them all out were the last Tabby would ever take in the manor.

50

Thirty-three years ago: the evening of the heist

Tabitha clutched her vet's tote bag in the passenger seat as the Caddy rocketed in reverse from the coach house. Widget let out a startled shriek from Tabby's shoulder, the bird's claws tightening so sharply that they bit through her shoulder pad.

As they shot backward down the dark driveway, Ursula yelled from the back, "Lights, Queenie! Switch on the lights."

Queenie flicked them on with a grunt, turning out into the road in a tight arc, before slamming to a stop, changing gears, and then accelerating again.

"Oh, please hurry," Ruby pleaded from next to Ursula.

"I'm going as fast as I can," Queenie replied, contradicting herself by then accelerating even more.

Tabby was grateful the top was up on the Caddy or else poor Widget might have been blown off her shoulder. "What's the emergency?"

"The horses all got sick suddenly. Magnus is frantic."

Tabby immediately discounted Potomac horse fever, since Magnus's property didn't border a creek or river, and thought equine herpesvirus unlikely since his horses hadn't traveled for shows or competitions recently. Magnus ran a stud farm, shipping his retired prize-winning stallions' frozen semen all over the world. Colic was a possibility if only one or two of them were sick, but that wouldn't explain all of them.

"He couldn't get hold of the county vet," Ruby added, "but knew you'd be able to help."

"We need to turn back," Ursula said. "Something terrible is going to happen. I just know it."

"For the love of the Goddess, Ursula," Ruby shouted. "Just shut it!"

As Queenie gunned it down the dark back roads to the farm, Tabitha thought that was probably a good thing since the county veterinarian, Vernon Cartwright, was an idiot. Tabby regularly butted heads with him at the very few conferences he deigned to attend, believing he'd learned everything he needed to know fifty years ago when he'd qualified and that there was nothing new he could be taught.

When they turned into Magnus's property, Queenie raced up the driveway, sending a spray of gravel flying in their wake as they bypassed the main house for the stables around the back.

Once they came to a stop, the women sprang from the car, and Widget took flight. As Ruby sprinted ahead of Tabby in her dazzling sequined party robe and festive high heels, Tabby registered Ruby's state. Despite the women's clothing, Ruby was still presenting as a man after her switch back during the celebration.

While this was something Tabby usually wouldn't have given a second thought to *inside* the manor, it was a completely different matter outside of it.

Tabby had never known Ruby to leave the manor presenting as a man. In all the time they'd known each other, if Ruby's powers failed her and she needed to leave the house, she'd dress in drag.

But tonight, with the surprise phone call and the urgency to get to the farm, Ruby must have forgotten what she looked like. And in all the commotion, Tabby had forgotten too.

As Ruby sprinted ahead of them, still the fastest of the women despite running in heels, Tabby saw Queenie's and Ursula's expressions change as they, too, noticed the problem. Ursula looked especially pale and clammy, like the realization made her feel sick.

Unlike with her other beaus, Ruby hadn't spoken to the women of the sisterhood much about Magnus. She'd gone on and on about how wonderful and gorgeous he was, how smart and kind, but she'd remained tight-lipped about the dynamics of their relationship.

While Tabby suspected things were serious between them, she doubted Ruby had confided her situation to Magnus, since it would mean admitting that she was a witch who had special powers, something the sisterhood has always agreed to keep secret so as to protect themselves.

And now, here Magnus was about to find out the truth, seeing Ruby as she really was, in a moment of high emotion and drama. Who knew how he might react, what he might do in shock? A man, thinking he'd been duped into having an ongoing relationship with what he saw as another man, could lash out in unexpected ways.

Tabby was just about to call out to Ruby to warn her when she saw it was already too late. Magnus, upon hearing Ruby calling his name, was striding from the stable. And Ruby was rushing to him with arms outstretched.

51

Thirty-three years ago: the evening of the heist

As Ursula watched Magnus and Ruby on their collision course, time slowed in a way that made her hyperaware of every single second unfolding. In that strange time warp, the moment did something wholly unexpected. It raised an axe above its head and brought it bearing down, three times in quick succession, cleaving the one Ursula into three distinct entities, much like she'd always cut the deck of her tarot cards into three separate piles.

The first Ursula, freed from the confines of her body, rose up into the night and hovered above their little clutch of key players as an objective observer who was able to see everything unfolding with a detached, almost clinical, air. This Ursula, who'd been a lifelong student of human nature—of its ridiculous follies and desperate yearnings, of its petty jealousies and stubborn pride—was interested to see how the drama might unfold and what it said about those involved.

The second Ursula cringed as the moment began playing out to its logical conclusion: a betrayed Magnus lashing out at the person who'd made a mockery of him. That same part of her wanted nothing more than to sweep the love of her life into her arms so as to spare Ruby the humiliation she was about to endure.

The second Ursula's hand was already reaching for her wand in case Magnus's reaction might manifest as violence. If it did, *that* Ursula would be honored to step in and protect Ruby. She was ready to prove her undying love in a grand gesture that could not be misunderstood as so many of her gestures had been in the past. That part of her was ready for the showdown and the moment of the truth. It would not let Magnus utter a word that might befoul Ruby's essence or detract from it in any way.

And then there was the third Ursula.

The scorned one. The one who'd been cast aside year after year after year, overlooked and taken for granted. She who'd given so selflessly—who'd loved so purely and unabashedly—and who now desperately wanted nothing more than for Ruby to feel as derided and contemptible as Ursula had for decades, ever since she'd first laid eyes on Ruby and fallen so desperately in love.

That third Ursula, that shadow one, stood rooted to the spot, wanting a front-row seat to Magnus's dismay and disgust. She needed to bear witness to his rejection of Ruby, which would prove once and for all that no one would ever love Ruby like Ursula did, that no one would ever understand Ruby like Ursula did, that no one would ever deserve Ruby's love as much as Ursula.

That Ursula wanted Ruby to be cut to the quick as punishment for everything Ruby had put her through. And to see Ruby break, because she'd chosen the wrong person when the right one had been there, by her side within arm's reach, all along.

It was all three of these Ursulas who circled the moment—either feeling nothing, feeling overly protective, or utterly vindictive—and who watched as Magnus spotted Ruby, stopping in his tracks with his mouth falling open. As Ruby tried to fling herself into his arms, he grabbed her, holding her at arm's length away from himself.

Ursula took a deep, shuddering breath as Magnus spoke.

"Ruby, darling, what happened? Are you quite all right?"

"I lost my powers earlier," Ruby said breathlessly. "It's a long story that I was planning to surprise you with. I'll tell you all about it later." She flapped her hand to show it didn't matter. "What happened with the horses?"

And then everything sped up, and Ursula was one person again, watching dumbfounded as Magnus drew Ruby in and kissed her forehead, clinging to her as though she were the most precious being in the world. And as he looked out over the top of Ruby's head for a second, what Ursula saw there was love. Absolute, unadulterated love. Which, of course, it couldn't be. Not after what she'd seen in the vision.

And then a frantic Magnus was leading them to the stables, speaking nonsensical words about suspected poisoning, and Tabby was pulling open her bag of antidotes. Time churned in a way that made Ursula feel sick to her stomach. She stood out of the way, her mind roiling with possible explanations, as Tabitha ran from one horse to the other, administering antidotes which she sprayed into their nostrils from what looked like an antique perfume bottle.

Ursula had no idea how much time had passed by the time the horses' mouths stopped foaming and their widened, panicked eyes grew calm. But eventually, they stopped rearing wildly on hind legs and bowed their heads to Tabby, listening as her frantic whispers of comfort became a gentle crooning of encouragement.

When Magnus's shoulders slumped with relief, it was over.

The horses were fine. Tabby had worked her usual magic. The deaths of seven beautiful stallions had been prevented.

But Ursula didn't understand what had happened. She couldn't grasp how everything had gone so spectacularly wrong. And then a woman's voice called for Magnus from outside the stables. Upon hearing it, Ursula was flooded with a sense of vindication, thanking the Goddess that the truth was about to be exposed and that Ruby was about to learn of Magnus's betrayal.

Magnus dropped his arm from around a heaving Tabby's shoulders and walked to the stable entrance where the woman—who was tall and slim, with her dyed blond hair cropped in a severe bob—stepped from the darkness.

She addressed Magnus. "Darling? Is everything all right?" The stranger was wearing a man's burgundy robe. As she looked from Magnus to Ruby, who'd joined him and was now clutching at his arm, the woman didn't need to ask who Ruby was when the question was so clearly etched on her face.

Ursula trembled, ready to swoop in and comfort Ruby when she learned the heartbreaking truth about the man who she'd given her heart to.

"It's better than all right," Magnus replied, voice graveled with emotion. "The horses have all been saved." And then he turned to Ruby, leading her forward. "Ruby, I want you to meet my twin, Caroline. Caro, this is my fiancée, Ruby."

Ruby flushed, suddenly self-conscious as she smoothed down her sequined robe that looked like it was awash with thousands of fireflies. She reached up, running a hand through her thinning red hair to tamp it down.

The woman looked startled for a moment, but then she smiled. Ursula was taken aback to realize that it was a true smile, not an ounce of guile or spite in it. "Ruby, I'm so happy to finally meet you."

"This isn't how I imagined it would happen," Ruby said.

"I'm not usually such a fright." She ran a hand over her jaw, all too aware now of the salt-and-pepper stubble.

"Nonsense," Caroline replied crisply. "You're as radiant as Magnus said you were."

As the two women embraced, Ursula stepped forward, intending to ask Magnus if she might use his telephone. A high-pitched wail suddenly pierced the night, and for a terrible moment, Ursula thought the awful sound was coming from the back of her own throat, a lament that would not be silenced. But then, the wailing continued, growing closer and louder, and bile rose up in Ursula's mouth to meet it.

52

Thirty-three years ago: the evening of the heist

Tabby's chest heaved from exertion. Having to rein in seven stallions without the help of halters or leads, all while dodging their flailing, had utterly depleted her. She'd needed to use both brute strength and her powers of zoopathy to try to calm them while, at the same time, trying to figure out where they were hurting so she knew which of Ivy's antidotes to administer.

Widget had helped immensely with that, the little crow's circling acting as a kind of triangulation for the echolocation Tabby's powers required. She was proud of her familiar and how helpful the bird had been, how intuitively she'd gone exactly where Tabitha needed her to be.

As Tabby stood hunched over, hands on knees, she closed her eyes and cast her sixth sense into the horses, one by one, as they slowly settled. She was gratified to feel their breathing ease and the fire in their blood cool. Their minds were calming and the pain in their bellies had dissipated. The antidote was working.

After reassuring herself that they would be fine, Tabby tried nudging herself deeper into their neurons, asking for permission to access their memories. Six of the stallions immediately blocked her, and respecting their wishes, Tabby retreated. One granted permission, letting her know he was gifting it out of respect for her powers.

As he opened up his recent experiences to her, what Tabby saw in them was Bart Gedney Jr.—slinking through the gloom from stall to stall, his weathered old face contorted with evil satisfaction—handing each horse a red apple that was just as shiny as his patent leather loafers.

And isn't that always the way? Tabitha thought grimly.

In all those fairy tales, children were cautioned against witches who might disguise themselves as ugly old women, ones who came bearing poisonous fruit in the guise of kindness. When in real life, the bad guys came in three-piece suits, not even bothering to pretend they were someone else. That's how confident they were that they'd get away with their misdeeds.

That son of a bastard, Tabby thought. *So that's what happens to those who refuse to sell up their land.* She wanted to call Queenie over to share what she'd discovered, but her head was throbbing too hard, the agony too acute to disturb with a flock of words.

As Tabby remained frozen, eyes still shut, she was distantly aware of Magnus's arm being thrown over her shoulders, followed by his sincere whispers of gratitude. After his arm fell away, the swell of conversation rose up around her. She was aware of it as a kind of excited buzzing, a swarm of rejoicing, which was then drowned out by a distant wailing that grew louder with every second.

In Tabby's spent state, she wasn't sure if the noise was out in the world or just in her head. She hoped for the latter so that it wouldn't spook the jittery horses even further. When she felt the animals' rising unease and understood the sound to be external, Tabby opened her eyes and stood, stretching the tension from her spine.

Widget swooped down from a rafter, settling on the perch of Tabby's shoulder pad. The crow quivered, as exhausted as her mistress. The wailing of sirens stopped abruptly, replaced by the slamming of doors and indistinct shouting. Flashing lights intruded upon the night, painting the scene in surreal splashes of blue and red.

Tabby made her way toward the commotion with the sensation that she was sleepwalking into someone else's dream. Ruby's dress was lit up like a disco ball, flinging shards of light as though throwing confetti at a wedding. It made Tabitha think there might be a real wedding soon with Ruby as the sisterhood's first bride. The thought made her smile with how right that would be, how utterly fitting.

"Put your hands up!"

Hearing the words, Tabby had the overwhelming urge to laugh. It was a command she'd gone fifty years without ever hearing once, and then, there it was, three times in one night. What were the chances?

It was impossible to discern who'd uttered the amplified instruction because of everyone blocking Tabby's view of the stable's exit. Plus, there were all those headlights, boring straight into her dilated pupils, blinding her while viciously poking at her headache.

Tabby watched, mesmerized, as the five silhouettes in front of her raised their arms in unison. The way their hands and fingers floated above their heads in the light strangely reminded Tabby of the anemones she'd studied while doing night dives in the Great Barrier Reef ten years before.

That got her thinking about that big Australian, Shane, the marine biologist she'd met during that trip, the one who she'd had such a big crush on. She could never think of him without a tinge of regret. It was a feeling she'd become quite companionable with, just as one never quite minds being attached to one's shadow. But, for some reason right now, regret made her feel prickly. And she realized she was sick of its tiresome company.

Tabby decided right then and there that she was going to go back to Australia to see what had happened to Shane. And if he was still free, and still interested, she wasn't going to push him away again. This time, she was going to let him kiss her—hell, she was going to *beg* him to kiss her, and she was going to wrap her arms around his burly barrel of a chest and ask him to whisper sweet nothings to her in that ridiculous accent of his—because what she was suddenly hyperaware of was that life was short, too short, a mere blink of the universe's eye.

And no sooner had Tabby made her mind up about it when she drew up alongside everyone. Magnus and Ruby were to the left of her. Queenie, Ursula and a strange woman she didn't recognize were to the right. Holding up a hand to shield her eyes, Tabby saw what looked, ridiculously, like six police officers with their guns trained on them.

And then it dawned on her. The police knew about the heist. Klepto's theft of the jewels must have given them away, and now here they were to arrest them for it. Except, the cops were motioning to Magnus with their guns, calling *his* name, and telling him to step forward away from the women.

But that was all wrong. Magnus had nothing to do with it, and someone had to tell them that.

As Magnus began taking slow strides toward the police vehicles, Ruby drew her wand and pointed it at him, probably to cast a protective shield. Tabitha stepped forward, reaching for her own wand while calling out to get the cops' attention so that they'd stop pointing their weapons at an innocent Magnus.

The first bullet took Tabby by surprise because it was such an affront, almost like a display of awfully bad manners. As it seared its way through the air just past Tabitha's ear, she was convinced that its existence was a terrible mistake, the result of a weapon accidentally discharging.

The second and third bullets punctuated the sentence of the first, making its meaning clear. The fourth bullet found Tabby's chest. There could be no misunderstanding that.

She fell, the kind of falling she'd last done as a child, head thrown back, eyes skyward, arms splayed, a reckless sprawling backward, submitting to gravity's supreme reign over a body. Her breath was snatched away as she hit the gravel; it was replaced by the kind of searing heat she'd so recently relieved the stallions of.

Turning her head to her left, Tabby witnessed a world tilted on its axis. Flashes of green light were erupting from Ruby's wand so that its tip resembled the cops' weapons. And then Magnus was running back to Ruby, throwing himself over her.

Tabby blinked, everything going hazy. When she opened her eyes again, it took a moment to make sense of the crumpled heap lying next to her.

There were too many arms and legs. She blinked again to clear her blurry vision. This time, Tabby could make out Magnus, who was collapsed over Ruby, a human shield. A hideous red stain was spreading rapidly across his back, dripping down onto Ruby's dress.

Turning slowly to the right, Tabby saw that the stranger had thrown herself down, trying to protect her head with her arms. She was shrieking something unintelligible, an animalistic sound of pure terror. Ursula was crouched low, pointing her wand past Tabby while muttering an incantation. From the green flares that emanated from the wand, Tabby could tell it was a protective shield, the same kind that Ruby had just tried to conjure.

Ursula half stood, raising her wand skyward, shouting, *"Gravis periculumis."*

As silvery-red sparks erupted from its tip, Tabitha felt the sisterhood's alarm as fine sand pouring through an hourglass, time relentlessly passing, never to be reclaimed.

Movement caught Tabby's eye, and she spotted Queenie crawling toward her on hands and knees. Queenie paused, paralyzed by the alarm. She looked panic-stricken, which was curious, since Tabby had never seen that particular expression on her friend's face before. Wasn't that the most peculiar thing? How you could know someone almost all your life and yet they could still surprise you?

Tabby angled her gaze heavenward, but instead of the stars what she saw was the moon of Queenie's face. She was mouthing something Tabby couldn't hear, but that didn't matter. She could taste everything Queenie was saying through her tears, which were dripping down onto Tabby's lips, anointing them.

And then the strangest thing happened.

Queenie reared back as Widget dive-bombed her. And then Widget was upon Tabby's sternum, her little head nestling into the part of Tabby's chest where the pain radiated from. The burning began to ease, and the darkness was bleached into a brilliant whiteness.

What Tabitha saw then, in those last moments, was something she'd never allowed herself to think about, the night both of her parents died, killed by one of the exotic animals they'd spent a lifetime abusing and exploiting as they profited from their smuggling.

Was it a cruel twist of fate, or karmic justice, that had given two such terrible people a child who could feel the pain of animals and who was therefore forced to endure every single injustice the creatures experienced at her parents' hands? Tabby didn't know.

All she knew was that as a child she'd been just as helpless as the hundreds of beasts that had passed through her parents' black-market business. The animals had all been mistreated and neglected, provided with only enough care to keep them alive, so that they could be sold to the highest bidders.

Which was why what she'd felt most was relief on the night a Bengal tigress, smuggled from India, had slipped free of her cage, which an eight-year-old Tabitha had been charged with securing. The mauling was terrible, but the price exacted was more than a fair one: two human lives in exchange for the lives of hundreds of animals.

After Tabby freed all the beasts from their cages, she picked up the falcizard egg and began walking, following the tigress for miles and miles to a place where she promised Tabitha safety. It was during that walk that Tabby resolved to dedicate her life to the care of animals, each breath of it serving as an atonement for the unforgivable harm her parents had done.

The violence of that night had robbed Tabby of words for the next two years. What were the use of them when the only ones she wanted to utter over and over again were *I'm sorry, I'm sorry, I'm sorry,* a lament to all the creatures she'd let down. What right did Tabby have to a voice when she hadn't been able to protect the voiceless?

As Tabby took her last breaths, the crow peered down at her, the marbles of Widget's inky eyes like twin galaxies above a dying Tabby. "You have been our voice for so long," Widget rasped, "and now I will be yours."

Finally, just like that, little Widget had something to say.

Moonshyne Manor Grimoire

Tabitha's Falcizard Dewormer and Tonic

Ingredients:

½ cup whole cloves
1 cup anise seed powder
1 cup black walnut hull powder
1 cup cayenne pepper powder
1 cup cinnamon powder
1 cup minced garlic
1 cup gingerroot powder
1 cup mustard seed powder
1 cup psyllium seed powder
1 cup rosemary leaf powder
2 cups sage leaf
2 cups thyme leaf
2 cups wormwood
1 gallon unicorn urine

Equipment:

A large cauldron

Instructions:

Mix all ingredients together in the large cauldron and bring to the boil. Let simmer for as long as it takes to read Thelma by Marie Corelli. Store in a cool, dark place. Administer to falcizards for 7 days, morning and evening, every 6–8 weeks and as needed.

Keep first-aid kit handy as the creatures do not enjoy the taste and are likely to express their displeasure.

Do not administer to any other animals or humans.

53

Saturday, October 30
Evening: twenty-eight hours left

By the time Widget has cawed the last of Tabby's memories, with Ursula and Queenie filling in some of the blanks, the crow's voice is hoarse. Widget has spoken more in the past half an hour than Ursula has heard the crow say in her entire lifetime.

There's a stunned silence, and then Queenie says, "It was Brad's father, Bart Gedney Jr., who poisoned the horses?"

Tabby nods, looking dazed. "I only just remembered," Widget says for her.

"That son of a bastard." Queenie's furious. "Three generations of Gedney men coming for us, so desperate for our land, and our neighbors' land, that they're prepared to kill and terrorize to get it!" Queenie looks like she's just getting warmed up, but as she's about to launch into another tirade, she spots Ruby, and her diatribe stalls.

Tears drip from Ruby's face. She's whispering something over and over again, whimpering as she rocks back and forth, clutching at herself. "Magnus. Oh, my darling, darling Magnus." Ruby hiccups, the grief so all-encompassing that it's manifesting as a physical expression, each hiccup sending shockwaves through Ruby's small frame.

And suddenly, Ursula can't stand it anymore. She's swallowed guilt like a self-prescribed poison, day after day for over three decades, never suspecting that it was the kind of beast, that once consumed, would begin to devour you in return.

Ursula lost Ruby after Ruby's arrest, but not wanting to accept that, Ursula told herself that they would find their way back to each other once Ruby was released from prison.

But Ruby will never return from prison. *Someone* has, but it's not the Ruby who Ursula's been waiting for. *That* Ruby has disappeared into herself, so deep inside the maze that she might never find her way back again.

Perhaps speaking the truth will be the equivalent of sending a flare up, because what Ursula realizes is that if Ruby has lost herself, then only the sisterhood can find her. They are the living libraries of Ruby's memories. They are the cartographers who helped draw up the maps detailing the landscape of Ruby's soul. If Ruby can't remember who she is, if she's lost her very Rubyness, then the sisterhood can remember *for* her; they can resurrect her through their recollections.

They have all borne witness to each other's lives for more than seven decades. In that time, they've experienced all of one other's heartbreaks and triumphs, their joys and disappointments. They've bickered and cajoled, apologized and compromised, pleaded and granted forgiveness.

What they will do now is remember, remember it all together, even the shameful parts. *Especially* the shameful parts.

Because the time for a reckoning will always come, won't it? Whether on earth or in an afterlife, there comes a time when the good we've done in the world needs to be weighed against the harm we've inflicted. Scores must be tallied. Hands must be shown. Bluffs must be called.

Ursula is ready for her moment of truth. Her only regret is that she's kept her secret for as long as she has.

She takes a shuddering breath and then whispers, "It was all my fault. Tabby and Magnus died because of me."

Her statement is met with blank stares, everyone taken aback by her declaration.

Ivy recovers first. "Whatever do you mean?" And then seeing Ursula's grave expression, Ivy whispers, almost too horrified to get the words out, "What did you do, Ursula?"

Her question conjures up a steady trickle of words in what was once a dry riverbed of a mouth. Ursula inhales deeply and then begins to speak. "At Tabitha's fiftieth birthday party, when I read Magnus's palm, I saw that he'd asked Ruby to marry him."

The women all gasp, turning to Ruby to check if that's true. When they realize she probably won't be able to verify it, they reluctantly turn back to Ursula.

But Ruby surprises them by saying, "And I said *yes*. We were engaged, but we didn't want to steal Tabitha's thunder by announcing it at the party."

Ursula goes on to tell them how, after they all returned from the heist, she'd answered a call from Magnus who wanted to chat with Ruby. As Ursula spoke with him, a vision came to her of the woman he was with, his lover right there by his side! The audacity of it took Ursula's breath away.

"How was I supposed to know it was his sister?" Ursula pleads with the women now, turning to look each of them in the eye. "I thought it was someone he was messing around with, that he was brazen enough to call Ruby with his lover sitting right next to him in his home."

Queenie has closed her eyes, as though she's trying to escape into prayer or meditation. The purple bracelet on her wrist burns brighter than it has before, its light intensifying hour upon hour. Ivy shakes her head, a slow and steady denial, a willful refusal to believe what she's hearing. Jezebel is frozen, like she's too stunned to move. Tabitha listens closely, understanding dawning on her face. Widget sways from foot to foot as Persephone stares at Ursula, the girl tugging insistently at a white curl while stroking her dog.

The manor itself is listening now. Ursula can feel it. How the walls have become more attentive, how the creaks and groans have gone quiet as the house takes it all in.

"I didn't want Ruby to marry a scoundrel," Ursula says, an entreaty for them to understand. "So I made a decision that I thought would save Ruby from having her heart broken *and* that would keep her with us. Where she belonged."

It's Queenie who puts two and two together. "The third necklace," she says, opening her eyes and nodding as though it all makes sense now. "I saw three necklaces when we arrived home and discovered what Klepto had done. But when Ruby took everything from the bag to go and hide it, she only saw two. I thought she was just confused, but she wasn't. You took the third necklace, didn't you?"

"And then you planted it at Magnus's house before phoning the cops to tip them off about the museum heist," Widget caws.

Ursula flushes to hear her deceit laid so bare. Hearing the truth of your actions, without the justification of the motivations that led to them, is like having your corpse picked clean by vultures. There's nowhere to hide. "While all the rest of you were getting ready for the festivities," Ursula says, "I flew to Magnus's house and crept inside while he and who I *thought* was his lover were distracted. I planted the necklace in a hiding place, and then I came home and made an anonymous call to the police. That's why I was late to the celebrations."

Jezebel groans, covering her ears like a child who doesn't

want to hear the kinds of gruesome tales that will keep her up at night. Ruby has gone still, her face like a book scrubbed clean of all its words, and that's who Ursula appeals to now. "I just thought Magnus would be arrested and put in jail for a few months. Months. I wanted him punished for what I thought he'd done to you, Ruby. I didn't mean for any of the rest of it to happen."

"That's why you told us you had a bad feeling about going to Magnus's place," Queenie says. "Because you *knew* the cops would be arriving at the stables any minute."

"How could I possibly have known that Bart Gedney Jr. had also made an offer on Magnus's place and that he'd poison Magnus's horses in retaliation for being turned down? I tried to stop you from going," Ursula says, sounding whiny even to her own ears. "Over and over, I asked you not to go, but you wouldn't listen."

"But instead of unmasking Magnus as a lying cheat, you realized the woman was his sister," Ivy says. "And yet you didn't do anything to correct your mistake."

"That's not true!" Ursula insists. "I was just about to go and call the police and tell them I, as the anonymous informant, was mistaken, but that's exactly when they arrived, sirens wailing." Ursula shakes her head, regret weighing down every word so that they drop like stones from her mouth. "How could I predict that Ruby and Tabby would pull their wands, and the police would mistake them for guns?"

"Yes," Queenie says bitterly. "How could you, as a white woman, know what would happen to a witch drawing her wand while Black? Both of them drew their wands, but notice which one they shot?"

Ursula winces. "I tried to conjure protective shields to stop anyone from getting hurt."

"No, you cast *a* protective shield for Ruby," Widget caws.

"It's impossible to cast multiple protective shields at once,"

Ursula says, defensively. "And you were already shot, Tabby. It was too late to protect you. I was trying to limit the fallout."

The statement hangs in the air, everyone recognizing it for the lie it is. Had Tabby not been shot yet, the person Ursula would have chosen to protect would still have been Ruby.

"But," Queenie says, trying to figure it out, "the cops never found anything on Magnus's property. They accused Ruby of being in cahoots with Magnus and said the two of them fired at them Bonnie and Clyde–style." Queenie looks at Persephone, explaining, "There were even some tabloid articles, like the one you saw, that claimed Ruby killed Magnus, Tabby and the police officer, when it was actually the police who shot and killed Tabby and Magnus." Queenie turns back to Ursula. "But they never wrote anything about the necklace or the heist because they never found anything."

Before Ursula can reply, Ivy puts the missing puzzle pieces into place. "During the confusion of the arrest and the ambulances, as Jezebel and I came rushing in response to your alarm, you snuck into the main house and took the necklace back, didn't you?"

Ursula wrings her hands. "I didn't want them to have anything they could use against Ruby during her trial."

"But she accidentally killed a police officer while trying to protect Magnus." Queenie speaks slowly as though trying to explain something to a child. "It doesn't matter what they found. She was always going to be sent away for a long time."

It's Jezebel who speaks up now. "That's where you got the fifty grand from, isn't it? You sold the necklace in town." And then she shakes her head. "It wasn't your savings you wanted us to have. It was blood money to assuage your own guilt."

Ursula's been telling herself all this time that she had the best intentions and only acted the way she did to protect Ruby. But the truth is that Ursula was acting in her own self-interest. A decision made on impulse, fueled by her own jealousy, led to the death of the woman she loved as well as that woman's fiancé.

There's no excusing that. Perhaps there's no forgiving it, either.

Ursula feels the weight of the sisterhood's judgment, but she can't process it all at once. For now, she turns to Ruby. "Ruby, I—"

But Ruby is no longer fully in this moment or the one in the past. Ursula can see it by how Ruby's vacant eyes are staring into a reality Ursula is no longer a part of. She can't decide if it's a mercy or a curse that the person she most wants absolution from can't ever grant it, not truly.

Ursula turns to Tabby, wanting to apologize wholeheartedly and sincerely for what she did. It's far too little, far too late, but there's a reason why that old adage *better late than never* holds true.

Late means that there was, at least, a reckoning. There was a moment in which a person stared into the darkest recesses of their psyches, at the monster that hides under the bed of themselves, and instead of closing their eyes to it—hoping, like a child would, that it would simply go away—challenged it to a duel.

But before Ursula can speak, Tabby holds up her hand and Widget caws, "I don't want to hear it."

Just like that, the sisters stand one by one, leaving Ursula, none of them sparing her a backward glance as they head out of the library. It's Jezebel who helps Ruby to her feet, ushering her out of the presence of the Judas who so thoroughly betrayed her. Widget flies ahead of Tabitha, an invisible umbilical cord tying the two together.

Ursula feels as though an arctic wind is howling through her soul. If they weren't losing the house, at least the sameness of the days ahead might allow her the hope that the sisterhood's forgiveness could eventually be possible. But at this point, will they even let Ursula come with them?

Persephone is the last one left in the room. Ursula can't tell if it's from politeness or awkwardness or something else entirely. When the white-haired girl finally stands and walks over, Ursula stiffens. She's unsure what to expect when an onslaught is what she deserves.

Persephone stands on tippy-toes and reaches out, hugging Ursula tightly before she, too, leaves, trailed by her little dog.

The manor heaves a sigh of disappointment. Ursula has never felt so alone.

54

Sunday, October 31
Evening: seven hours left

It's the sisterhood's last night in the manor. By midnight, the property will no longer rightfully be theirs, and the wrecking ball arrives at nine tomorrow morning. But what Queenie finds even more inconceivable than that is that they're all spending this last night apart, all the witches having withdrawn to their own rooms, like battered boxers retreating to their corners after a particularly brutal round.

Since Ursula's astounding confession, a pall has hung over the manor, an emotional smog that refuses to lift. Queenie considers calling a final meeting since it's All Hallows' Eve, a powerful magical night when they should be in the forest, observing their sacred rituals and paying tribute to the Goddess.

But she quickly dismisses the thought. The injured need time alone to lick their wounds; if nothing else, Tabby's creatures have taught Queenie that. And forcing the sisters out of the womb of the house into the increasingly hostile woods—where Tabby's creatures have become almost feral in her absence—feels like a callous thing to do, especially since it will leave Tabby alone, the one sister who most desperately wants to be in the forest. They may all be apart, but they're still under the same roof. Queenie thinks that has to count for something.

The manor is drafty, its most precious contents already removed. Queenie and Ivy oversaw the last packing up of it this afternoon, ensuring the items with the most sentimental value all magically fit into the tiny moving van parked outside.

As Queenie walks its hallways now from bedroom to bedroom—a lonely sentry whose job it is to ensure that all is well—her footsteps echo like gentle chastisements. Dust and cobwebs—survivors of the great cleanup operation before Ruby's arrival home—have been exposed. What remains is mostly watermarks and mold, sun-bleached wallpaper and scuffed wood, the manor's battle scars dating back to a time before the sisterhood lived within its bosom.

"I'm sorry, old girl," Queenie murmurs, running her hand along the hallway wall on the third floor. "You deserve so much better than this."

She doesn't set the sconces blazing as she usually would, thinking it a kindness to allow the house to be seen this last night in a more flattering light. But despite Queenie's good intentions, the pulsing light of her bracelet is getting brighter and hotter by the minute. It illuminates the shadows as it burns against her skin, a brand to remind her that she sold her soul to the devil.

And that he's coming to take delivery of it in five hours' time.

Queenie thought she'd be more unsettled about it than she is. Perhaps it's reaching this ripe old age that's given her some perspective. When you're young, you think you're never going to die, but it's actually a miracle Queenie's made it this far, considering her penchant for making things explode. She's certainly been luckier than her parents were.

Those on death row are granted a favorite last meal, something to help swallow all that regret, making it more palatable. But Queenie has very few regrets. Beyond wishing that she could have saved the manor for the sisterhood, there's nothing else she would've done differently. Her last few hours will be spent not ticking items off a bucket list but continuing to try to keep them all together. That's all she wants now. That and to save Persephone from Charon.

Queenie pauses at Jezebel's closed door. She expects to hear sounds of wild coupling like she did last night after Jezebel snuck in a young buck. That's how Jezebel deals with most of life's knocks—or by throwing things (but aren't they almost the same thing? Throwing a plate against a wall and throwing a body against another?).

But instead, what Queenie's greeted with is the murmur of voices, Jezebel's and Ruby's. Queenie smiles to think that two of the sisters aren't alone after all and that Jezebel is with someone who can nourish her soul rather than just her flesh.

When she reaches Ursula's door, Queenie considers turning and heading back the way she came. There are too many emotions playing a game of tug of war inside her: fury and hurt, sorrow and dismay. There's a part of her that wants to banish Ursula, to tell her she's no longer part of the sisterhood.

But that's the betrayal speaking.

You don't stop being someone's family just because your sister behaves in a way that's bewildering to you. That's what makes them family, the ties that exist and can't ever be severed, even if you sometimes want to take a chain saw to them.

Besides, didn't Queenie always suspect there would come a time when a reckoning was inevitable? If hell hath no fury like a woman scorned, then Hades knows no havoc like that wrought by a woman tipped over the edge of reason by her own jealousy. Queenie and Ivy have always been in agreement that love makes people unpredictable and, therefore, dangerous.

And so Queenie leans in, ear to the door. She's not sure what she expects to hear, weeping or pacing, the distinctive snap of tarot cards being laid down. She rears back when a song begins playing, coaxed from the record by the gramophone's needle. Ursula must have retrieved it after Queenie packed it. The tune is Fats Waller's "It's a Sin to Tell a Lie," the first song Ursula ever played to cheer Ruby up just after her arrival at the manor so that she could turn back into a girl.

Queenie shakes her head grimly at the irony. If that wasn't a hint of what was to come, some kind of foreshadowing of future events, then she doesn't know what is. The universe can't be accused of not having a dark sense of humor.

After taking the west-wing stairs down to the second floor, Queenie knows not to bother to head for Ivy's room, with its tree-house bed built into a large oak that Ivy conjured to grow indoors. Ivy will, of course, be in her greenhouse, saying goodbye to her plants, hardly any of which they can take with them.

Ivy packed as many seeds and cuttings as she could, determined to begin another greenhouse at the new rental property that Persephone helped them find, but Queenie is aware of how devastated Ivy is to not only leave the plants she's spent a lifetime growing but also knowing they'll all be destroyed by the wrecking ball.

Queenie can't bear to witness Ivy's sorrow, especially knowing it was her own ineptitude that has led to Ivy losing what she considers to be her children. And so she doesn't pause in the conservatory's doorway. Instead, she takes the grand staircase down to the library, needing to talk with Tabby.

But when Queenie finds her old friend seated in there, forehead bent toward Widget's, trying to feel the contact of her familiar, words fail her completely. Instead, she's horrified to discover tears welling up, bursting their banks, and overflowing before she's able to stop them.

They're so self-indulgent that Queenie tries to shove the tears back into their ducts, telling herself she doesn't deserve to cry. She can't stand people who feel sorry for themselves, especially when they've brought whatever catastrophe down upon their own heads, making them less victims than perpetrators of their own suffering.

"Come in, Queenie," Widget rasps, distracting Queenie from her self-flagellation.

Queenie enters the library and sits across from Tabby. It feels strange being in here with so many of the books and parchments gone. The room is like a mouth missing most of its teeth.

"What is it?" Widget asks, head cocked.

"I wanted you to know that I'm heading down to the lab. I'll be spending the next few hours working on a device that might enable us to take you with us tomorrow," Queenie says. "Persephone gave me the idea after she told me about some contraption called a proton pack used in a movie called *Ghostbusters*." She smiles, not wanting to give Tabby false hope but also needing her to know that Queenie is doing her best to save Tabby and keep the sisterhood together. "Will you come down later and let me test it?"

"I appreciate it," Widget caws, "but I'd prefer you didn't."

"What?" Queenie cries. "Why?"

"I can't be in this limbo anymore, Queenie. I have no idea why I'm stuck here or what's holding me back, but I want to move on," Widget translates for Tabby. "If I don't have the manor walls keeping me in anymore, there's always the chance I'll be released."

Released to what? Queenie wonders. *What if it doesn't work and you're just stuck in the rubble? Or, worse, confined to haunting Men's World forever?* But these aren't thoughts she can share with Tabby.

She tries to mask her own pessimism by saying, "You might just have some company on that journey."

"What do you mean?" Widget asks.

And so, Queenie tells Tabby about Charon, the price he's demanded for the failure to deliver the Heka Wand of Isis and what she's planning to offer up instead of Persephone. "I know he wants youth, but I can offer him decades of magical experience which, if freely given, is more powerful than something taken." She takes a deep breath and then adds, "I'm also going to offer him the Moonshyne Manor Grimoire."

A sisterhood's grimoire is their most prized possession, and it's not something another witch or wizard can steal. It can only be used if given voluntarily. While the sisterhood will feel its loss greatly, it's not as if they have daughters who they're saving it to hand down to. After their deaths, the grimoire will go to waste anyway; it will probably be tossed away by some clueless bureaucrat who will be tasked with clearing out their rental property to make space for the next tenants.

"I'm really hoping the grimoire will sweeten the deal," Queenie says.

There's not much that she's grateful for right now, but one biggie is that Persephone is safe at home with her father. The Ferryman can't take Persephone from her own house: she'd have to be here at midnight with the witches in order for the transaction to take place. That's not to say he can't go after Persephone there, but it will make it harder, bringing attention to Charon and the magical world in the process. Queenie hopes Persephone's absence will further encourage Charon to accept her counteroffer.

"If you give your soul to Charon," Widget says, "it won't be coming with me anywhere. It will be going with him to work whatever dark magic he needs you for."

"I know," Queenie says weakly. The only way she can go through with it is not to think about it.

There's a sound from the foyer, a creak that distracts Queenie. She's about to stand and investigate when Widget says, "I can't stop thinking about what Ruby said about the fire."

"Me too," Queenie says glumly. Trying to solve the mystery is infuriating, like trying to scratch an itch that keeps moving just out of reach. "Everything that gives off a flame has been checked multiple times—"

"Wait!" Widget croaks, her voice charged with excitement. "What about the bilious room?"

Queenie's jaw drops. "The pyramid stove in the bilious room!" Why didn't she think of it before? Ruby, being the superior bilious player, is the only one who can open the pyramid since it's the winning goal that releases the flaming crown.

She's about to stand and head straight there when there's a banging at the door. If Brad Gedney and the wrecking ball have come early, Queenie is prepared to use magical force to stop them, and to hell with the consequences. The banging comes again, louder this time, so that it feels like it's pounding against her head. Queenie stands and marches to the door, reaching for her wand. The others dribble down the stairs behind her, summoned by the noise.

When Queenie flings open the double doors, she isn't surprised to find Brad Gedney on their doorstep. What's a shock is seeing Ruby standing next to him, his arm interlinked through hers, an expression of terror on her face. An even bigger shock is seeing Brad brandishing a wand.

55

Sunday, October 31
Evening: six and a half hours left

Brad Gedney is enormously gratified by how Queenie stands gaping at the strange tableau he and Ruby make.

Ivy races down the last few steps of the grand stairway. "What's the meaning of this?" she demands. "Release her immediately." Ivy's wand is in her hand, and her swollen knuckles are white with the force of her grip.

When Brad doesn't obey, Ivy raises her wand and shoots off a hex. Though it's directed at him, it's Ruby who lets out a cry of pain when the spell lands.

"Cousin Ivy," Brad says, stepping across the threshold, pulling a squealing Ruby along with him, "I'd suggest you drop the wand. Same goes for all of you." He looks from one woman to the next.

Queenie, clearly thinking that Ivy's aim was off, raises her own wand and fires off another spell. Once again, it deflects off Brad and hits Ruby, making her writhe in pain.

"As you can see," Brad says, "I've worked a spell that means any harm you try to do me will hurt Ruby instead."

Queenie's hand flies to her mouth, and she winces. Ivy looks furious but is helpless to do anything about it.

Brad is careful not to meet Jezebel's eyes for too long; he knows about her powers of seduction and needs to guard against giving in to them. She is undeniably a most enchanting woman, a vixen who could addle a man's brain.

He smiles when he spots Tabitha, letting his gaze settle upon her. "I'm sure you don't want *another* of your friends meeting a fatal accident," he says, winking.

Tabitha glowers back.

"Where's that familiar of yours?" he asks, knowing that Tabitha can conjure magic through it without using a wand.

"She's out hunting," Queenie replies on Tabitha's behalf.

"Crows don't hunt at night," Brad says. "They're defenseless after dark."

"This one does. And she's not defenseless. She'll be in the forest where she'll have backup." Queenie looks pointedly at his scar, as though she's figured out where he got it.

"What's that on your wrist?" Brad asks, distracted by the pulsating purple light. He's never seen anything like it, and it makes him nervous. There's so much about magic that he doesn't know and hasn't been able to learn. It's just one of the many things he resents them all for.

"Witchy jewelry," Queenie replies. "I can conjure one for you, though you don't strike me as a man who likes old-lady bling."

"Nice try," he says, recognizing a trap when he sees one.

Brad tightens his grip on a squirming Ruby, revolted by touching her. He's repulsed by her advanced age, by her helplessness and disorientation, by her ridiculous gender confusion—an affliction he associates with millennials and Zoomers, who think it's cool not be able to reach a fucking decision about whether they're men or women—and he's also disgusted by how utterly trusting she's been of him.

He sees Queenie eyeing his wand with a puzzled expression, and he answers her unasked question. "Ruby gifted it to me since we're engaged, apparently," he says, snorting at the ridiculousness of it. "She gave it to me when she came out to meet me the night after she arrived back home. You didn't do a great job of keeping an eye on her, did you?"

As Queenie balks, Brad grins and muses how it serves the interfering bitch right, thinking she had everything under control. She did a good job of running the distillery despite all the breakdowns and issues he created, he'll give her that. But she rated herself too highly, thought she could manage everything by herself like some kind of stupid girl boss.

"I'll give you all three seconds to drop your wands," Brad says, "after which I can't promise Ruby will still be alive if you don't."

Ivy reluctantly drops hers. It's quickly joined by Jezebel's and Ursula's wands. Queenie is the last to add hers to the small pile on the floor; it clatters with finality as it hits the wood.

Brad mutters an incantation, and the wands erupt into flames, kindling for a sulfurous black fire that quickly burns itself out. At the sight of Ivy's stony expression, he laughs. "What, dear cousin? Did you think you were the only person in the family with magical powers?"

"Your father and grandfather were magic-deficient," Ivy says tersely. "I thought you came from similar stock."

"She thought you fired blanks like the rest of the men in your family," Queenie says, goading him.

Brad ensures he's calm, almost meditative, when he replies. "It's true. They were both weak men, unable to summon any power at all, but my own immense powers have more than made up for it. It's like they were lying dormant, generation after generation, until they could find a strong-enough lightning rod."

His father and grandfather were unable to take on the sisterhood, first when they were just a gaggle of girls and then when they were middle-aged biddies. But he's not. The fight ends here. This Gedney will be the victor. And the Men's World development he'll be making millions from is just the icing on the cake. Avenging his family for the theft of a legacy that was rightfully theirs is the first prize.

Brad looks around the foyer and beyond. The manor and grounds should have been left to his grandfather, not to Mirabelle, and certainly not to Ivy after her. It's because Mirabelle used sorcery to make her grandmother favor her that his grandfather hated all kinds of magic, passing that hatred down to Brad's father, who wasn't pleased when he discovered his only son was a wizard.

Bart Jr. tried to beat it out of Brad, thanks to Ivy and her coven. But look at him now, doing what the old bastards couldn't do, and doing it all by himself. Not like Ivy, who had all of Mirabelle's magical tutelage and support, and yet who was still stupid enough just now to give up her wand.

"Enough chitchat," Brad says. "As fun as it is to catch up on the family news, I'm here for the Heka Wand of Isis you stole during the heist."

Ursula gasps.

"What wand?" Jezebel asks, face full of innocence. *Trust a harlot to manage to look that angelic.* "Stolen in what heist?"

Brad feels a stirring in his loins which he has to resist the pull of. "Cut the crap. I was there that night. I saw everything." When Jezebel looks dubious, he adds, "Young man standing just outside the museum entrance? Hat pulled down low? Reading a newspaper. Ring a bell?"

Ivy gapes at him in growing realization. "That was you?" She does a quick calculation. "You were what? Eighteen then?"

She shakes her head, agitated. "How did you know what we were planning?"

"I know a lot of things," Brad says, smiling mysteriously.

He won't admit that he'd been sneaking around the manor a lot back then, so desperate to learn how to use his powers that spying on the women had become second nature to him. It's how he got the scar on his face, being attacked by one of those hideous beasts of Tabitha's after following the women into the forest one night to watch their rituals.

Brad's father had wanted him to poison Magnus's horses that night, but having been outside the open parlor window eavesdropping on the day that Ruby made her big announcement and they all began to plan the heist, Brad wasn't prepared to miss out on it, and so he'd told his father to do the dirty work himself.

As soon as he heard about the forbidden spell and how powerful it was, he knew he had to get his hands on both the spell and the wand. Brad's plan had been to steal it from the sisterhood after they'd already pulled off the heist.

It should have been easy enough, stealing from old women, but then Ruby hid the treasure and got herself arrested. And no matter how many times he broke into the manor over the years, Brad was never able to find the wand despite finding and memorizing the spell in their grimoire. What he learned from his ongoing spying was that the witches had no clue where it was, either.

He'd gotten the idea two years ago to visit Ruby in prison, in an attempt to befriend her so he could extract information. But he quickly discovered her mind was riddled with more holes than a hunk of Swiss cheese. Still, he'd hoped she'd give him something valuable, even by accident, and so he'd persisted.

At first, Brad had wanted to get his hands on the manor so he could search for the wand himself, certain Ruby would eventually tell him something useful. But then, after she just kept speaking about the safe fire—and after he'd searched the manor multiple times during the break-ins without any result—Brad realized that what he had to do was light his own fire under the witches and crank up the heat. That way, *they'd* be forced to do the heavy lifting for him in terms of the search.

Hence the spectacle of the wrecking ball and the ticking clock to motivate them to find the one thing that could save them. And now, with just over six hours to go, Brad is counting on them to have found it.

"Where is the wand?" When he's met with blank stares, Brad shrugs. "You don't want to tell me? Fine."

As he prods the wand at Ruby so hard that she cries out, Ivy rushes in. "We don't know where it is. We've looked everywhere. Do you think we'd be packing up to leave our home if we'd found the bloody wand?"

He can tell she's not lying: it's a gift he has, a part of his powers, to see through most people's bullshit. The witches' ineptitude enrages him. They had one job: find the wand. And they haven't managed to do it, even though their livelihood and home are at stake, not to mention the survival of their ghost buddy, Tabitha.

His vision blurs, goes crimson-black with rage. Brad lets go of Ruby's arm and reaches out and grabs at her hair, yanking it back. She whimpers as her head snaps backward. "Then, I guess there's no reason to keep the freak around any longer," he growls.

As he opens his mouth, preparing to utter a curse, Queenie shouts, "I know where the Heka Wand is!"

"Don't lie to me," Brad spits, pulling Ruby's head back even further, exposing her throat as he digs the wand deeper into her sternum.

"I'm not lying," Queenie says, speaking slowly and maintaining eye contact as though she's dealing with something wild and unpredictable. It gratifies him that she's smart enough to be afraid of him. “Tabitha actually figured it out just a few minutes ago. We were about to go get it when you arrived.”

Brad shoots a look at the ghost. While she emanates hostility, she isn’t giving off any deceptive vibes. Neither is Queenie, though the other women are clearly hearing this information for the first time and suspect it’s a ploy.

“Let Ruby go, and I’ll tell you where the wand is,” Queenie says.

Brad laughs. “Take me to it. And then we’ll see about Ruby.”

56

Sunday, October 31
Evening: six hours left

Persephone pats her pocket, the solid shape in it reassuring. She closes the window of the YouTube video on her laptop and gathers up the papier-mâché, plaster cloth and crafting paint, putting them all in one of her desk's drawers.

Checking the time, she sees it's 5:30 p.m. There's only six and a half hours to go until midnight so there's no time left to lose. It would normally be difficult sneaking out of the house on a Sunday at this time, but tonight won't be a problem.

Her father is downstairs in the dining room with John Hathorne, the bank manager, Cotton Mather, the reverend, and a few developers, financiers and construction people. They're all poring over plans for their stupid Men's World development, certain that the witches of Moonshyne Manor won't be able to come up with the money in time to prevent the demolition from going ahead bright and early tomorrow morning.

Persephone's father tried to get Persephone to play hostess to his guests, asking her to serve up drinks and snacks and generally play the dutiful daughter to the powerful mayor of Critchley Hackle. But when she told him she would rather give them all food poisoning than serve the patriarchy in any way, Will Stoughton had flapped his hand at her, poured himself a triple whiskey and told her to make herself scarce so as not to embarrass him.

She considers stuffing pillows under her blanket, so he might be fooled if he comes up to check on her or kiss her good-night, but Persephone can't remember the last time he did that. It was long before her mother died, back when he was still a happy person and a good father.

Most teenagers Persephone knows would kill for this kind of freedom, to have parents who aren't constantly hovering, but all Persephone wants is a father who is so interested in her wellbeing that he'll overstep boundaries to keep her safe.

She swallows back the lump that rises like a tide in her throat, telling herself it's a waste of time yearning for something she can't have. Persephone may not be accepted at home or at school, but that's okay. She's most unexpectedly carved out a place for herself within the sisterhood. It doesn't matter that the girls at school would die laughing if they knew the people Persephone most hangs out with are all in their eighties. She never knew any of her grandparents, so it's kind of like hitting the grandmother jackpot.

And besides, the witches of the sisterhood are way more interesting and accomplished than any of the vapid popular girls who're all just so basic. Now that she's finally found her people, Persephone is terrified of losing them. The rental farm property is fifteen miles away. That's not somewhere she can easily reach on her bike, and it's not like her dad will drive her there. There's no major public transit in Critchley Hackle, either, since everyone's encouraged to have their own patriotic gas-guzzling, planet-destroying trucks.

Persephone desperately needs to stay close to the witches, so helping them isn't exactly a selfless act. But sometimes it's okay to do good things for selfish reasons.

She calls Ruth Bader Ginsburg up to her bed, fastening a clean crochet collar around her slim neck. As she does, Persephone looks up at a poster of her hero, the real, notorious RBG, who's looked down, many a night, at a miserable Persephone, lying in bed, trying to cry quietly.

Persephone believes in guardian angels and silently thanks RBG for delivering the witches to her when she most needed them. After all, it was Ruth who inspired Persephone to join The Young Feminists of the World Association. And it was Persephone's wanting to uphold their values that led her to protest against the wrecking ball at Moonshyne Manor.

She slings her satchel over her shoulder and checks her pocket again. She's spent hours on her project, getting it just right, and she has a really good feeling about it. If anything will have the power to trigger Ruby's memories, then this has to be it.

Satisfied, she slaps her thigh. "Come," she says to Ruth's namesake. "We have work to do."

57

Sunday, October 31
Evening: six hours left

"Stand against the wall over there where I can see you," Brad commands, and the women comply, shuffling together next to the pyramid stove like they're preparing for an identification lineup in the bilious room.

Brad may have destroyed their wands, but unlike the rest of the sisterhood, Jezebel and Ivy can do magic without them. He can't possibly know that, so Jezebel is biding her time, trying to think of a way to take Brad down without harming Ruby in the process. She catches Ivy's eye and can see by the determined gleam in it that Ivy is doing the same.

"You two," Brad says, motioning at Jezebel and Ivy. "Hands up." When they reluctantly obey, he flicks Ruby's wand, sending coils of rope spiraling through the air before they coil around their wrists. "Thought I didn't know about your secret tricks?" he asks, smiling in that slimy way of his.

Damn it, Ruby, Jezebel thinks. *Did you tell him everything?* She knows she shouldn't be mad, and that Ruby can't help it, but it still feels traitorous.

As the rope pulls right, Brad nods at Jezebel and winks. "From what I've heard, you enjoy being tied up." He has that gleam in his eye, the one Jezebel knows all too well.

"Only voluntarily," Jezebel retorts. "And only by real men who know how to properly dominate me."

He flicks Ruby's wand, and it's like a giant invisible palm cracks against Jezebel's cheek. She reels back, instinctively trying to raise her hand to her stinging face, but the constraints make it impossible.

"Maybe that will teach you some respect," Brad says, gloating.

There's a crackling sound, as though static is building itself up from the air's molecules. Sparks begin to erupt from Jezebel's aura, her fury supercharged. But without her wand or her hands, she has no outlet for her rage. Ursula murmurs soothing words from next to her, trying to calm her down.

It doesn't work and so Jezebel thinks of Artemis, of the one kiss she allowed him to think he'd stolen but that she'd granted more freely than anything she'd ever given. His face is the balm she needs; she feels the rage simmering rather than bubbling over.

Brad ignores the fireworks display of Jezebel's anger, looking at Queenie instead. "Okay, we're here now. Where's the wand?"

Queenie points at the pyramid stove. "We think it's in there."

"So? What are you waiting for?" Brad demands. "Go open it."

"The only way to open the pyramid is by winning a game of bilious. That's why Ruby hid the jewels in there. She was the best at the game, the only person who could consistently get the pyramid to open and release the crown of flames that goes to the victor."

Brad takes in the room properly for the first time, noticing the scorch marks, the pinball-style paddles aligning with the six huge pockets of the billiards-type table, the mesh masks and chain-mail gloves, and the metal basketball hoops positioned on the opposite sides of the room. He looks from all of it to Ruby, that shit-eating smile spreading on his face like a disease.

"Well, she sure as hell isn't going to win this time," he says. "It will be like taking candy from a baby."

Jezebel can imagine Brad Gedney doing literally that and taking enormous pleasure in it.

"So get to it," he says, laughing. "Kick her ass so I can get the wand."

"It's not that simple," Queenie replies. "Firstly, she may not want to play—"

"I want to play," Ruby interjects from next to Brad.

Ruby's tears have dried, and she doesn't look so cowed anymore. Though Brad's still gripping her tightly, the wand stabbing into her ribs, Ruby's expression is one of tentative happiness, almost like a memory of joy. She must be remembering how much she loved this game, how much of a thrill it brought her as she and Queenie played, hour after hour as teenage witches and then later as adults.

"Did you hear that? She wants to play." There's mockery in Brad's voice, like Ruby's a child who wants to partake of some adult pursuit.

"We each need wands for the game," Queenie says. "And you've destroyed mine."

Brad thinks it over for a moment and then shoves Ruby away, confident that none of them can do anything to him thanks to his protective spell. He extracts his own wand from his suit pocket, pointing it at Ruby's. After muttering an incantation, the wand replicates in his palm. He then strokes its twin while whispering to it, releasing a black shimmer like a glittery fog. "Neither of these can be used against me, so don't try any funny business."

Brad hands Ruby's wand to her and then its clone to Queenie.

Ursula takes two steel mesh masks and two pairs of chain-mail gloves from the hook. She passes them across to Ruby and Queenie. Queenie puts hers on, but Ruby looks at them blankly, clearly at a loss as to what's expected from her.

"Here, I'll help you." Ursula fastens the protective mask to Ruby's face before pulling on the gloves for her. After a moment's hesitation, Ursula takes another two masks off their pegs, securing them to Ivy's and Jezebel's faces since they can't move their hands. Jezebel tries to meet Ursula's eyes to thank her, but Ursula keeps her gaze averted like a penitent.

"What are you doing?" Brad asks Ursula.

"The game is a cross between basketball, billiards, table tennis and squash," Ursula replies tersely, "if the balls used in those games were made of fire. It can be dangerous." She nods at the scorch marks on the walls. "They don't even have their hands to protect themselves." And then she adds, "You can always send the rest of us outside to wait for you."

"Nice try," Brad says. "I want you all where I can see you." He waits a beat and then says, "Give me the protective gear as well." Jezebel can tell he's trying not to look nervous.

Ursula hands a mask and gloves to him.

"So how does the game work?" he asks.

"First one to twenty-one wins," Queenie replies, "but only if you're leading by five points. If not, you keep playing until one of you has a five-point lead."

"And how do you score a point?"

Queenie explains how, when the game begins, and then after each new point is scored, a fireball is released from the top of the pyramid stove, shooting up at the roof, counting as a serve. Each player gets two turns in a row to respond to the serve, using their wand to direct the fireball.

They can use their wand to target the fireball itself—directing it to ricochet where they want—or they can target one of the paddles to swipe at the ball. The aim is to either get the fireball to land in one of the six pockets of the table or into their opponent's hoop, with each of these individual goals scoring one point. If they don't score in one movement of the wand as they respond to their serve, the other player has a turn to target the fireball. They play this way until one of them scores.

After a player has scored three table-pocket goals in a row, a fireball will erupt back out of its pocket at a paddle above it. If they're then able to score a hoop goal from that, they get three additional points, automatically putting them six points in the lead, winning them the game. The victor's winning shot opens the pyramid stove, releasing the crown of flames that then settles on their head.

"You're allowed to get the fireball to bounce off the roof, walls, table and floor in your trajectory toward a pocket or hoop, but you can't bounce it off your opponent or spectators," Queenie says.

Brad's expression is dazed when he says, "Sounds simple enough." He rubs his hands together. "Let's get started."

Despite everything, Jezebel can't help feeling a surge of hope. This is the closest they've gotten to finding the Heka Wand. If they can somehow overcome Brad Gedney, they'll finally have the means to save the manor.

As Queenie points her wand at the pyramid, Jezebel, Ivy and Ursula all step back in unison. The only person not worried about getting caught in the blazing cross fire is Tabby, the one who stands to lose the most if Brad makes off with their treasure.

58

Sunday, October 31
Evening: five and a half hours left

The first serve erupts from the top of the pyramid, the ball of flame blazing like a meteor entering the earth's atmosphere. Ruby won the coin toss, so it's her turn to respond to the serve. As the fireball hits the roof, Queenie winces, worried about what Ruby's reflexes will be like.

But it's instantly obvious there's no reason for concern. Ruby points her wand at a paddle, getting it to swipe at the fireball which rockets toward the hoop behind Queenie. Before Queenie has a chance to block it, the fireball disappears in a poof of smoke.

"Holy shit," Queenie mutters, impressed.

"One, nil," Ursula shouts, having appointed herself the scorekeeper.

"Is it my turn now?" Ruby asks, smiling.

Since each player gets two turns in a row to respond to the

serve, it is Ruby's turn again, and Ursula tells her as much. The second fireball shoots from the top of the pyramid, and when the ball of flame hits the roof, instead of Ruby directing a paddle to flip it at the hoop, she aims her wand directly at the ball, bringing it slamming down onto the table. The ball is incredibly springy: it bounces twice before plopping neatly into one of the middle pockets.

"Two, nil!" Ursula yells.

"Is it my turn now?" Ruby asks.

"No, darling. It's Queenie's," Ursula says gently.

Queenie can't help but marvel at Ruby's coordination. Ruby can't seem to keep track of whose turn it is, and yet she makes an extremely convoluted game that she hasn't participated in for decades look like child's play.

Queenie recalls a journal article she read recently about how studies showed that playing table tennis activated up to five areas of the brain in Alzheimer's subjects. The article said the sport stimulated overall awareness, enhancing players' motor skills, and effectively improving that function of the brain. The study concluded that Alzheimer's patients could experience functional improvements in the brain's frontal lobes by playing the sport.

But there's obviously muscle memory involved as well. Some instinctive reflex that's activated by going through these kinds of motions that were once so automatic that they required no conscious thought. Ruby looks to be in her element, flicking her wand in response to the fireball in ways that predate her illness. She looks like a geriatric Olympic athlete who's been called upon to perform in the arena one last time, and she's rising to the occasion in a way that's astonishing.

While Queenie's overjoyed to see Ruby return to some semblance of her old self, she's also conflicted. The better Ruby plays, the sooner Brad Gedney will have the Heka Wand. And Queenie can't help but hope that the longer the game goes on, the more likely she is to come up with a solution to their problem.

As Queenie takes her turn, she's distracted by Charon's bracelet burning against her flesh, its light now blazing a fierce white. She has to force herself to push past the pain of it and concentrate on the game. They fall into a rhythm, alternately scoring points. Despite it being decades since Queenie played, she finds that it's easier to get back into the game than she would have expected. She can't make the old showy shots, diving spectacularly like she used to, but she's still pretty good for an old broad.

Even as Queenie's body responds to the game, her mind churns through possibilities. Ruby and Queenie can't use either of their wands against Brad, and Ivy and Jezebel's hands are literally tied, meaning they can't work their magic that way, either. Ursula's hands are free, but she doesn't have a wand.

Where's Widget? Queenie wonders. Tabitha can conjure certain spells through her familiar, but the crow has to be in the room for that to work.

When Queenie catches up to Ruby's score, tying at twenty-two all, Brad yells for a time-out. "What the hell are you doing?" he demands, his face screwed up in anger.

"I'm playing the game." Queenie wipes sweat from her brow.

"Why? You want to let Ruby win so we can get the Heka Wand. Stop playing to beat her."

"That won't work," Queenie says. "The game only works—"

"Shut up! And let her win!" he insists, his scar scrunched up in a knot, and his eyes bugged out.

"But—"

"No *buts*," he yells. "Stop trying!"

Queenie shrugs, pissed. "Okay, fine." The idiot will find out soon enough why that's a waste of time. In the meantime, Queenie can catch her breath.

"When is it my turn to play?" Ruby asks.

"Now, darling," Ursula replies.

Ruby responds to the next serve, and Queenie pulls back her efforts, barely trying to score points, making it clear that she's letting Ruby win. Her wand flicks are sloppy, and she stands stock-still, not even trying to dive to get the best vantage points or block Ruby's shots.

Within three minutes of playing this way, after Ruby has gained a five-point lead that should win her the game—with the score being twenty-seven to twenty-two—the fireball stops ricocheting around the room. It floats to the middle of the ceiling and hovers there before sputtering out, a heap of ash landing on the table.

"What's going on?" Brad asks, looking to the pyramid. "Why isn't it opening?"

"I tried to tell you," Queenie says, shrugging.

"What?"

"This is a game to the metaphorical death." Queenie crosses her arms, thinking how much she'd love to play this game against Brad himself, setting his hair alight, maybe giving him a matching scar on his other eyebrow. "You don't play bilious unless you're prepared to give it your absolute all, everything you have, to try to win. The game knows when you're going through the motions, and it won't tolerate it."

"That's such bullshit," Gedney protests. "It's just a stupid game."

Queenie shrugs as if to say *I don't make the rules*, quietly gratified by his ignorance. He may have magical abilities the sisterhood didn't know about, but between them they have hundreds of years of magical knowledge that's been passed down by a long line of experienced witches. It's scant comfort, but it's something.

Finally, Brad shakes his head, annoyance etched into the furrows of his brow. "Okay, fine. Get on with it, then."

Queenie walks over to the pyramid, placing her hand against the hole through which the fireballs erupt. She closes her eyes and says, "I'm sorry for disrespecting the game and the hallmarks of good sportsmanship. I promise to do better."

The pyramid considers the sincerity of Queenie's apology. And then it thrums, and she yanks her hand back. The game begins anew, and a fireball is lobbed to the ceiling.

Where the hell is Widget?

"A hundred and fifty-three to a hundred and fifty-one," Ursula croaks, sounding as exhausted as Queenie feels, which makes Queenie want to smack her, since all Ursula's done for the past four hours is stand there yelling out scores.

Everything hurts: Queenie's ankles, calves, knees and hips; her fingers, wrists, elbows and back. She's too old for this shit, for this taxing kind of exertion. Women in their eighties aren't meant to push themselves this hard. And yet Ruby shows no sign of stopping which means Queenie can't, either.

What the hell did Ruby do in prison to keep fit? Spend her days doing victory laps around the running track in the yard?

Queenie shoots yet another pointed look at Tabitha and then at the door, wondering for the umpteenth time why Tabby hasn't summoned her familiar. With Brad's fear of birds, Widget could really come in handy, both as a distraction and to take Brad's wand from him. That's what they need: *his* wand. It's the only one they can use against him.

Tabby keeps mouthing something at Queenie which she can't interpret. Her damn eyesight isn't what it used to be, and she isn't a lip-reader.

Brad catches Queenie staring at Tabby. "Waiting for something, Queenie?"

"No," she says, glowering at him.

"Liar. You're hoping that crow will come save you." He laughs. "Pity I foresaw that little complication and put a blocking charm on the door. Haven't you noticed how the fireball hasn't bounced out of the room once?"

Shit! Queenie mentally kicks herself. She absolutely should have noticed that. Widget hasn't come to their rescue because the crow can't pass the barrier of the door.

A fireball ejects from the pyramid and play resumes.

"For god's sake, how much longer is this going to take?" Brad demands ten minutes later, frustration in his voice.

"It's impossible to say," Ursula replies. "Some games are over in minutes while others can go on for hours. Their record is twenty-seven hours, and that game only ended because Queenie fell asleep on her feet."

"I didn't fall asleep," Queenie gasps as she swats at the fireball and scores. "I tripped and hit my head against the table and got concussed."

"When is it my turn again?" Ruby asks for what feels like the thousandth time.

Ursula sighs. "Now, darling."

There's a whoosh as another fireball is released from the pyramid. It's followed by the squeak of the paddle, and then Ruby grunts as she dives to get the angle she wants.

After the clatter of the fireball entering one of the table's pockets, Ursula declares, "A hundred and sixty-four to Ruby and a hundred and sixty-one to Queenie."

Ruby's leading by three points; she needs two more to win. She's standing hunched over, hands on her knees. Sweat drips from her forehead and dampens her armpits. She's flushed, and her breathing is labored, but she's smiling despite the awful circumstances and the fact that she must feel utterly spent.

When the fireball ejects from the pyramid, Ruby straightens, flicking her wand in an elaborate movement. A paddle swipes at the ball, swatting it down, like a slam dunk. The fireball disappears into one of the table pockets. And then it shoots straight back out again. Ruby lunges, flicks her wand at another paddle, which snaps, sending the fireball careering at the hoop.

It looks like it's going to sink, but then it bounces back out again. It circles the rim of the hoop in excruciating slow motion before toppling gently inside.

Ursula shouts, "A hundred and sixty-seven to Ruby, and a hundred and sixty-one to Queenie. Ruby wins the game."

"Fucking finally!" Brad yells.

Queenie digs a hand in her side, trying to numb the pain of the stitch as she gasps for air. There's the old familiar blasting of trumpets, the victory anthem, and the side of the pyramid facing the table suddenly drops open, blue flames erupting from within. The flames shift and twist, rearranging themselves into a shape as though invisible hands were performing origami with them.

What results is a crown of fire. It rises and floats across the room, settling itself upon Ruby's head. She beams as it anoints her, the blue light from the crown causing her perspiration to glow, making her look utterly radiant despite her obvious exhaustion.

Just then, there's a loud clatter from just outside the bilious room's door, causing all heads to snap in that direction.

59

Sunday, October 31
Evening: an hour left

"Run," Ursula yells, seeing something that Queenie can't because of the angle she's at. Before Queenie can move, Brad bolts outside. When he returns, he's dragging a startled Persephone behind him.

Queenie goes cold at the sight of the girl.

No. No. No. No.

There's only an hour left until Charon arrives to claim either the wand or the price he's demanded in its stead. The bracelet's heat sears her wrist. With Gedney about to make off with the Heka Wand, this is the last possible place Queenie wants Persephone to be.

"And who is this little spy?" Brad asks, holding Persephone by the collar of her red coat.

"It's Sarah-Jane Mortimer," Ruby replies, smiling at Persephone.

"It's your *friend's* daughter," Queenie says, trying not to sound as panicked as she feels. "So you'll want to think twice about harming her in any way."

"My friend?" Brad scoffs, making it clear what he thinks of such a ridiculous notion.

"The mayor, Will Stoughton. He won't be very happy knowing you've laid your hands on his kid."

Brad's grip on Persephone eases up. "Huh." He gives it some thought and shrugs. "It's nothing a bit of memory modification can't fix, though I probably won't even bother. Who do you think her father's going to believe? The man who's made all the town's dreams come true or a stupid teenage girl?" And then he smiles. "You've actually come at a most opportune time, child. I don't trust these witches not to be setting me up for some kind of trap. Go over to that pyramid, and bring me whatever is inside it."

"Leave the girl," Queenie says, starting to head for the pyramid. "I'll go—"

"Stay right where you are." Brad points his wand at Queenie.

Queenie freezes, holding her hands up.

"Go," Brad instructs Persephone.

Persephone shoots a look at Queenie, trying to communicate something that Queenie can't interpret before she heads for the pyramid. When she gets to it, she kneels down, hesitating for a second before plunging her hand inside. It's as Persephone's retrieving something that Widget suddenly swoops into the room. When Brad left the room, he must have broken the protective shield placed over the door.

Widget heads straight for Brad Gedney's face. Spotting the crow, he shrieks, shielding his head like he did the first time he encountered Widget. The crow circles, about to dive-bomb him again, and Queenie prepares to pounce on Brad while he's distracted. As she's about to make her move, a red light erupts from the tip of his wand sending Widget plummeting in a death spiral.

The women all cry out, Tabby rushing at Widget, but Brad points his wand at Persephone. "Stay where you are, or I'll kill the girl."

Everyone freezes, eyes focused on Widget who lies splayed on the floor, a lone feather circling the air before it comes to settle on her chest.

"Bring me the treasure," Brad commands.

Persephone stands, both hands full, and walks over to Brad. She's looking at the necklaces really strangely, like she's trying to figure something out. When she gets to Brad, she tries handing him the jewelry first. He swats the pieces away, reaching for the curved ivory wand, which he snatches from her hand.

He stares down at it, turning it over in his hands, an expression of glee spreading across his face. "Ladies, it's been a pleasure doing business with you." And then he looks at Ruby. "It goes without saying, Ruby, that the engagement is off." And with that, he throws his head back and laughs, turning and walking from the room.

As the women rush at Widget—Ivy's and Jezebel's movements awkward because of their tied hands—the wall-sconce flames go out, plunging them all into darkness. Ruby's crown of blue flame is extinguished. Queenie's pulsing bracelet is the only light in the room.

"Untie my hands, so I can conjure light," Ivy says, somewhere to Queenie's left.

"Claresce," Queenie calls out, holding the twin to Ruby's wand aloft. But the spell doesn't work.

There's chaos in the room, the women tripping over one another, banging into the table. Voices cry out but are quickly muffled by the density of the inky air which thickens and clots, like the room is being flooded with black tar. As the darkness begins to smother Queenie, her guts turn icy with terror. *The*

Ferryman has come early, and Persephone is still here. There's no way to stop him from taking her.

"Queenie," Charon says, his voice wheezing like bellows from all corners of the room.

There's a collective intake of breath, the women fueling the fire of their terror.

"I believe you have something for me?" Charon prompts.

"You're an hour early," is all Queenie can think to say.

The darkness brushes against her arms like sandpaper. It's the manifestation of Charon laughing. "You looked busy. I thought it best to collect while I could get your full attention."

"I was just about to go and get the wand back," Queenie says. "If you could come back—"

"Are you saying you don't have it? Again?"

"I don't, but if I can just go after Brad—"

"Then, I'll have the girl." The darkness squeezes against Queenie's ribs.

"The girl?" Ivy croaks, horrified.

"What the hell?" Jezebel exclaims.

"No!" Queenie yells. "Not the girl. Take me instead." Queenie gags on the darkness seeping into her mouth, spits it out. "I know youth has power, but I'm a powerful witch. And if you take me, I'll give you the Moonshyne Manor Grimoire as well."

Queenie ignores the witches' gasps. She holds her breath, waiting for Charon's answer.

"I'll be allowed to use your forbidden spells?" he asks, his voice taking on a rasping quality, the way Queenie imagines a lion would speak.

"Yes. Take me, not the girl, and you can use my own magical powers *and* the forbidden spells."

"No!" a voice shouts from nearby.

It's not Charon who's spoken. It takes Queenie a moment to

realize it's Persephone. "You don't need to take her," the girl says. "I have the Heka Wand."

The women gasp again, the sound rippling across the room. With the air so dense, Queenie can feel it as butterfly wings against the back of her neck.

"Persephone," she says, "you can't lie to Charon—"

"I'm not lying," the girl says. "I swapped out the real wand for a decoy that I made. That's why I came here tonight, to show Ruby the decoy wand to see if it might jog some memories loose. I got the idea after Ruby thought I was my mother. I figured if the sight of my mother's coat could trigger her to remember someone she barely knew from decades ago, then something that looked and felt like the wand might help her remember where she hid it."

Persephone continues speaking, overtaken by a kind of nervous verbal diarrhea, explaining how she googled an image of the wand and then checked out some YouTube videos, experimenting with papier-mâché and plaster cloth, using crafting paint and an engraving pen to finish it off. Mindful of the mistakes Queenie made as they prepared for the heist, Persephone says she even made it the right weight and everything, believing the key to triggering Ruby's memories was absolute faithfulness to the original.

"Let me see it," Charon says, and Queenie hears Persephone gasp as the artifact is snatched from her by the darkness.

There's silence as Charon evaluates the curved ivory wand with its engraved female deities. Finally, the darkness releases its grip on Queenie's throat. "It is the real Heka Wand of Isis," Charon declares. "Saved by a little girl." He chuckles. "My, how things have changed, Queenie."

With that, he's gone, as is Queenie's bracelet, which dissolves like mist as the darkness dissipates. The wall sconces burst into flame again. A bag of cash sits on the floor next to the pyramid stove, the half a million dollars Charon agreed to pay.

But no one rushes to the money. They all scramble for Widget who has miraculously not been trampled in the dark. Ursula's struggling to untie Ivy and Jezebel. Tabby's on her hands and knees on the floor, tears streaming down her face as she tries to pick the crow up. Her hands slide through the bird over and over, not finding purchase.

Queenie picks Widget up for Tabby, holding the crow out to her mistress. "I'm sorry, Tabby," Queenie whispers, as she strokes a limp black wing. "I'm so, so sorry."

"The birdie's just sleeping," Ruby says from behind them, smiling in that sly way of hers.

Queenie thinks Ruby's confused, but then Widget stirs in her hands, the crow getting unsteadily to her feet.

"I zapped the birdie with a spell before that bad man could hurt her," Ruby says.

The women let out a collective whoop of joy, alternately rushing Ruby to envelop her in a group hug and crowding around Widget, nuzzling her.

"You were going to die for me," Persephone says from next to Queenie, awe in her voice. "Rather than let Charon take me." There are tears in her eyes.

Queenie waves it off like it's nothing. "I didn't want to accept your help, and yet you still gave it. It's *your* help that saved us."

"Everyone needs help sometimes." Persephone says it like it's the simplest thing in the world.

And suddenly, Queenie realizes, it is. It really is.

"I don't mean to break up this love fest," Ivy says, voice clipped and raw. "But we only have ten minutes to get this money to the bank, which will be closed at this hour."

"We don't need to go to the bank," Persephone says, pulling away from Queenie. "We just need to get it to my house. That's where they all are." But then her face darkens. "But it will take longer than ten minutes to drive there."

"Then, we'll fly," Queenie says.

<u>**Moonshyne Manor Grimoire**</u>

Ivy's Instructions for Making a Broom

Begin by choosing a tree based on the magical properties of its wood.

Choose a special occasion such as your birthday, a full moon or one of the seasonal festivals when you will take what you need from the tree to make your broom.

Ask the tree for permission to take a branch and twigs, and honor it by leaving an offering of fruit or water. Bless the branch and the twigs, and consecrate them through smudging with sage. Bind the twigs to the branch with a rope of your choosing or with copper wire. Carve Wiccan symbols of your choice on the handle. You can also adorn it with bells and ribbons or add the feathers of your familiar in the bristle bouquet. Gently blow on your broom, from the bristles to the end of the handle, so that it may carry and protect you.

Sweep with it at the entrance of a cemetery.

60

Sunday, October 31
Evening: six minutes left

Persephone clutches Queenie's waist, the bag of cash wedged between her chest and Queenie's back. Her eyes stream from the wind buffeting her face as she peers around Queenie. Persephone frees up a hand to clamp her hair back so she can see beyond the corkscrew curls flopping in her eyes.

They're on Queenie's souped-up Harley-Davidsonstick. All the witches, except Tabby and Ruby, are zooming on their own slower brooms behind them. Queenie's hands clutch the raised handlebars as she veers around trees, chimneys and satellite dishes.

"There," Persephone says pointing down at her house, relieved to see all the cars still parked in the drive. "It's that one."

Persephone's stomach lurches as Queenie swoops down, aiming the Harley-Davidsonstick at the pathway leading up to the front door. The landing is less bumpy than Persephone was expecting. "That was so sick," she says, dismounting from the broom, clutching the bag of money. The broom keeps hovering there, even though it doesn't have wheels to stand on.

As the rest of the women touch down around them, Persephone pulls her phone from her pocket. "We're going live on TikTok," she says, holding her phone up. The women all regard her blankly. "That way, everyone can see what's about to go down, so there can be no cover-ups."

She sends a quick text to Reggie Collins, that reporter from the other day, whose details she saved in case she'd need them down the line.

Hi Reggie. It's the mayor's daughter. Watch my TikTok live right now. You're gonna want to cover this story.

There are three minutes to go. Persephone follows Queenie, camera held up, as Queenie bangs on the door. The witches are fanned out behind them. Persephone's father answers a few seconds later wearing a scowl, which Persephone is careful to capture on her video.

"What the hell?" Will Stoughton gapes first at Queenie and Persephone and then at the witches behind them.

"We've got your half a million dollars," Queenie says. "I know John Hathorne is here, so we're making the home delivery to him instead of the bank."

"Nice try," Persephone's father says, recovering. "But your time is up."

"No, it's not. They still have two minutes," Persephone says, pushing her way inside past Queenie, making her father retreat. She narrates to the camera all the while. "We're here at Mayor Will Stoughton's home in Critchley Hackle, where the women of Moonshyne Manor are delivering the half a million dollars they owe to Hunter Thompson Bank. They had until midnight to make the outstanding payment of their debt, and now, with two minutes to midnight, they're making good on it."

Persephone zooms in on the money in the bag and then holds the camera up to film the faces of all of the men clustered in her living room, looking like deer caught in headlights.

She walks up to John Hathorne, zooming in on his astonished face. "Will you be accepting this payment, Mr. Hathorne, or will you be trying to find reasons to screw over these little old ladies whose home you're trying to steal?"

Persephone swivels the camera to take in all the witches, winking so they know what's expected. Queenie suddenly hunches over, looking unsteady on her feet, while Ivy stoops low to appear fragile and waiflike. Ursula takes on an expression like she's eaten bad fish, and Jezebel manages to look slightly less like a bombshell.

"Are you going to try to go ahead with building this ridiculous development you've approved despite their still officially owning the land?" Persephone leans over the table, filming all the plans.

"Shut that thing off," Will Stoughton yells, trying to grab Persephone's phone. "Switch it off right now, Phony!"

As Persephone struggles with him, the strangest thing happens. A spark erupts from her fingers, jolting him. He yelps, withdrawing his hand, staring at Persephone with horror but also a dawning recognition. While Persephone is shocked by the spark, her father isn't.

And isn't that just the darnedest thing?

61

Monday, November 1
Just after midnight

As Queenie races ahead on her Harley-Davidsonstick, her flapping robes make Ursula think of windy laundry days, clean sheets snapping fractiously on the clothesline.

Ursula's fingers ache from the cold seeping into her arthritic joints. She wishes there'd been time to prepare for the flight. The fall night is too frigid to be gallivanting around without being properly dressed. She looks forward to thawing out next to the fire, a rare glass of port aiding the process.

Ahead of her, Queenie begins her descent, the lights in the bilious room and library guiding them home. Ursula's always loved seeing the manor and sprawling grounds from this vantage point, but it's even more special tonight, knowing how close they've come to losing it all. There's no guarantee the bank will accept their highly unusual deposit, but Ursula has a good feeling about it.

Queenie lands near the porch and dismounts. By the time Ursula lands behind her, the front door is already open, Tabby peering out while Widget circles Queenie, undoubtedly catching up on the news. Ursula's heartbeat stutters as Ruby steps through the doorway, heading down the stairs. She appears to have recovered from the grueling bilious game earlier, though she'll probably feel the worst of it tomorrow. Three gentle thuds sound behind Ursula in quick succession, the rest of the sisterhood landing.

"Why are we parking our brooms here?" Jezebel asks, breathless after the flight.

"You can all go park yours in the coach house. I just wanted to catch Tabby and Ruby up before I head out again," Queenie replies. She's still in possession of Ruby's wand from earlier, and she's peering at it like she would some intricate piece of machinery.

"Where are you going?" Ivy asks, looking windswept with her glowing red cheeks and the hair from her braid having come loose, framing her face.

"After Brad Gedney."

"But why?" Ursula yelps, her serenity from a minute ago evaporating entirely.

"How long do you think it will take him to realize he has a fake Heka Wand? How long before he'll be back here again, launching another surprise attack? And then another and another?"

"It's best to go on the offensive," Ivy says, nodding. "Take him by surprise."

"Exactly," Queenie replies. "He's never going to stop gunning for us. It's time to eliminate the threat once and for all."

In that moment, Queenie reminds Ursula of how Mirabelle looked the night she and her sisterhood flew out to avenge the murder of Ursula's mother. *Women can't always rely on the legal sys-*

tem for justice, Ursula recalls Mirabelle explaining before they'd left. *Sometimes we have to take matters into our own hands.*

"How do you even know where to find him?" Jezebel asks. "The Gedney property was sold years ago."

"I'm thinking we can try some reverse geolocation magic," Queenie murmurs, turning Ruby's wand over in her hands. "Since he used his own wand to prevent Ruby's from working any magic against him, it might be possible to use her wand to pinpoint where his currently is." She looks up at Ivy who's come to stand next to her. "What do you think?"

Ursula can see the wheels spinning in both Queenie's and Ivy's brains. They confer, murmuring in that scientific shorthand only the two of them understand. She catches words like *frequency*, *localization*, *signal* and *data extraction*. After a few minutes, they seem to reach agreement that it could be done if they use the right spell.

Finally, Queenie grips the poles of Ruby's wand with both hands and closes her eyes. *"Aperi."*

For a few seconds, nothing happens. And then the wand struggles in Queenie's hands. She lets go of it, stepping back. The wand quivers upright in midair, spinning this way and that as though in the hands of an invisible baton twirler. And then it flips over, settling horizontally. Its tip twitches, pointing in a southeasterly direction.

"It worked," Ivy exclaims, slapping Queenie on the back. "It's become a compass!"

Queenie looks both dismayed and relieved. "It's going to lead me there."

"No, it's not," Ursula says, shaking her head. "It's going to lead *us* there."

Queenie opens her mouth to object, but before she can utter a word, Ivy says, "We're going with you. End of discussion."

"Your days of having to take care of everything by yourself are over," Jezebel says. "Do you hear us?"

Queenie nods, swallowing hard.

"Can we please just grab coats and gloves first?" Ursula asks, teeth chattering. "I'm freezing my tits off."

The women laugh, heading inside to layer up. When they return, Ruby is standing outside, her broomstick clutched in her hand.

"What are you doing?" Ursula asks, ready to shepherd Ruby back inside.

"I'm coming with."

"I don't think that's a good idea, Ruby," Ursula says, thinking that Ruby's confusion over Brad being Magnus could cause unnecessary complications.

"I want to come with you," Ruby says, jaw set. She mounts her broom and takes off. Despite Ursula's misgivings over Ruby's ability to fly after all this time, Ruby's instincts kick in as strongly as they did with bilious.

Ursula looks to Tabby, the only one of them to be left behind. She hates that Tabitha can't join them.

"What?" Widget caws from the porch banister. "Of course I'm coming!"

Adventure calls the group of six just as it did so often in their youth. And they rise up into the night to answer it, taking flight.

62

Monday, November 1
1:00 a.m.

The wand has led them to a palatial property on the outskirts of Critchley Hackle. The mansion has twelve-foot walls and electric gates monitored by security cameras, none of which prevent the witches from landing on an enormous second-floor balcony that overlooks row upon row of grapevines.

And because Brad Gedney is so cocksure of himself, Queenie doesn't even have to use an unlocking spell on the door. She just opens it and walks right in, the sisterhood and Widget close behind her.

Finding Brad in a mansion this size should be difficult, but it isn't. Instead of trying to navigate the maze from room to room, they just follow the sound of his echoing cursing two floors down to the basement. As Queenie peeks around the corner into the room he's in, she's expecting a lab, like hers or Ivy's; instead, what they find is a chamber in the shape of a heptagon.

It's seven walls are covered floor to ceiling. The adornments include gilt-framed portraits as large as king-size beds, taxidermied heads of each of the Big Five, as well as other majestic creatures long extinct, awards and trophies of all shapes and sizes, framed newspaper and magazine clippings, certificates issued by prestigious institutions, and dozens of photographs of the three generations of Gedneys posed with so-called very important men, mostly politicians and high-powered businessmen.

Conspicuous by their absence are books. Not one leather-bound tome can be found in the entire room. Nor a ratty paperback, either, for that matter, from what Queenie can see.

Centered in the room, however, is a thirteen-seat oval table. It's buffed to an ominous shine, a reddish-purple gleam that brings to mind viscous internal organs. Above the table, taking up the whole of the ceiling, is an elaborate fresco of a heptagram painted in swathes of mainly gold and blue. It's embellished with intricate Celtic symbols, as well as writing that looks like Tolkien's Elvish and runic-type letters resembling chicken scratches. Through it all are woven strings of Latin words and Roman numerals.

Brad Gedney is seated in a high-backed chair that resembles a throne. His elbows rest on the table, and his hands are threaded through his hair. "Fuck's sake," he growls, reaching for a nearby paperweight and pitching it at one of the walls. It crashes against a framed photo of Brad shaking hands with Donald Trump. The picture topples to the floor. "What's the secret ingredient?"

He picks up his wand and taps it against the table as he reads aloud from a piece of paper. Queenie's shocked to realize that he's listing the ingredients of the forbidden spell, the one that Ruby was going to use with the Heka Wand to allow her to present as a woman permanently.

How the hell did he get his hands on it? Queenie wonders. He must have seen their grimoire, memorizing the spell from it.

Queenie turns to look at the sisterhood who are clustered behind her. The electric light in here isn't forgiving like the flickering light cast by the manor's flames. It's harsh and intrusive, highlighting the sisterhood's wrinkles and gray hair, liver spots and swollen joints.

Age has not been kind to them physically, but then, that's not its job, is it?

Age's sole purpose is to gift us more years in which to experience the minefield that is living. Along with that, it grants us the perspective to know that by the end of it all, it doesn't matter a damn whit that we no longer look like our younger selves. Because here's the thing: we *are* no longer those supple, youthful, foolish people. We're that much older and infinitely wiser, war-weary and battle-scarred. We've become survivors and warriors, and as Ruby will tell you, you should always, *always* look the part.

Queenie raises an eyebrow at her sisters, who nod in answer to her unspoken question: they're ready. Ursula takes Ruby's hand, pulling her close.

Holding Ruby's wand aloft, Queenie steps into the strange room, muttering, *"Veni."*

Brad's wand is yanked from his grip, shooting across the space between them. Widget swoops to grab it in her beak, flying down to hand it over to Ursula. The wizard's mouth drops open. They were right to go on the offensive: the last thing he expected was for the witches to fight back.

"I'm afraid that spell's not going to work for you for four reasons," Queenie says, quickly closing the gap between them despite how strongly her muscles protest. "The first is that you don't have the real Heka Wand." She nods at the wand resting next to him. "That's a fake made by a girl who was smart enough to do more homework on the wand than you did."

Brad goes pale, looking incredulously from Queenie to the artifact.

"The second is that it isn't a full moon. You can only work that kind of powerful magic aided by a moon whose energy is at its peak. And the third is that you can't steal a spell from another witch's grimoire. The spell won't work for you unless it's freely given."

"Well, how the hell was I supposed to know that?" Brad asks, face contorted with rage. "None of you said anything about it."

We would never say anything to you! Queenie thinks, before suddenly understanding. *No, of course we wouldn't.* But he knew all about the heist and the spell, and who knows what else? *Not because he's a powerful wizard but because he's a little sneak who's been spying on us for years.*

As the women surround Brad, Widget circling overhead, it's Ivy who responds. "The sad thing is that if you had just come to me, asking for help, I would have given it. I would have been happy to take you under my wing and mentor you."

Brad sneers. "I didn't need your help."

"On the contrary. I'd say your failure to work this spell proves otherwise."

Brad jumps up, looking like he's about to strike Ivy. Before Queenie can conjure a protection shield, Jezebel shoots off a spell. Brad's arm freezes in midair.

"You really need to learn how to control that temper of yours," Jezebel says and tuts. "I'd suggest turning whatever the fuck this hideous space is into a rage room." And then she stares at the paperweight and broken frame on the floor. "Though, you'll need to work on your target practice. I'm guessing that wasn't what you were aiming for."

"What were you wanting to use the forbidden spell for?" Ursula asks.

"None of your fucking business," Brad spits, fruitlessly trying to wrestle his right arm down by tugging at it with his left.

Ursula shrugs, walking over to the piece of paper. *"'The most powerful wizard in the world,'"* she says, reading the part where the witch or wizard manifests what it is they most want. She whistles. "Quite ambitious, aren't you?"

"And quite stupid too," Queenie says. "The fourth reason the spell won't work is because the conjurer of the spell has to give up all their magical ability after working it. That's the secret ingredient."

Brad issues a string of expletives, his face contorted with rage. When he runs out of curses, he turns to Ruby and takes a deep breath, forcing a smile. "Ruby, darling. You'll help me, won't you? You'll help your darling fiancé, Magnus?" The freezing spell expires, and his arm drops to his side.

Ruby gazes at him, smiling and nodding. "I will, my darling, I absolutely will."

Queenie's spirits sink. It was a mistake allowing Ruby to come along.

"You'll conjure the spell for me, giving up your power, won't you?"

Ruby nods, but then her expression changes, and she shakes her head, confused. "You're not my Magnus."

Brad lunges for Queenie then, grabbing at her locs. He pulls her back by her hair, ramming Queenie against his chest, as he wraps an arm around her neck.

Brad turns them around so that Queenie is a human shield between himself and Ivy, Ursula and Jezebel.

Ignoring Ruby behind them, Brad strains with his free arm, reaching for his wand that Queenie's holding. His arms are longer than hers, and he's also so much stronger. As his fingers close over her hand, trying to wrestle the wand from her grip, she drops it, kicking it away. It skitters out of sight.

"You try firing off any spells, and I'll snap her neck," Brad calls out as he retreats, dragging Queenie with him. "You don't need magic to kill someone. Especially not someone this old and decrepit." He looks up, glaring at Widget who's hovering nearby. "Keep that fucking bird away from me."

Queenie struggles for air, but her squirming just serves to make him tighten his grip. The witches are frozen, unable to get a good vantage point to shoot off a spell that won't accidentally hurt Queenie. Her vision blurs, and panic rises in her chest as her legs give out. She's not taking in any air. She's not breathing.

"Mustela," Ruby calls out from behind them.

Queenie barely hears the spell over the sound of adrenaline whooshing through her veins. What she feels is the blessed relief of an arm falling away from her throat. And then she's falling backward, nothing behind her to prop her up anymore.

There's a commotion as she hits the ground. Something with sharp claws scampers over her chest.

"Clude," It's Ivy's voice this time.

Queenie blacks out for a moment, and when she comes to, Ursula is leaning over her, eyes wide as she checks Queenie's vitals. "I'm okay," Queenie croaks, struggling to sit up, her head pounding and throat raw. She's astonished to see a weasel throwing itself against the bars of a cage.

Jezebel walks past Queenie, bending down to look at the creature. "Excellent job, Ruby. There," she says, satisfied. "Now he finally looks the part."

63

Sunday, November 7
Afternoon

When a guest announces themselves at the door for the first time in a week, six old women and a geriatric crow are drawn from all corners of the sprawling manor. They descend upon the foyer, the source of the commotion, where they're happy to find a beaming Persephone, bundled up against the chill, clutching a quivering Ruth Bader Ginsburg.

"All hail the conquering heroine," Queenie says to a loud round of applause as she lets Persephone in.

Persephone ducks her head, blushing though she's thrilled by the warm welcome. When she looks up, she does a double take at the sight of Tabitha. She can see her, actually *see* her this time, instead of just feeling her presence.

Tabby winks at her, and Widget caws, "How lovely to finally be seen by you."

Queenie leads the women into the parlor. Jezebel sets about

making everyone drinks, while the old women fuss over Persephone, offering her a seat next to the fire, and inviting Ruth Bader Ginsburg up onto a footstool.

Jezebel hands Persephone a virgin cocktail they've concocted just for her. "It's called the Future Madam President."

Persephone stares at the glass in her hand, at a loss for words.

"Thanks for joining us for our meeting," Ivy says.

Persephone coughs past the lump in her throat. "I wouldn't have missed it for the world." She walks over to Widget, who's perched next to Tabitha's seat. "Are you okay after that hella wicked fall?" she asks the crow.

"Splendid, thank you," Widget replies. "Ruby cast a most excellent stunning spell that saved my life."

Ruby beams at the praise, walking over to pet the crow's head. "Nice birdie. Good birdie."

That's when Persephone spots a cage in the corner of the room. She goes over to take a look, bending to see what's inside. At first, she thinks it's a little dachshund, because of its elongated body, but upon closer inspection she sees that it's a weasel. The creature is cute, but when she smiles at it, it hisses, and she jumps back.

As everyone settles down, Jezebel sends the rest of the cocktails floating across the room. Persephone's gratified to see Ruby and Ursula sitting next to each other.

Ivy raises a glass to Persephone, but before she can speak, the phone trills, and Ursula stands to answer it. "I'm sorry, but we're just in the middle of something," Ursula says. "Can I take a message?" She listens for a second and then covers the receiver, calling out, "Jezebel, it's Artemis. He wants to know if you're still on for your second date tomorrow night?"

Jezebel blushes and nods, looking ridiculously like a schoolgirl experiencing her very first crush.

When Ursula returns, Ivy tries again, holding up her glass to Persephone. "Thanks to you, and the uproar caused by that video on TokTik, er... Tic-Tac-Toe...or whatever that thingy is called, the bank accepted our deposit, and we're all squared up. The Moonshyne Manor and Distillery are saved!"

They all send their glasses flitting across the room to clink against Persephone's.

"My father was livid," Persephone confesses. "He grounded me for a week, which is why I couldn't visit sooner."

"It's fine," Queenie says, waving it off. "Ruby and I were both so stiff after that epic game of bilious that we're only just walking properly again."

Persephone tugs at the stalk of a maraschino cherry, plucking it out of her drink to take a bite. "Brad Gedney disappeared, along with all of his funding, so the development can't go ahead, despite the town suggesting they build it elsewhere."

She expects the witches to be surprised by this, but they aren't. And that's when Persephone notices the fake Heka Wand of Isis she made. It's sitting right there on the coffee table. "How did you get that back from Brad?"

Queenie smiles grimly. "Let's just say we tied up some loose ends. There's only so long we can allow ourselves to be tormented by the men of one dysfunctional family." She shoots a dark look at the caged weasel, before waving her hand dismissively. "But that's not why we invited you to join us. First, we wanted to congratulate you on discovering your powers. I couldn't understand why Charon wanted you as his payment if I couldn't deliver the Heka Wand, but it all makes sense now. He saw your powers before we did. A young witch who hasn't yet used her magic is an incredibly powerful being."

Persephone shivers as she thinks about how close they came to having Charon claim her. She understands now why Queenie was so gruff all those times, why she didn't want Persephone hanging out at the manor.

"Your powers came in pretty late, but that's not unheard of," Queenie adds. "Your mother's magic came in late too."

"My mother?" Persephone yelps.

It's Ivy who leans forward and tells Persephone what they've figured out, which is that it was Persephone's mother, Sarah-Jane Mortimer, who came to see them after strange things began happening to her when she was sixteen. "We gave her some tutelage, showing her how to harness her powers. She was a talented witch and showed a lot of promise, but she stopped coming three years later after she met and fell in love with someone. Your father, as it turns out."

"Sarah-Jane didn't think he would love her if he knew about her powers," Queenie continues, "and so she stopped coming for lessons. We didn't hear from her again for ages, until she came to see Ivy about a tincture that would help her get pregnant with you."

"She didn't tell me about the cancer," Ivy says quickly, "or I'm not sure I would have helped her. But then there wouldn't have been you, so perhaps it's a good thing she kept that secret."

Jezebel adds, "Some of us thought you looked familiar, but we didn't put it all together until this week when we compared notes."

That gives Persephone a lot to think about. Her mother was a witch, but her father never knew.

Queenie clears her throat, interrupting Persephone's thoughts. "We have a confession," she says. And then she tells Persephone about how the witches have been drugging the townsmen for decades, slipping their special elixir into the Moonshyne Manor alcohol, assuming the men of the town would drink it in moderation. "We never thought about what might happen in the event of extreme grief, when someone might drink more than usual as a coping mechanism."

"The elixir was always meant to calm them down," Ivy says. "Just a few sips are enough to make them docile. But imbibing it often, and in excess, would have the kinds of effects you've spoken about, a complete withdrawal from life."

It's Ursula who says, "You can't just blame your father for his behavior toward you this past year. I'm afraid we bear the blame for that."

"We've stopped drugging the booze," Jezebel says. "It wasn't right to control people in that way, and we're sorry for the hurt we've caused you."

Persephone nods. Having seen firsthand how worked up the men were when they descended on the manor, she understands why the witches felt they had to do it. She's upset, of course, but she knows that sometimes terrible consequences can come from the best intentions. And if her father's withdrawal can be explained, if it wasn't his fault, then there's hope for them going forward.

Plus, if he didn't know about his wife's powers, then he was never given a chance to learn more about them. People fear what they don't understand. Perhaps if Persephone lets her father in, showing him exactly who she is and allowing him to be a part of her journey, he'll surprise her. One thing's for sure: he can't rise to the occasion if Persephone doesn't at least give him the opportunity to do so.

She understands why her mother didn't tell him about being a witch: she was scared of being rejected. But pushing people away and locking them out before they can hurt you is the one way of ensuring everyone loses. That's not how Persephone chooses to live. Her father may have been violently antiwitch up until now, but that's only because he wasn't aware he already knew and loved two of them.

What happens when *the other* reveals themself to be one of your own?

"We want to offer you our magical guidance and training," Ursula says. "If you want it, that is."

"Are you kidding me?" Persephone asks, thrilled.

"Only if you teach us your own magic in return," Jezebel says. "I especially liked your card tricks."

"Deal," Persephone says, grinning. And then she turns serious. "Can I see those two necklaces? The ones Klepto stole during the heist?"

"Uh…sure," Queenie says, confused by the sudden change of subject, but figuring Persephone has a good reason for asking. She stands and heads for the chest of drawers, retrieving the jewelry from among the good silver. "Here you go," she says, handing them over.

Persephone puts them down next to her, all of her focus directed at the gold and jade necklace with the strange froglike figurine on a pendant. "Just as I thought," she says, grinning wildly.

"What?" Ivy asks.

"When I was researching the Heka Wand of Isis to make a replica for Ruby, I went down a rabbit hole of sites dedicated to artifacts believed to be magical. That's where I saw this necklace. It said that it belonged to an Aztec goddess and that the piece is believed to be missing after it was incorrectly classified forty years ago as regular Aztec jewelry and sold to an undocumented private collection." She hands the piece across to Jezebel for her to look at.

There's a stunned silence which Widget finally breaks. "Who knew Klepto had such a discerning eye?"

"Pity we couldn't find it when we desperately needed the money. Sounds like selling it would have saved us." Jezebel runs her thumb over the jade.

It's Ursula who joins the dots first, realizing what it is that Persephone's getting at. "If it's a powerful artifact, then Ruby could use it in the forbidden spell to make her transformation complete."

They all turn to look at Ruby who's dozed off.

"How long until the next full moon?" Ursula asks.

"Twelve days," Ivy replies.

"Beaver moon," Jezebel adds, wriggling her eyebrows suggestively.

"It's not that kind of beaver." Queenie tuts, but she's smiling.

"Do you think Ruby will have the power or presence of mind to conduct such a complicated spell?" Ursula asks.

"I don't know," Queenie replies. "There's something about being back at the manor with us that's making her stronger. Haven't you noticed how she seems to be making small improvements every day?" She looks to the others who nod, daring to hope that Queenie's right. "Either way, isn't it wonderful that Ruby at least has the option?"

"It's time for dinner." Jezebel ushers them all from the parlor to the dining room where the ten-seater table is laden with roast vegetables, soups, freshly baked breads and a roast chicken for Queenie, who's the only meat-eater in the manor.

They sit talking and eating for another hour, the witches each coming up with ideas for what they want to teach Persephone. Ivy wants her to learn plant magic, whereas Queenie wants her to learn how to use magic to invent. Tabby says she already has a way with animals, so perhaps that's what she should focus on. Ursula wants to test how clairvoyant Persephone is, while Jezebel explains that seduction is a magical art form that's wholly underrated, though she's only prepared to teach it to Persephone once she's eighteen, and only if she's fully into it.

Ruby pipes up. "Sarah-Jane will have her own particular power. She just needs to wait until it reveals itself."

When the time comes to leave, Queenie offers to give Persephone a ride home on the Harley-Davidsonstick. As tempted as Persephone is, she has to decline since she came here on her bike. "Next time," she says, hoping Queenie will teach her how to ride the broomcycle by herself one day.

"Have you ever flown in a plane?" Ivy surprises Persephone by asking.

"Yeah, quite a few times, when we went on family vacations. Why?"

"Tabby's talked me into accepting an invitation from the University of Edinburgh to give a talk about biodiversity next month," Ivy replies. "I'm more than a bit nervous about the flight."

"It's a lot more comfortable than a broomstick," Persephone says, laughing. "You can even try for a nap. And they serve drinks and food."

"That actually sounds quite nice," Ivy murmurs.

It's Tabby and Widget who usher Persephone and Ruth Bader Ginsburg out ahead of the others straggling behind. "Thank you for saving the manor," Widget caws. "No one's more grateful to you than I am."

Persephone accepts the gratitude with a dip of her head. "Are you still angry with Ursula?" she asks, voice pitched low.

"I understand why she did what she did," Widget says. "But it's complicated. It will take a while to mend those fences."

"You were waiting all this time for an apology," Persephone says. "Just from the wrong person. I'm sure Ursula wants to tell you she's sorry."

"Oh, she does," Widget rasps. "I just don't want to hear it."

"Because you're still so upset?" Persephone asks.

"Because I'm scared it will set me free," Tabby replies through Widget. "I've decided I'd like to hang around a little longer. Now that we're all reunited." She smiles, looking sheepish. "Maybe see Ruby finally transition permanently."

Persephone nods, understanding completely. She reaches out on impulse, wanting to comfort Tabby with a hug. As she leans in, Persephone realizes what a stupid gesture it is, how utterly futile to try and embrace a ghost. And how rude too, like initiating a handshake with an unsighted person. But before she can pull back, Persephone connects with something.

Tabby's eyes widen at the contact.

For thirty-three years, Tabby has lived as a specter, as insubstantial as a sigh, even less so since you can at least still feel an exhalation against your cheek and be warmed by another's disappointment. No matter how much she's yearned for contact, Tabby hasn't been able to feel reassured by Widget's claws against her shoulder or by the sisters' body heat nearby. Having zero sensation for so long has numbed her. She now feels like someone paralyzed from the waist down who's just felt a pinprick against the sole of their foot for the very first time.

Through her desire to offer comfort, Persephone's discovered her particular power. As she embraces Tabitha, the ghost clinging to her, Persephone can feel all of Tabby's despair and frustration, her anger and fear radiating from her in waves. But what she can feel as well is hope.

And hope burns the hottest.

64

Twelve days later
Night of the full moon
Midnight

Ursula pulls her lined cloak tighter around herself, grateful for the layers of thermal underwear she thought to don beneath her winter robe. She tilts her head back, gazing up into the night sky. The full moon is at its summit directly above them, luminous as though lit up from within, the giant crystal ball of the deities.

"I'm freezing my bazoombas off," Queenie mutters from behind her, teeth chattering.

"Oh, Queenie, stop complaining," Jezebel chides. "We used to do this in the buff seventy years ago, remember?"

"Proving once and for all that teenagers aren't that smart," Queenie replies.

"Hey!" Persephone chirps. "I'm a teenager, and I'm, like, appropriately dressed for this weather. If you were all once stupid enough to get frostbite while running around naked, that's totally on you."

The forest releases them into the clearing where the ritual circle is. Queenie points at a boulder that's paler and less weathered than the rest. "That one's yours, Persephone." She says it shyly, like it's a gift she doesn't want the girl making a big deal of, even though it really is.

"It's amazing, thank you." Persephone looks more thrilled than any teenage girl should ever be when presented with a big old hunk of rock.

Queenie smiles warmly at the young witch who's wearing new red robes, sewn by Ruby using fabric repurposed from Persephone's mother's coat.

The sisterhood was complete at six until it wasn't, and then the manor brought them a seventh. Ursula is surprised by how much this new addition has energized the women, who'd resigned themselves to the fact that they had no progeny. There's so much wisdom to impart, so much they have to teach the girl. It's given them renewed purpose, an injection of good old-fashioned oomph.

Widget swoops overhead, late to the party after having stopped to greet forest friends. Tabby can't join them, but she's at least able to experience everything through her connection with her familiar. Once Widget settles on Tabby's boulder, all heads turn to Ruby. It's her big moment, one that she's waited more than thirty-three years for. They were nervous that she wouldn't be up for it but, in typical Ruby style, she's risen to the occasion. Her mind is as unclouded as the sky, which is the best they could've possibly hoped for.

It seems Queenie was right. There is something about being among the sisterhood that's helping Ruby remember herself and, through remembering, reclaim her power.

Ruby smiles, but it's not one of her vacant ones they've come to know so well. It's a nervous smile, one that's charged with an understanding of the gravity of the occasion. "I'm ready," Ruby says, nodding. She runs a hand over the sandpaper of her jaw as though bidding farewell to an old friend.

"Then, let's do this." Queenie claps her hands, setting everyone in motion.

Ivy conjures the cauldron while Jezebel demonstrates how to work the spell to ignite the ritual fire. "You'll have to do this one day," she tells Persephone, "so watch closely."

Ursula summons the cart carrying all the ingredients, and it sails a few inches above the ground toward the middle of the circle.

Finally, it's time.

Ruby walks to the cauldron with slow, measured steps. She nods at Ursula who joins her. Ursula unwraps the purple silk that covers the Moonshyne Manor Grimoire, thinking how wonderful it is that they now have someone to pass the book down to. She undoes the buckles and clasps, turning to the last pages so that Ruby can access the spell she needs.

In a reedy voice, Ursula begins reciting the instructions to Ruby as she gently guides her. "We'll begin with the liquid ingredients. First the gallon of rainwater from Puerto Rico. Then the half a gallon of urine from a black rhino."

Ivy, Jezebel and Queenie help Ruby with the ingredients, the long list of which includes an orchid, a thousand-karat tanzanite stone, three drops of Cuchumatan golden toad saliva, one drop of scorpion venom and ten tears shed by a virtuous man.

"I hope these were all ethically sourced," Persephone mutters. "Can you get fair-trade rhino pee and frog spit?"

"Those weren't the problem," Queenie whispers back. "You try finding a virtuous man. I almost felt bad about making him cry."

Ursula shushes them, continuing to read. "Now add an eyelash from a ruling British monarch."

"What the hell?" Persephone yelps.

"Don't worry about it," Queenie says, winking. "Liz was totally cool with donating it."

Ursula gives them both a dirty look while reminding Ruby to stir the cauldron's contents clockwise with the wooden paddle after each ingredient is added.

When they get to the last two, Widget picks up the Aztec gold and jade necklace in her beak, flying it to Ruby.

"You need to drop it into the middle of the cauldron, being careful not to make a splash," Ursula explains.

Ruby takes the necklace from Widget, before holding it out and gently lowering it in.

"Good," Ursula says. "Now it's time for the secret ingredient, the sacrifice." Her voice quivers as she says it. "You'll need to use your wand to withdraw your magical powers."

The forest comes to life around them, every sound amplified as the witches fall silent. There's the clicking and chirping of strange nocturnal creatures hunting. The wind runs its spindly fingers through the trees, most of which have already shed their leaves. The branches creak and sway as owls hoot and scavengers forage.

Ruby closes her eyes, reaching inward. She lifts her wand, swishing it in a convoluted figure eight that's struck through at the end with a kind of exclamation mark. She then points it at her heart. *"Ego…ego…"* She shakes her head.

"You've got this, Ruby," Ursula murmurs. "Take your time."

Ruby nods and takes a deep breath, trying again. "*Ego sacrificium*…um…*ego sacrificium*…" But it's no use: she can't remember what follows.

"It's *ego sacrificium meum magica*," Ursula whispers. "Like we practiced, remember?"

Ruby nods and tries again, but she stammers, tripping over the same part, her face crumpling with frustration. Ursula looks down at the cauldron. The mercury-silver color of the potion is beginning to darken; they're running out of time. If they miss their window, this will all have been for nothing. The ingredients were incredibly difficult to source. This is not a spell they can just work again at the next full moon.

Taking in Ruby's stricken expression, love wells up in Ursula like a tide answering the siren call of the full moon. Ruby *is* her moon. There is no resisting the pull of her. "I'll do the spell for you," Ursula says.

"You can't work it for her, Ursula," Ivy replies. "The person who works the spell has to make the sacrifice."

"I know," Ursula whispers, nodding. "I know that."

"You'd have to give up your magical powers," Jezebel adds, as though Ursula doesn't understand the magnitude of what it is she's offering.

Ruby looks at Ursula with widened eyes that are filled with tears. Ursula lets go of the grimoire, setting it floating next to them. She steps toward Ruby and reaches out, wiping Ruby's tears away with her thumbs. And then she takes Ruby's hands, staring deeply into her violet eyes. "Rubilicious Faloolah Minx Betwixt," she says, "I have loved you since the moment I first laid eyes on you. And I have loved you with every beat of my bewitched heart ever since. I don't just love you, I am in love with you. I have always been, and I always will be."

Ursula's heart claps its rapturous applause, relieved beyond measure to finally have its truth so plainly spoken.

"I am so sorry for what I did, and for taking Magnus from you. I wish with every fiber of my being that I could bring him back from the grave. But since I can't, let me do this for you. Let me sacrifice my powers to make your deepest wish come true."

Yes, Ursula's heart whispers. *Yes. Yes. Yes.* She reaches for her wand, Ruby's beautiful face blurred by Ursula's own tears. Ursula does the figure-eight movement, punctuating it forcefully with the exclamation point, because she's never been so certain of anything. And then she points her wand at her heart. *"Ego sacrificium meum—"*

"No!" Ruby's voice is anguished as she grabs at Ursula's hand, snatching the wand away before Ursula can do the unthinkable.

Ruby cups Ursula's cheek with one hand, searching her face just as she did on the night they first met as little girls all those years ago. And then Ruby leans forward slowly and kisses Ursula, gently, reverently. The kiss is everything Ursula imagined it would be, both hollowing her out and filling her up.

"I forgive you, Ursula," Ruby says. "Stop punishing yourself." They aren't the words Ursula has always wanted to hear, the ones she dreamed Ruby would say one day. But they're the exact ones Ursula *needs* to hear, the ones that will set her free from the guilt and remorse that's plagued her for more than a third of her life.

"Thank you," Ursula whispers. "Thank you for forgiving me."

Ruby nods, resting her forehead against Ursula's. When she finally pulls away, Ruby points her wand at her own heart and says, *"Ego sacrificium meum magica."*

The potion begins swirling and bubbling in the cauldron, creating its own churning current.

Ruby's voice is strong and steady as she addresses the Goddess, asking for that which her heart most desperately yearns for. Ursula scoops a ladle full of potion from the cauldron, pouring it into a chalice and handing it to Ruby. Ruby holds the chalice up to the moonlight, uttering the incantation. *"Muta in donum volutissimum."*

And then she takes a sip, grimacing at the acrid taste. Ruby gags but forces herself to keep the potion down. She gulps and retches, gulps and retches, until the chalice is finally empty.

As the sisterhood watches, a silvery mist envelopes Ruby. It swirls around her, iridescent and shimmering, draping her with moonlight. When it finally clears—the breeze carrying it off—Ruby is transformed.

"Do I… Do I look like me?" Ruby asks, her hands flitting to

her face, alighting there like a pair of moths before they come to rest briefly against her hips and then her neck. "Am I me again?"

"Why don't you see for yourself?" Ursula asks, conjuring a gleaming mirror in front of Ruby.

Ruby looks at it like it's a portal to another world, which in many ways it is. Stepping up, she gazes at her reflection with an expression of wonder. Her hair has grown longer, and her bristly stubble has disappeared. Her chin is narrower, and her cheekbones are higher. Ruby's nose is more tapered, and her features have softened. Her body is once again made up of hills and valleys instead of the prairie it had so stubbornly returned to.

Ruby's hands trace all the changes, tears trailing their way down her cheeks.

"There she is," Ursula says, joining her at the mirror. "There's our Ruby."

The rest of the coven join them there, wrapping their arms around Ruby and each other. Widget lands on Ursula's shoulder, nuzzling her beak into Ursula's neck.

"It doesn't feel the same without Tabby," Ursula says sadly, stroking Widget's head. The women all murmur their agreement. "Let's go celebrate with her."

They wend their way back through the forest, trailing behind Widget, whose wings are quicksilver in the moonlight.

"What's the plan for Weasel Brad?" Persephone asks, using the nickname they've all come to adopt for him. "Do you plan on keeping him in that cage forever?"

"Why not?" Queenie huffs. "He wanted the manor so badly. Would it be so terrible if he got to live out the rest of his days in it?"

"Be careful what you wish for," Jezebel agrees, "or you will surely have it."

"He's too dangerous to set free," Ursula says, arm looped through Ruby's, guiding her around a tree stump. "But none of us are very keen on keeping him in the cage, his beady eyes constantly trained on us. Tabby's giving some thought to whether he can be released to the forest under the supervision of the falcizards."

As they ascend the porch steps, the manor welcomes them into its bosom, Tabby and Ruth Bader Ginsburg waiting at its threshold. Tabby marvels at Ruby's transformation, congratulating her friend on the fulfillment of a decades-long wish. The joy is written so plainly on Tabby's face that Widget doesn't even need to translate for her.

"I guess I should fly you home," Queenie says to Persephone, checking the time and noting that it's almost three in the morning. "I'm sure your father's waiting up for you. It was good of him to let you come."

"At least it's not a school day tomorrow, so you can sleep in," Ursula adds.

As Persephone picks up Ruth Bader Ginsburg and then bids the sisterhood farewell, the women all unconsciously lean in to one another. Even Tabby, who can't feel the sisterhood's touch, scoots in close, trying to rest her head on Queenie's shoulder.

Clearly reluctant to leave just yet, Persephone pulls out her phone. "Let's take an ussie to commemorate tonight."

"A what now?" Queenie asks.

"It's like a selfie, but with all of us."

"This kid assumes I know what a *selfie* is," Queenie mutters from the corner of her mouth.

Persephone laughs, joining the women, who then crowd around her. She holds up her cell phone, trying to get everyone in, dog and crow included. "I'm not going to tell you to smile or the patriarchy wins," Persephone says.

But they do all smile, even Tabby, though it must be said that Ruby's smile is the most radiant of all.

★ ★ ★ ★ ★

ACKNOWLEDGMENTS

A book is much like a potion in that it requires the right combination of perfect ingredients in order to make it work. Lucky for this novel, I was blessed with a smorgasbord of the finest ones available.

Firstly, a great big thank-you to my agent extraordinaire, Cecilia Lyra, who helped me bulldoze my way into a story that's been quietly percolating for years. I couldn't have written this book without CeCe's brilliant insight and ongoing encouragement. This was a wonderfully collaborative process, which made the whole experience much less lonely than it might otherwise have been. I am in awe of CeCe's talent and how epically fierce she is.

Thanks as well to the brilliant Carly Watters for so generously sharing her expertise and support, as well as the involvement of the whole P.S. Literary team who championed me and the story along every step of the way. David and Curtis, you went above and beyond, and I'm incredibly grateful for your involvement.

To K. Dishmon, thank you for your amazing, insightful notes and for being such a kind and sensitive reader. You made this a much better book! Thank you as well to the lovely Viv Monterroso for being a wonderful sensitivity reader and for guiding me in terms of ensuring that I did Ruby justice. It was such a joy working with, and learning from, you!

Then a great big thank-you to my brilliant editor, Nicole Brebner, at MIRA Books, for loving Queenie, Ivy, Ursula, Jezebel, Tabby, Ruby and Persephone as much as I do. Nicole immediately understood what I was trying to do, and it's always such a gift to work with someone who shares your vision and is as excited by it as you are. Thank you for working so damn hard on this, Nicole, and for making it look so easy when I know it's been like juggling tigers while hopping one-legged through a swamp.

Thanks as well to the awesome MIRA Books team who have so wholeheartedly embraced my motley crew! Vanessa Wells, thanks for making me look good during the copy editing, as well as for saving me from myself when it came to my atrocious Latin. Erin Craig, you designed a cover that made me gasp with delight. Thank you for all the work that you put into it! Audrey Bresar, thank you for being such an excellent champion of the book and for being so utterly fabulous. We are *so* doing that champagne scavenger hunt one day! Cadence King and Loriana Sacilotto, thank you so much for going above and beyond to get us to the finishing line! A huge thank-you also goes to Colleen Simpson, Emer Flounders, Alice Tibbets, Ashley MacDonald and Margaret Marbury for all your hard work ensuring that the witches got into all the right hands—I honestly can't thank you all enough! To each and every member of the team: thank you for your sleight of hand and for knowing all the magical words to open any door.

As always, I am nothing without my writing groups who continue to teach me how to be a better storyteller. Thank you to the awesome BACKSpacers: Alek Trpkovski, Cristina Austin, Kira Mahoney and Suzy Dugard. And to the fabulous ChiTos:

Alicia Maini, Kevin Kilmartin, Lisa Rivers and Sarah Mae Dalgleish. Thanks as well to Caroline-Sweetie-Faloolah Gill, Kath Jonathan, Bronwen Broomberg, Emily Murray and Tracey Pieterse for always being such marvelous cheerleaders. Thank you to the members of my awesome book club for your incredible support and for allowing me in even though I've greatly brought down the tone of it. Lisa Rivers and Suzy Dugard, extra gold stars and an erupting glitter cake go to you both!

An enormous thank-you as well goes to all the amazing Bookstagrammers, book bloggers, BookTokers, booksellers, librarians, book clubs and readers who make my job possible. I can't express how grateful I am to you for everything you do to support authors. You are my rock stars.

Thank you to my "bestie in a Tessie," Brendan Fisher, for crying at my ending and for designing all of my floor plans so I could make Moonshyne Manor come to life. Thanks, too, for being my unpaid photographer, social media wizard and all-round Renaissance man. I will never be able to repay my enormous debt to you, my friend.

To Jean Dow, thank you for bringing your brilliant expertise and insight to checking all my potions and recipes. Charmaine Shepherd, I honestly don't know what I'd do without you, my bokkie. Thank you for always being my biggest fan and for making me believe that anything is possible. You are the Ivy (with a bit of Tabby thrown in for good measure) to my Queenie. Your sisterhood has inspired this one!

Thank you to my lovely parents, my wonderful family (immediate and extended) as well as all of my amazing friends for their ongoing support. There are too many of you to mention by name, but I am hugely grateful for each and every one of you, especially when you go rogue and rearrange bookshelves to ensure that my books are front and center, before photographing evidence of your skullduggery. Leana Marais, you are an absolute angel.

To the witches, thank you for getting me through a really tough time. Your shenanigans are what got me out of bed every day.

Finally, to Stephen, who is the swish to my flick, the tuck to my roll, the cadabra to my abra and the light to my shadow… I promise you this: if we ever win the lottery, I'll try really, really hard not to give away more than we win.

A LETTER FROM THE AUTHOR

Dearest Fabulous Reader,

I started writing *The Witches of Moonshyne Manor* back in January of 2021 when Toronto was cold and dark, and we were in the midst of yet another pandemic lockdown. But despite how bleak the world felt, spending time with the Moonshyne Manor sisterhood was like holding my hands up to a roaring fire (the lovely, crackling kind that warms every inch of you—your soul included—as opposed to the dumpster kind that sometimes mirrors the state of the world). The fever dream six months it took me to write the novel felt like a vacation. (That is if you have a penchant for taking vacations at retirement villages, surrounded by cranky, horny, irreverent old women who heckle you constantly to *Get back to work, missy! This book's not gonna write itself!*)

Most people I know, women especially, are horrified at the thought of getting older. But I'm a Capricorn (and we're apparently born ancient, getting closer to our true age every year), so I can't wait for my seventies and eighties. It's the only reason I eat revolting kale and do my ten thousand steps a day—because I want to be around then, not just for the senior discounts, but for that epic moment when the bras come off and the muumuus come out.

I speak to a ton of book clubs, many of which are made up of retired women, and what I delight in is how few f*cks they have left to give. If they don't like a plot twist in one of my books, they'll yell, "What the hell did you do *that* for?" And then, because they think they're muted, they'll yell it again, only louder. All while instructing their husbands to get off their lazy asses and pour them a damn drink. My favorite part of any Zoom session with them is the first fifteen minutes, where they don't give a sh*t that a famous author (hey, this is *my* author letter, and I can elevate my status however I want) is sitting there waiting for the discussion to begin. That's when they chat about how CBD oil is likely to clear up Iris's boob rash, or when Shanice can cha-cha again after her hip replacement, or where Louise should hide her husband's Viagra this time around.

What occurs to me is that we've all grown up identifying with some awesome character or another at various stages of our lives. I was first a Kristy (*The Baby-Sitters Club*) and then a Miranda (*Sex and the City*) and then a Dorothy (*The Golden Girls*). But then media and literature mostly stopped showing me what else I could be after my midfifties...like women stop existing after a certain age, like we don't have so much to look forward to. Which, as Jezebel will tell you, is utter bullsh*t, especially if you (like me!) have big plans to age as disgracefully as you possibly can.

The great news is that you won't be on that journey alone. As women, we've been looking out for each other since we were little girls. In our twenties and thirties, our friends became our family, getting us through our worst breakups and biggest career disappointments. They also kindly held our hair back for us when a few too many of those tequila shots did U-turns, making mad dashes for freedom. Sisterhood is one of the greatest gifts we can give one another, at any stage of life, and this book is a celebration of that (#AgingGoals #AgingDisgracefully #SisterhoodGoals #BadBitches). And if we can all support and encourage each other, while simultaneously bringing down the patriarchy, then why not? It's all in a day's work, just another item to tick off that never-ending to-do list.

I hope that you love the sisterhood as much as I do, and that they give you something to look forward to as you keep on kicking ass and taking names, growing into your power as you age. I'm not saying the witches are likely to hex you if you don't love them, but I'm also not making any promises that they'll behave. More importantly, I really hope you have an Ivy, Ursula, Jezebel, Ruby, Tabitha and Queenie in your life. And that you see yourself in at least one of these amazing women. May you also know a Persephone who gives you hope for the next generation of women who will be raised to be just as badass as you are.

And may you fight for the Rubys of the world who need our support and allyship.

Warm, witchy regards,

Bianca

PS: Looking for fun book club content? Head over to my website, www.biancamarais.com, to take the quiz to discover which witch you are! Find *The Witches of Moonshyne Manor* playlist to liven up your gathering, as well as recipes and games that everyone will enjoy!